Blanche
Passes Go

VIKING

75 years

Also by BarbaraNeely

Blanche on the Lam
Blanche Among the Talented Tenth
Blanche Cleans Up

BarbaraNeely

Blanche Passes Go

VIKING

VIKING
Published by the Penguin Group
Penguin Putnam Inc., 375 Hudson Street,
New York, New York 10014, U.S.A.
Penguin Books Ltd, 27 Wrights Lane, London W8 5TZ, England
Penguin Books Australia Ltd, Ringwood, Victoria, Australia
Penguin Books Canada Ltd, 10 Alcorn Avenue,
Toronto, Ontario, Canada M4V 3B2
Penguin Books (N.Z.) Ltd, 182–190 Wairau Road,
Auckland 10, New Zealand

Penguin Books Ltd, Registered Offices:
Harmondsworth, Middlesex, England

First published in 2000 by Viking Penguin,
a member of Penguin Putnam Inc.

1   3   5   7   9   10   8   6   4   2

Grateful acknowledgment is made for permission to reprint Shola Olunloya's
recipe for Muscat Sauce ("Blanche's Gig from Hell Dessert Sauce"). By
permission of Shola Olunloya.

PUBLISHER'S NOTE
This is a work of fiction. Names, characters, places, and incidents either
are the product of the author's imagination or are used fictitiously, and any
resemblance to actual persons, living or dead, business establishments, events, or
locales is entirely coincidental.

LIBRARY OF CONGRESS CATALOGING-IN-PUBLICATION DATA
Neely, Barbara.
Blanche passes go / BarbaraNeely.
p.   cm.
ISBN 0-670-89165-7
1. White, Blanche (Fictitious character—Fiction.   2. Afro-American women—North
Carolina—Fiction.   3. Women detectives—North Carolina—Fiction.   4. Caterers and
catering—Fiction.   5. North Carolina—Fiction.   I. Title.
PS3564.E244 B58 2000
813'.54—dc21   99-462184

This book is printed on acid-free paper. ∞

Printed in the United States of America
Set in Janson Text
Designed by Kathryn Parise

*To the dearest and the finest:
my brother, Bryan Neely*

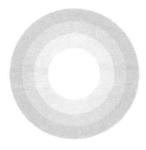

Acknowledgments

Thanks to the following for their invaluable, clarifying, thought-provoking, insightful comments and editing: Babs Bigham, Pam Dorman, Nancy Falk, Roz Feldberg, Regina LeJeune, Susan Hans O'Connor, and Phyllis Wender, with very special thanks to Dick Cluster, Shelley Evans, and Pamela Harkins. Thanks as well to Jeanne Bracken for her research; Lisa Dodson for camp stories; Vernelle Jordan for helping me to understand; Joycelyn Moody for her menu advice; Ariel Rogers for her detective advice. Particular thanks to Chef Shola Olunloya in Philadelphia, for his recipe and dinner menu. Finally and primarily, undying gratitude to HWMIAP: Jeremiah Cotton.

Blanche
Passes Go

Getting There

Blanche noticed him the moment he stepped into the railroad car. His short beard glowed silver against his dark, dark face—the kind of face that would look good in an ad for high-end cognac or $2,000 watches. He stood erect in his blue, gold-trimmed uniform. The fingers of his left hand curled around his lapel. He could easily have been the captain of a luxury liner if not for the ticket puncher in his right hand. He looked around the car before moving forward. Blanche watched him work for a few moments.

The adults stopped fiddling with their bags and children and gave him their full attention. As he took their tickets, he cautioned them not to move about the train without one of the seat checks he tucked in the slot on the overhead luggage rack. He patted each of the children on the head like the Pope giving a blessing. He moved with a dancer's grace to the bump and shift of the train.

An involuntary hum vibrated the back of Blanche's throat. She reached in her bag for her ticket, then raised her head to find him looking right dead in her face. His eyes were the color of burnt sugar. He held her gaze while he moved toward her, his slow smile widening. Since she wasn't the age, the color, or the size generally considered beautiful in America, when a man smiled flirtatiously in her direction Blanche usually looked around her, sure that there was a younger, thinner, lighter-complected woman nearby for whom the smile was meant. But this smile was definitely directed at her blue-black, size-sixteen, going-gray self. It warmed her insides. She thanked the Ancestors that there were still men around who liked a woman with some meat on her.

"Good morning, ma'am." He took in everything about her that could be seen before he reached for the ticket she held out to him. Blanche didn't see what he did with it. She was too busy admiring his large, muscular frame and trying to identify that spicy, warm scent wafting from him. She liked a man who went to the trouble to smell good. This man smelled lickable. When she looked up at him, a smile warmed her eyes but barely lifted her mouth, just in case he was only trying to make a sister his age feel welcome on the train.

He leaned over her seat and spoke softly: "I see you're going all the way to North Carolina, ma'am." His voice had a hint of gravel in it.

Blanche turned that hum in her throat into an "Umm-hum." She was tempted to add that she was looking forward to going "all the way" but decided against it. If anything was really happening here, let him run it for a while.

"It'll be a pleasure working the Silver Star knowing you're on my run, ma'am." He tipped his cap and moved on. He hadn't tipped his cap to anyone else.

Well! She fanned herself, still grinning. When she'd cooled down a peg, she raised her head above the seat in front of her and looked around. She'd been so busy giving all of her attention to the conductor she hadn't checked out the other passengers in the car. From her seat, all she could see was the elderly white couple directly across from her—all pink and white and matching khaki pants and plaid shirts—the bulk of the man in the seat in front of the couple, and the tops of heads in seats farther along. Under normal circumstances, speculating about who the people around her might be would have been one of the head-games she played to keep herself occupied on this long train ride. But circumstances could turn out to be better than normal. She might have another game to play, a much more interesting one.

She settled into her seat, even though she was as keyed up as a cat eyeing a frisky mouse. She was lucky to have a double seat all to herself. She unzipped her small plastic carryall bag and dug around her reused cookie tin of ham sandwiches and plastic container of fried chicken. She took out her book, and her thermos of tea. Her old green slippers were wrapped in plastic in the very bottom of her oversized black handbag. She'd planned to put them on once the train got under way but now changed her mind. She didn't even pretend to have any reason for this other than wanting to look her cutest for the conductor. Good thing she'd decided to wear her black skirt and a decent blouse.

They were leaving Providence, Rhode Island, when he came through the car again. She was reading *What a Woman's Gotta Do*, by Evelyn Coleman. She loved the kick-ass opening and was eager to get deeper into the book, but she wasn't able to give it her full attention right now. She looked up the second the door clanged shut behind him and didn't have time to look down before his eyes met hers. He smiled. So did she.

He stopped beside her seat. "Good book?"

Blanche breathed in some more spicy and warm. "I just started it, but I hear it's real good."

"Your lucky husband a reader, too?"

Blanche didn't hesitate. "Don't have one."

"I'm a widower myself." He grinned like he knew that was good news. He pointed to the golden plaque on his chest. "Thelvin, Thelvin Lewis."

She'd noticed his name tag but had purposely avoided looking at it. She wanted to hear it from him first. Maybe because she so often felt the need to defend her own name, she'd come to believe something could be learned about people from how they said their names—with pride or indifference, as though presenting a gift or calling down a curse. Thelvin Lewis said his name as though he knew it was special.

"Blanche White." She held out her hand; his was warm and blanket-soft.

"North Carolina your home, Miss Blanche? I swear I hear pine trees rustling, the way you say your name."

And to think she'd been dreading this long ride. Blanche crossed her legs.

"I live right over in Durham myself," Thelvin said after she told him she was going home to Farleigh, where she'd been born. "You planning to be down home for a while?"

Blanche explained how it was that she was free for the summer. She watched herself calmly telling him about the whereabouts of the niece and nephew she'd been raising since her sister's death—Taifa off to Amber Cove Inn in Maine to make beds and wait tables, and Malik to Outward Bound and then to Vermont and the environmental camp where he'd be a peer counselor. "It's supposed to teach them how to survive in the woods and trust each other."

"You must be worried half to death!" Thelvin said, to Blanche's delight.

"Yeah, but I'm determined not to let them know that!"

"So—you taking a little vacation down home, hunh?"

"I'm really going down to help my friend who's a caterer. It's Farleigh's bicentennial, so she's got plenty of business." Blanche didn't add that maybe going into the catering business with Ardell would turn out to be exactly what she wanted to do when the kids were gone from home and she was free to leave Boston permanently. She also didn't mention that she was going home to find out if Farleigh was or could be made safe enough for her to live there again if she should choose to do so.

Thelvin checked his watch. "Uh-oh. I better get moving! I'll be back to see you, Miss Blanche. If that's all right."

Blanche was truly tickled by this little bit of flirtation, whether it led anywhere or not. Flirting was like any other skill: use it or lose it. She sighed and relaxed into the slight motion of the train as the backs of factories, the dime-sized yards of quarter-sized houses, heaps of dead cars, and scraggly greenery rushed by her window. She felt herself loosened from the world outside the train, simply skimming the surface like a water bug on a pond. Her mind raced ahead to where she was going.

She was amused by trying out for a cooking-and-serving job—like the work was something new to her—when she'd spent her whole working life cleaning and cooking in other people's houses. She was also halfway between excited and nervous about being her own woman for a while after so many years as the hub of her family. Oughta take a lesson from Taifa and Malik, she thought. As they'd gotten closer to leaving for the summer, both of them had seemed about to burst with the desire to be already gone. Neither of them had expressed a drop of concern about going to stay someplace where they had no family within easy reach. Of course, she'd been the very same when she was their age. It was easier to rush off to who you were becoming than it was to walk back to where you'd left a part of yourself and try to revive it. Life was a forward-moving thing. Trying to go back was like swimming upstream with rocks in your pockets. But even though Malik and Taifa were eager for their summer away, they'd made it clear they'd have preferred for her to stay at home, holding their rooms and meals and regular home life at the ready, like a comfortable robe they could slip into after their adventures in the wider world.

Three years ago, when Ardell came to Boston with her proposition that the two of them go into the catering business in Farleigh, Malik and Taifa had just settled into school and friendships in Boston. They were in their third school system in nearly as many years. Blanche wouldn't consider asking them to move again. So Ardell had started the business on her own.

"Half of it's yours whenever you're ready," Ardell had told her. But Blanche wasn't sure she wanted it. She enjoyed doing day work, setting her own hours, working for whomever she liked and dropping clients when they plucked her nerves or otherwise treated her in ways she didn't appreciate. Working alone suited her, too, with no one else's habits or needs to consider. She enjoyed cooking, though, which is what she'd mostly be doing if she went in with Ardell, and she certainly wouldn't mind making more money, if catering could provide that. But pleasure and money weren't the only considerations. There was also David Palmer.

She'd lived in Farleigh for at least another year after it happened. She'd sworn that she'd get even with him someday, somehow, but for the first few months she'd traveled the streets and worked with her eyes down, fearful that she'd see him. She'd thanked her Ancestors for shielding her from the sight of him. She'd cried with relief when Ardell told her he'd left town, then she'd left herself. Over the years, as time and distance forged scar tissue tough enough to dull the pain of what he'd done to her, thoughts of revenge had faded, too. But there would be little distance between them now. He was already back in Farleigh, and she would be shortly. She would just have to see.

"Can I help you in any way, Miss Blanche?" Thelvin asked when he found her walking the train to stretch her legs.

"Thank you, I'm just fine."

"I can see that, Miss Blanche. A blind man can see you don't need no help with being fine."

By the time they reached Baltimore, Blanche knew that Thelvin had three children—two boys in their late twenties, one in California and the

other in New York, and an older, married daughter down in Savannah—
that he rented an apartment from his mother, who lived in Rocky Mount,
and his phone number.

"I got a answering machine," he'd told her, "so you can always leave me
a message."

By the time the train reached Fredericksburg, they'd decided to meet
for dinner, day after tomorrow, unless Blanche had to work. She was to
call him. She wondered at meeting Thelvin—a man with all the early signs
of being decent and interested as well as good-looking—while she was
purposely heading toward a man who was scum. Had the Ancestors put
Thelvin in her path as a reward for doing the right thing by going to Farleigh, or as a consolation prize?

The trees rolling by the train window were fully dressed in early-
summer leaves. Blanche felt her whole body yearning toward the warmth
of North Carolina, toward the smell of the South—the scent of life and
death distilled into a fine wine with a green and floral finish. She would be
in Farleigh all summer. Praise the Ancestors.

Getting Settled

Blanche spotted Ardell as the train was pulling into the station in Selma, North Carolina, the closest stop to Farleigh, and was startled by the tears that sprang to her eyes. Her emotions were getting closer and closer to the surface, she'd noticed, just about the time her night sweats had become a regular thing. She meant to ask her mother how she'd managed menopause, although it was unlikely she'd get a useful answer. Ardell saw her at the window.

"Blanche! Blanche!" Ardell waved wildly and jumped up and down. Light reflecting off her oversized glasses made her look momentarily blank-eyed, like Little Orphan Annie of the old funny papers. She looks the same, Blanche thought as they grew closer, but different, too. Maybe it was just that she'd never seen Ardell in a suit before. Although her hair was still natural, it was more slickly cut, with a part down the middle. It made her long, hawk-nosed face seem thinner, more serious. Of course, she was grayer, too.

Ardell smelled of something lemony. She wrapped her long, lean arms around Blanche and pulled her close. Blanche was sure she could feel energy flowing through Ardell's body like an electrical current. They hugged each other for a long time, kissed repeatedly, and talked at once, until the train pulled out and the platform was suddenly quiet.

"Girl! I can't even tell you how glad I am to see your big behind!"

Blanche slapped herself lightly on the butt. "You mean my *fine* big behind, don't you, Miz Bow-Legged Power Suit?"

They laughed their way toward Ardell's old blue Dodge. "I was gonna get a new one," Ardell said as she wrestled with the back passenger door, "but I found a great deal on a van for the catering business. Wait till you see! It's got shelves and compartments for bottles and all."

They piled Blanche's bags in the back of the car.

"Trip okay?"

"Um-hum."

As Ardell pulled out of the parking space, her headlights swept the car parked in the last spot in the lot.

"Ooh-wee! Purple Passion!"

"Where?" Ardell looked around.

Blanche pointed at the couple in the car—a white man and woman kissing as though they hadn't been together for a long time or wouldn't see each other again for years. The man raised his head and glared at Blanche through glittering dark eyes as if she were looking in his bedroom window. All she saw of the woman was a pair of startled eyes and a high forehead. Blanche turned away from him toward Ardell.

"I met somebody on the train, but aint no sense talking about him until something happens."

"Like hell!" Ardell pulled out onto the road.

Blanche laughed, then told Ardell everything as they drove the short distance to Farleigh.

"Girl, moving back down here might be the right thing for you in more ways than one!"

Blanche was about to remind Ardell that she was just there for the summer when Ardell made an unexpected turn down the small dirt street, not much wider than an alley, that ran behind Washington Street.

"The Miz Alice!" Blanche jumped out of the car and walked around to the front of the small bungalow. "I'd almost forgotten about this place."

Ardell walked up the stoop and unlocked the door.

The last time Blanche had seen the little two-room bungalow they called the Miz Alice it had been full of chairs with broken legs, chests with missing drawers, and tables with cracked tops—furniture Ardell's Uncle Russell had planned to mend someday. He was a fine carpenter, but a busy one. Blanche looked around the Miz Alice: The wooden headboard was carved with bunches of grapes on a twisting vine. The mission-style chairs and small sofa were both covered in deepest purple with throw pillows in blue and green.

Blanche waved her hand at the furniture. "Mr. Russell's repair projects?"

Ardell nodded. "Surprised?"

"It's perfect!" Blanche had prepared herself for being a roomer at Miz Alexander's boarding house, keeping someone else's rules and hours. It was that or live with Ardell or with her own mother. While Blanche and Ardell were closer than some blood sisters, they had very different ways of doing things: Once a tube of toothpaste was opened, Ardell didn't think it was necessary to put the top back on it. "Saves me the time of having to take it off again," she'd once told Blanche. And although Blanche agreed it was important not to waste water, she doubted she'd ever be convinced only to flush the toilet every third time she peed. Of course, there was really no possibility Blanche would have stayed with her mother—unless she was trying to end her relationship with the woman. So having the Miz Alice for the summer was a truly lovely surprise.

The Miz Alice was named after the woman who'd first rented the place, some months after Ardell's Uncle Russell had dug up his backyard, laid the foundation, and built what he'd called "part of my old-age pension." The neighbors had sniggered and signified. Who was going to rent a little bitty place like that? Wasn't a single family around that didn't have at least a couple of kids. This place was hardly big enough for one. But Miz Alice had shown up in Farleigh from somewhere north just like she'd been sent for, having left wherever she'd been with one suitcase and no inclination to talk about her past. She'd lived in the snug little house—one big room with living/sleeping quarters at one end, a kitchen alcove at the other, and a tiny bathroom tucked on the side—until she'd died a couple years after Ardell's uncle. The place had stayed in the family.

After Ardell had gone, Blanche walked around, opening cabinets and peeking in the bathroom. Ardell had thought of everything from dishes to a back brush. There was even half a roasted chicken, pasta salad, milk, juice, eggs, butter, and bacon in the refrigerator, and she'd arranged to have the phone turned on tomorrow morning. Blanche reminded herself to call Thelvin—as if she were likely to forget.

She ran her hand along the grain in the oak bureau and looked at herself in the mirror. She saw fifty looking back at her. Fifty. She tried to find its meaning in her different yet same-as-always face. She knew it had changed over the years. Some days she could see her twenty-year-old self peeking out, all damp-eyed hope and eagerness. Other days she saw only Mama's face where her own should be. Fifty. She smoothed the gray hair at her temples. Fifty and free. She tried to picture herself alone in their house in Boston but couldn't, probably because she had no intention of staying there. She'd already begun to prepare Taifa and Malik for her giving up the house once they were in college.

"But where will we stay during the holidays?" Taifa had asked.

"Wherever I'm living," Blanche had told her.

"But where'll that be?" Malik wanted to know.

"And what if we don't like it?" Taifa added.

Blanche had been unwilling to say what was on her tongue, that Malik and Taifa would only be visiting her, so whether they liked it or not was immaterial. Though she hadn't said it, the thought had thrilled her. She didn't feel quite the same when it came to *their* freedom. She probably wouldn't have let Taifa go off to Amber Cove alone if the three of them hadn't stayed there with the Crowleys a few summers ago. The Crowley kids were friends of Taifa's and Malik's from the year they'd gone to private school. Their parents had a cottage at Amber Cove and their mother, Christine, was there this summer, too. She'd agreed to keep an eye on Taifa. One of Malik's favorite teachers was a part of his whole camping thing, so she was less concerned about him. And, she admitted, Malik was a lot more like *her* than Taifa was.

Blanche put her clothes away, then took a shower followed by a soak in the tub. She used a bucket of the water she'd soaked in to wipe the floors, careful to get into every corner as she put her mark on the bungalow. Madam Rosa, her old spiritualist up in Harlem, said the proper way to mark and protect a house was with your urine. Blanche had tried it. Once. For days afterwards, she'd found herself constantly sniffing to make sure her house didn't smell pissy. So she'd made up her own ritual, just as she'd put together her own spiritual practice, including reverence for her Ancestors and the planet, and seeking energy from trees and healing from the sea. Some things she'd learned from African, Afro-Caribbean, Native American, and Asian ways of having a spiritual life, but she always added her personal twist. Until she'd come up with her own rituals she'd been hungry for ways to demonstrate her belief that there was more to life than she could see—ways that didn't require her being a member of the Christian or the Muslim or any other religion that had played a part in African slavery. She also had no time for any religions that said she needed a priest or priestess to act as a go-between or worshipped a god called He. She was her own priest and goddess.

As her last act of the evening, she pressed her gray dress with the black stripe. She planned to wear it tomorrow evening, to her first gig with Ardell, or, rather, with Carolina Catering—a first gig that could launch her new career.

Mama

As promised, a man came and hooked up the phone the next morning. Blanche's first call was to leave the new number for Taifa at the front desk of Amber Cove Inn. She didn't try to call Malik, since she knew he was still on his Outward Bound trip.

Blanche had allowed Taifa and Malik to convince her not to call them unexpectedly, setting up dates to talk to them instead. But she'd also given them each ten postcards, already stamped and addressed to her at Ardell's. After she left her number on Christine Crowley's machine at Amber Cove, Blanche called Thelvin. She got his answering machine and smiled at the sound of his voice. She left her number and confirmed their date. Now it was time for Mama. It had been too late to wake her up last night.

Opening her mother's front door was like stepping back in time. There was the old slip-covered sofa, the balding blue armchair, the brass floor lamp with its fringed shade. As always, an army of doilies and antimacassars covered every surface except the floor and made the room look like it was frothing at the mouth. But it was Miz Cora's nearly nonstop tirade that made Blanche feel as though she'd lost forty years. It was the same tongue-whipping Blanche had been getting since she was old enough to make her own decisions. Only this time it wasn't about what Blanche was doing but where she was staying.

"It's just like you, Blanche," Miz Cora said when Blanche told her about the Miz Alice.

Blanche watched her mother slap a hot iron down on a cotton slip. As usual when she was angry, Miz Cora seemed about two feet taller than her actual four-foot-eleven-inch height.

"You always did have to be different!" Miz Cora turned the slip over and attacked it again.

"Even when you was a chile, you went your own way irregardless of other people's feelins. It aint a nice thing in a woman, Blanche." Miz Cora folded the slip. Her nut-brown eyes snapped at Blanche like angry turtles. They were almost the exact color of her skin.

Blanche sighed and wondered how it would be if just once her mother started a conversation with something other than a put-down. She looked good, though. Mama's face had obviously aged as much as it intended to, since her looks hadn't changed in ten years. She seemed a little lighter-skinned. Was she losing her color along with her hair? She'd also picked up a pound or two, but was still thin as a feather compared with Blanche. Her plumper hips and arms gave Miz Cora a softer look, but there wasn't anything cuddly about Mama.

". . . friend or family aint good enough for Miss High and Mighty Blanche to stay with!" Miz Cora was saying when Blanche tuned back in. "I can understand why you might not want to stay with Ardell. You know what people's like round here. What they gon say? Two women sleepin in the same bed when they don't have to. It aint natural." Miz Cora spread another slip across the ironing board.

Blanche rolled her eyes to the ceiling and sighed but warned herself not to say anything. When Mama was this wound up, any interruption was like throwing dry kindling on an open fire. Better to wait till the flames died from lack of oxygen—when Mama needed to stop and take a breath.

"Mama, I didn't want to cause you one extra lick of work. And you know how you are, always wanting to fix my favorite food and not letting me lift a finger," Blanche said, remembering how her mother had worked her like a slave the last time she'd stayed in this house.

Blanche could almost see her mother shrinking down from her angry height to her normal size.

"Humph. Well, humph. You coulda stayed with Ardell," Mama said, reversing herself. "Prob'ly hurt the chile's feelins, her bein your best friend, she . . ."

Wait a minute. Had Mama taken her sarcasm as sincere? Might as well play out the possibility—if she could do it without choking. "But, Mama," she cut in, "Ardell knows what you're like. Didn't she spend as much time at our house as she did her own? She knows what a fine table you set and how you keep your house. She'd run herself ragged trying to do for me like you would. That's why I can't stay with either one of y'all."

"Humph, well, humph." Miz Cora folded the last slip and moved on to a pillowcase. "You sure don't want to be livin on that chile's greens! Much as I love Ardell, every time I eat her greens I git gas somethin fierce. They aint cooked long enough, for one thing, and she probably don't put enough . . ."

Blanche relaxed her shoulders and nodded as though she were paying attention. If only it was always this easy. Maybe she needed to keep thinking up little pieces of flattery to chill Mama out, like throwing red meat to a lion. Still, by the time her mother was through with her, all Blanche was fit for was a long nap. Welcome home!

First Gig, First Sighting

Blanche watched Ardell directing the three waitpeople as they set up the buffet table, lit chafing-dish candles, and laid out plates and silverware, glasses and napkins.

"Clarice, I asked you to fan these out like this." Ardell quickly rearranged the napkins, then patted the slightly crestfallen Clarice on her shoulder. "Don't fret. You'll get it right next time." Ardell moved on to inspect the bar.

All business, Blanche thought in a proud, "Go, girl!" way. It looked as though Ardell had found both the work she wanted to do, and a deep well of know-how to go with it. Ardell couldn't cook a lick but she'd hired some of the best cooks around to work for her on contract. She supplied ingredients, developed menus with their help, and paid them either by the hour or the product. Blanche had listened with awe as Ardell had explained the bidding-and-billing processes, menu tastings for potential customers, then launched into the pros and cons and trials of working with the part-time staff—students from North Carolina Central and Shaw University, the funny ways of her cooks, and the lowdown on the two people she employed full-time as wait-and-cleanup crew—Clarice and Zeke.

Clarice was in charge of overseeing the heating and presentation of the food—on instructions from the cooks. Clarice was a woman in her mid-thirties. She reminded Blanche of a plump, rich-brown mink, quick and wide-eyed with a quivery nose. Ardell had said that Clarice grew up on a farm with parents who had told Clarice she was slow-witted. Ardell thought this was her parents' way of keeping their only child at their side, since Clarice had turned out to be a quick study and a hard, steady worker. "She may look and sound kind of dithery, but she's not," Ardell had said. "She don't lose it when things don't go right. But she's just as country as she can be! Soon's her parents died, Clarice decides to live her dream and move to the city. So, check this, she comes here to Farleigh! But being country don't add up to being slow," Ardell had said. "Girl wasn't here three months before she'd hooked up with Jimmy Henry. You remember him, Jeanette's baby brother."

Zeke, with his drill-sergeant walk and scraggly mustache, tended bar, waited table, and was in charge of breakdown, in which everyone, including Ardell, participated. Zeke had left Farleigh over thirty years ago and had recently moved back with his wife. Their kids were grown and gone. Whatever had happened to Zeke outside of Farleigh had turned him into a man who didn't like to look people in the eye. Blanche could tell from the tightness in Ardell's voice when she talked about him that Zeke was not her favorite person. "He's smart and he's real good when he's good," was all she'd say when Blanche asked her how she felt about him.

Right now, Ardell honchoed setup but was training Clarice to take this over. Catering was uniform work. Zeke and the two boys from the college were in black pants, white shirts and gloves, red bow ties, and bolero jackets. The boys would be circulating with glasses of champagne and Zeke would handle drinks at the makeshift bar. Clarice and the three girls who'd be serving trays of canapés wore shiny black uniforms with small white aprons. Ardell had told Blanche to wear her own clothes.

"Tonight, you just watch and get a feel for how things work," Ardell had told her. "And maybe pitch in if we need you."

So that's what Blanche was doing, beginning with noting the care with which the van was loaded so that when it was unloaded at the job site, the tablecloths came out first and were immediately put in place. The chafing dishes came out next and were set up and heated without delay.

The food—scallops wrapped in bacon, mini Brie tarts, crab-stuffed mushrooms, shrimp dumplings, and various fruits and cheeses—was being served at one of the many balls being held this summer to celebrate Farleigh's two hundredth birthday.

Tonight's affair was at the home of Jason Morris and his wife, Nancy. They lived in the Morris clan's ancestral mansion, which, along with most of its furniture, had been built by slaves. Everybody in Farleigh knew of the Morris family, its being one of the state's oldest and including such pillars of the South as slavers, Indian-killers, Confederate generals, and diehard segregationists. But Ardell said this generation saw itself as the leader of the New South. Of course, they still occasionally named their sons Braxton and Zebulon, in honor of their Confederate, slaver ancestors, and they still didn't invite their string of mulatto relatives with the same looks and last name to sit down at the family table.

"New South," Ardell had told Blanche, "means sending their kids to integrated schools—long as aint no more than one or two colored children present—instead of sending them to all-white Christian academies like they used to do. New South is celebrating Martin Luther King Day without mentioning that their daddies wanted to kill him, and hiring outfits like us for a lot less than they pay the big white caterers. New South *aint* about getting up off none of that power or big bucks, and it sure don't mean doing a damned thing for the real poor. The New South is where they capitalize Nigger."

Blanche would have been surprised if it were otherwise. This was still America, after all.

Jason and Nancy were also co-chairs of the Farleigh Bicentennial Committee. Jason wasn't around at the moment, but his lady wife was dogging Ardell's steps—asking questions that said she was nervous about Ardell's ability to do her job. Blanche wondered how long Ardell would put up with it. Less than a minute later, Ardell gave Blanche a pleading look.

Blanche headed Nancy off and corralled her toward one of the delicate-looking gold-and-white chairs just off the dance floor. "Ma'am, why don't you have a seat here? You must be bushed, what with all you've had to do."

Like getting your hair done and getting on Ardell's nerves, Blanche added to herself. "I'll make you a nice cup of tea." She took another look at the woman. Nancy's eyes glowed feverishly; she was breathing a little fast. "Maybe a nice glass of sherry would be more fortifying?"

"Oh yes, please! That would be lovely," the woman said as though the governess had unexpectedly offered her a cookie. Blanche watched her almost wiggle with pleasure. She wasn't so much a plain woman as a plain-seeming one. Something about the way she ducked her head when she spoke. The happiness she showed at the simple offer of a glass of her own wine reminded Blanche of a dog more accustomed to being kicked than stroked.

Nancy Morris pushed a stray tendril of wispy hair behind her ear. She gazed up at Blanche with a smile as she took the glass of sherry from the tray Blanche held out to her. She took a sip, sighed, and leaned back in her chair.

"It's my first ball, you see. We've had parties, of course, but my mother-in-law always . . ." She looked around the gold-and-white mirrored room bigger than the parking lot in Blanche's housing development back in Boston.

Blanche wondered if Nancy Morris would ever have occasion to understand the luxury of having nothing worse to worry about than hosting your first dance.

A white woman with heavy legs and a pale, waxy face entered the ballroom and came toward them. She walked like she didn't think she belonged in the room: her eyes lowered, her hands folded at her waist, and almost a curtsy when she got Nancy's attention. In an accent heavy in high-note endings, she told Nancy she was wanted on the phone. Trophy help, Blanche thought. Probably Nancy's imported personal maid. Ardell had told her it was all the rage among the area's rich to have a white servant with a foreign accent.

"Ladies' maids, nannies, social secretaries," Ardell had told her. "But not cooks. These whitefolks know who cooks what they like, the way they like it."

When Nancy's back was turned, the woman gave Blanche a you-are-lower-than-mud kind of look, then sniffed and tossed her head. Blanche wondered if this was a case of aping the attitude toward blacks that the woman saw in her employers. She knew from experience in other households that people who came to America later in life often bought into the racist hype about blacks as a way of proving they were real Americans. Blanche impulsively thumbed her nose. The woman fluffed herself up, spun on her heels, and marched out of the room behind her mistress.

The sound of breaking glass sent Blanche hurrying from surveying the layout of the elaborate refreshments setup off the ballroom back to the kitchen. She pushed open the kitchen door. "Everything okay?" She could see that it wasn't.

A tall, muscular white man had Clarice pinned in the corner. She tried to duck under his arm but he lowered it and pressed closer, laughing all the time.

"Get the hell away from her." Rage deepened Blanche's voice. Her breath felt hot in her mouth. The man turned his head toward her. There was something familiar about him. His eyes glistened; dark brown hair fell over his forehead. Blanche could see him sweating. He looked at her as though he knew her voice wasn't one he had to obey. He didn't release Clarice. Blanche looked around for a weapon.

"What's going on here?"

All three people in the room turned toward the man and woman who'd just entered the kitchen. It was the man who'd spoken. The woman was Nancy Morris. Blanche assumed the man was Nancy's husband, Jason.

The other man quickly stepped away from Clarice. "No problem, Big Bro," he said. "We were just havin a little fun, weren't we, gals?" He looked from Clarice to Blanche, both of whom stared at him as though he were a talking dog-turd.

"You the only one having fun, mister," Blanche said.

Jason was across the large room in four steps. He grabbed his brother by the arm. "Get out of my way, Seth." Jason pushed his brother aside and turned to Clarice. "Are you all right, miss?" he asked. "Here"—he gently guided Clarice to a chair, then knelt in front of her—"did he hurt you? Are you . . ."

Clarice nodded her head without looking at him.

Jason Morris glared at his brother, who smirked in a way that made Blanche want to spit on him.

"Apologize. Now!" Jason said.

Blanche noticed that Nancy Morris was staring at her husband with what seemed like amusement in her eyes. Blanche wondered what it was about this scene that the woman could possibly find funny. Nancy opened her mouth as if to speak but didn't. Jason stood and faced his brother. They were like light and dark photographs of the same person, Jason pale-eyed and curly blond, Seth with dark eyes and limp, almost black hair. Yet their noses, the size and set of their ears, the shape of their chins and bodies were all the same.

"I said apologize." Jason sounded even less like a man willing to take no for an answer than he had the first time. Seth looked from Jason to Nancy. She turned away, no doubt embarrassed to have her brother-in-law forced to apologize to a servant, and in front of others. It just wasn't done—which sent Jason right up in Blanche's estimation.

Seth finally gave Clarice the same smirk he'd offered his brother. "Sorry about that." He turned and sauntered toward the kitchen door with his hands in his pockets. Blanche half expected him to start whistling. He looked back over his shoulder as he left. Something about the tilt of his head or the light triggered Blanche's memory. She knew why he'd seemed familiar: she'd seen him before, and she remembered where, too.

Jason stared after Seth until the kitchen door swung closed, then turned to Blanche and Clarice. "I can't tell you how sorry I am that such a thing should happen in my home. I hope you will accept my apology and that of my wife and family. There is no excuse for my brother's behavior and I will not attempt to make one. Now if you'll excuse us."

Nancy Morris listened to her husband's speech with folded arms. Her look reminded Blanche of someone watching a magic trick and trying to figure out how it was done. It was not the kind of look Blanche would have expected from the mousy little worrier to whom she'd served sherry earlier.

When the door swung closed behind them, Blanche went to Clarice and put her arm around the woman's shoulders.

Tears rolled down Clarice's cheeks. "Nasty-assed thing!" Her nostrils quivered. "Waited till I was in here by myself, puttin his hands all . . ." Blanche could smell Clarice's rage, like hair burning.

"When Mr. Henry hear 'bout this, he gon grab that white man and . . ." Clarice made motions with her hands as though she had them wrapped around Seth's throat. She stopped suddenly and gave Blanche a teary look full of panic. "I aint gon tell him, though. Mr. Henry don't need that kinda trouble, he . . ." Clarice's lips trembled so fiercely she couldn't continue.

Blanche was thrown back to the days just after she was raped, when she had longed for the solace of telling her then boyfriend, Leo, what Palmer had done to her. She hadn't told him for the same reason Clarice wouldn't tell Mr. Henry about Seth. Blanche pulled Clarice to her and hugged her hard, as if that could protect them from the pain of this piece of black women's old race knowledge: their rapes and mistreatments at the hands of powerful white men could also cost them the black men who loved them. There were more local stories than either woman wanted to remember of what had happened to black men who'd attempted to defend their daughters and wives, mothers and sisters. But that didn't mean nothing could be done about Seth.

"Maybe we'll get a chance to fix him something special," Blanche said. "Just a little something special on his plate or in his drink in payment for what he did to you." Blanche remembered times when she'd used just this method after some insult from an employer that she couldn't address directly without losing a job she needed to keep. She shut her mind against the memory of the time she hadn't fought back.

Clarice heaved a clearing sigh and nodded. "Yeah, a real special somethin." She forced a grin through the last of her tears.

"Shoulda stabbed that fucker in the nuts!" Ardell said when she heard about the Seth incident.

"Not till we get paid. He's our client's brother, remember?" Blanche told her how Jason had forced Seth to apologize, then added: "I seen that Seth before, and he was acting like a booty-hound then! He's the man I saw with his tongue down some woman's throat at the train station. Remember, Ardell?"

"Oh yeah. That was him? Wonder who the woman was."

"I didn't get a good look at her. Just hair and big eyes."

"I bet it wasn't that very pregnant wife I saw him come in with."

"Well, at least his brother made that dog apologize," Clarice said.

"And me and Clarice got our own special way of dealing with Seth," Blanche told Ardell.

Ardell looked from one to the other. "Less I know about it the better, I think."

The guests were about to arrive when Jason came back to the kitchen. His wife was with him. Blanche assumed he'd come back to say whatever he'd planned to say when he'd caught his brother acting like a dog in rut. This time Nancy's expression matched her husband's in relaxed affability.

"My wife and I just wanted to tell you how pleased we are that your company is participating in the Farleigh bicentennial celebrations. You know, it's not enough to simply end segregation. It's not enough to rest on the great progress we've made in the South. A share of the pie is what full citizenship and equality . . ."

Blanche and Ardell gave each other a "Can you believe this shit?" look. Blanche understood what Jason thought he was saying about economic development for black folks, but what she was hearing was a relatively young white man, with inherited wealth and power and all the privileges that go with that profile, telling them that he and Ardell were equals because a little black catering outfit had a contract to serve white people while they partied, as black people have always done. And the contract was just a one-time thing. There'd been two years of fund-raising events for the bicentennial—all of them catered by white caterers.

". . . and thank you in advance for what I am sure will be a wonderful repast."

Repast? Give me a break! People were ever amazing. In the little time she'd known this man, she'd seen two different people in him: one who was concerned and kind to Clarice; another who'd been so furious with his brother that she'd half expected them to come to blows; now here he was sounding like a bad politician with an icicle up his butt. She wondered who he really was. She watched with amusement as he looked from face to face. Did he expect them to applaud, or break out in a heartfelt rendition of "Old Black Joe"? Ardell let him feel the weight of their silence before she stepped forward.

"We certainly do appreciate this opportunity to be a part of the bicentennial by bidding our services right alongside more established caterers."

Blanche took Ardell's last comment as a reminder to Jason that all he'd done was clear the doorway. Ardell had gotten through it by being good and willing to cut her profits to the nub.

When Jason left, Nancy stayed behind.

"My husband . . . We just hope that this . . . the earlier incident won't . . ." She pulled her head in so far her chin seemed to rest on her neck; she looked up at them without raising it. "My brother-in-law is sometimes too . . . gets overly . . . I hope we can keep this confidential?" She looked quickly from face to face and took their silence as the answer she wanted to hear. "Well, that's fine, then." She hurried out of the room.

"Whitefolks!" Blanche, Ardell, and Clarice all said at once and burst out laughing, even though it wasn't the Morrises' whiteness but their lameness that was laughable.

When Blanche went back out into the refreshment alcove off the ballroom, there were about ten or twelve people milling around with drinks in their hands and another thirty or forty dancing to a small band in the ballroom—heads bobbing like corks in a sea of black tie, sequins, and satin. She was fascinated by the lack of color in the women's clothes. There were some lovely gowns but they were all pearl or white or a middling shade of blue. If there was a red gown in the room, or one whose tulle, satin, seed pearls, or modest décolletage was not interchangeable, she couldn't find it. She noticed that two of the three black women guests were wearing dressy leather shoes. She began to check out the white women's feet. There was a pair of leather shoes. There another. She gave these leather-shoes-wearing women—black and white—a closer looking over. Their gowns seemed expensive enough, although there were more skintight fits than among the other women present. A couple of the men with the leather-shoe women were wearing business suits instead of tuxedos. They also had larger hand gestures and worse haircuts than the other white men standing and dancing around. Blanche figured these folks were the race/class-diversity guests: people invited as symbols of the New South's integration of both blacks and up-from-working-class whites. But shoes are one of the ways you know who's who in the class club, she thought. It was possible for some everyday people to get a good education, so having gone to Yale or Harvard wasn't always enough to identify you as one of the serious haves. But Yale didn't teach you to have your cloth shoes dyed to match your ball gown, or the difference between formal and semiformal wear. She always cracked up when she heard some (usually overrich) white politician going on about classless America—a country where only one class counted.

Blanche spotted Seth Morris standing at the bar, relaxed and laughing with another man as though he hadn't just been caught assaulting Clarice. The man with Seth had his back to Blanche. He raised his hand to get the bartender's attention. "Bourbon and branch," the man said.

A stomach cramp nearly doubled her over. The light grew dingy; a smell, bitter and fruity, like milk about to turn, stung her nose; the music went flat; and she was suddenly cold. The pleasant buzz and hum of people talking and laughing rumbled ugly, like a mob forming. She covered her mouth and hurried toward the kitchen, vomit burning her throat. Someone spoke to her; she hardly heard and didn't heed. She yanked the back door open and ran down an unlit driveway, her heart and her footfall beating like call and response. Ardell caught her by the arm and jerked her to a stop. They both stood panting for a moment.

"It's him," Blanche said. "He's in there."

Ardell didn't need an explanation. "Oh shit! I knew we shoulda talked about this. But you never seemed to want . . ." She put her arms around Blanche and hugged her close. Then she took her car keys from her pocket and gave them to Blanche. "You go on home." Blanche almost dropped the keys. Her hand was slippery with sweat.

She sat in the car for a minute or two, chastising herself for being so weak. She'd thought she was prepared to see him, had come to Farleigh to face him somehow. Yet the sound of his voice, the knowledge of his presence, was a boil erupting in her brain, oozing poison as though it were only yesterday that David Palmer had raped her at knifepoint. Her head slammed against the headrest, propelled by memory so sharp she could smell the lavender bubble bath in the tub she'd been soaking in at Palmer's sister's house, where she was supposed to be working. What had she been thinking about in the moment before he'd pushed back the bathroom door? She raised her hands to her aching skull, clawing at his hands as she'd done back then, trying to loosen her hair from his grip. Slipping, banging her knees and legs against the tub, trying to get on her feet, too shocked and scared to scream. Then the knife. The knife: long, slim, pointed; carvings on its fancy bone handle—the kind of knife a boy got for his twelfth birthday. The kind of knife that stopped all struggling, that made her repeat, "Please, don't cut me, please," over and over and over again, as though the words could protect her from a slit throat, a pierced heart. Once again, she watched herself pleading for her life while parts of her were being stolen and murdered. When it was over—when he had grunted and poked and shivered his sperm into her, then finally fled—for just a flash, for just a fast beat of her heart, she'd been grateful that he had only raped her. For this alone she would hate him until the moment after she died. Suddenly she felt as though she'd been frozen for the last eight years, as though her life were a game of Monopoly in which she was stuck at Go. Certainly she had gone on with her life and she'd done all right with what she had to work with. But she could see now that a part of her was still back there, curled up like a broken child on that bathroom floor.

Her throat clogged with the same questions that had plagued her the day it had happened: Why hadn't she locked the bathroom door before she got in the tub? Would she have had the courage to fight him if he'd caught her with her clothes on, in the kitchen, with its large variety of possible weapons? Was she wrong about how she would have been treated by the police and courts if she'd reported him and pressed charges? Was she wrong in her belief that to do so would have meant the end of her working in white people's homes in Farleigh? Blanche leaned her head against the steering wheel, amazed that this old wound could be so easily reached and ripped wide open simply by the sound of his voice.

What would have happened if she hadn't run away just now, if she'd turned and faced him? Her knees knocked together and her hands trembled. Her weakness made her cry hot, stinging tears that left her feeling no better. She started the car and drove home.

She couldn't rest. She checked the windows and door locks three times and was glad the place was too small to have an entrance that was not within her view.

She heard voices outside. She turned out the lights and stood listening, a butcher knife gripped in her hand, her ears and eyes concentrated on the partially open window: a man and a woman arguing, like lightning and thunder. "No!" the woman shouted. Another victim? "Godamnit!" from the man. A thin wail, sad and scared, made Blanche flinch. That makes three of us tonight, she thought. A door slammed. A car started, then sped past her house and around the corner. Quiet. Blanche turned on the lights, the radio. No. She could hear better with the radio off, hear someone sliding up to her door, trying the knob, scrambling around the bungalow trying to peek in through the space between the curtains and the windowsill. She wedged a chair beneath the front-door knob, and thought about iron bars for the windows. Maybe a dog. Pacing the floor, sweat cooling on her forehead, she gave a little shriek when the phone rang. She picked up the receiver, but didn't speak.

"Hello? Hello?" A man's voice. "Hello, Blanche? Is that you?"

Blanche let out the breath she'd been holding. "Thelvin, hey." She worked at sounding as if she'd just been mindlessly flipping through a magazine. "How you doin?"

"Everything all right?" he asked as though his fingers were on her wrist, charting her racing pulse.

"Why you think something's wrong?"

"Well, you're home, for one thing. The message you left on my machine said you were working tonight. And you sound kinda . . ."

"If you didn't think I was home, why'd you call me?" She could hear suspicion thick as fresh cream in her voice. She reminded herself that Thelvin wasn't David Palmer. He was a different man. A different kind, even a different color of man. But right now it was only the man part that mattered.

Thelvin cleared his throat before suggesting, "Maybe I oughta hang up and call back." His voice was as careful as a person trying to cross the highway during rush hour.

Blanche wanted to explain, to tell him it wasn't about him, but she wasn't sure this was true. Maybe some other woman was catching hell from Thelvin; maybe he had similar plans for her. In the region of her mind where fear didn't run things, she knew she was being unfair. But that section of her brain wasn't currently in control.

"I'm sorry, Thelvin. Mood I'm in, I shouldn't have answered the phone."

"Anything I can do?"

"No. I'll be okay after a good night's sleep." She hesitated, then: "But why *did* you call if you didn't think I was home?"

"Oh. I thought maybe you might have an answering machine, too. I wanted to tell you I got to cover for a brother whose wife's got sick. So I can't keep our date."

"Oh. Okay." She was both relieved and disappointed. She wanted to see him, but right now a date with a man she didn't really know wasn't something she could look forward to.

Thelvin cleared his throat again. "Okay, then. I'll call you when I get back."

"Okay."

"Blanche? Are you sure you're all right?"

"I'm fine, Thelvin, just fine. Have a good trip. Bye."

Of course she felt like a fool after she hung up. Man must think I'm some kind of nut case.

The phone rang again before she'd walked away from it.

"Hey, Ardell," she said when she picked it up.

"I been calling you." Ardell's voice swung between worry and irritation.

"I was talking to Thelvin."

"Humm. How'd he know you were home?"

Blanche was too accustomed to their thinking alike to be surprised. She told Ardell what Thelvin had said about an answering machine and added: "Sorry about taking off on you like that, Ardell, but I . . ."

"Don't worry about it. Like I said, we shoulda talked about it."

"Why didn't we?"

"I tried to, remember? But you kept changing the . . ."

"I won't run again," Blanche told her. "He aint keeping me from nothing."

"Humm, well, better to run from him than kill him, I guess."

"Better for which one of us?" Blanche asked. He'd already killed the woman she'd been before he raped her. Would murdering him change her much more than he already had? When she hung up the phone, she went straight to bed—with all the lights on.

She slept hardly at all. Every new night sound required a period of attention until it was identified as something other than David Palmer in search of seconds. Somewhere in the drifting place between waking and sleeping she understood that she needed a ritual, something that would let her drop all the baggage she was carrying from that awful day. She fell asleep wondering what that ritual would be.

Number Four,
Cake, and the Lay of the Land

"A local girl was found dead in Briarmount Woods, outside of Farleigh, last evening."

Blanche's eyes flew open. She turned her head and stared at the clock radio. Her body clenched like a fist as the reporter somber-toned his way through a report of the murder of Maybelle Jenkins, age twenty-two, hit on the back of the head with a blunt instrument and dumped over an embankment. Number four, Blanche whispered, as though there were a straight line or chain connecting her, Clarice, the woman she'd heard cry out last night, and now this dead girl. Had this girl been raped as well as murdered? She'd read somewhere that seven hundred thousand women were raped every year in the United States. Had this girl been one of them? For once, the idea that she was not alone did not comfort her. She stared at the radio, then turned it off and rolled out of bed. She needed to talk to her Ancestors right now, but she hadn't yet set up her Ancestor altar.

She hadn't brought all the items from her home altar, just enough to give this temporary one the same feel of being a part of the everyday world yet larger and deeper, and somehow connected to her, like a centuries-

long umbilical cord tying her to all of her bloodline. She got a cardboard
box and set it on its side so its flaps formed doors. She draped the box in a
red scarf and spread a white one inside, tacking it to the sides and back so
that it formed a little grotto in which she placed stones, a small bowl of
water, and the pictures of her dead relatives from her home altar—she'd
had a number of them copied onto one sheet of paper. She hung multicolored beads around the neck of the black, potbellied wooden figure that
represented her oldest Ancestors, older than the first known mother—the
one whose DNA scientists said most people shared. She set this figure in
the center of the altar and placed two white candles in front of the box.

She paused when she was through, trying to decide how to talk with her
Ancestors about what she was going through without whining or asking
for special favors. She knew she didn't need to explain it to *them*. They
knew about rape, they knew about fear, and they hadn't been stopped by
either. They'd found ways to fight back—from running away to killing as
many slavers as they could, from aborting the slaver's issue to hexing his
penis so he'd never want to touch that particular woman again, to putting
pepper in the slop pot and spit in the soup. They had not run from their
enemies, except to rest up and find another way to fight. And there it was.
It was as if the answer to last night's question was being whispered in her
ear: Find a way to fight back. She was suddenly sure that the ritual she
needed to rid her life of David Palmer was to take action against him—not
in a legal way, or even by getting in his face. All he'd have to do was deny
it. She had no proof. No. She had to find a way to get to him so that he
would really suffer. It was that or leave town right now, and she was no
more about to let him scare her back to Boston than she was about to dye
her hair purple and get green contact lenses. She had no idea how she was
going to cause David Palmer grief, but she was sure her Ancestors had
guided her to this decision. A way would present itself.

She called Ardell to tell her about this Palmer revelation.

"Humm. About time! But first I want to know how you're feeling. You
were in a pretty bad way last night," Ardell said.

Blanche saw herself running from the sight of Palmer, afraid to turn
around for fear she might see his face. His eyes. Last night, she'd felt
trapped, as though Palmer had allowed her a long lease on herself that he
could end the moment he decided to kick in her door, put another knife to
her throat, and take over her body again.

"Blanche?"

"I'm . . . I'm going to be okay. Seeing him like that . . . I was just caught off guard. I need to do something about him, is all. I see that now. When it first happened, I swore I'd get back at him some way. Then . . . I don't know. After I left here, I thought . . . I didn't expect the fear! I thought that was done and . . . But I ran. I ran."

"Humm, well, like you said, you were caught off guard. But you'll be ready for him from now on."

From now on? Blanche recoiled from the phrase even though she knew Ardell was right. They were working for his social set. He'd be at more than just that one bicentennial event. She'd likely be seeing a lot of him.

"And I'm damned proud of you," Ardell said. "It's past time for you to do something about him." Ardell had never agreed with Blanche's decision not to bring charges against Palmer.

"Yeah, well, I still don't know *what* I'm gonna do."

"You will. We'll think of something," Ardell said.

Blanche took comfort from the sound of that "we."

"You hear about that girl they found dead in the woods?" Ardell asked.

Blanche's arms felt suddenly chilly. "A little. On the radio."

"Yeah. White girl. I feel sorry for any person dying like that," Ardell said, "and you know it's gonna cause a whole heap of trouble."

Blanche knew what she meant. "Yeah, I guess, even in the New South, when a white woman's killed lots of whitefolks still automatically think black."

"Damn! I sure hope none of the wait-staff boys get picked up! Or that shifty-eyed Zeke. I shoulda fired his behind before now. I can't keep letting his sick and out-of-work wife be the reason I put up with him. Next bit of trouble and he's out."

Blanche couldn't think of a better reason for putting up with Zeke and said so.

"I got a business to run, I can't let . . ." Ardell sounded as defensive as a cheating husband caught with his paramour. "What're you getting at, Blanche?"

Blanche hesitated. She didn't want to get Ardell's back up any higher, but she couldn't help but think about that woman who'd been the talk of Harlem when Blanche lived there. The woman, while on welfare, had always been in the government's face agitating for more help for the poor.

She'd organized tenants in the projects to demand better maintenance and demonstrated until the city put a child-care center in her neighborhood health clinic. Then she'd won the lottery for three million dollars, become a Republican, spoke out against the lazy poor, and moved to a gated community. "Some differences between being the boss and being the worker are bad for everybody."

"Humm, well, we'll see how you feel about that when you're a partner. I gotta go. My other line is clicking. I'm expecting a call from a client."

Blanche hung up the phone and added what it meant to be the boss to the list of things she and Ardell would likely be talking about for years to come.

Blanche did some stretches and push-ups, showered, dressed, and ate some toast and yogurt. She had time for a second cup of tea before Ardell picked her up. They were going to visit the cooks.

Blanche wondered if Ardell would bring up their telephone conversation, but she obviously had other things on her mind when she arrived.

"You gotta help me with these old girls, Blanche."

Ardell drove them toward the outskirts of Farleigh.

"Half the time they're too evil or ornery to even speak, and when they're not, they're . . . well, I don't know, odd, I guess."

"Odd how?"

"Humm, there's their names, for one thing."

"Well, I know their last name's Hasting and they were always called Miz Monday and Miz Tuesday. What else is there to know?"

Ardell nodded. "Those are their real names. But that aint . . . Wait. Just wait. You'll see."

Blanche wondered if Ardell was exaggerating to make Blanche feel needed enough to say yes to a partnership in Carolina Catering.

Ardell turned off the highway onto a road with fields on both sides covered with the bright-green fuzz of some crop just coming up. The air was so fresh it seemed to sparkle.

"They still cook just fine," Ardell went on, "but something aint right. Maybe it's knowing I can't cook that makes 'em treat me like a child or . . . I don't know. Something just don't feel right. You know what I mean?"

Of course, Blanche understood. Just because you didn't see or feel a mosquito didn't stop its bite from being real. Blanche was now sure there was something about the elderly sisters that was making Ardell uneasy. She was curious about what it might be. Blanche hadn't seen them for more years than she could recall. Like most people, she'd never been able to tell them apart, except on those days when they wore different hairstyles. Both sisters were members of a breed of mostly dead famous black women cooks in big plantation houses around the region. When Blanche was a girl, the society and food columns in newspapers across the state had often gushed over the feasts the Hasting sisters had prepared for their employers and their guests. Nowadays, young black women with those kinds of skills took themselves out of Farleigh and other such towns to Atlanta and Winston-Salem, where they opened their own restaurants, or ruled the kitchens of other people's. Blanche remembered hearing that the twins were once pressured by the Governor's wife to give up one of their secret recipes to be included in a high-toned charity cookbook being done by an upper-crust ladies' group. The twins had refused but had given the very same recipe to a bunch of black parents putting out a cookbook to raise money for a new playground.

Now, standing in front of them, Blanche wondered if it were really possible for the Hasting twins to have the exact same deep wrinkles coursing down and across their round, pudgy faces. It wasn't only their wrinkles that were the same. Everything matched—button-round eyes and pillowy hips and bosoms, long, strong-looking fingers, rosy brown complexions— everything except their hair. One of them wore an old-fashioned pageboy. The other had her hair pulled back in a tight little bun. Although their eyebrows and the wisps of facial hair above their upper lips were silver-white, the hair on their heads was blacker than pitch.

"Well, look who's here, Eighteen, and she . . ." the one with the pageboy began.

"Got somebody with her, Seventeen," said the one with the bun. They turned to Ardell:

"Who is . . ." Seventeen-pageboy began.

"Your friend?" Eighteen-bun added.

Ardell gave Blanche a see-I-told-you-so look before introducing Blanche to the two women.

"We know your mama and knew . . ." Miz Seventeen said.

"Your daddy when you and your sister, God rest her soul . . ." her sister added.

"Was just bitty girls," Seventeen said.

They both looked Blanche over as though they were quality-control inspectors. When they'd finished, they nodded to each other.

"Y'all," said one.

"Sit," said the other, as she and her sister lowered themselves to the purple horsehair sofa.

"Is you home," Seventeen said.

"Visitin your mama?" Eighteen asked.

"Yes, ma'am—I mean, ma'ams," Blanche said. "And helping Ardell out with the catering business."

The sisters looked at each other for a few moments, then back at Blanche. "Help her out," the one with the pageboy said.

"How?" said the one with the bun.

"Oh, just kinda pitch in," Ardell said before Blanche could answer. "You know, keep things moving, make sure your fine food's served right, check on the clearing-ups and so forth. I need somebody 'cause it's so busy now, you know, with the bicentennial and all the parties and the . . ."

Blanche didn't know why Ardell didn't want the twins to know Blanche was also a cook, but it was clear she didn't.

The sisters gave each other another nod, then turned to Blanche with identical sweet half-smiles on their faces. They rose from the sofa in unison.

"We gonna make y'all . . ." said one.

"A nice cup of tea," said the other.

Both women went off toward the back of the house.

Blanche could hardly wait for them to leave the room. "What's up with this number calling?" she whispered.

"See? I told you they were odd. They're twins, right? But one was born on the thirty-first of December, 1917, just before midnight. The other one was born on the first of January, 1918, just after the new year began. So, they call each other Seventeen and Eighteen. It was Miz Minnie who told me how it works. I didn't know what the hell was going on first time I came out here. On top of that, Miz Minnie said sometimes they tell people they're cousins. Now, what's that about?"

Miz Seventeen poked her head into the living room. "Y'all come on through," she said.

"And have a sit-down," Miz Eighteen added over her shoulder.

Blanche followed Ardell down a short, dark hallway to a room crowded around a huge claw-footed dining-room table, six chairs, a sideboard, and a china closet. Everyone, except lean Ardell, had to squeeze by the furniture to get into the chairs.

"Well, now," Miz Eighteen began after she and her sister had arranged tea, cups, and cookies on the table. She opened the small spiral notebook beside her plate. "Let me . . ."

"See what all we need," Miz Seventeen said, and eased the notebook closer to her own place.

Eighteen reached for the notebook. "Last time you . . ."

Miz Seventeen snatched the notebook and put it on the other side of her teacup, out of Miz Eighteen's reach.

"But last time you . . ." Miz Eighteen began again.

"Now, Eighteen, I *am* the oldest, so I'll handle this. You pour the tea."

"I poured the tea last time and the time before that," Miz Eighteen complained. "You said that . . ."

Miz Seventeen angled out of her chair. "Excuse us, please." She smiled at Blanche and Ardell and turned toward the kitchen, holding the notebook tight against her bosom. Her sister followed her.

Ardell and Blanche could hear the sound of loud, emphatic whispering from the next room, but couldn't make out any actual words. Blanche wanted to move closer to the kitchen to listen, but she was afraid of being caught. When the twins returned, Miz Seventeen still had the notebook and a triumphant gleam in her eye.

"Now. Like I was saying"—she gave her sister a sidelong look—"we done made a list of what we need to fill this here order you had that gal drop off t'other day." While her sister poured tea, Miz Seventeen pulled a stubby pencil from her apron pocket and wet its tip with a flick of her tongue. "Five pounds of chocolate, two quarts of cream, a box of salt, two boxes of baking powder and powdered sugar, twenty-five pounds of butter . . ."

Twenty-five pounds of butter?! Blanche cut her eyes at Ardell, who was too busy writing down what she was being told to notice. Ardell had told Blanche earlier that the sisters were to make five yellow cakes, some yeast rolls, and petits fours. But twenty-five pounds of butter?

Ardell read the list back to them. When she was done, the twins stared at her as if waiting for Ardell to speak. When she didn't, the sisters looked at each other, then turned back to Ardell. "Make that thirty pounds of butter," they said in unison.

"That sure is a lot of butter," Blanche said.

The sisters locked Blanche in their sights. "Well, that's why they . . ." began Miz Seventeen.

"Call 'em butter cakes!" her sister added.

Blanche ducked her head and bit her lip to keep from howling with laughter. Ardell was right about something being up with these two but they were more crafty than weird. Blanche wondered if the twins were simply stocking their own larder with the extras collected from Ardell, or did they have a little grocery business on the side?

When they were back in the car, Blanche explained what she thought was going on.

"I knew it!" Ardell shouted. "I knew something was up with those two witches! But I never thought they was outright thieves, not two upstanding old colored ladies like them! I'm gonna have to do something about those two! You really can't trust nobody no more. What about Mr. Broadnax? You think maybe he's ripping me off, too? I know you remember him and his smoked turkey and that smoked fish he does! Melts on the way to your mouth! He's another character. I'll swing by his place on the way back to town."

Blanche shook her head. "Unh-unh. I got to get some groceries and . . ." She hesitated for a few seconds. "And I want to go out to the mall to get an answering machine."

Ardell grinned when she dropped Blanche off at the mall. "Get a good one, now. Y'all don't want to miss none of them new-boyfriend calls."

"Go on, girl!" Blanche flipped Ardell a wave and walked away.

She bought an answering machine and some groceries, stopped by the hardware store, and caught the bus. As soon as she got home, she hooked up her new machine. She could hear Ardell teasing her as she worked. It was a pleasure to have someone to be teased about.

The out-of-doors was loudly calling her name by the time she'd finished with the answering machine. It was time she walked her street anyway, mingle with her surroundings, maybe meet her neighbors.

There were only three other houses along Rush Road—the formal name of Blanche's street, although everybody called it Miz Alice Way. The other three houses were all larger than the Miz Alice, two on Blanche's side and one across the street, next to the weedy lot that was directly across the street from Blanche.

Blanche spoke and introduced herself to the woman sweeping her porch next door.

"You Miz Cora's girl," the woman said. She looked older than Blanche but, depending upon how many kids she'd had and what kind of other work she did, could have been ten years younger. "I'm Gwennie Borran, useta be Greeley. My oldest sister, Loretta, and your sister, Rosalie, God rest her soul, was girlfriends."

Blanche didn't pretend she remembered Gwennie but she was pleased to be already known on her street. She knew Miz Mary and Miz Rayna had lived in the next house until they'd died within days of each other. They were supposed to have been cousins, but Blanche, and pretty much everyone else, had assumed their relationship was a more intimate one. The curtains at the window and an open carton on the porch said someone else lived in the house now, but no one seemed to be at home. Blanche walked beyond the houses to where the street met some woods, then turned around and walked back on the other side of the road. There was no sign of life at the house on that side of the street, but the bad vibe she got from the house nearly knocked her to her knees. She hurried across the road to where Gwennie was pulling weeds out front and asked who lived there.

"No-count Negro from Mobile or somewhere. Got a wife and three sweet girls. He aint shit. I know you heard him the other night." Blanche reheard the wail that had pierced the air while she was on Palmer alert. She rubbed at the goose bumps on her arms and felt a tug on the chain of harmed women she'd imagined earlier.

". . . makes me sick," Gwennie said. "Gets drunk and . . ." The phone rang in Gwennie's house. As she turned to go inside, she motioned for Blanche to wait, but Blanche decided not to. She'd heard all she wanted to know about that house and the people in it. She walked back toward the Miz Alice.

The red light on her new answering machine was already blinking when she went in. She took the instruction booklet out of the drawer and checked to make sure she wouldn't Erase when she wanted to Playback. There was one message:

"Hey, Blanche. It's Thelvin. I'm coming home tonight. You up for a little dinner and dancing tomorrow night? I'd sure like to see you. Leave me a message that says 'Yes.'"

Blanche examined herself for remnants of the flash of distrust she'd felt when Thelvin had called last night. It was gone. In the light of day, she knew there were men and then there were David Palmers. She'd spent years relearning this distinction.

She called Thelvin's number and left him the message he said he wanted to hear, adding that she'd look for him around six unless she heard otherwise.

She spent the rest of the afternoon putting a chain lock on her front door and hammering nails into the window frames so the windows couldn't be raised high enough for a man to crawl inside. She put one of the foot-long lengths of pipe she'd bought beside her bed, and the other just inside the front door, in case she needed to bash somebody's brains out. She put the hunting knife under her pillow. She felt a little safer when she was done, but not really better. Her fortifications reminded her of how women were told to stay off the streets after dark when a rapist was loose in the community. She always thought it was men who should be locked inside.

She turned on the radio, then turned it off when the newscaster began talking about Maybelle's murder. Blanche didn't know why this unknown young white woman's death upset her so much. Was it the timing—waking up to hear about Maybelle's murder the morning after seeing Palmer—that made this death seem so personal somehow? If so, her extra distress was just more proof that David Palmer was taking up too much space in her mind. Her current life seemed to be stepping aside to let the past run her: run her scared, with the little hits of flashback that had begun searing her nerves and making her heart race; run her paranoid, look what she was doing right now, with locks and nails; run her hateful, with fantasies of Palmer in pain. She knew rancor and fear were bad for her, not just for her mind, but her body as well—this was the kind of shit that made a person sick, the way she'd been after the rape: talking to herself on the street, moaning so loud in her sleep that she woke herself up. She thought of calling Ardell, to try to talk away some of the pressure she was feeling. But she didn't want to talk about it. She didn't want to be relieved of the stress. She just wanted to be shed of David Palmer and the poison he poured into her life. I got to get rid of him, she told the Miz Alice. I got to.

She felt a surge of relief and pleasure when the phone rang. She already knew who it was as she always did when someone she cared about called her or was about to knock on her door.

"Hey, sweetie pie," she said, only to have a recording tell her to push 1 to accept the charges.

"Hi, Mom," Taifa said when they were connected, and then yawned.

"Tired, hunh?"

"Am I ever! On top of working in the restaurant all day, we had a fire drill in the middle of the night, and I had to go into town for gel for my hair and . . ."

"But you're okay?"

"Yeah. Hungry. We're going out for pizza." She yawned again.

"Who's 'we'?"

"My roommate, Charlotte Boyd, and this other girl, Marcia Lamb. They're both from Connecticut."

"Tell me about your room."

"Oh, wow, Moms! They've built this whole new part since we were here and all the girls that work here live in a bunch of rooms in the new part. It's deeply cool."

"Have you seen Christine Crowley, or anybody else you know?" The faces of people she'd met at Amber Cove flashed across Blanche's mind. At least two of them brought a fillip of remembered pain—but only the memory of it.

"I saw Mrs. Crowley at lunch. She asked about you. And that older lady you liked was with her. I can't remember her name."

Blanche didn't want to remember it, since the liking had all been on her side in the end. "What's your work schedule?"

"I think it's going to change a lot, but right now I'm waiting tables at breakfast and lunch and doing cleanup in between, so I work six-thirty to three, half-hour for lunch. I get Thursday and Monday off."

Sweet Ancestors! The child would be worn to a frazzle. She'd never done any real physical work before. "You're going to have to take care of yourself, Taifa. Eat right. Get enough sleep. Some exercise."

"Yeah, I guess so." Taifa yawned again.

Blanche wanted to tell her not to be ashamed to say the work was too much if it came to that, but she knew Taifa was the Queen of Picking Up

Vibes. She would know without being told that Blanche doubted she could handle the job.

"So you got your own place, hunh?"

"Yeah, it's great," Blanche said. "I'll tell you all about it next time. You need to get some food and some rest."

Taifa gave her the number at Amber Cove. "It's in the hall, so let it ring a long time."

"Okay, honey. You take care of yourself and . . ." Blanche caught herself about to launch into the kind of wear-clean-underwear-wash-well-and-don't-talk-to-bad-boys kind of mother-talk that she'd hated and hardly heeded as a teen. "And have fun," she said instead.

"Are you okay, Mama Blanche? You seem kinda, I don't know, your voice sounds . . ."

Speaking of picking up vibes. The girl was so focused on herself—her hair, her clothes, her future and plans—that she hardly seemed to have room for a thought about anyone else. Yet some part of her was always on duty, listening, watching, feeling people like a thermometer taking their temperature. Had she thought Taifa wouldn't notice the tightness in her voice? Blanche could hear it herself, like a scream caught in her throat since the night she saw David Palmer.

"Oh, I'm tired, too," she said. It wasn't all the truth, but at least it wasn't a lie. "A good night's sleep'll do us both good. I'll call you on Thursday."

"Okay, Moms. See ya."

"Love you."

"Love you, too, Moms. Go to bed!"

"Good idea."

In her dreams, Mr. Broadnax and the Hasting twins were in bed together in pretzel formation. Mama was walking around the bed trying to get them to put money in the collection plate, and Taifa was flipping through the whorls of Blanche's brain as though leafing through a book. And outside of it all and everywhere in it, like bad-smelling fog, was the presence of David Palmer.

6

High Tea and Hot Date

It was the kind of rainy morning that turned her bed into a cocoon of comfort, an island of coziness against the damp. But her alarm clock said, Get up and get ready for work. Blanche rolled over and stretched. At least she wouldn't have to worry about running into Palmer on today's job. She headed for the bathroom.

She was ready when Ardell came to pick her up. They were serving high tea to ten of Farleigh's wealthier old girls—which meant spending most of the day making scones in Ardell's industrial-sized oven and assembling watercress, smoked-salmon, and deviled-egg sandwiches while Ardell drove out to the Hasting twins' house. She was going to deliver the ingredients for those much-buttered cakes. But the order only included half the requested butter, so Ardell had another job to do there as well.

Blanche watched her fingering the stem of her spectacles—something Ardell only did when she was uneasy. Ardell had wanted Blanche to come along with her to see the twins, but Blanche thought it would be embarrassing enough for the old girls to be confronted by one person about their thievery. Now she wondered if that one person was up to it.

"Ardell, it aint disrespectful to call people on cheating you, even if they are old."

"But they're the best cooks around. Carolina Catering couldn't . . . Suppose they get mad and won't cook for me no more? Even if you wanted to stay, you got to go back to Boston till your kids are gone. What'll I do if they . . ."

"Aint nobody else beating down their door to cook for them, Ardell, or they wouldn't have time to cook for you. It aint their quitting you need to be worrying about, but whether you can get them to stop stealing you blind."

"Oh sweet Jesus, why me?!"

"'Cause you just what you said you wanted to be. The boss." Blanche didn't try to hide her glee. Ardell returned to playing with her eyeglasses.

"Watch your pocketbook!" Blanche called as Ardell headed out.

"Knowing those two, I'd better hang on to my liver. They may have a little transplant business on the side, too."

Blanche breezed through the baking and sandwich-making and was ready for Ardell when she got back—looking as though she'd been rolled down a hill. Even her hair was rumpled.

"Damn! What did they do to you?" Blanche pulled out a chair for Ardell to sit down.

"Girl! Those two old biddies is a mess! I hope I'm half as sharp as they are when I'm their age! Wouldn't admit a thing, of course. Although they did do a real nice little-old-ladies-who-get-confused number."

"Well, they know you're on to them. That might at least slow them down."

"Oh, they promised to be more careful with their measuring and recipes in the future. That was after I told them I was cutting back using them this summer. Give them time to think about what kinda relationship they want to have with me. Then they asked about you."

"Oh yeah?"

"Um-humm. Just as soon as I started talking about the extra ingredients they're ripping me off for."

"That means they know I dimed on 'em."

"Yep. Good thing you didn't go along. Both of us liable to be buried in their vegetable garden by now."

The tea party was held in a big old house that looked as though nothing had been changed in it since 1880. The ten women at the tea party were advertisements for shades of blue: slightly blued hair, watery blue eyes, blue-tinted bifocals, blue-veined hands hungrily clutching plates of sandwiches. They spoke in voices brittle as water crackers and heavy on wistful sighs. Blanche barely heard them. She was seeing Thelvin tonight. She was as excited as a sixteen-year-old. This was not only her first date with Thelvin, it was the first one she'd had in longer than she chose to remember. And it was a *real* date: dinner, dancing, the whole kit and caboodle, as her grandmother used to say. And she needed it. She needed to see herself in the center of a forward-moving life. There was much more to her than what had happened to her one day in one bathroom. Thelvin was a part of where she was going, not where she'd been. He reminded her that she was still her whole self.

After work, Blanche showered, then ran herself a bath into which she dropped four glycerin balls of sandalwood-scented bath oil and slipped into the tub. She wanted to feel soft and smooth and smell like more. She'd decided to wear her green dress that buttoned down the front, her brown-and-green sandals and straw bag. She liked the way the skirt of the dress swung when she walked. She had earrings almost the exact color of that dress, too. She lay back in the tub and let her legs float to the surface while she wondered how this evening would go and whether she would like Thelvin less or more when it was over. She cautioned herself not to expect too much. Thelvin was just a real man, not a dream one. She also cautioned herself not to treat him like she suspected him of being guilty of everything she was afraid of in a man—something she'd struggled through after she was raped. She could still remember the day when she'd healed enough to seek male company.

She went to the door when she saw Thelvin driving up. The earlier rain had washed the evening to a sparkling sheen. She didn't invite him in; she had her purse and jacket on her arm when she opened the door. The luscious smell of him leapt across the threshold and made her want to touch him. They grinned at each other.

"I missed you." Thelvin looked serious.

Blanche lowered her eyes. She'd been thinking about him, too, but wasn't sure it was such a good idea at this point.

"I'm looking forward to this," she said. "Jimmy's Place was still a farm when I lived here."

Jimmy's was twenty miles outside of Farleigh, which put it close enough to Hancock, Larkstone, and Dolly Point to draw customers from those towns as well as from Chapel Hill, Raleigh, and Durham. The building was born a barn—one of the farm buildings where Jimmy's daddy and granddaddy had housed their mules, cows, pigs, and chickens. The year Blanche left for Boston, Jimmy had come home from Chicago to take care of his ailing daddy, who had somehow managed to hang on to the land. When his father died, Jimmy leased out the fields and opened the club. None of the customers knew if the place was legal, and no one cared. What mattered was that black folks had a place to go to eat, drink, and, more important, to dance—not hip-hopping, house-music-loving youngsters, but people for whom the blues was the listening and dancing music of choice. Thelvin told her blues groups from all over the South came to Jimmy's. Tonight, Little Sister and the Bad Boys from Charlotte were playing.

Inside Jimmy's there were no traces of the former manure gutters, troughs, and feed passages. A dense cloud of cigarette smoke seemed to be holding up the loft. The air beneath the cloud smelled of fried chicken and greens.

It was early when Blanche and Thelvin arrived. The band wouldn't start for at least another hour. Even so, the place was already more than half full. Blanche and Thelvin snagged one of the last small tables that ringed the dance space. Behind the tiny bandstand, wide swinging doors led to the kitchen. A bucktoothed waitress with serious hips and a sweet voice came to take their order.

Blanche hesitated. She hadn't realized fried chicken was the only meat Jimmy's served. She wasn't all that eager for what usually passed for Southern-fried chicken in public places—too much grease and not enough seasoning on a piece of chicken old as her mama was usually the case. But what choice did she have? She didn't want Thelvin to think she was too cute to eat with her fingers, and she was hungry.

Both Blanche and Thelvin ordered lemonade. She'd considered a gin but felt heady enough without it. She wondered if Thelvin was a teetotaler. She'd find out, of course, but didn't want that to be the first question out of her mouth. She looked around the place while they waited for their drinks.

The long bar and tables were dotted with black people—mostly couples at the tables and men at the bar—in various stages of dress-up. Their ages ranged from that young honey across the room in the leather miniskirt and halter top—she couldn't be more than sixteen, could she?— to the man in the corner with the aluminum three-toed cane and head of pure white hair. He was dressed in a black suit with a pink shirt and flowered tie. Blanche felt the excitement of that special Saturday-night energy created by people hoping for a good time, a new love, at least a good dance partner, but most of all looking to drop for a bit all that worried and vexed them in the everyday.

"So how was your trip?" she asked at the same time Thelvin asked her how the catering business was going.

"You first," he said.

They laughed over Blanche's account of her visit to the Hasting twins.

Thelvin turned serious when he said: "My trip would have been easier if it hadn't been for you. I kept thinking about you, wondering if . . ."

The waitress returned carrying two tall glasses with a straw in each. "Chicken coming right up."

"To the best of people," Thelvin said. They clinked glasses.

"I haven't been out this way in a long, long time." Blanche sipped from her lemonade.

"My sister lives not too far from here," Thelvin said. "She and her husband got a small farm. Nice place."

"I always loved to visit folks' farms when I was a kid. All those smells is what I remember most."

"We can take a ride out to Ernestine's one Sunday. You'll like her."

Blanche just smiled. It was him, not his family, she wanted to know.

"Is she your older or younger sister?"

"Older. I'm the baby. My brother, Devon, was born between me and Ernestine. What about you?"

Blanche told him about her one and only sister, dead at thirty-five from cancer. "I already told you about the two children I inherited when she died."

"But no kids of your own, hunh?" he asked.

"Yeah, I know. It's unusual," she said, understanding his tone. "I just never really wanted to have any. For all the good that did me."

"Wait till you get to be a grandparent! Nothing stranger."

"Some folks seem to think it's wonderful. They say you get to be to your grandkids what you couldn't always be to your kids."

Thelvin didn't look convinced. "Yeah, maybe. But I aint talking about the parent you. What I'm talking about is the deep-down you. See what I mean?"

She nodded. She knew: the you who looked in the mirror in amazement that that gray-haired person could possibly be the same you that you'd been seeing since the first time you ever looked in a mirror.

"How do you handle it?" she asked.

"It handles me. I just hang on and hope I don't . . ."

The waitress plopped two overflowing plates of fried chicken, mustard greens mixed with kale, and candied sweet potatoes in front of them and went off to bring back a plate of white bread, a jar of hot sauce, and a small dispenser of vinegar. To Blanche's surprise and delight, the chicken's crisp skin gave way to tender, moist meat that she chewed slowly, trying to identify each of the spices that tingled and swelled in her mouth. They both ate in silence for a few moments, in deep appreciation of their food.

"Finish what you were saying, about hoping you didn't . . ."

Thelvin looked puzzled for a moment then: "Oh yeah! About being a grandfather." Thelvin looked over her head, his eyes brimming with feeling she couldn't read.

"I just hope I don't make a fool of myself. That's what I was going to say." Thelvin put a forkful of greens in his mouth.

Blanche waited for him to finish chewing. "Make a fool of yourself how?"

Thelvin shrugged. "I don't know. Tell the grandkids my name's Thelvin, not Pop-Pop, or that the 1960s and '70s weren't a million years ago."

Feeling old, Blanche thought. "But you wouldn't really be making a fool of yourself, just telling the truth."

Thelvin glanced toward the bandstand. "Looks like the band's about to start."

Blanche toyed with whether to press Thelvin to continue their grandparent line of talk and decided against it. He'd told her enough about his unhappiness with being older, his confusion between honesty and foolishness, and the short distance he was prepared to let her see inside of him right now. That was okay. She had no plans of laying her soul out for after-dinner inspection either. They gave themselves over to cleaning their plates.

The waitress cleared the table and then came back: "Y'all havin dessert? We got sweet potato pie, peach cobbler, and vanilla ice cream." She looked at them with question marks in her eyes, her pen poised over her pad. They both ordered the cobbler and the ice cream.

The Bad Boys played the first set alone: a balding man on the drums, a dredded brother on guitar, and one with a close cut and bedroom eyes on bass. The saxophone player wore a tuxedo jacket but no shirt, and looked like chocolate candy. The piano player was a big man whose fingers appeared too thick for the keys but certainly didn't sound like it. People were on their feet after the first licks of the first song.

When Little Sister stepped on the bandstand, she was so hot steam seemed to rise from her hips as she switched them across the stage in a sequined silver dress that clung to every crack and curve of her body. She was a firm, fleshy woman with big wide lips, a long nose, and large round eyes. She looked like she'd smell of earth and allspice. During one of her do-it-to-me-slow-and-long numbers, Blanche and Thelvin rose and squeezed themselves in among the gyrating bodies on the dance floor. Blanche could feel the muscles in Thelvin's thighs as they moved to the slow-grind tempo of the music. Little Sister moaned from somewhere way down deep and Thelvin pulled Blanche closer. He took a deep breath and let it out slowly.

"You smell like cake tastes."

Blanche purred as though she'd been a cat in another life. Whether it turned out that she and Thelvin hit it off in a long-term way or not, she wanted to see him long enough for her to offer him all the cake he could eat. She eased her hips back from him a little bit.

When they went back to their table, Thelvin called the waitress and ordered a scotch and water. Blanche asked for a gin and tonic and watched Thelvin's hand as he tapped time to the music on the tabletop. Jimmy's was nearly full now.

"You ever wish you could speed up time?" Thelvin took her hand to lead her back to the dance floor.

"I know it aint smart," she said, "but I guess everybody does it some-time."

"You right. It aint smart. But I can't help wishing we'd already known each other for long enough to . . . I don't know . . . be more easy with each other or . . . You know what I mean?"

"I guess that's another thing people can't help doing," Blanche said. "Trying to put their best foot forward when they meet someone they . . ."

"Yeah, that's what I mean."

He moved his hand to another spot on her back and left the old spot damp and lonely.

As the night wore on, they picked up each other's style and moved to-gether in a way that made their dancing sparkle. Blanche couldn't remem-ber the last time she'd had such fun. Thelvin was singing along with Little Sister's version of "Going to Chicago" as he swung her around. Dancing and the little bit of alcohol he'd consumed loosened Thelvin up just enough for him to open his tie and lie back in his chair like some kind of king or prince being entertained by the masses.

"Having a good time?" he asked her, and picked up her hand.

"Oh yes."

"Good enough to try it again?" His eyes were serious.

"Sure 'nuff."

"And again, and again?" His voice was as grave as his eyes.

Blanche frowned. The question was a real one. "If I'm supposed to." She gently took back her hand, aware that it felt like a rescue operation.

They were both quiet on the way home. Blanche wondered if Thelvin was thinking ahead to what would happen when they got to her place, or looking back to when they were plastered together on the dance floor, or maybe he was thinking about how his back ached or about calling his mama tomorrow.

Thelvin slowed his car as it rolled down the hill toward the gentle curve onto Miz Alice Way. Squares of golden light shone from the windows of the one house on the other side of the road. Moonlight lent silver to the deep night green of the trees. Blanche rolled her window all the way down. Frogs and crickets sang backup and warm-up for each other, and the smell of moist earth flooded the car. Blanche's heat-and-moisture-seeking body could hardly wait to get out into the night.

Thelvin stopped the car in front of her door and turned off the engine.

Blanche shut her eyes for a moment and willed Thelvin not to spoil the evening by treating her like a piece of meat he was bent on beating tonight. She clamped her teeth against hurrying through her thank-you-it-was-fun-goodnight routine and leaping out of the car. She prepared herself to make sure there was no part of no he wouldn't understand.

Thelvin reared back in his seat. "Chicken was good, wasn't it?"

Blanche burst out laughing. Thelvin gave her an amused and puzzled look. What had made her think he was a pouncer or a beggar, or one of those other dogs you had to beat off with a stick?

"The company was good, too," she said.

Thelvin leaned over and gave her cheek the merest of glancing kisses.

"I leave first thing tomorrow morning. I won't be getting back for a couple days, but I'll call you, okay?"

"Umm-humm." She reached for the door handle. "Don't get out."

Thelvin ignored her and got out of the car. He was on the passenger side before she could move. Blanche frowned up at him but Thelvin didn't notice. He held out his hand for hers. She sighed and took it and let him help her out of the car, even though it was much easier to manage alone. He walked her to her door.

"Sweet dreams." He gave her a look that had a bed in it, but no sleep.

Blanche didn't know if it was going to be a sweet night, but she had a feeling it was going to be a hot and sticky one.

She was trying to decide if she wanted a nightcap when the phone rang.

"I hope you didn't think I was going to wait till tomorrow," Ardell said when Blanche answered the phone.

Blanche settled back in her chair. "It was nice. Real nice. We went to Jimmy's Place. Danced our butts off."

"And?"

Blanche hesitated, trying to decide where to begin. She thought about the way Thelvin had looked at her as though she filled his entire field of vision; about the ease she felt in his company; the sexual spark between them. "He opened the car door for me when he took me home."

"Humm. It still happens, I guess."

"You don't get it."

"What's to get? You mean he leaned over you, opened the door, and booted you out while the car was still moving?"

"I'm serious, Ardell."

"Yeah? About what?"

Blanche wasn't sure how to answer. She was talking more from her feelings than from her mind. "Maybe if I hadn't told him I'd get the door myself it wouldn't have bothered me so much."

"Humm. Most women I know would love to have a man open their car door. Are you sure this aint more about David Palmer than it's about Thelvin?"

Blanche thought for a few moments: It was true that being raped had made her more suspicious of all men. At first, simply being in their company had made her jaws clench so tightly she could hardly speak. So she'd gone out of her way to spend time alone with men she trusted until she'd regained some ease and as much trust as she was going to. She'd never been big in the trust department and saw no reason for that to change—not until there was intelligent life on earth. But there was something else going on here, too.

"I'm not saying there's anything wrong in a man opening doors or always paying for everything, if that's what you're into," she said, "but you ever notice how close being protected and taken care of are to being held prisoner?"

"Girl, you notice it enough for both of us. This aint the first time the subject's come up. I think you focus on this stuff to keep a man from getting close to you."

"Well, I just think there's a message in all that gentlemanly business."

"And what kinda message is that again?"

"You know what I'm talking about, Ardell. A message that I'm a weak, not-too-bright female who aint got sense enough to get out of a car on my own, that I can't take care of myself and need somebody to protect me."

"I know that kinda stuff makes you crazy, Blanche, but he's just being polite, girl."

"You mean like saying 'thank you' and 'please'?"

"Yeah. Kinda like that."

"Well, then, how come it aint polite for both men *and* women to take turns opening the door for each other? How come it's always the woman who has to be the helpless one?"

"Humm, well, you got a point there, I guess. But I still think you're looking a gift horse in the mouth."

"Yeah, right. Like you're any more interested in being treated like a helpless ball of fluff than I am. And on top of that, he asked me whether I was willing to see him again, and again, and again!"

"So he likes you and wants to see you some more. What's the problem with that?"

"Ardell! That aint a first-time-out-together question. He don't even know me, and for all I know, he could have ten dead women stacked up beside his kitchen table."

"Give the man a chance, Blanche. Don't decide he's a dirty dog just 'cause he pants a little bit. See what I'm sayin?"

"So now you do romance counseling. If you know so much about it, how come you . . ."

"Forget it," Ardell snapped. "Just forget I mentioned it."

"Unh-unh, time to shut up when we git to *your* business."

"We only got to my business 'cause you can't stand having me in yours. And you know why? 'Cause I'm right, that's why!"

"So you say," Blanche told her. "I just want to make sure I got some idea who Thelvin is before I . . ."

"Yeah, well, you can go too far with that, you know."

"Yeah. And you can not go far enough with it, like that last little fling of yours. What was his name? Lloyd? Floyd? Tell me again what he wanted you to do with his underwear?"

"All right, Blanche. I got more to do than chitchat about the past. I'll talk to you later." Ardell rang off.

Blanche chuckled, but she took Ardell's remark seriously enough. Despite what she'd told herself before her date with Thelvin—about not being overly suspicious—was she being too hard on him? She'd had a really good time and enjoyed his company, not to mention his dancing and attention. Yet she'd decided to give Ardell the bad news instead of the good. Why? Was she doing that thing some Asian people did, calling out "Bad rice!" to convince the gods not to mess with their rice fields? Maybe she was afraid Thelvin was too good to be true and didn't want to be disappointed. Maybe Ardell was right: she needed to watch herself, even if she wasn't prepared to admit it out loud.

Death and the Hitchhiker

In the next days, Blanche felt weighted down by stories about Maybelle Jenkins's death. The newspapers, TV, and radio were full of what a nice, upstanding young woman Maybelle had been, even though she came from a family of backwoods rowdies known for petty thievery, heavy drinking, and light work. The newscasters said Maybelle was different: she'd finished high school and had a job in a high-priced dress shop over in Chapel Hill where she was well liked and known to be saving her money to go to fashion-design school.

But what really stretched Blanche's nerves was watching Ardell's prediction come true in the suspicious looks whitefolks gave the black men who mowed their lawns and delivered their groceries, certain that one of them, dazzled by his desire to defile white womanhood, had dragged poor Maybelle into the woods and played out whitefolks' version of every black man's fantasy, then killed her. Black folks were equally sure some white male, lacking the morals and common decency of a rabid dog, had given into his basest desires and taken what Maybelle wouldn't give, then killed her. This despite the fact that none of the reports said a word about rape.

No matter what black folks thought, whitefolks were in charge of the investigation, which meant, as Ardell had foretold, every black male who had a functioning penis and some who didn't were hauled downtown for questioning. Stories of strip searches on the sidewalk and men dragged off to jail without shoes or pants gushed through the community like water from a broken hydrant without any sense of how many of the stories were true. Blanche couldn't stop herself from wondering if there would have been a similar reaction had she reported David Palmer. Would he have been searched or dragged off to be questioned by men who only wanted a flimsy excuse to hurt him? Even she had to laugh at the very idea.

"Mr. Henry say it aint true," Clarice had told Blanche and Ardell regarding the rumor that the police had arrested a black man. Clarice's boyfriend, Jimmy Henry, was the janitor and gofer in the Sheriff's Office, so the catering staff got the news before most folks, black or white.

The falseness of the rumor did nothing to stop women in Blanche's community from being sharper with their sons, as if irritated at their boys for having been born black and male into a world where their name was Enemy Suspect. Blanche was sure the crackdown on black men would prompt many black couples to reach for each other with a bit more abandon than usual, fearful that this might be the last time. The memories of innocent black men dragged from their beds and lynched or otherwise murdered for being black were as fresh in black people's minds as yesterday's newspaper.

Carolina Catering was serving a buffet supper after an orchestra concert when Clarice arrived winded and wide-eyed with the next piece of the Maybelle story:

"Sheriff lookin for that Bobby Larsen for killin Maybelle Jenkins. Mr. Henry say Bobby was s'posed to be her boyfriend and he the one found her and Maybelle's daddy tell Sheriff Maybelle and Bobby had some kinda fallin out. Mr. Henry say somebody else tole Sheriff they saw Bobby hitchhikin down the highway headed for Greensboro. If he aint do nothin, what he runnin for, Sheriff say. But Mr. Henry say naw, 'cuz Bobby's mama was the one stuck up for that black girl bein picked on over at the farm show some years back." Clarice loaded a tray with the ham-and-cheese hors d'oeuvres Blanche took from the oven.

"Clarice, that aint got squat to do with Bobby killing that girl," Blanche told her. "Lotta women are raped and murdered by somebody they know.

A lot of them somebodies is called the-man-in-her-life," she said, although it wasn't true in her own case.

Ardell put a sprig of parsley on the salmon mousse before Clarice picked it up. "Humm. I'm just glad the Sheriff got somebody to focus on and that that person aint black. Thing like this could ruin my business. You know how these folks like to blame all of us when one of us does something wrong."

Blanche didn't so much disagree as she was surprised that Ardell, who had a son, would think first of her business. Of course, her son was down in Atlanta, out of this harm's way. Still . . . "I'll take these in, and check on things." Blanche picked up the tray of canapés.

Blanche knew she could have let Clarice or Ardell take the tray to the front of the house, but she'd been serious about refusing to let Palmer keep her from anything. She took a deep breath. There was no way of knowing which of these events David Palmer might attend, so she always had to be ready. But the man she ran into this time made her break out in a grin. She saw him at the same moment he saw her, and both their faces were washed with delight. Blanche set the tray down as he hurried across the room. He wrapped his arms round Blanche so tightly her ribs ached. Over her shoulder, she watched other guests watching them with interest. Probably think I'm the old family nursemaid, Blanche thought.

"Blanche, Blanche, Blanche," he whispered as he rocked her like a lost child just found. He finally let her go and stepped back. "Oh, Blanche! I am so glad to see you!"

"Mumsfield, you sure are looking fine, honey." And she meant it. Age had sculpted grooves and hollows that relieved his moon-round face of any babyishness. His once palest-blue eyes had deepened to a darker shade with more bittersweet in it. The slant of his eyes, evidence of his mosaicism—a mild form of Down's syndrome—made him look mysterious. How old was he? she wondered as they beamed at each other. Twenty-eight? Thirty? He looked distinguished in black tie, like a junior banker. He was still into suspenders. When she'd first known him, when she was working for his mad, murderous cousin and hiding out from the Sheriff, Mumsfield had worn a different color suspenders for each activity—one color for fixing the car, another color for driving, and so forth. She was a tad disappointed to see that tonight his suspenders were black, like those of every other man in the place.

"I'm sorry I did not know you were in town, Blanche," he said.

"Well, it aint as though we run in the same set, honey."

Mumsfield nodded. "Yes, Blanche. Cousin Archibald explained that it was better not to try to find you when you left. I missed you very much, Blanche. But now you are here." A grin split his face before he turned serious again. "I hope you still like me and want to be my friend, Blanche."

Friend! Blanche was always amazed at how some people threw that word around. She'd had employers who'd introduced her to guests as their friend. It wasn't a term Blanche used lightly. There were lots of people—from those she liked well enough to those for whom she felt deep love—that she did not consider friends. Mumsfield was one of them. She thought there ought to be another word, one that allowed for concern and affection but didn't include the mutual trust, soul-bearing honesty, and responsibility to guard each other's back that she considered to be the heart of friendship. She'd been through this once with Mumsfield when she'd worked for his people. Despite the distance she'd tried to maintain between them, Mumsfield had latched on to her as though she'd held out her arms to him. She understood why he wanted them to be friends: because of his Down's syndrome, much of the world treated him the same way it treated her. So he knew what it meant to be invisible, to be assumed to be the dummy in the room, to be laughed at because of parts of himself over which he had no control. This gave them something in common. But she didn't think mutual mistreatment was a basis for friendship. Still, he'd done her a kindness when she'd worked for his people, and she'd always be grateful—which made him more than just an ex-employer.

"Well, well, what a pleasant surprise!" Archibald Carter, Mumsfield's cousin, lawyer, and money manager, shook Blanche's hand. "Welcome home."

"It's good to be home," she said, although she wasn't altogether sure this was true.

"Has Mumsfield told you his big news?" Something went wrong with the way he said "big news."

Mumsfield smiled as though determined to show her all of his teeth. "Yes, Blanche. I am getting married!"

Archibald didn't crack a smile.

"Well, congratulations, honey," Blanche said, "I hope you'll be very happy."

"I will, Blanche. I want you to meet Karen, Blanche. She is coming with her mother. She will be here soon, I hope." He looked around the room as if to see if she might have already arrived, then excused himself before Blanche could tell him this wasn't a good time.

Archibald watched him for a moment, then turned to Blanche. "Don't worry, I'll explain that you're busy." He gave Blanche a full look. "Many times I've thought of you, my dear. Many times. And lately . . ."

Blanche wondered what was up. Something surely was.

"I, uh, wonder if I might . . ."

A silver-haired matron, like a snowball wrapped in yellow satin, walked up and took Archibald's arm. "Archibald, dear. You must come and meet my nephew and his charming new wife in from Sweden," she said as though he'd been talking to the wall instead of to Blanche. Blanche slipped away, still wondering about that current she felt running beneath Archibald's words.

Phone Calls and Philanthropy

It was too early to talk to anybody when the phone rang her out of a dream of swimming in the ocean with a porpoise, or seal, or some other sleek black creature that felt like silk when it brushed against her body. She groped for the phone.

"Yeah?"

"Did I wake you, Blanche?" Archibald's voice was so wide awake and cheery it made Blanche evil.

She didn't bother to ask him how he, one of the richer, better-connected citizens of Farleigh, got her phone number. "If you was worried about waking me up you wouldn't be calling me at six-thirty in the morning."

Archibald chuckled. "Quite right. I was much more concerned with speaking to you than with your rest."

"About Mumsfield."

"How did you know?"

"Just smart, I guess, even at this hour."

Archibald cleared his throat. "Perhaps I shouldn't have called quite so early. I do apologize."

"And I accept. Now, what's up?" She waited for Archibald to get over being talked to as though he were just any old body.

"Ahem, yes, well. It's about his engagement. If I may speak confidentially . . ."

"You can speak any way you want. I'll decide whether it's confidential after I hear it."

"Yes, well. I suppose . . . I'll have to trust your judgment on that."

"You don't have to. You could just not tell me." She never understood why people acted like they were doing you a favor when they wanted to tell you some tacky business that didn't have doodly-squat to do with you.

Archibald cleared his throat once again. "Well, the problem is . . . You see, this marriage really won't do, Blanche." Archibald's voice was full of looking-down-your-nose. "This young woman is simply not suitable."

"How come?"

"Well, her father has already informed me that once Mumsfield joins his family my services will no longer be required, as if I'm some sort of old family retainer who can be . . . Not that such a thing is possible, but the very idea, the suggestion that . . ."

Blanche yawned. Money, of course. What else got rich folks' blood boiling at such an early hour? Archibald just didn't want to lose control of all that money his cousin Mumsfield had inherited.

"What does Mumsfield say?"

"You know what the boy is like, Blanche. He thinks she's some kind of angel."

"Maybe she is. None of us get to pick our family. She don't have to be like her daddy."

"It's not just the father. Her older sister married a man still in mourning for his first wife and old enough to be her grandfather. Of course, she's running through his money. She made him a laughingstock in Farleigh, then insisted they move to Florida, where he has no friends and no one to . . ."

Blanche didn't have a drop of sympathy for some old geezer who'd bought himself a youngster but didn't want to pay the price. "Sisters aren't always alike any more than parents and children."

"Yes, but in this case I'm sure . . ."

"Why you telling me all this?" Blanche inched toward the edge of the bed. She had to pee, and she wanted to wash her hair before she met Ardell.

"I know you're fond of the boy, Blanche, so I was wondering if you might be willing to help me convince him to at least wait a while. They've only been seeing each other a few months."

Fond of the boy? She liked him well enough, but did that equal fond? She wondered if Archibald's calling Mumsfield a boy had anything to do with his views on Mumsfield's readiness for marriage.

"I don't even know the woman. How can I try to convince him not to marry her? Anyway . . ."

"Well, actually," Archibald interrupted, "I was hoping you might provide some information that would convince him."

"How? What kind of information?"

"Oh, you know. Despite your well-taken comments about not choosing one's family members, there is a chance that this young woman herself is not above reproach. Indeed, it's not quite accurate to refer to her as a young woman. She's at least five or six years Mumsfield's senior. Surely she has some past, some . . ."

"Sounds to me like you need a detective."

"Yes, yes, I thought of that. But then, when I saw you the other night, it occurred to me that you might be better suited to . . . the people who have information might be more willing to talk with you than to some stranger."

"You mean the help."

"Exactly. Who else is likely to have more information than . . ."

"So you want me to collect dirt from the servants on Mumsfield's girl-friend without telling him I'm doing it."

"I wouldn't put it in such harsh terms, my dear. Let's say I'd like you to help me ensure that Mumsfield doesn't get hurt."

Blanche was sympathetic to Archibald's desire to make sure Mumsfield's fiancée wasn't out to take him. She could also see how Archibald might consider it part of his job as Mumsfield's money manager and lawyer.

"Have you told Mumsfield how you feel?" She knew from the long silence that he hadn't.

"He's quite touchy where she's concerned," Archibald said at last.

"Well, I'm quite touchy about sneaking around trying to find reasons to rain on somebody's parade, especially when that somebody considers himself my friend."

"I understand your reluctance, Blanche, and I assure you, I wouldn't re-sort to such methods if . . . Mumsfield is like a son to me. We both know what a wonderful person he is, kind and generous and really quite wise in his own way. But to other people . . . Well, why would a normal woman choose to marry . . . I couldn't bear to see the boy hurt, emotionally or fi-nancially."

Blanche agreed to herself that it would take a so-called normal woman as special in her own way as Mumsfield was in his to see deep enough into him to want to be his wife. But Mumsfield was rich, which made him prime husband material even if he had collard greens for brains. Anyway, being normal among some of the families down here included all those who were toilet-trained and could count all their fingers without help. Blanche shook her head, even though Archibald couldn't see her. "I'm sorry, Archibald. I just don't think I want to get mixed up in this."

"He's very fond of you, Blanche. He was despondent for months after you left. He wanted to hire someone to find you. Of course, I knew you wouldn't want that, wouldn't want to take a chance on the Sheriff also finding you. He was quite put out about your having escaped from that jail sentence, so . . ."

So I did you a favor, now you do one for me. "Let me think about it, Archibald," she said, more to get him off the phone than anything else.

"Please do, Blanche. This Palmer woman simply is not right for Mums-field and I know there's some . . ."

Blanche shot off the bed like the mattress was on fire. Every cell in her body came to attention. "Who? This who?"

"Palmer, Karen Palmer, the woman Mumsfield intends to marry. She . . ."

Blanche interrupted him. "Does she have a . . . a somebody in her fam-ily named David?"

"Yes. A brother. The family owns the . . ."

"Listen, Archibald, I gotta go. I'll call you back later."

Blanche staggered to the bathroom to pee, then sat on the side of the bed while she considered the news that Mumsfield was engaged to David Palmer's sister. At moments like this, people's lives seemed to her like a basket of yarn of different colors and sizes all tangled together, running over, under, and between each other, creating knots and loop-backs that no one could design or predict. Who would have figured that her need to get back at David Palmer and Archibald's questions about Mumsfield's coming marriage would be woven together into a single coil, a single way to satisfy both her need and Archibald's? But here it was: She would use Archibald's money and interest in Karen Palmer to learn all that she could about David Palmer. He had put a knife to her throat and threatened to cut her if she dared to resist him. What else had he done? What secrets did he want kept? She was willing to bet he'd done evil more than once. Maybe he'd raped other women, or left the scene of a hit-and-run, or lied in court. Somewhere in the musty corners and back halls of David Palmer's life there was something she could use against him, and she intended to find it. And she would use it any way she could to bring him down. She felt calmer and more sure of herself than she had for days. She knew what she was going to do, and she knew how.

She reached for the phone book. She found the numbers she needed, but it was still too early to call.

She brushed her teeth, and made herself get down on the floor to stretch her muscles and do three sets of twenty sit-ups and thirty push-ups. While she worked her body, her mind roamed around her decision not to tell Archibald what she knew about David Palmer. Even if rapists ran in the family, it wasn't likely that Karen was one, given that most rapists were men. As far as Blanche was concerned, what David had done had nothing to do with Karen. Blanche knew what it felt like to be held responsible for other people's crimes just because you belonged to the same racial group. Wasn't this a similar kind of thing? She could just hear Archibald asking Mumsfield if that was the sort of person he wanted at the family table, as if Karen had created her brother. Blanche stopped mid-stretch. There was another reason why she didn't want to tell Archibald about Palmer.

Although she felt sure Archibald would happily use her rape as a club to beat Karen off of Mumsfield, she doubted Archibald would take the rape seriously enough to do anything else with the information. Would he make sure that women in his circle knew that Palmer was dangerous? Would he see that Palmer was cut from the our-kind list? Or would he tsk-tsk, pat her on the shoulder, and maybe give her an extra bit of bonus for her pains? After all, if assaulting poor black women could get rich white males ostracized, half the dinner parties in town would be short some guests. As for Mumsfield, he would have sympathy for what had happened to her, but she was sure it wouldn't make a crumb of difference to his marriage plans. She rolled over and did her push-ups before she rose from the floor.

Of course, she praised herself mightily when she finished her exercises. It had taken her getting knocked around by a couple of thugs and over two years of starts and stops to get to this point. Now she only grumbled about exercising every other morning, which meant she was halfway to making it as much a part of her daily ritual as brushing her teeth. And it was worth it. She hadn't lost a speck of weight, but a whole lot of flab was gone. When she flexed her upper arms, nothing wobbled, and the muscle that rose was firm and round. She could also run a couple of blocks without panting if she had to, and stairs never gave her any trouble. As an adult, she'd had a mostly good relationship with her big black body, but having muscles had turned that relationship into a love affair.

She climbed in the shower and unbraided her hair. She hummed E. C. Scott's "Queensize Bed" as water poured over her head and body. While she washed and shampooed, she thought about Mumsfield. She admitted to being surprised when he'd told her he was engaged. She was a tad irritated with herself about that surprise. Just because he had Down's syndrome was no reason Mumsfield shouldn't marry. She'd spent enough time with him to know that, though he wasn't like most folks, he wasn't less than them, only different. She oiled and cornrowed her hair while it was still wet and marveled at its woolly softness, as she always did.

After a Cheerios breakfast she made her first call.

"Hey, Mumsfield, how you doing?"

"Blanche! I was going to call you, Blanche!"

"Oh yeah?"

"I think of you many times, Blanche. I remember everything, Blanche. All of it."

Blanche knew Mumsfield was talking about what had happened years ago while she'd worked for his family—back when she'd been hiding out from the Sheriff in Mumsfield's household. Mumsfield had done her the favor of not telling his people she didn't belong there, and she'd helped him find out what had happened to his beloved aunt. Blanche looked at the small gray-green rock sitting on her windowsill—one of the first things she'd unpacked—and remembered when and why Mumsfield had given it to her: a remembrance of their other connection, poor dead Nate, who they'd both cared about.

When she'd first met Mumsfield, Blanche had chafed against the gut-level connection she'd felt with him. She'd been lucky enough to be born without a mammy gene or a case of Darkies' Disease, but she didn't press her luck by trying to befriend her employers' families. Even so, she knew how easy it was to slip into a Darkie crouch, eyes lifted toward the employer as loved one. Darkies' Disease was like any other—nobody planned to get it. It just crept up on some people when their emotional immune systems were damaged from having had to grin at one too many insults or otherwise kiss ass to keep a job they probably didn't want but couldn't live without. Or people caught the disease from their parents, or grew into it out of their own self-hatred. Her connection to Mumsfield had been as much about her circumstances as anything else. Once she was safe, any link she'd felt to him had faded, although she still had warm feelings for him.

"Will you please come to lunch, Blanche? I want you to meet Karen, my fiancée. You will like her, Blanche. I know you will," Mumsfield said.

"What's important is that *you* like *her* and *she* likes *you*."

"Yes, Blanche. That is true, Blanche. But other people . . . If you like Karen, Blanche, then maybe other people will like her more."

Blanche was flattered but not fooled. "Other people like who?"

"Archibald, Blanche. Archibald does not like Karen. But if you like Karen, Archibald will like Karen more. I know it, Blanche."

"Did Archibald tell you he didn't like Karen?"

Mumsfield hesitated. "His eyes told me, Blanche."

Of course. If Mumsfield waited for people to give him information, he wouldn't know his nose from his nuts. Nobody bothered to tell things to a person with Down's syndrome living in a part of the world where almost every kind of difference was ridiculed. That's why Mumsfield was nearly as good at reading people—the language of the way they moved, the tone and undertone of their voices, their frowns and tics—as Blanche herself was. It was a skill shared by most invisible people.

"I wouldn't say he doesn't like her, exactly," Blanche told him. "Archibald's real concerned about you and Karen getting married, Mumsfield. He asked me to see if I could find out some things about her."

"Are you going to do it, Blanche?"

"I wanted to talk to you first."

"If you do not find anything bad about Karen, then Archibald will like Karen more."

"But what if I do find something bad?"

"I know she is a good person, Blanche. I know it."

"Okay, Mumsfield. But don't tell Karen. She might get so mad at Archibald they can't be friends later on."

"Yes, Blanche, I understand, Blanche. Now, will you please come to lunch, Blanche?"

She liked the idea of lunch at a home where she'd once served the meals, and was eager to get a look at Karen Palmer.

"Sure, honey. When do you want me to come?"

They made a date for the following week.

Blanche made two more calls—to detective agencies in Chapel Hill— then got Archibald on the phone.

"I'll do it. I'll ask around about Karen Palmer for you." Blanche didn't mention that she wasn't just going to be asking around about Karen or that Karen wasn't even her main interest. She didn't mention that she intended to collect information on David Palmer and sift it fine as cake flour.

"It'll cost you what you'd pay a detective," she added. In for a penny, in for a bit more.

"I'm delighted, Blanche. I . . ."

"You understand what I said, don't you?" Blanche interrupted. "I'll do it for the same price you'd pay a detective." She held her breath.

"As I recall, you always did drive a hard bargain, Blanche. I'll see what such services would cost and . . ."

"I already checked." She quoted him the fifty-five-dollar-an-hour rate she'd just been given.

"It's a deal."

Blanche relaxed. "Before I start quizzing other folks, tell me what you know about Karen Palmer and her family."

Archibald was silent for a few seconds, in which Blanche could feel his desire to save Mumsfield from a bad marriage and to remain Mumsfield's financial handler doing serious battle with his social reflex not to talk about his class to people who weren't in it.

"Look," she told him. "If you don't trust me with what you already know, you need to make sure you really want me to get in these people's business."

When Archibald finished sputtering about how it wasn't anything against her personally, and how sorry he was, he was ready to talk.

"Well, let me see, now. I've checked the family's corporate financial holdings and dealings as best one can. Nothing of note there, or at least nothing with a paper trail. You know they own the BonBon department-store chain. There was some talk when old man Palmer took over the whole chain. He had a partner that Palmer managed to buy out at a nominal price. There was talk of undue pressure, if not extortion, but never any proof of what Palmer might have had on the man. Their headquarters are over in Chapel Hill. David Palmer, the only son, works alongside his father. As I told you, the oldest daughter is down in Florida wasting her husband's money."

Blanche tried to picture this woman for whom she'd been working when David Palmer raped her. She could see the bathroom as though she used it every day, but the woman and the rest of the house were gone from memory.

"As for Karen," Archibald was saying, "her only work is doing the sort of things such ladies do, I suppose. They all live on the family place, just there off Main Street."

"And the son?" she asked, holding her voice level by will.

"Youngish, single, reasonably attractive, and, of course, wealthy. So few of this sort of young man stay in the area. A good catch, as they say, although I've always found him somewhat limp. Perhaps that's why he's still available."

"Limp?"

"Perhaps 'bland' is a better word."

"Never married?"

"Seems to me there was an engagement some time back. I don't recall to whom. A local girl, I believe. A lot of gossip when they called things off. I don't recall why now. I'm afraid I'm not that interested in the peccadilloes of the young. Unless they're clients, of course."

"How does old man Palmer get along with his kids?"

"Like any other father these days, I suspect. He doesn't understand them any more than they understand him. But they do all live together. I get the impression the old man wishes his son were somewhat more lively where the ladies are concerned. Wants the next generation born early enough to mold them himself, I suspect. The mother is well meaning, a bit sanctimonious."

"Is that all?" she asked, sensing that it wasn't.

"Well, there'd been some tension between the son and Palmer elder, but that seems to have eased."

Blanche leaned forward. "Oh? What kind of tension? About what?"

"The old man can be rather overbearing. I suppose . . . It was an unpleasant incident. Years ago now, so . . ."

"Tell me."

"Well, old man Palmer once slapped the boy. In public. Everyone saw it. It was quite . . ."

Blanche took an instant liking to the old man. "In public, hunh?" She knew this crowd would rather die than have anything ugly happen where others could see it. "Must have really pissed his daddy off."

"I would think. But, as I said, they seem to have resolved their differences. The boy went away for a while after that. I never did hear what the fight was about."

"Okay, Archibald. That'll do for now, but I'm going to need some pot-sweetening money. Maybe four hundred dollars. I can't be taking up folks' time asking a lot of questions about things they aint supposed to know, let alone talk about, without at least helping out with their bills."

"Yes, of course," Archibald said. "I'll have a messenger drop it off. Cash, if that's all right with you."

Blanche gave him her address and mentally patted him on the head for not arguing with her. "I'll call you when I got something for you," she told him before she hung up. "Sooner if I got reason to."

Blanche immediately called Ardell.

"Humm, well, I'm glad you're finally doing something about Palmer's nasty ass!" was Ardell's response to Blanche's plan to find out all she could about David Palmer. "I just wish it was, you know, more direct—like taking a contract out on him."

"Which I wouldn't do, even if I could," Blanche said. "It wouldn't be a bad idea if I believed in a hell where he'd suffer forever, but I don't. And if I'm wrong, well, if he's going to be in pain, I want to see it. So what'd be the point in killing him?"

"So now what?"

"Why you got an attitude, Ardell?"

"Well, for one thing, I don't like the idea of you being mixed up with that Archibald and that other white boy. You almost got killed when you lived with that family! I don't even know why you'd . . ."

"Forget about Archibald. He's just my cover story. 'Course I'll check around on Karen," Blanche quickly added, "but . . ."

"I don't know, Blanche. It seems like a long shot. I mean, what do you think you can find that . . ."

"Well, let's start with what he likely loves most: How much money does he have? Where does it come from? Does he need some? Does he gamble it away? Does he buy women *and* rape them? Is his daddy in his shit about something? Does he do drugs? And who does he run with and where? Anything and everything, I guess." A buzz of excitement began in Blanche's feet and worked its way into her stomach and chest, where it set her lungs and heart to vibrating. "Somewhere there's something I can use against him. I know it. I can feel it. And I know I'm going to find it, too."

"Humm, yeah, well, that's a whole lot of knowing. I hope you're right. I guess it beats doing nothing. Like you say, if there's any dirt out there you're the one to find it, crazy as you are about sticking your nose in other people's business."

Ardell's lack of enthusiasm for her plan made Blanche all the more determined. "I'll show you," she told the Ardell in her head. She made herself a cup of tea, then found a pad of lined paper and a ballpoint pen advertising Jackson's Plumbing Supplies. She sat at the kitchen table, sipping tea and making a list of what she wanted to know, and put it in her handbag when she was done. She'd stop by the drugstore before she went to see Miz Minnie.

Halfway out the door, Blanche turned back. She'd better call Taifa now, even if it was a little earlier than they'd planned. She had a feeling, or at least a hope, that it would be a busy day. She reached for the phone.

Blanche had always expected that as Taifa got older their shared experience as black females in a world that disrespected both their sex and their color would give them a special connection that Blanche was sure was impossible with even the most understanding and decent of males. But as Taifa moved toward adulthood, Blanche had begun to wonder if there weren't going to be as many things to separate them as there were to bring them together.

Blanche liked Taifa's determination. It was her destination that was the problem. Taifa liked well-off people and intended to travel in their circles. She'd picked up all the manners and attitudes she needed to blend in with them, which was very different from where Blanche thought Taifa was headed as an early teen bent on fitting into the 'hood. That loud, baggy-jeans phase was over by the time Taifa was fifteen—gone the way of too-big earrings and cracking gum. She liked expensive things and had learned to shop at sales and upper-end consignment shops. She dressed as though Mummy and Poppy had pots, but in a style very much her own. Instead of trying out for cheerleading, as she'd talked about doing since she was nine, Taifa had joined the Fencing Club. She'd wanted to pledge to the junior chapter of a national black sorority with a history of color prejudice, despite its good works. Blanche hadn't been able to hide her disappointment. She'd tried to raise both Taifa and Malik to understand that black people couldn't afford to separate from one another on the basis of nonsense like skin color, that only as a group could they make things get better for everybody.

"You come from a long line of women who couldn't have joined that sorority if they'd wanted to because they were too black and did the wrong kind of work," Blanche remembered telling Taifa, who hadn't been impressed. Blanche rarely pulled rank. It was easier on her nerves to negotiate, try to work out a happy compromise. But there were some things she wasn't prepared to half-step about. She'd let Taifa know that if she was going to be the kind of woman who needed to belong to exclusive organizations she was going to have to wait until she was grown to join them. Even this summer job at snooty, color-struck Amber Cove was all about being around the so-called right crowd. Many of the girls who took summer jobs at Amber Cove were the children and grandchildren of well-off blacks whose families felt they needed the experience of work, if not the money. Taifa had described it as a good place to make contacts. Blanche didn't know what she could do about Taifa's attitude beyond making sure Taifa understood that more than didn't mean better than and keeping her fingers crossed. She pitied parents who thought they had more control than that.

"Hi, Moms." Taifa yawned into the phone.

"Still tired, I see."

"Girls who've worked here before say I'll be over it soon."

"You mean you'll get over being tired from work, or get over being tired from hanging out all hours?"

"Moms! Get serious! It's really hard work. That first week I was so tired when I got off I could hardly make it to bed."

Good. No time to get into anything. "Otherwise, how's the job going?"

"Great. I love being back here. And I'm making fabulous tips!"

Blanche shook her head. The idea of going back to Amber Cove after having had her feelings seriously hurt there was so far down her list of things to do she couldn't even see it. But Taifa had loved the place from day one.

"How are things going with you and Aunt Ardell?"

"Oh, just fine. We're doing a lotta business." Blanche hesitated. "Although I have found a little more time to enjoy myself than you have."

"You two been hanging out, hunh?"

"Not exactly." Blanche told Taifa about meeting Thelvin and their recent big date.

Blanche could feel Taifa coming to attention over the phone.

"Why didn't you tell me about him when I called last week?" Taifa sounded as though Blanche had forgotten to mention a new birth in the family.

"Well, we were both tired and . . ."

"Humph! What does Aunt Ardell think about him?"

Blanche blinked: Taifa's "Humph!" sounded just like Mama's.

"They haven't met yet. Why'd you ask?"

"Well, I mean, you just met him and . . ."

Blanche grinned. "Yeah? So?"

"Well, every time I bring a boy home, you always ask, 'Do we know anybody who knows him? Who are his people?'" Taifa imitated Blanche's very tone. "So who knows this man and who're his people?"

Blanche laughed. "Yeah, you're right, Taifa. I do need to check him out and I will. I do know his daddy is dead and his mama lives out in Rocky Mount. He's a widower with three grown kids and a sexy smile, okay?"

"Sexy? Did you say *sexy* smile? I never heard you say . . . Well, I guess you're planning to see him again, hunh?"

Blanche was having fun. She'd grown used to being the one trying to find out if the boy of the moment was a troglodyte or a mass murderer and hoping Taifa would care if he was. She'd all but forgotten how it felt on the other side of the fence. She supposed she could run the I'm-the-mother thing that put an end to all questions, but she'd always thought it was unfair when Mama did it to her. And it had only made her more de-termined to have her questions answered, one way or another. Mama's mail would have gotten a lot less reading and her bureau and night-stand drawers a whole lot less searching if she'd given young Blanche straighter answers.

"No need to get all motherly, Taifa. I like him well enough, so far, but who knows what'll happen? Next time I talk to you I might have forgot-ten his name." But don't bet any money on it, she added to herself.

They talked a few more minutes about Taifa's room and job, the Miz Alice, their respective eating habits of late, and Taifa's shopping plans.

"Don't forget, you're supposed to be saving for school."

"I know, but one of the girls here has a car. We might go to an outlet mall. You know I can always find a bargain! Speaking of cheap, when's Peanut Head get done crawling through the muck?"

"Your brother's not cheap, he's just careful. He leaves Outward Bound for camp day after tomorrow."

"From one mud puddle to another. It's creepy. Just thinking about sleeping in the woods and stuff makes me feel all slimy!"

Blanche had no idea where Taifa's nature squeamishness came from. Malik and everybody else in the family was happy to play in the dirt. Mama said Taifa's prissy ways came from the Waterses, her hincty grand-parents on her father's side. Blanche had never cared for them either, but she doubted they were to blame for Taifa's stuck-up attitude since the Wa-terses had all but lost touch with Taifa and Malik.

When Taifa hung up, Blanche felt sure that, if Malik could be reached, Taifa would be calling him right now to tell him about Mama Blanche's new man. She grabbed her handbag and headed up Mulberry Street toward downtown and the drugstore.

When the word got out that the Sheriff intended to arrest Bobby Larsen for Maybelle's murder, relief floated over Farleigh like a rose-scented cloud that even seeped into the drugstore. The whole town seemed ready to get beyond this particular madness.

"Y'all come back now, heah?" the blue-haired white woman whose family owned the drugstore told Blanche as she left with the jar of Vase-line she'd forgotten to get the day before. On the last occasion, this same woman had stared at her as though she were positive Blanche was the mother of the wild-eyed black buck who'd killed poor sweet Maybelle. Now Blanche rolled her eyes and sucked her teeth at the woman, just as she'd done the day before. She stopped by the Miz Alice to pick up a pie before she went to see Miz Minnie.

Working the Net

Blanche helloed her way down Miz Minnie's street, smiling and nodding at her neighbors. Miz Minnie was the community's most reliable source of information. She knew practically everyone in black Farleigh and most of the old-line white folks who had money enough to hire help. There was something about the woman that made people want to talk, even though they didn't know they wanted to, and to tell her things they certainly had no intention of mentioning. This meant she knew everybody's business. She'd been known occasionally to use that information to convince husbands that their wives would indeed leave if they had one more drink or fling or hit of that pipe; to cajole children into staying in school to spite the lives they were forced to live at home; to push those who could to take their lives in their own hands and move on to bigger and better.

Blanche half expected to find Miz Minnie's old wooden-slat house boarded up or fallen down, and the old woman living with one of her kids. But there was the house and there was Miz Minnie sitting on her porch in what looked like the same old rocking chair, wearing, if not the same, then certainly a very similar grease-stained housedress and a pair of too-large men's bedroom slippers. Her blue head-scarf was tied so tightly it gave

Blanche a headache just looking at it. Miz Minnie was rocking slowly, watching her neighbors doing their gardening and car-washing rituals as though they were her personal home-entertainment unit. Her porch sat right on the ground, gray and weather-beaten but brimming with pansies and daffodils in every conceivable type of container from coffee can to bedpan.

"Afternoon, Miz Minnie."

"Afternoon to you, daughter. I heard you was back in town."

"I sure am glad to see you, Miz Minnie. I bought you a apple pie, I know you got a fondness for them."

"Why, thank you kindly, daughter. Put it in there on the table if you don't mind. I'll have me some later. You want some? There's ice tea in there. Bring us a glass."

Blanche did as she was told, tiptoeing through Miz Minnie's shotgun house like she was afraid she might disturb its dark and aged neatness. She found glasses and the iced tea and poured them each a glass. She didn't bother to look for sugar. She knew Miz Minnie's tea would already be well sweetened. She carried the tea outside.

Old thing's about the color of beef jerky, Blanche thought, looking at Miz Minnie, and likely just as tough. How old is she? Way older than Mama. Older than old. Her husband died when I was just a kid and he was ancient then. Unless she was a child bride, she must be . . .

"Ninety-six," Miz Minnie said, and cackled over Blanche's expression.

"Aint no magic to it, daughter. Person lookin like they tryin to count the wrinkles on your face is most like wonderin how old you is." She lifted a tin can from beside her chair and spit a long slim stream of tobacco juice into it.

"I'm looking for information about somebody," Blanche told her when they'd passed the time of day.

"Why you lookin?"

Blanche had been expecting this question, but she'd thought Miz Minnie would want to know who first. No sense lying to Miz Minnie; she could sniff out a lie better than a cat could smell mice.

"It's somebody who did me harm."

Miz Minnie rocked for a bit. "That's reason enough. Who he is?"

"Why you say 'he'?"

Miz Minnie looked at her and snorted. "You got your list?" A snaggle-

toothed, tobacco-stained grin lit up Miz Minnie's face at Blanche's stupe-
fied look, although Blanche shouldn't have been surprised. Everybody
agreed Miz Minnie usually knew what you wanted before you asked. That
was part of what made her so easy to talk to.

Blanche unfolded her list of the jobs of people around David Palmer:
maid, cook, bartender, barber, banker, shoeshine man, tailor, mail carrier,
laundry person, and gardener—all in close contact with him and/or his
belongings, although it was unlikely he noticed most of them—unless they
were young women.

"Palmer, yes." Miz Minnie nodded her head. "Now, Mary Lou Pa-
chette useta work for his people. In the kitchen. She passed, and Dorothy
Dotson took over the cookin. Aint no sense talking to her, 'less you wants
him to know you askin. She what you call a house nigger." Miz Minnie
aimed another jet of tobacco juice at her can. "Whole family's thataway.
Daughter works there, too, so you aint gon git nothin outa they house
people."

Damn! Blanche lowered her head to hide the tears prickling her eyes.
As she became more menopausal, tears seemed to be her first response to
everything. Of course she was disappointed. The people who worked in
the Palmer household were the first people she'd wanted to talk to. She
sighed and wrote down the names attached to some of the other positions.
Miz Minnie also gave her the names of some other folks who might be
helpful. Blanche then sat politely listening to the old woman talk about
the weather and how Farleigh was changing.

"I sure do thank you for your help, Miz Minnie," Blanche said when
she thought it was about time to leave.

"Glad to do it, daughter. Man aint got no right to put his hands on a
woman don't ask him to."

"I never said he touched me."

Miz Minnie shifted her jawful of snuff from one side of her mouth to
the other. She raised one butt cheek and tugged at her cotton dress.

"'Course you did, chile. Lookit how you sittin there."

Blanche looked down at her arms, held close to her sides; her legs,
crossed at knee and ankle and pulled in under her. She was leaning forward in her chair, almost rolling herself into a ball, into a woman with all
her tender, most often wounded parts protected.

Miz Minnie leaned over and patted Blanche's arm. "It's all right, daugh-

ter. Everything you doin you s'posed to be doin. This your time to step up
for yourself."

"What you mean, Miz Minnie?"

"You know what I mean, daughter. If you don't you will. You will."

Blanche left Miz Minnie's feeling as though she'd just been sworn in to
her own army. She was over her disappointment about the Palmer help.
There were plenty of other ears and eyes working around him that could
help her. When she got home, she found a heavy cream-colored envelope
slipped under her front door. Twenty twenties wrapped in a plain sheet of
white paper. Thank you, Archibald. She put the money away and took out
her notebook again. Who should she call first? She decided on two people
she knew and one she didn't.

First she called Miz Minnie's great-niece who Miz Minnie had told her
was married to the Bueles boy, who was cousin to Jack Moses, whose sister-
in-law was Mary Lee—a bright, St. Augustine's College–educated young
woman. She was a senior clerk at Farleigh National Bank. Miz Minnie's
niece gave Blanche Mary Lee's phone number.

Blanche hesitated before she punched it in. This was her first call, the
first time she was willingly bringing some part of David Palmer into her
life. It felt strange, risky. Yet necessary. If she could get Mary Lee's help . . .

No one answered, but at least she'd made the call. A start. She tried
Curtis Martin next. Miz Minnie said he was one of the trainers and
masseurs over at Silver's Gym in Chapel Hill, where boys like Palmer
pumped iron and such. Curtis had been a year ahead of Blanche in high
school.

"Sure, Blanche!" Curtis said when she called and asked if he remembered her. "Leo's girl, right? I was on the football team and the wrestling
team with him, remember?"

"Miz Minnie gave me your number," Blanche said, in a hurry to move
away from talk of Leo. She wondered how long it would take folks to stop
linking her name with Leo's now that he'd married someone else.

"I want to talk to you about somebody I think uses the gym," she said.
"It won't take long, and I'll make it worth your while."

"Damn! I'm on my way to work, but what about Saturday? I'm off on
Saturday. Come on by. Anytime." He gave her his address before he hung up.

Blanche was hungry, but she felt like she was on a roll. She picked up
the phone again and called Mr. Bennie, who shined shoes at Magnon and

Kramer's, where better-off white men had their hair cut. As a girl, Blanche ran errands for him and his wife. At the mention of money, Mr. Bennie told her to come by as soon as she could.

Mr. Bennie was in his garden, turning dirt with a trowel, when Blanche got to his house. He reminded her of an unfolding extension ladder as he rose to greet her.

"How you, Mr. Bennie?"

"I'm fair to middlin. What about your mama, how she?"

"She fine, Mr. Bennie. Just fine. I don't want to keep you. . . ." Blanche explained what she was after.

"Oh yeah. Been knowing that boy 'fore he was born. I could tell you aplenty."

Blanche took a folded twenty from her pocket. "Why, thank you, Mr. Bennie. I sure appreciate you talking to me." She slipped the money into his hand.

"Something real sad about that boy," Mr. Bennie told her. "Didn't useta be like that. I remember him from a chile, happy as a puppy, even as a teenager. Now he like a person with a hole in the middle."

"You think maybe he's got some kind of trouble? A woman, maybe? I heard . . ."

"He's what you call a dutiful son. Don't run across youngsters like him. Nowadays, children go off, don't think about they old people, whether they's sick, or needs anything."

Blanche remembered Mr. Bennie had a daughter and a son who'd left town before she did. It sounded like they might not have been back since.

". . . volunteer fireman, too. Saved them two little girls trapped in that house couple years back. He respectful to me. Always."

Blanche forced herself to listen to Mr. Bennie compliment Palmer. After all, nobody was totally bad. Hadn't the slavers and overseers who'd whipped and raped little African children and their mothers brought flowers to their own wives and bounced their own babies on their knees? Loving their children and their wives didn't make men like Palmer any less terrible, it made them bigger monsters.

"'Course, aint nobody perfect," Mr. Bennie said.

Blanche crossed her fingers behind her back.

Mr. Bennie shook his head from side to side. "Aint fittin for a man rich as him to be so tightfisted when it comes to tips."

Blanche swallowed her disappointment and relaxed her hands. "You ever hear anything about the rest of his family?"

"That oldest girl, she's down Florida way, you know. Ran off, with old man Gibson, I think it was. They say the youngest one's 'bout to marry somebody too dumb to even know how much money he got. Imagine that."

"Thanks for talking to me, Mr. Bennie." Blanche was glad she'd only given him twenty dollars. Even if it wasn't her money, she wasn't prepared to pay much for nothing, although she'd be glad to give him more if he'd tell her something worthwhile. She decided to try one last time:

"So you aint never heard anything about David Palmer having trouble over a woman, or money, or anything like that?"

Mr. Bennie slipped the twenty in his pocket. "Don't do to be gossiping about people. I don't hold with it!"

Blanche glared at him. Old hypocrite. She forced her mouth into a smiling pose.

"It sure does my heart good to know a honest man like you who can't be bought is in the world. Y'all take care, now, Mr. Bennie."

She'd gotten the opposite of what she'd wanted, but maybe she hadn't yet talked to the right people: women.

Disappointment made her restless, so she continued walking around town, into comfortable old neighborhoods where no blacks lived. She wasn't concerned about appearing suspicious. Most of the people who worked on these streets looked like her.

If she had it in mind to go by the Palmer place, she wasn't aware of it until she was half a block away. The huge white house with its gigantic columns seemed to step out onto the pavement and bar her way. She considered walking in another direction, then remembered what she'd told Ardell about how Palmer wasn't going to keep her from anything. A big black car pulled up to the house. The driver got out and stood on the pavement by the car. The front door of the Palmer place opened. Blanche braced herself for the sight of her enemy but, instead of hurrying away, crossed the street and slowed down.

Old man Palmer came out first. Stout, sparse steel-gray hair and a suit to match. He wasn't particularly tall, but seemed to float above the short, plump woman with rounded shoulders who followed him and was likely his wife. David Palmer came next. Blanche flinched and squinted her eyes, blurring his image. She knew all too well what he looked like. Karen came last, walking as though she needed a push from behind. The old man turned his head and said something to the others. He reminded Blanche of the kind of king-of-the-walk rooster that shows up in comic strips. Only there wasn't anything comical about him and his brood. Yes, he was all puffed up and poked out, and, yes, his family hung back like they wanted to be in position to kiss his behind, but they also looked ready to be dumped on at any moment. Blanche remembered what Archibald had said and pictured David Palmer being slapped by his father in public. Old man Palmer surveyed the street with an air of ownership, then nodded to the driver waiting by the car. The other three kept their eyes down. Ashamed to be seen with him? Or maybe he didn't allow them to look up. Blanche could almost see misery puddling around the four of them like muddy water staining their expensive shoes. She watched the car drive down the street and turn the corner and felt suddenly full of smiles: it did her heart good to see David Palmer under someone's heel.

The Gig from Hell

Blanche couldn't imagine what had happened to the lemon curd. She'd packed it in three large plastic containers and set them at the far end of the loading table in Ardell's kitchen, along with the cream and butter that needed to be put in the cooler in the van. She searched the cooler for the third time. The cream and butter were in there; the lemon curd that was to be drizzled over the apple tart made with almond pastry crust and almond cream was not. Ardell went through all the other food. Clarice looked on the shelves in the van and other places the lemon curd had no business being, like in the boxes of plates and cocktail forks. She didn't find it either. By the time they accepted that the lemon curd was really missing, it was too late to go back for it.

They were trying to decide what to do about it when Zeke showed up smelling as boozy as closing time at Miz Mackey's blind pig. He stumbled across the room and hiccupped.

"Don't jump all over me!" he barked at Ardell. "I know I'm late, I know it!"

Ardell looked up at him. She didn't speak or blink or even seem to be breathing. Blanche watched Zeke's little bit of fight-pecker go limp and soft under Ardell's stare. Blanche had never yet seen a man, or more than a few women, who could stand up under that glare of Ardell's.

"Get the bar set up, then start laying out the cutlery," Ardell told him.

Zeke looked so beaten Blanche might have felt sorry for him if he hadn't been making more work for everybody.

Blanche loaded a tray with arugula salads for Clarice to take to the front of the house. Was that a toothpick in one of the salads? Sweet Ancestors! It was. Were there any more? There was another one. And . . . "Oh shit!" How the hell did they get in there? It didn't matter now. "Ardell! We got a problem here."

Fortunately, the waiters and waitresses arrived just then, and Ardell set half of them to work going through each salad to make sure there was no surprise ingredient in the rest of them. The other half were sent out front to begin serving the canapés. Blanche opened a bottle of the Beaumes de Venise dessert wine. Muscat sauce would do just fine. She separated egg yolks into a large mixing bowl and tucked the bowl against her hip while she whisked the eggs with sugar until the mixture was light and pale, then whisked in some of the muscat. She put the bowl over a pot of simmering water and whisked till it thickened, then transferred the bowl to a pot of ice cubes and water, whisking until it cooled. She'd add the whipped cream and lemon juice just before serving. She began breaking and separating eggs for a second batch.

"Hello everyone, hello!" The white woman who entered the kitchen just as Blanche was setting the second bowl of muscat sauce to cool was tall and busty. She had the kind of wide-open eyes that looked like they could read minds. Her satin dress caught the light and became the hard pearly-blue casing of the help-eating mantis. Everyone turned to face her. The wait staff instinctively stood with their rubber-gloved hands behind their backs, blocking her view of the table where the salads were being probed.

"Mrs. Clifford, how may I help you?" Ardell stepped toward the woman.

"Just checking up," she said with a toothy smile. She stretched her neck to see beyond Ardell, but there was only the row of grinning staff to be seen.

"Why, everything's just fine, Mrs. Clifford. Right on schedule. Are your guests enjoying the hors d'oeuvres?"

"Oh yes, they are quite wonderful. Quite." Mrs. Clifford looked at Ardell, and Ardell looked back.

"Well, I'll just leave you to it," Mrs. Clifford said when it was clear no one was moving until she did.

Once Mrs. Clifford had gone, Ardell turned to the staff. "And there you have the key to good catering." She struck a pose. "Never let them see you strip-search the lettuce! Thanks, y'all."

Once the salads were de-toothpicked, dinner got to the table without a ripple. While the guests ate mushroom soup, mixed green salad, and roast sea bass with corn and leeks in red wine sauce, Blanche joined in the breaking down—that constant cleaning up—by checking the bathrooms, the sitting room, the den, and other rooms for stray glasses or napkins, half-eaten canapés. Since she knew everyone was at dinner, she didn't knock on the closed door of what turned out to be the library.

Blanche's mouth formed a wide but silent O. The young white woman leapt up from her chair as though Blanche had caught her trying to steal it. Everything about her said she was not a regular visitor—from her home-permed, frowsy blond hair to her clunky-heeled, wannabe leather shoes. She was a good-sized girl with wide hips and the kind of muscular calves old folks called piano legs. Her yellow, ruffled dress ended just above two oddly wrinkled knees, like large pink cabbages. It was not a big-woman-friendly dress, and Blanche wondered what could have possessed her to buy it, let alone to wear it.

"Excuse me. I thought everyone was at . . ."

"I got here too early, see. I thought I was s'posed to be here at . . ." She took a step toward Blanche. "They ready for me now, ma'am?"

Blanche liked the way she said "ma'am." Somebody raised her right. "Ready for . . . ?"

"The naming ceremony, I guess that's what you call it. For the shelter. Poor dead Maybelle's daddy—her mama's passed, you see—asked me to . . . Her brothers, they didn't want to come because they . . ."

The girl's half-sentences were like pieces of a puzzle with parts broken off. Blanche moved them around in her mind, imagining various versions of the unsaid bits, trying to make sense of why this young woman was sitting in the library while all the other guests were having dinner. And hadn't every place at the table been taken when she'd peeked into the dining room? She remembered Ardell telling her that there was going to be an announcement about a new women's program tonight, but what did that have to do with dead Maybelle?

"I'm Blanche White, with the catering service. Are you a relative of Maybelle's?"

"No, ma'am, Miz Blanche. I'm Daisy Green. Maybelle was my best friend since the first grade. It's nice, them naming the new women's place after her, aint it? Maybelle'd like that, havin something named for her, I mean."

Blanche figured Daisy was standing in for Maybelle's brothers, who weren't willing to come be grateful to the gentry for using their dead sister's name. Since Maybelle's murder was taking attention away from the bicentennial celebration, it looked like the folks in charge had decided to put their show in Maybelle's spotlight. Which didn't include having the likes of Maybelle's friend at table.

"We was like that, me and Maybelle." Daisy made the usual two-crossed-fingers gesture. "Here." She opened her plastic handbag. "Here's a picture of the two of us on my birthday." She handed Blanche a dog-eared snap-shot of Daisy beside a delicate, shapely honey-blonde with big eyes, a turned-up nose, and a rosebud mouth. They were dressed alike, in the very dress Daisy had on now. It looked fine on Maybelle, showing off her petite figure, but it made Daisy look like a white whale playing dress-up. Blanche wondered whose idea it had been for them to dress alike.

Blanche handed back the photo. "I'm real sorry about your friend."

Daisy looked as though she might cry, but didn't. Blanche hurried on.

"It looks to me like it's going to be a while before anything gets cranked up. You want something to eat?"

Daisy bobbed her head. "I sure wouldn't mind. I was too nervous to eat 'fore I left home." She pressed her hand to her stomach. "I'm right peck-ish now, ma'am."

"Be right back."

"These folks is lower than snake shit," Blanche told Ardell, then explained about Daisy. She fixed the girl a tray of assorted canapés and added half a bottle of Tattinger.

"*Real* champagne?" Daisy asked when she'd read the label, her eyes widened until the hazel was totally surrounded by milky white.

"Maybelle was always goin on about how she had champagne a lot and . . ." Daisy stopped talking and took a sip from her glass. Her eyes widened again. "It feels like it's dancin in your mouth!"

Blanche remembered the first time she'd tasted good champagne and her promise to buy herself at least one bottle a year. She hadn't kept that promise lately. It was only alcoholic grape juice in the end, so she hadn't missed much, but it was a promise tied to her old and growing desire to poke her head out into a world wider than the one she'd known so far.

She didn't see Daisy again until the girl was standing by the fireplace in the drawing room. She stood between the hostess, Mrs. Clifford, and a green-gowned young woman with curly brown hair and glasses who looked like a younger Mrs. Clifford. Blanche assisted the other help in passing glasses of champagne and ginger ale to the guests for a toast. Mrs. Clifford gently requested everyone's attention. Daisy's face was now as rosy as her knees. Maybe a glass of champagne would have been better than half a bottle.

Miss Green Gown was speaking: ". . . very, very proud to be able to tell you that, thanks to an extremely generous gift from Mr. and Mrs. Jason Morris, the long-dreamed-of battered-women's shelter for this area is about to become a reality." She smiled and held up her hand to quiet the applause, then beckoned Daisy closer. "As you know, we have all suffered the tragedy of Maybelle Jenkins's untimely death. Therefore, we have unanimously agreed to name our new shelter the Maybelle Jenkins Women's Shelter!" The woman grinned as her crowd applauded themselves for their good deeds.

"This is Daisy Green, Maybelle Jenkins's best friend," Miss Green Gown said. "She would like to say a few words on behalf of Maybelle's grieving family, who, understandably, could not be with us tonight."

And a damn good thing, too, Blanche thought, unless they brought along their own dinner!

Daisy looked slowly around, as though searching for one particular person to talk to. Blanche thought maybe the champagne had rinsed away Daisy's speech, but she needn't have worried. If anything, food and alcohol seemed to have slowed Daisy down so that she appeared more graceful and gracious. Her remarks were brief: "Thank y'all on behalf of my best friend, Maybelle Jenkins. She'd be proud to have her name on that shelter. I'll miss her all my life."

"Thank you, Daisy," Miss Green Gown dismissed her and turned to her friends. Daisy hesitated, then made her way to the side of the room.

"Now I would like to introduce the first director of the Maybelle Jenkins Women's Shelter, our own . . ."

Blanche went back to the kitchen. Watching folks congratulate themselves gave her heartburn. And wasn't it a bit weird to make a martyr out of the girl without knowing just how she died?

"I still can't get over those people not inviting that girl to dinner," Blanche said.

The job was finished, and she and Ardell were settled on the love seat in the Miz Alice, drinks in hand and chips nearby.

"Some people just don't know what it means to have class. But I don't intend to let that stop me from squeezing a decent living out of these suckers!" Ardell chomped on a chip.

Blanche looked at the half-circles of shadow beneath Ardell's eyes and the little frown that never seemed to leave her forehead these days. "I see you working your tail off. Is that all you're doing? I know you aint exercising or getting enough rest. I bet you aint even taking the time to read, are you? And whatever happened to Douglas, from over Chapel Hill?" Blanche asked her.

Ardell shrugged. "Just didn't work out. Maurice says I'm too bossy."

"Well, he would, wouldn't he?"

Maurice was Ardell's grown son, a backup singer down in Atlanta who was now into poetry slams. Since he'd first learned to make sentences, Maurice and Ardell had been battling over which of them was going to get the last word.

"Maybe I aint the only one who's too picky," Blanche teased.

Ardell shook her head. "No, it's not that. It's time. I just don't have the time. When I'm not working, I'm thinking about work and . . ."

"And you don't want to be distracted. Right?"

Ardell leaned forward and set down her glass. "It's like this. I don't plan to mind another white woman's child, solder another wire on another board, clean another office building, or help another old party onto a toilet." Ardell ticked the jobs off on the fingers of her right hand. "I aint planning to work that hard for that little no more in life, and I expect this catering business to be my means of doing better, whatever it takes to make that happen."

Blanche looked at her old friend and marveled at how much there was still to learn about someone she thought she could read like the morning paper. There were obviously some inside pages that she hadn't gotten to, even after all these years. Or maybe they were new pages just being added.

"Never seen you like this before." She passed Ardell the chips.

"Aint never been like this before." Ardell leaned toward Blanche. "I like being the boss, Blanche. Not just knowing I'm in charge the way you do when you work somebody's kitchen or house. But being the boss in ways that these people I'm working for can't miss. They can't *not* see me, *not* speak to me, *not* treat me like a professional. They have to talk to me, consult me, listen to my advice. For the first time in my life, I'm the out-and-out expert. And I like it."

"I could care less what they think," Blanche said. "It's how they *act* that's important. Including how they pay. They can think I'm the world's biggest fool as long as they act like they know they need me and pay me what I tell 'em."

"Humm, but don't you get sick of always being in the background? I mean, yeah, being a caterer is background, too, but they call you in 'cause they know they can't do the party, or dance, or wedding by themselves. They need a caterer. People who hire you to clean for them, well, most of them could do it themselves if they wanted to, so . . ."

"So what? Need means different things to different folks. People I work for need me whether they can or can't clean their own place. Some aint got the time, some need me 'cause it aint cool for them to do their own housework, or they just don't want to. There's a whole lot of reasons why people need me."

They were both quiet for a minute in which Blanche could almost see them settling into their old groove. Since the second or third grade they'd been pronouncing each other's ideas and opinions as brilliant or bullshit and speaking their minds. But recently they'd mostly lived in different parts of the country. They still talked on the phone regularly, but long-distance phone rates put a damper on lengthy, deep conversations. It felt good to know this one could go on all night if they wanted it to.

"Humm, but what you're doing for people you work for aint important like a wedding or a fancy dinner party."

"You're talking about prestige," Blanche said, both surprised and irritated to realize Ardell's sense of herself was still so closely tied to her line of work. "You think being a caterer has more prestige, and that's what you want."

Ardell gave her an unreadable look. Finally, she shrugged. "Aint nothing wrong with that," she said as though she expected to be challenged.

But she was right. There wasn't anything wrong with wanting status. It was what a person was prepared to do to get it that was the problem. And she had a feeling Ardell was ready to go to some places she herself wasn't. Or maybe she just envied Ardell's clearsightedness about what she wanted and her determination to get it.

"Hey, your light's blinking." Ardell pointed to the answering machine. "Maybe it's your main squeeze."

Blanche pushed the play button: "I don't need to call nobody on the telephone to talk to no machine. I got a plenty machines right here in my own house—toaster, TV, radio, refrigerator—I can talk to 'em anytime I want. I aint got to call nobody up to talk to no machine. This is your mama. You call me."

Ardell laughed halfway off the sofa. "Miz Cora near 'bout crazy as you!"

"All right, now, be careful. That's my moms you talking about."

"Don't you mean telling the truth about?"

"I wonder what she wants. She usually just hangs up without saying anything and lays me out about the machine when I call her. Must be important. But not enough to wake her up, or she'd have said so."

It was nearly dawn when Ardell left and they'd covered the conversational globe from prestige to the pros and cons of younger lovers. Blanche went to bed feeling very glad to be down home.

11

The Hunt and the Culprit

"Good thing you aint stayin here," Miz Cora said when Blanche got her on the phone the next morning. "Your cousin's comin to stay a while."

"Cousin who?"

"Sauda, from the islands."

"Who? From where?"

"From the islands, you know, my mother's people."

Blanche remembered the Christmas cards from somewhere in the Caribbean that her mother sent and got every year. And weren't there regular letters, too? But, like much of the rest of Miz Cora's life, she'd never really told Blanche much about these relatives from . . . "Where they live again?"

"Angelica, and one of your cousins's comin here."

"On vacation?"

"Unh-unh. Goin to that art school over there by Chapel Hill. Got a scholarship, her mama say. Aint that somethin? She was gon stay in one of them dormitories, but I wrote back to her mama and told her, Send that girl right on here to stay with me, since my own chile's too hincty to . . ."

"How she related to us exactly?" Blanche hoped Miz Cora was excited enough to drop her guard.

"My grandmama was from Angelica. She had a sister, Rose, who stayed on the island to take care of the old people. There was a brother, too, but he died of the consumption in the army. Now, Great-Auntie Rose had a daughter 'bout the same age as my mama, and she had a bunch a kids, including Rosalie, who was born same day as me. She who your sister was named for. Me and Rosalie been writin each other off and on since grade school and never seen each other. Now one of her granddaughters is comin to stay with me. Aint that somethin?"

She's lonely! Blanche thought. Mama was always so busy, so involved in her church, cooking, working in her garden, it hadn't occurred to Blanche that her mother was wanting for human company. Was this why Mama had been so disappointed Blanche wasn't staying with her? If this woman were anyone but Mama, would I have realized she's lonely sooner? Guilt worried Blanche like a pack of fleas. Maybe she *should* have stayed with her mother. It would only have been for the summer. But if she stayed in her mother's house for a couple months, she'd have to spend half the winter trying to undo the ankle-socks mentality that came from living under Mama's roof and rules.

"What's her name again, this cousin?" Blanche asked.

"Sauda. Sauda Leon. Pretty name, aint it?"

"Sure is. When she coming?"

"End of next week. Give me plenty time to make some new curtains for the back room."

Didn't think it was necessary to make no new curtains when she thought *I* was coming to stay, Blanche thought.

"Maybe git rid of some of that old junk your grandma left you and . . ."

"Mama! Don't go messing with my things, now. I'll come over and . . ." The words were hardly out of her mouth before Blanche realized that Mama had set her up to say them. As soon as Blanche hung up, she vowed that when Taifa and Malik were grown she would treat them like people she wanted to know, and not like marks she needed to con into doing things for her. The best way to get Mama off the brain was to get on with her own business. She called Mary Lee, the young woman who worked at Farleigh National Bank. This time Mary Lee was at home.

Blanche introduced herself and explained how she'd gotten Mary's number. "I was wondering if I could maybe come by and talk to you for a couple minutes. Something I need to know. About the bank."

"Well, I'm just senior clerk, you know. I don't handle mortgages, or loans for . . ."

"Yeah, I understand that, but if you've got the time, I'd really appreciate it." Blanche tried to think what to say to convince Mary to see her. Something told her money wouldn't work. Maybe the same thing that would work on her would work on Mary. "It's very important and personal, or else I'd just ask you on the phone."

Mary didn't hesitate a second. "Okay. Can you come by in about half an hour? I need to go by the church later on and . . ."

"I'll be there."

Blanche did a little dance when she got off the phone, grateful that she wasn't the only curious soul on the planet. She just hoped Mary's curiosity didn't come up with questions for her that she wasn't ready to answer.

Mary Lee turned out to be a long-faced, slender, light-brown-skinned young woman with Dacron braids and beautifully manicured hands of the clear-polish variety. They settled themselves on Mary's blue denim living-room sofa in a house not much larger than the Miz Alice. It felt steamy, as thought someone had just taken a shower.

Blanche looked at Mary and considered buttering her up—congratulating her on her job and how hard she must have worked to have gotten it in a town where few black people had front-of-the-house positions. But there was something about Mary's straightforward gaze and calm manner that made Blanche sure Mary wouldn't appreciate it. Blanche also had a feeling that what she was going to ask Mary Lee to do needed a better reason than somebody-wants-to-know. But first she had to find out if Mary could help her.

"Mary, I need to ask you to do something. I wouldn't ask if it wasn't important." Mary crossed her arms. Blanche went on. "I'm trying to get as much information as I can on a man I'm sure's got an account, probably more than one account, at your bank. I'd just like to know how money comes in and out of his accounts and if anything looks unusual. I thought maybe you could help me."

"You mean you want me to look at his bank records!?"

"You can do that, can't you?"

Mary's eyes widened. "Well, the information is there, Miz Blanche, but I can't just be going in people's files like that! It's not legal."

Blanche backed up. "It's not particular information I'm looking for. I'm just trying to find out if he's having any kind of money troubles, anything that might show that . . . cashing in his stamp collection, or . . . I don't know, honey. You'd know better than me."

Mary was silent—her unwillingness a high, wide wall between them. Blanche hoped she was right about how to put them on the same side of that wall. She took a deep breath, and looked directly at Mary: "This man has caused at least one poor black woman in this town a lot of very personal grief and pain."

"You mean rape?"

Blanche nodded.

Mary Lee looked off in the distance, a frown wrinkling her forehead.

"I don't want you to do it if there's any chance you could get caught. But if you can do it *safely* . . ."

Mary still didn't speak. Blanche's hopes diminished even further. Then:

"My little cousin was raped a couple years back. She's not the same. Probably won't ever be. Give me your phone number, Miz Blanche. I'll call you in a few days. But you got to promise me you won't . . ."

"Mary Lee, I don't even know you, let alone know what you're talking about."

Mary nodded again.

Blanche blinked back her tears and reached out to squeeze Mary's hand. It was moments like this that made her believe wholeheartedly in the connection between all the black women in the world. She knew the feeling would fade, smudged by a run-in with some sister whose circumstances forced her to focus solely on the need to do whatever was necessary to survive and who was rightly angry about it. But when she looked at Mary Lee, that sister thing was so strong Blanche could almost touch it.

At the same time, she knew there was a way in which she'd gotten Mary to trust her by telling, if not a lie, not the full truth. She promised herself not to mention to anyone else what Palmer had done until she was ready to say he'd done it to her. She wasn't sure why this was important, but she knew it was.

Instead of going home, she decided to take Curtis Martin up on his invitation to come by anytime on Saturday.

He lived in a squat brown house on First Street. Its small patch of front yard was a mini-playland of tricycles, blocks, sandbox, roller skates, and a portable playpen with a beat-up, one-eyed stuffed rabbit propped against its side. An echo of whoops of laughter, screams of pain, and shrieks for the sake of sound seeped from every toy. Blanche's nerves were glad the little owners didn't appear to be at home. Curtis came out when she knocked.

"Hey, Blanche. How you doin, girl?"

"Nothin to it, Curtis. How you been?"

They sat on the low front stoop. Curtis yawned and rubbed his head, covered with hair so short it looked like chin stubble.

"Just trying to keep body and soul together." He stretched his thick legs out in front of him. Through his tee shirt Blanche could see the muscles rippling down his front, washboard-style. His arms reminded her of young tree trunks.

"You moving back down here?"

"Don't know yet. Thinking about it."

"I'd leave tomorrow, if it wasn't for Geraldine and the kids." Curtis yawned again. "So—what can I do you for?"

Blanche silently thanked him for getting right to the point. "It's about David Palmer. I'm trying to find out who he hangs out with, who his friends are, what they talk about, things like that."

Curtis gave her a narrow-eyed look. "Why you so interested in him?"

"I'm helping out somebody who wants to know what the boy and his people're up to. He figures folks like me and you know more about the people we work around than they know about themselves. 'Course, I won't be saying where I got my information." She slid a folded twenty-dollar bill across the stoop to get things moving.

Curtis picked up the money, winked, and started talking.

"Friends, hunh? Well, I guess you could call 'em friends. They come to the gym together, work out together, and hang out together from what they say, so I guess that makes them friends."

"Why you say it like that, like they aint real friends?"

"None of that bunch of cream-filled, looking-down-they-noses chumps got no *real* friends. Least not far's I can see. Whichever one of 'em aint there is the one they all dis. Every one of 'em's got somethin nasty to say about every other one of 'em and right in front of me, too. Like I'm too stupid to hear."

"Yeah, that's why we know all their business. What they got to say about David Palmer when he aint around?"

"They laugh about some girl who walked out on him. Says he aint been able to keep a woman since. Too nice, they say, whatever that means."

Blanche nearly screamed at the idea of David Palmer as too nice.

"Let's see, what else? They talk about how his daddy's on his ass."

Blanche liked the image. "Why's that? His daddy some kind of iron butt, or . . . ?"

"I aint sure. Seems like his old man's uptight 'cause of something Palmer did a while back."

"Oh yeah?" Blanche leaned toward him.

"I heard Jason Morris say something about how whatever it was that Palmer did was a long time ago and his old man needs to get over it."

"He didn't say what it was?"

Curtis shook his head.

"Anybody else ever mention anything about this?"

Curtis rubbed his head again. "I aint sure. Sometimes they signify about Palmer's days at L.U."

"What's that mean? Louisiana University, maybe?"

"Naw, all them suckers went to Tobacco U."

Which was a nickname for Duke University that Blanche had seen scrawled on walls, along with "Duke Is Puke" and "Nuke Duke."

"Then what?" she asked.

Curtis shrugged. "Maybe it's about what his old man's got against him, maybe it's something else."

"So which one of those suckers he hangs with is Palmer tight with? That Seth Morris?"

"Unh-unh. The other one. The brother, Jason. He just don't hang out as much. He's another one under Daddy's thumb, but for different reasons. Maybe that's why him and Palmer hangs together. I tell you, the way Palmer looks at Jason sometimes makes me wonder."

"Really?"

"Nah, not really. It sounds like the two of them been friends since they was kids. You know how it is sometimes."

Blanche thought about herself and Ardell and was offended that a shit like David Palmer should have the privilege of friendship.

"They may not be doing that thang, but if Jason's around, Palmer's in his face. The other brother, Seth, he's just a hanger-on, him and guys like that Houston, the one they call Reds, and the Morley brothers."

"So it sounds like Palmer's got at least one good friend."

"Well, I'd say Jason's got a friend in Palmer. Jason aint got nobody's back but his own."

Blanche remembered the scene in the kitchen with Jason, Seth, and Clarice. "I'd have thought Seth was the shaky one."

"Oh, he is. But Seth's just a big, ignorant, rich good old boy. His brother is something else. There's always somebody on duty in there."

"Palmer ever talk about money troubles, or debts, or . . ."

"All them rich boys poor-mouth. To hear them tell it, they aint got a pot nor a window. Nothin but bullshit. They may have to wait for their old people to die before they get the real big bucks, but every single one of 'em got a high-payin job and stocks and shit worth a thousand times what you and me'll ever make. That's why, when I git 'em on the massage table, sometimes"—Curtis made a gesture with his hands as if burrowing deep into taut muscles with the knuckles of his bent forefingers—"I like to give 'em a real deep massage, real deep. So for once they know what pain is."

"Ooh, I like that!" Blanche appreciated the image for a few moments before she spoke. "He gamble?" she asked.

"Nah. Not to speak of. Football pool, poker game, but not the real stuff you talking about where you need it like a wino needs wine."

Blanche nodded. "So what about Palmer and women?" she made herself ask as casually as she could.

"Well, aint a whole bunch of women use the gym. Only been lettin 'em in a couple years. Lotta the men still don't like it. If a woman shows when Palmer's there, he's always the one who makes sure nobody bugs her, even if she act like she come in there to *be* bugged!"

"Is he going out with anybody?"

"Just taking women in his crowd to parties and shit. Lotta this bicentennial stuff. I don't hear him talk about nobody special. Mostly they talk about making money and whores. They all into whores. Go down Greensboro to do their thang."

Blanche felt a rush of sympathy for women who needed money bad enough to have sex with Palmer to get it.

"So what do *you* think of him, Curtis?"

"Cheap. Aint never tipped more than ten percent and don't give out no holiday tips like the other regulars either. Other than that, he aint no worse nor better than any of the rest of them white boys who use the gym."

Blanche remembered Mr. Bennie making the same complaint against Palmer. "What else?" she asked, feeling something unsaid.

Curtis hesitated. "I don't know. Something funny about him."

"Funny ha-ha?"

Curtis shook his head. "Nah, funny strange. It's like, even when he's laughing with his boys, I don't know, something about him . . . like his dog just died or . . . you know, like they say, he's all by hisself in the crowd."

"What about the rest of his family, ever hear anything about them?"

"Well, let's see. His sister's 'bout to get married. You probably heard that."

Blanche acknowledged that she had. "They talk about that at the gym?"

Curtis rubbed his belly and laughed. "Yeah, one of 'em said he hoped the Palmer girl's fiancé likes used goods. 'Very used,' somebody else said. All of 'em cracked up. 'Course, they wouldn't have said no shit like that if Palmer was around. He dotes on that girl. Talks about her like she's the last virgin and his mama the first saint."

"Anything else?"

Curtis shook his head. "Not that I can think of."

"Well, I really appreciate it, Curtis. You been a big help." Blanche slid him another twenty before she stood up.

"Thanks." Curtis pocketed the money and squinted up at her. "You know, I sure was surprised when Leo and Luella hitched up," he said, bringing them back to where he'd started when she phoned him. "I thought for sure you and Leo . . ."

"Yeah, well, people change same as times, Curtis. You know how it is." She dusted the back of her skirt. "Thanks for helping me out. If you hear anything interesting from Palmer or about him, there's more of them twenties where those came from."

"You got it, Blanche. You take care now, girl. And tell Leo I asked about him." Curtis chuckled and turned to go inside before Blanche could respond. Blanche shook her head. Some things never changed. In some folks' minds she'd be linked to Leo until they both dropped dead and beyond. She hoped she wasn't fooling herself about not being one of those people.

The pieces of information she'd just gotten from Curtis batted against her brain. She'd gone to Curtis expecting not only to find out who Palmer hung with, but also to have the fact that he was a low-down skanky dog verified by somebody who had a chance to watch him. But the man Curtis talked about didn't sound like the knife-wielding rapist she knew. It had been nearly eight years since he'd raped her, and she expected that he, like everyone else, had changed. But had he become a totally different person? She gave a hard shove to what the answer to this question might mean.

Blanche had to hustle to be ready for the picnic Carolina Catering was working that afternoon. The picnic was being held near the Eno River, in a large public park—a section of which had been roped off for their private party. A stream burbled not too far from where they'd set up the outdoor tables. Closer still was a large, round, low stone building called the Teahouse because it was supposed to be shaped like some teahouse in Japan. Its rough stone walls were only about waist-high, leaving the building open to the out-of-doors and the green light of the nearby woods. The floor was of some kind of slate with built-in openings for plants of various types and sizes. A large ficus grew up through an opening in the center of the roof. A wooden bench circled the tree. Nestled among the plants were statues of Japanese figures made of what looked to Blanche like bronze and some marble ones as well—all with the feeling of knowingness that seemed to radiate from every Oriental statue she'd ever been near. A tall white shoji screen hid the water pipes and plant equipment. Blanche took charge of covering the wooden picnic tables with tablecloths and setting up a few small tables and chairs in the shady cool of the Teahouse's overhanging roof.

The picnic was an hour away from starting when Clarice arrived, huffing and waving to them before she got close enough to speak. "Guess what, y'all? Guess what?" She didn't wait for anyone to answer. "Sheriff caught that Bobby Larsen. The one Sheriff say killed Maybelle Jenkins."

Tears sprang to Blanche's eyes so quickly they were on her cheeks before she knew they were coming. She excused herself and found an empty bathroom. She closed the door behind her and leaned against it. She let her tears fall freely. Sweet Ancestors, thank you! It was as if Maybelle's killer's arrest was a sign that she would be able to bring her own attacker to something that at least passed for payback, if not justice.

She was expecting the knock on the door when it came.

"Blanche?"

Blanche opened the door and let Ardell in.

"You all right, baby-girl?" Ardell stroked Blanche's arm.

Blanche nodded. "It's just . . ."

"I know. Maybelle, Palmer, all that is mixed up in your head. You got some heavy shit going on right now, but you don't have to go through it by yourself."

Blanche put her arms around Ardell and held on. "What would I do without you, Ardell?"

"Humm. You'll never know, I can tell you that."

Another tap at the door. Blanche and Ardell looked at each other.

"What y'all doin in there?"

Blanche and Ardell grinned at each other. "Just a second, Clarice, we're having sex right now," Ardell said, then quickly opened the door so they could see the look of shock and interest on Clarice's face.

"Y'all ought to be 'shamed of yourselves, sayin somethin like that. Anybody coulda heard you!"

Ardell steered the still-complaining Clarice back to work.

Blanche blew her nose, washed and dried her face and hands, and looked at herself in the mirror over the washbowl. Her face seemed blurred, as though her features were resettling, as though there was some new part of herself growing up and out. She hoped it was full of spunk and fire.

Clarice started talking the minute she saw Blanche approaching: "Mr. Henry say Bobby say he didn't do it. He was huntin's what Bobby say. With some big-shot hunter from up north, 'cept big shot aint come to say Bobby's tellin the truth or not. That's what Mr. Henry say."

Blanche sucked her teeth. "Lotta so-called boyfriends out here think they own a woman's life and can end it when they want to."

"I guess you right. Lord knows plenty of these mens aint nothin but dogs in dress-up. I'm just glad Mr. Henry aint like that."

• • •

Blanche felt drained by the time she headed home, like she'd been riding a roller-coaster: up to help from Mary Lee and Curtis, down to work, up over Bobby's arrest. She was looking forward to a nice long bath with plenty of bubbles and a long session with her book. She dug in her bag for her door keys as soon as she was on her street, but she could see that she had company: three little girls sitting straight as a fence across the top step of her stoop. One squinted like she needed glasses; the second one had a Band-Aid on her knee; the third little girl's eyelashes were so long they looked false. Sisters: they wore the same mammy-made blue floral-print dresses and Made in China cloth Mary Janes. The one in the middle reached for her sisters' hands at the same moment they looked up to see Blanche heading toward her stoop.

"Hey."

Three pairs of big brown eyes stared, then blinked. Then, all together, they rose and, still holding hands, formed a single file down the side of the stoop farthest from Blanche.

"Hey! Where you going? We haven't even met yet!"

The girls flowed by her like oil around the bottom of a hot frying pan. Hands still clasped, they ran around the corner. A door shut with a bang from the opposite direction, and Blanche automatically turned toward it. A woman slipped out of the lone house next to the garden on the other side of the street. The wail house, Blanche thought, curious to see who that voice belonged to. The woman looked both ways.

"Doretha? Murlee? Lucinda?" she called in a voice too small to reach around the corner. She stepped out into the street and walked toward Blanche.

Blanche waited for her to come closer, then raised her hand, about to shout out that the girls Blanche was sure she was looking for had gone around the corner. But the woman turned her head away from Blanche and hurried by in a way that said, Don't speak. Blanche could think of a lot of reasons to avoid a neighbor you knew, but not a new one. Of course, calling your children to come home to a place where you, and therefore they, were in danger might make you want to avoid talking to anybody. Blanche had a flash fantasy of herself on the stoop waving wildly at the woman, screaming at her to do what Palmer's knife had stopped Blanche herself from doing; to do what Maybelle had not been able to do:

"Run! Run! Run!"

Party Hearty

Blanche was glad she hadn't realized it was Thelvin on the phone before she picked up the receiver. At least he hadn't yet moved into the level of her affection where she knew when he was calling or knocking at her door. Things hadn't gotten that far, thank the Ancestors. But they had gotten far enough for her to be thinking about him a couple of times a day.

"We're okay for tonight, right?" he asked.

"Looking forward to it."

"Me, too. But it's not the party I'm talking about."

Corny but cute.

"You sure know how to make a person feel good."

"Oh, you aint seen, or should I say 'felt,' nothin yet."

"I hope that's a promise," she told him. "Because I'm holding you to it."

Blanche was in a serious party mood when Thelvin arrived. She hadn't done any partying in over a year, and this was the first one she'd been to since she'd come back home.

"Want a drink before we go? Beer, gin, iced tea?"

Thelvin chose tea and wandered around the room while she fixed it. He eyed the closed cardboard box that held her altar but didn't say anything. He looked at her book lying on the table, the rock souvenir Mumsfield had given her years ago, the pictures of Taifa and Malik on the small shelf.

"How's work? You like riding the train?"

"Sometimes. Most of the time. Except when some white boy thinks I stole his brother's job and tries to treat me like I don't know what I'm doing."

Blanche remembered reading about some racism problems at Amtrak. "You get a lot of that?"

Thelvin shrugged. "Enough."

She handed him a glass of tea with a lemon-peel curl and a sprig of mint floating on top. Thelvin looked at the glass, then smiled up at her in a way that made her think he appreciated the extra touches.

He nodded toward the picture on the shelf. "Good-looking kids."

"And as good as they look." Blanche didn't try to keep pride out of her voice, so she prepared herself for a session of your-kids-aint-got-nothin-on-my-kids, a ritual parents performed as naturally as a peacock fanned his feathers. She figured Thelvin must not have any pictures of his kids on him, since he didn't whip them out.

"My daughter, Maggie's going back to college, even though she's got two kids, you know. And did I tell you? Martin, my oldest, just got promoted to assistant manager of city planning up there in Albany."

Blanche waited for the update on the other son.

"Rog, the youngest, he's a pharmacist in San Diego. Doing just fine for himself."

"Both boys are still single." Thelvin laughed. "Both of them got more women than . . ." He looked at Blanche and stopped talking. The proud-papa grin disappeared, too.

"Now, Martin's a Big Brother, too." Thelvin cleared his throat. "And Rog coaches a Little League team. I raised them to give something back, all of them."

Blanche was impressed with how easily and quickly he'd read her feelings on this subject. She was also curious to see how he was going to try to explain away sounding like banging women by the pound was something to boast about.

"I wasn't trying to say a lot of girlfriends is a good thing." Thelvin looked at Blanche as if for approval. "They both old enough to be settling down."

Blanche held her face in neutral.

"When I was their ages, I was trying to find the money to pay some-body to take care of them so I could keep working, and wondering how we would manage if I got sick. I guess I'm just glad they got more freedom," Thelvin said.

"Is that what freedom is? Being able to have a lot of women?"

"Uh-oh. I really did put my foot in it, didn't I?"

"It's not your foot that worries me."

Thelvin's smile slipped away. "Hey, I'm sorry. I didn't mean no offense. But, I mean, having sex is what young people do, isn't it? I thought that's what they were *supposed* to be doing."

Blanche thought about it for a second. "You're right. It is what people are supposed to be doing, young or old. It's the how that worries me. Taifa's just coming into her womanhood. Knowing there are men out there just waiting to add her to their list of jumped bones scares me half to death, even though I know it's something women have been dealing with forever. And I don't even like the idea of her *speaking* to somebody who wants to have sex with lots of people in these days of AIDS."

Thelvin was slowly nodding his head. "Yeah, I see your point. My daughter married so young, I forgot how . . ."

Blanche raised her glass. "To parents!" She watched relief loosen the muscles in Thelvin's neck. He swigged from his glass and walked toward her.

"We got plenty of time, you know. The party could go on to all hours." He slipped his arm around her waist and kissed her. The tip of his tongue was cool and tasted of mint. He set their drinks on the table so they could involve more than just their mouths in the action. She could feel a pulse throbbing through his penis pressed against her thigh. The heat from it spread across her crotch, up her belly, to her chest, where it hardened her nipples. She pressed even closer when his hand roamed across her behind. Appetizer, she said to herself, then pulled back. Time to go. She went to the bathroom and wiped the moisture from between her legs.

The party they were going to was just three blocks away, so they left Thelvin's Buick behind and strolled over to Branch Street. The night air took up where Thelvin had left off and kissed Blanche's cheeks and caressed her arms and legs. Crickets and other night creatures played accompanying love songs. It was the kind of sweet, velvety evening that made people lower their voices and walk softly, as if they might frighten the night away.

The party was at Carl Stillwell's. Blanche hardly remembered Carl, but she and his younger sister, Melva, had run with the same crowd in high school.

"We played baseball in the summer league," Thelvin had told her when he'd invited her.

Blanche knew Leo, her old lover, was already at the party before Thelvin rang Carl's bell.

Thelvin gave her a sharp look. "What's wrong?" he asked, surprising Blanche with his ability to read her. Carl opened the door before she had to answer.

"Looka here, looka here!" He hugged and pummeled Thelvin and pecked Blanche on the cheek. "I remember you, old wild thing! You and Melva and Ardell. MELVA! Come see who's here!"

Blanche looked quickly around the room. She didn't see Leo, but she felt him like a vibration just under her heart.

People Blanche hadn't seen since she'd been back and, therefore, hadn't seen for years called out and waved to her. There were also plenty of "Hey, man"s and shout-outs to Thelvin as they made their way into the living room. Thelvin left Blanche with Melva and headed to the kitchen for drinks.

Blanche leaned against the wall. "How you been, Melva? I aint seen you since the dinosaurs died."

"I know that's right." Melva's big lips made her face look bottom-heavy, despite her high forehead. When they were kids, Melva had tried to hold her lips in to hide their size. Now they were outlined in deep red and colored in with a lighter shade, as if to highlight them. Good for Melva.

"What you been doing for yourself, girl?"

Melva pulled herself up sharp. "Got me a hair salon. 'Beauty by Melva.'"

"Oh yeah?" When Blanche had lived in Farleigh, Melva was doing hair in her basement on weekends and working at the cigarette plant over in Durham during the week.

"Yeah, girl. Lot more black people moving in around here, 'cause we so close to the Research Triangle, you know? So, when they start talkin that New South stuff about black enterprise, I went for some of that money and opened me up a shop." Melva paused. "In the new mall!" She said each word with emphasis and offered her palm to be slapped. Blanche obliged.

"Hot damn!" Blanche didn't approve of processed hair, but she did approve of black business in the malls, where the money walked by. "Now, that's what I call movin on up!"

"Yeah, girl. It's good." Melva nodded her head and grinned. "Real good. I even got me some white customers and a couple of Hispanic women. Lots of them movin in around here, you know." She looked up at Blanche's plaited hair. "We do cornrows, Senegalese twists, extensions, all that. Come on by. I'll give you a free sample."

"I'll be there," Blanche said, knowing that she wouldn't. She didn't even like being around the kind of chemicals that women put in their hair. She kept waiting for reports to come out on the relationship between brain and scalp cancer and hair dyes and permanents. She already knew there was a connection between all those hair-straightening poisons and black women's programmed hatred of nappy hair. She didn't like to be around that either. She paid attention to Melva's hair—kinky at the roots with straightened bits sticking out on the sides, she didn't want to guess what was going on in the back. Every hairdresser she'd ever met had a hairdo that would be greatly improved by putting a paper bag over it.

"How's Junior?" Blanche pictured a big, freckle-faced man with the kind of sleepy-eyed, loose-jawed face that fooled people into thinking he was stupid.

"Still just as sweet as he can be. He'll be here later. Got his own hauling business now, you know. Doing real well, real well. Talkin 'bout let's have another baby. I told him, 'Yeah, if you the one's gon carry it and be its mama.'"

"How many kids y'all got?"

"Two bad-assed boys. You got your sister's kids, right? How they doin?"

"They fine. Both of them off working this summer."

"Lord! Don't they grow up fast!"

Sometimes too fast and sometimes not fast enough, Blanche thought.

"I heard you was back, working with Ardell. How's it going?"

"Well, business sure is good. And Ardell got that catering thing down to a bust-out."

"She coming tonight?"

Blanche shook her head. She'd mentioned the party to Ardell, but Ardell said she intended to sleep away her evening off.

"Speaking of business," Blanche said, "you got any clients who work for the Palmer family?"

"Who owns the BonBon? Wasn't the son the one engaged to that Gregory girl?"

Blanche pushed herself away from the wall. There was something here, she could feel it. "When was this?" The flutter in her stomach was so strong she put her hand on her belly to calm it.

"Aint no sense interrogatin me, 'cause that's all I remember. Might not even have been him, but I'm pretty sure it was." Melva took Blanche by the wrist and pulled her down a hallway. "Patsy'll know. She worked for them Gregorys. If she's here, I know just where she'll be."

Melva opened the door into a bedroom full of people talking quietly, lolling on the edges of the bed, the bureau, and anything else leanable. Everybody's eyes swiveled toward the door to see who was coming in. The smoke in here smelled different from the cigarette smoke in the living room. The music on the clock-radio was mellower, too. Blanche didn't mind. If she was going to breathe secondhand smoke, this was no doubt better for her than the name brands they used to make down the road in Durham.

Melva looked around the room. "Patsy in here?"

"Aint seen her," somebody said.

"Well, she must not be here, then," Melva said, " 'cause this is definitely her spot."

"Hey, Blanche!" someone called from the corner by the bureau.

Blanche and Melva stayed a while, talking to more people Blanche hadn't seen in ages. She kept moving around the room so the joint never reached her. She'd occasionally taken a toke or two before she'd become a parent. Once Taifa and Malik were in her care, she'd given it up— not because she thought there was anything wrong with adults using marijuana; she just figured that parenting was easier when it was an example thing. Maybe she'd add a future toke to her list of emancipation presents.

"If Pasty knows anything, I sure would like to hear it," Blanche said when they were back out in the hall. She dug in her handbag for a piece of paper and a pencil. She wrote her phone number down and gave it to Melva.

"You still aint said why you so interested in these folks."

"Somebody I know wants to know what some of them Palmers are up to. I'll make it worth her while," she added, knowing this would distract Melva from more why-type questions.

"Ooh. Money. This is serious shit."

"And all on the QT. Aint nobody gonna know who said what. That's a promise." Blanche decided to go all the way. "The middlewoman gets her cut, too."

"You speaking my language and singing my song, girl. I know Patsy'll be by the shop for a touch-up soon. I'll be gettin back to ya." Melva folded the paper with Blanche's number on it, put it in her bra, and gave Blanche her number.

Blanche asked the way to the bathroom. While she peed, she ordered herself just to wait until she'd talked to Patsy, but she couldn't stop the surge of hope that maybe Palmer's fiancée had quit him for reasons he wouldn't want known. She felt not light-headed but light-bodied. A sample of how she'd feel when she was finally done with him? She washed and dried her hands, straightened her skirt, and took a deep breath. Party time.

The living room was even more packed than when they'd left. Blanche didn't see Thelvin. Or Leo. She could tell from the red lightbulbs and Funkadelic blasting from the stereo that it was a serious party for younger old-heads. She intended to get right down with it. She let George Clinton's groove drain the tension from her back.

"Well, look who's here!"

Blanche's back stiffened; she didn't turn around or need to. Luella's voice reminded her of a mouse with a megaphone. How did Leo put up with that high, loud squeak every day?

Luella sidestepped until she was in Blanche's view. Blanche grinned. Luella had gained twenty-five pounds, easy, and Luella was the kind of woman who believed in skinny.

"I heard you was back," Luella squealed.

Blanche just looked at her. She hadn't liked Luella since they were children. Luella had been one of those cute, caramel-colored girls who called Blanche names like Pickaninny and Tar Baby. She might have changed some of her more evil ways, but Blanche was sure that underneath those extra twenty-five pounds lurked the same prissy-minded, color-struck hussy. And she certainly aint giving or getting no head, Blanche thought and smiled at the memory of the last time she'd been alone with Leo.

"I can't imagine what Farleigh's got for a city-living woman like you, Blanche White."

Blanche tried to hold her tongue, but something in Luella's trapped-mouse voice begged Blanche to tease her, to hurt her feelings, to make her cry.

"Oh, I can think of one person worth coming back for," she said.

Luella's eyes darted from Blanche to Melva, as if she were afraid Blanche might say just who she had in mind. Melva looked like she was waiting for the pie-throwing contest to begin.

"I hope you don't think . . ." Luella began in her Olive Oyl voice, then stopped and stared over Blanche's shoulder.

"Hello, Leo," Blanche said, just as he put his arms around her waist from the rear. Her body seemed to press against him without moving a muscle.

"Good to see you." He tightened his arms around her and kissed her ear, then jumped back as though he'd been singed when he realized his wife was watching. And Luella *was* watching: eyes wide, her mouth tight as a skinflint's wallet.

"Luella was just asking me what could have brought me back to Farleigh. Then you walked up." Blanche grinned at him. Leo harrumphed and er-ed and ah-ed but was finally saved by Thelvin's arrival.

"Hey, everybody." He handed Blanche and Melva their drinks and waited to be introduced.

"Leo's an old, old friend," Blanche said, then flipped her hand in Luella's direction. "That's Luella, his wife."

Thelvin shook hands with both of them, spoke to Melva, then put his arm around Blanche's waist. If he'd done this at another time, Blanche would have moved away. She didn't hold with women on leashes, whether the leash was leather or a warm brown hand. But right now . . . She shifted her hips and snuggled a bit closer to Thelvin and winked at Leo even while she was telling herself to behave.

"Well, you certainly didn't waste no time," Luella said to Blanche, but smiled at Thelvin with such happiness and relief he might have been her missing brother returned to the bosom of the family.

Melva was trying not to laugh. Leo looked as shocked as if Blanche had just unzipped his fly. Luella took Leo's arm.

"Y'all stop by sometime," she said, tugging at Leo, her voice finally pulling him out of his state of stun.

"Yeah, anytime, anytime. Y'all come on by. We'll . . ."

Luella dragged him away before he could finish. Melva looked from Blanche to Thelvin and decided to ease away, too.

"Old, old friend," Thelvin said. "That must take y'all back to high school."

"Um-humm." Blanche was deciding what if anything to tell Thelvin about Leo but was more interested in how much Thelvin wanted to know.

"Close friends, or just friends?" Thelvin was smiling but there was some tightness around his eyes she hadn't seen before. It had been a while since she'd heard that tell-me-the-truth/tell-me-what-I-want-to-hear whine men developed when they feared somebody else might be getting a piece of the pie.

"You mean now or in high school?" She gave him a wicked, keep-on-if-you-dare grin.

Thelvin looked at her for what seemed a long time. Blanche thought about his already well-developed ability to pick up on her vibe. Is that what he was doing now? Trying to feel her feelings? Could he tell that her jealousy alarm was beginning to flash? She'd installed it right next to her bullshit detector as soon as she'd understood the harm that jealousy could do. A woman she'd worked for up in Harlem had helped her understand that a lot of times jealousy was the first sign of a man's feeling like he had the kind of ownership that allowed him to blow your brains out if he was in a bad mood or if he thought you were being a bad girl. And it aint nothing to play with, she reminded herself, thinking about the way she'd let Thelvin hug her just to tweak Leo's last nerve.

Something shifted in Thelvin's eyes. The tightness around them disappeared. He took Blanche's hand and held it between both of his.

"You know what? Forget I asked that question."

Good move, Blanche thought. Very good move.

"You wanna dance?" he asked.

And they did. First to a song fast enough to release them from the last of the tension of their previous conversation, and then to something that brought them belly to belly, wrapped in a tension of another, more delicious kind but not so powerful as to keep Blanche from wondering if Leo was watching. When the music stopped, Thelvin went to the bathroom and Blanche made a slow circuit of the party. She didn't know why she was surprised so many people she'd grown up with were living in Farleigh—more than when she'd last lived here. She'd read that lots of blacks were giving up the phony integration in the big cities, North and South, for places where they could breathe and grow. But could she breathe here? Could she grow while living in the same town as David Palmer? Was Luella right about her being a city woman now? She wound her way back to Thelvin—without going near Leo, despite the tug.

Blanche and Thelvin were on the dance floor, repeating their slow drag to something by Teddy Pendergast that should have been sold with a pack of condoms, when Leo tapped Blanche on the shoulder. "Just wanted to say good night."

"Night."

Thelvin pulled her closer and executed a turn that took Leo out of her sight. Boys will be boys, she laughed to herself.

On the walk home, Blanche wondered how to tell Thelvin that she didn't trust herself to let him in her house because she wasn't sure she was ready for sex with him yet. To say it was to imply that she knew he wanted her—which she did, but she didn't want to sound boastful. And she wasn't ready for any questions about why she wasn't ready to have sex with him, since half her reasons couldn't be put into words. She was operating on one of those wordless commands that boiled up from somewhere deep inside of her and were never wrong, even though she didn't always heed them.

"Can I come in?" Thelvin asked when they reached her door.

"I don't think so, Thelvin. It's pretty late, and I don't want to rush things. And if I let you in now . . ."

Thelvin grinned as though she'd actually invited him into her bed. "Well, thank you," he said. "I consider that a real compliment." He put his arm around her in a brotherly way, gave her a quick hug, and let her go. "I sure like being with you, woman," he said, walking backwards toward his car. Blanche watched him drive off and wondered if she'd made a mistake about being ready.

Later, in bed, she slipped her hand between her legs and relieved some of her craving—at least for the moment. It was probably a good thing he was going to be away for a week. Give her some time to cool down. She didn't want to scare the man to death.

13

Out to Lunch and
Under Orders

A familiar-looking young brown-skinned woman answered Mumsfield's door and smiled like she knew something Blanche hadn't told her.

"Yes, ma'am. He's expecting you."

"What's your name, honey?" Blanche asked.

"Christine, Miz Blanche, Christine Potter."

Of course, how could she have missed that Potter nose? This was Leo's brother's child. That accounted for the knowingness in the girl's smile. Blanche wondered just what she'd heard about Blanche's relationship with her Uncle Leo. She certainly wasn't going to ask. The important thing about her relationship with Leo was that there wasn't one any longer. Until the party, she hadn't seen him for nearly two years. The last time they'd met, he'd paid her a surprise visit in Boston and they'd spent the day in bed. Leo had tried to keep something going after that, but Blanche wouldn't have it. It wasn't simply that he was married, but that he'd married that limp Luella when Blanche was prepared to be his long-term lover, if not his wife. All right, maybe not his live-in, but at least his part-time long-term.

Leo's niece showed Blanche down the black-and-white marble-floored entry hall. Blanche was pleased to have totally forgotten what Mumsfield's family's house looked like. She didn't want to use up precious brain cells storing the layout of ex-employers' houses. But she was sure the feeling in the house was different from the crazy, stressed vibe in the place when she'd worked there.

"Blanche!" Mumsfield came down the hall. He gave her one of his boa-constrictor hugs but not before she noticed his suspenders. Orange for eating? Blanche looked over Mumsfield's shoulder at his fiancée. Karen Palmer reminded Blanche of a pale bird: pigeon-breasted and thin-legged, with fluffy brown hair and an air of being ready to take off. She wore an odd expression; Blanche thought she saw surprise or confusion, and was that fear in Karen's eyes? There was something familiar about her, too, especially her eyes. Of course, they were like her brother's.

Mumsfield turned Blanche toward Karen and introduced them.

For all Blanche's talk about no one being able to choose her family, she realized she didn't want to shake Karen Palmer's hand—invisible flecks of dried Palmer skin left behind on her fingers, falling into her food. Didn't Archibald say Karen and David were close?

"How do you do?" Blanche kept her hands at her sides but tried to make her voice friendly.

Karen looked at her for a couple of beats, as though she expected Blanche to say something else, something Karen didn't want to hear. She seemed relieved when Blanche remained silent. Blanche had no idea what that was all about, but once it passed, Karen perked right up.

"Why! Well, this is a . . . Mumsfield told me he wanted me to meet an old friend but I had no idea . . ."

"I did not tell her it was you, Blanche," Mumsfield said.

No wonder she looked surprised, Blanche thought, and smiled at Karen.

"Yes, well, he has spoken of you, and it certainly is a—" Karen's hands flew from her sides to her hair to her neck to a short bout of wrestling with each other—any- and everywhere but in a position to shake Blanche's hand. Fine. They were in agreement on that, even if their reasons were different.

"Why, I'm so pleased to meet you," Karen finally said.

Blanche thought she looked more like she had a toothache or needed a toilet than pleased.

Mumsfield ushered them into the room dominated by a large sofa in a blue, beige, and gold fleur-de-lis pattern. The walls were covered with portraits of men who, according to their dress, were long dead, and pictures of the countryside.

Mumsfield touched Blanche's arm. "Would you like a drink before lunch, Blanche?"

"No, thanks, Mumsfield, honey." Blanche squirmed to get comfortable in an overstuffed chair. Mumsfield and Karen sat on the sofa.

"I'm afraid I don't have too much time," Karen said.

From the look on his face, this was news to Mumsfield. "But Karen, I thought we—"

"Oh my, did I forget to tell you? Why, yes, I've got a meeting. About the bazaar?" She looked from Mumsfield to Blanche. "You know, the Farleigh Daughters of the Confederacy Bazaar?" She gave Blanche an especially toothy grin.

Since it wasn't necessary for Karen to volunteer any of that information, Blanche figured this must be her way of announcing what she was. The Farleigh Daughters of the Confederacy Bazaar was a whites-only event that used to be held downtown—Main Street was blocked off and off limits to all but whitefolks for two days. In the late fifties, the NAACP filed a discrimination case and won. But the good Daughters were not to be outdone: they moved the bazaar to the spacious lawns of one of the members' homes and made it a private whites-only event. Well, if that's the way Karen wanted to play it:

Blanche grinned right back. "Oh yeah," she said. "The Farleigh Daughters of the Confederacy—in my neighborhood they're called the Klanettes. Of course, I'm sure you girls are better behaved." Blanche gave Karen's outfit a slow looking over. "And a little better dressed . . . I guess."

Karen's eyes got narrower, her cheeks and neck were mottled with red, and Blanche could swear she saw the woman's head bobble in shock, like one of those hound dogs people put on the ledge inside the back windows of their cars.

Mumsfield looked from Blanche to Karen, a frown beginning to crease his forehead.

"Lunch is ready, Mr. Mumsfield," Christine said from the doorway.

Blanche felt like a midget in the high-backed, hard dining-room chair.

The three of them were huddled together at the end of a table long enough to seat thirty.

Karen seemed to have regained some composure by the time they were seated, and they talked of the weather while Leo's niece served the salmon, new potatoes, and braised Brussels sprouts. Blanche was determined to turn the conversation toward topics that might give her a glimpse of Karen and Mumsfield's relationship, since that was why she'd come.

"Will y'all be living here after you get married?" she asked, breaking the silence created by something she only now remembered about Mumsfield: his total concentration on his food.

He chewed and wiped his mouth before he spoke, looking all the time like someone suffering from pig-out interruptus, despite his good manners.

"We are going to live in the country house, Blanche. You remember."

A flood of memories of what had happened to her in that house filled Blanche more fully than the meal.

Karen broke into Blanche's thoughts: "Why, you were the maid at the summer house, isn't that so?"

Blanche continued to chew her potatoes a bit longer than needed. Mumsfield reached over and took Karen's hand. "Blanche worked there, but she was always my friend."

"Yes, dear," Karen said. She gave him a melty look. "I only meant . . . Well"—she looked over at Blanche—"why, it must feel quite different. I mean, being a guest instead of . . ."

Blanche wiped her mouth before she spoke. "Oh, quite different. For one thing, being the maid is dirtier work than being a guest, and people's manners are *usually* better when you're the guest."

Karen looked at her watch. "Oh me! I'll be late!" She patted her mouth with her snowy napkin. Mumsfield rose and pulled out her chair.

Blanche was irritated that her time had been taken up sparring with Karen instead of trying to sense whether Karen really cared for Mumsfield. But what did caring mean to a bigot like Karen? Karen didn't have the kind of beauty or sexiness that usually went with the term gold digger or heartbreaker, but looking like a sweet old granny hadn't stopped Margaret Thatcher from being vicious.

Blanche watched Karen as she rose to leave.

"Why, I'm so glad to have finally met Mumsfield's, uh, friend," Karen said, looking just over Blanche's left shoulder and sounding as sincere as a TV commercial.

"Why, thank you, Karen, honey. I hope y'all will be very happy. And I can't wait till you get settled in the country house so I can come on out and sit on that big ole front porch with my feet up and just enjoy your hospitality."

Blanche wondered if anybody had ever broken his neck doing that head-bobble thing. Girl's so pale she looks like she's seen a ghost—or is one. Blanche pursed her lips to keep from laughing. There'd been a time when Karen's Klanette attitude would have depressed her for days. That was before she was old enough to understand that both race and racism were invented by white people and didn't have a thing to do with her. However, she did like to remind them of the cost of their stupidity when she got a chance.

"You take care now, Karen, honey," she said. "I'll be waiting for my invitation to the wedding." Blanche called out as Karen was leaving the room: "I'm gonna make Mumsfield promise me a seat right up front. Right next to your mama."

"Why! . . ." Karen looked from Blanche to Mumsfield and back. "Why, I'm sure I . . . we . . ."

Mumsfield put his arm around Karen's shoulders and ushered her to the front door, murmuring to her as they walked away. Blanche doubled over in silent laughter.

Mumsfield's face was full of distress when he came back. "I am sorry, Blanche. I did not know, Blanche. If I knew Karen was prejudiced, I would have talked to her. I will talk to her, Blanche," Mumsfield said, demonstrating the understanding of people that had drawn them together years ago. She had a feeling it was the rare white person who could both see prejudice in those he cared about and speak on it.

"And what will you tell her, Mumsfield, honey?" she asked him.

Mumsfield frowned at her. "That it is silly not to like people because they are different from you," he said with impatience, as though she well knew the answer and was testing him.

"Um-hmm," Blanche said, but she thought that Mumsfield's talking-to and about five years living as the only white person in a Georgia town might change Karen's mind.

"I want you to like her, Blanche. Now you cannot."

Blanche was relieved at not having to find a gentle way to tell Mumsfield that she thought his fiancée was a racist bitch. But beyond that, what could she say? She couldn't tell him she thought Karen was fine for him, as though being a racist weren't something that seeped through your whole life like the stench of sewer water rising in the basement.

"She will listen, Blanche. She will understand. I know she is a good person, Blanche, even if she . . ."

"Mumsfield, honey, I don't think it's possible to be a good person and be prejudiced against black people the way Karen is. I understand what you mean, but please don't ever call her a good person in front of me, not as long as she's the way she is."

"She will change, Blanche, you will see."

Sounds like fantasy city to me, Blanche thought.

"I got to be going, too, Mumsfield. We're catering tonight, and I got plenty work to do." She rose, smoothed down her skirt, and picked up her handbag. "Thanks for the lunch, honey. It was scrumptious. I'm just going to step into the kitchen and speak to Miz Claudia." Blanche had heard from Miz Minnie that Miz Claudia ruled Mumsfield's kitchen.

Blanche had no trouble finding her way there, but Miz Claudia was slumped over her newspaper at the kitchen table having a quick nap. Blanche waved to Leo's niece and went back to join Mumsfield.

Mumsfield wouldn't let Blanche leave without promising to come to dinner soon. "Just you and me," he said. He leaned over and kissed her cheek. "I will help Karen to change her mind, Blanche. Then you will like her, I know you will."

Blanche warned herself not to praise him. People ought not expect or get praise for doing the right thing any more than they got praise for breathing.

"Maybe so, honey, maybe so. But it aint nearly as simple as you make it sound."

Mumsfield giggled. "Well, if she does not understand, you can sit on the porch of the country house until she does."

They laughed together.

Mumsfield insisted that his chauffeur take her home. He was a young white man who also looked familiar.

"Where I know you from?" she asked.

He tilted the rearview mirror so that he could see her. "I useta live out Hokeysville, near Mr. Mumsfield's summer place. Delivered groceries, worked on cars, ma'am."

Of course, the smart-mouthed grocery boy. Hadn't she put a curse on his penis for talking fresh to her? Had it worked?

"Got any kids?" she asked.

The young man blushed and glanced at her in the mirror again. "No, ma'am, not yet, anyways. No wife. But I got a girl."

Well, the curse didn't seem to have crippled his love life completely, although working for Mumsfield certainly had improved his manners and attitude. Maybe she was selling Mumsfield short by thinking he couldn't help Karen change.

When she got home, Blanche hurried toward the blinking light on her answering machine:

"Hey, Moms. It's me. I'm in camp. I'm glad you got a machine. I'm okay. I'll call you, like Friday. See ya."

Malik's message dissolved a rod of concern stiffening her back that Blanche hadn't even been aware of—evidence of that parent-worry thing she'd come to realize would likely live in her in one form or another until she died—like a lingering cold she couldn't throw off. When the children were small and using up every moment when she wasn't working for money, she'd soothed herself with a one-day-they'll-be-grown fantasy. Now that they were practically grown, instead of trying to convince them to be careful of strangers, pick up their toys, and eat their okra, she was now urging them to use condoms, to avoid hard drugs, and to become their very best selves. Different topics, more stressful topics. Who started that bullshit about parenting getting easier as the children got older? What parenting lost in intensity it picked up in worriation.

The next message gave her something else to worry about:

"Leave," a voice hissed on the machine. "Leave right now."

When her heart stopped thumping so loud she could hardly hear, Blanche played the messages again, preparing herself for the second one while Malik's message replayed. Then there it was. Just four ordinary words, but so full of threat they made her want to run. Though she couldn't tell if it was a man or a woman, she was pretty sure she knew who it was. It could be a wrong number, but she didn't think so. She thought it had everything to

do with what she'd been doing. Who had she told about looking for information on David Palmer? Who might have told him? She didn't even
have to think about it: that little old weasel, Mr. Bennie. She'd bet money
on it. She poured herself a small drink. Her hands were shaking just a bit.
She looked around the Miz Alice. Safe. Secure. In here. But out there . . .
She called Ardell.

"In a way, I'm glad it happened," Blanche added after she told Ardell
about the message on her machine.

"What!?"

"Well, don't you see, Ardell? It means I'm on to something. Palmer
wouldn't be leaving threatening messages on my machine if he didn't have
something to hide."

"Humm, well, maybe it's because he raped you that he wants you to
leave town, to make sure you're not going to bring it up or do anything
about it."

Blanche shook her head. "He knows there's nothing I can do to him.
Even if I had proof, it's probably been too long ago for the law to care. It's
gotta be because I'm asking questions!"

"How you think he found out?"

Blanche told Ardell her Mr. Bennie theory.

"Butt-sucking old buzzard. I never did like him much."

"His wife was nice."

"Musta scared you half to death. I'm gonna come get you. You can
spend the night here."

"No. I told you he aint keeping me for nothing, and he sure aint running me outa my house!"

"You sure, Blanche?"

"I don't know. Maybe. Yes, I'm sure, for now. But I bet this is just the
warm-up. He'll wait a day or two at least to see if I leave."

"Then what?"

"Then that's when I start getting scared."

"Well, you'll just move in with me?"

"I don't know. We'll see."

There was a click on the line.

"Uh-oh, gotta go," Ardell said. "I'm waiting for a couple of calls, and
this is liable to be one of 'em. Come on over."

"No. Don't worry, Mommie, I'll be okay."

"All right, Miz Smart Ass, but if you get another threat, you call me. You hear me, Blanche?"

"Yes, Mama," Blanche said in a little-girl voice, and hung up before Ardell could say anything more.

She wasn't pretending to be unconcerned. She was still caught in the aftershock of the rocket of fear that had shot through her when she first heard the message. But it wasn't nearly as strong as the surge of excitement created by her certainty that David Palmer had something he didn't want her to know. She just had to find out what it was before he decided to do something more direct than just ordering her out of town.

14

Worriation, Hypocrisy, and a Secret

Blanche woke with David Palmer worrying her mind like a popcorn hull lodged between two back teeth. For all her show of bravery to Ardell, Blanche had spent an uneasy night, waking any number of times to feel for the knife beneath her pillow, to listen for noises that shouldn't be there. Now she rolled out of bed and showered beneath a rush of water as hot as she could bear it, then turned it to cold. Her skin squeaked when she was done. She dried and oiled herself, and her hair, quickly gathering it into a knot on top of her head. At her Ancestor altar she struck a match and began speaking as the first tendril of smoke from the stick of incense curled toward the ceiling like an undulating gray snake.

"Ancestors, I come to you this day in need of the strength to right the wrong done to me, and the courage and speed to do it before I get caught." The thought of being once again in Palmer's clutches would have rocked her if she hadn't just then felt the strong presence of her Ancestors around her. She closed her eyes and felt the weight of Palmer shifting from her back and shoulders to her upper, then her lower arms. She raised her arms and shook them violently out to the sides, throwing the heft of him from her body to dissipate in the air around her. His shadow remained, like a film across her left eye, but she could feel her Ancestors telling her that it would not always be so. Soon, very soon, she would be done with him.

But despite the Ancestors' help and the added incentive of a threatening phone call, she was still reluctant to make more Palmer calls. Curtis had put her off with his lonely nice-guy talk about Palmer. The man she wanted to hear about was a rotten rapist, not the dutiful son Mr. Bennie had gone on about. Which was why she had to keep moving, keep talking to people until she found somebody who knew the David Palmer she knew.

A young woman answered her first call. She said Miz Letitia was having her hair done so she couldn't come to the phone. Blanche pictured one of those late-afternoon hair-fries that used to go on in her mother's kitchen and those of her friends: one of them straightening and curling the others' hair to the accompaniment of women signifying, sneaking a little nip, and telling stories that had made young Blanche laugh and learn. Miz Letitia was one of the best seamstresses in town. Miz Minnie had said she did work for the Palmer women. Blanche told the young woman on the phone that she'd be sure to call back.

Blanche could feel her shoulders tightening, a bit of headache above her right eye, a feeling that she was purposely playing in dog shit. But she forced herself to press on.

No one answered the phone at Mr. Jim's house. He was gardener to the Palmers and a lot of other rich folks in the area. Blanche couldn't help feeling relieved. No more Palmer right now. She tried Ardell's number. Both lines busy. Ardell had mentioned she had to call a woman about catering her wedding and had some ordering to do. The way Ardell was working these days, she was probably trying to do both tasks at once. The thought of Ardell working away moved Blanche to wash the fifty carrots for the carrot tulips she needed to make for a job they were doing tomorrow. She got them out, washed and patted them dry, but couldn't stand still long enough to work on them. I need a walk, she thought. The carrots went back into the refrigerator and Blanche headed for downtown in search of deodorant and hairpins.

She'd always liked downtown Farleigh. Wasn't much to it, although there was a bit more than when she'd lived in town. Three stores that had been boarded up when she'd left for Boston were now a boutique, an antique shop, and a sweets bakery. The tree-shaded wooden benches along the sidewalks were comfortable—perfect for a nice session of people-watching. And something about the low two-story buildings added to the friendly feel of the place.

"Champagne lady!" someone shouted behind her. Blanche turned around to see who was being called. She was surprised to see a young white woman galumphing toward her. A pink-and-yellow floral-print dress bouncing around her substantial thighs.

"It's me, Daisy Green!"

Where did she know this girl from? She was close to six feet tall, wide and muscular, too. Yet there was something defenseless about her, as though she could be seriously wounded by a word.

"You remember!" the young woman said just as Blanche realized who she was. "You gave me some real champagne at that ceremony for that new women's place named after my friend Maybelle Jenkins?"

"Oh, hey, Daisy. How you doing?"

Daisy hadn't seemed nearly so tall at the dinner the other night, as though those unwelcoming surroundings had actually made her shrink.

"I'm sorry, ma'am, but I forgit your name."

"Blanche, Blanche White." She waited for the usual double-take.

Daisy nodded. "Got me an aunt named Blanche. Lives over by Fay-etteville."

You never know, Blanche said to herself. Of course, Daisy probably didn't even realize that her name meant white twice.

Daisy lifted her pale, fine hair off her neck and let it slip back into place. "It sure is humid!" She looked over her shoulder and perked up. "Come on in here and let me buy you a Coke, Miz Blanche. For bein so nice to me t'other night." Daisy was pointing to a little restaurant a few doors away.

Blanche looked the place over. She didn't want a Coke, especially from this greasy spoon that had Poor Working White Folks' Hangout written all over the grimy plastic lace curtains at the cloudy, finger-marked front window. She could smell the oilcloth tablecloths and the overused grease without opening the door.

"Weren't you headed somewhere?" she asked, hoping Daisy was on some errand she'd momentarily forgotten.

"No, ma'am, I was just on my way home. Today's my half-day at the cleaners." Daisy took Blanche's arm and tugged her toward the restaurant. Blanche decided it was easier to give in than to fight all this gratitude.

They both ordered cherry Cokes from a waitress who looked from one of them to the other as though she wanted to ask them what they were doing together. Blanche had expected some pop-eyed reactions. For all its blooming downtown and spreading out, Farleigh was still a small Southern town where the Daisys and Blanches did not generally meet in restaurants for gabfests over Cokes. But Blanche decided it was good for her to be there. She'd been thinking lately about how she only knew and hung out with people who were like her. When she'd lived in Harlem, she'd spent time with Puerto Rican and Cuban women as well as an occasional Asian or African woman she met through work. She missed seeing the world from other colored people's eyes and tasting it through their food. Daisy wasn't colored, but she sure as hell wasn't white in the way the people they both worked for were. Blanche thought it a special shame that so many poor white people had been suckered into believing black people were their enemy, instead of seeing how both groups were being screwed by the same pale rich guy. Daisy may not have worked all that out, but she was obviously ready to have a Coke across the color line, which was unusual enough in Farleigh to make her interesting.

The waitress never looked or spoke directly to Blanche, although every other person—all of them white—looked her over as though she had wings, or more likely a tail. Once they were served, as naturally as the sun's passing overhead, their conversation turned to Maybelle.

"I keep thinking about how she . . ."

Blanche interrupted before Daisy got too choked up. "Sounds like her boyfriend did it."

Daisy shook her head. "Bobby didn't do it, Miz Blanche. I know he didn't. He really loved Maybelle." Daisy sipped her cherry Coke and blinked at Blanche over the glass. "I mean really, really loved her." The hint of something like envy in Daisy's voice piqued Blanche's interest.

"Then he must be real broke up," she said. "Bad enough to have your girlfriend die, especially like Maybelle was killed, and then to be arrested for killing her yourself . . ."

Daisy nodded. "He's in a bad way, awright. I went to see him down the jailhouse yesterday. He looked so sad and hurt, I wanted to . . ."

Blanche didn't press Daisy to continue her sentence. They both knew where it was going.

"She was my best friend." Daisy's cheeks were flushed. Misery whined in her voice.

Blanche nodded. Poor thing. Having a crush on your dead girlfriend's boyfriend who'd been arrested for the girlfriend's murder had more shades of guilt and complication involved in it than there were feathers on a duck's behind—which made Blanche quite curious about how it was all going to go down. She figured she was like Daisy's seatmate on a cross-country bus—a stranger Daisy could talk to about her secret love for Bobby without worrying that word would get back to people who knew her and would think her feelings out of line.

"Well, I hope everything turns out the way you want, Daisy, honey, but you know they say nine times out of ten the boyfriend's the one who . . ."

"No, Miz Blanche. Not this time! You just wait until the man Bobby was huntin with that night shows up."

"Daisy, do you *really* think there's any such hunter?"

"There is, Miz Blanche, I know there is, and that aint all, no." Daisy leaned over the table toward Blanche. "Bobby wasn't the only one who . . ." She stopped talking as suddenly as if a hand had been clamped over her mouth.

"The only one who what?"

Daisy's cheeks were deep red now; she moved her hands to her lap. "Talkin outa turn," she said. "Papa always say it's gonna be my downfall."

Blanche was so curious she could almost feel her nose twitching. She leaned back in her chair and looked around the room, trying to seem as casual as possible. "Yeah, well, I know you think Bobby didn't do it, but I can't help wondering if he really does have an alibi. I mean, where's this hunter?"

"He'll show up, Miz Blanche, you mark my words. Anyways, Bobby can prove . . . he . . ." She stopped talking again and looked twice as stricken.

Blanche was truly curious now. "Girl! You really believe that! Guilty people always say stuff like that, pretend they know who did it and hope somebody's silly enough to believe them."

"Bobby's not like that! He's not!"

"Yeah, right. If Bobby can prove somebody else killed Maybelle, why don't he just tell the Sheriff?"

Daisy looked around the room, then down at the table, before she spoke. "He . . . the Sheriff aint no friend to Bobby. He's always messin with Bobby and his brothers. Always accusin them of . . . Bobby don't trust him. He's gonna give the information to . . ."

"Daisy! He tells you he got proof, but he won't use it to get hisself out of jail, and I know he didn't tell you what it is he knows. You sure are gullible, honey."

"He did, too, tell me what it is, but I can't tell nobody! He . . . he knows . . . He found somethin! When he found Maybelle. You'll see!"

Blanche believed her, but admitting it wasn't the way to get Daisy to talk. "Something, hunh? He found something? Like what? A driver's license? A note saying, 'I'm the one who did it'? Come on, Daisy."

Daisy looked at her with eyes full of tears. Uh-oh. She hadn't meant to push the girl this far.

"I done already said too much!" Daisy pressed her lips together.

"Sure, honey, sure. Let's just pretend you didn't say a word." Blanche pushed Daisy's Coke a tad closer to her. If what Daisy said was true, it would all come out soon enough. Blanche watched as Daisy delicately sipped Coke through double straws.

"Well, it was nice talking to you, honey. But I need to get rested up for work tonight. Another one of them bicentennial dos."

"Y'all take care, now," Daisy told her as they parted on the sidewalk.

Blanche watched Daisy's square-hipped, flat-butt back as she bounced down the street and wondered whether loyalty to Maybelle's memory or the hots for Bobby would win out.

She went home, changed her clothes, and opened the refrigerator. The sight of those carrots waiting to be carved convinced Blanche this was a good time to call her mother.

"Hey, Mama. It's me, Bl—"

"I know who this is! You think I'm so simple-minded I don't recognize my own chile's voice? I knew what your voice sounded like before you did. Bawled like a stuck pig for the first couple days, till my milk started to flow good, then you just . . ."

Blanche felt herself drying up as though each of Miz Cora's words was a little leech sucking the blood right out of her veins with each of Miz Cora's stories about baby Blanche's eating, pooping, playing, and sleeping habits. Blanche thought about interrupting, but what good would that do?

Mama would likely take up the subject of being interrupted and talk on that for another half-hour.

"... were six months old 'fore I could git you to stop doin it. But that aint why you called me. You must be wantin something, 'cause I know you aint just called to say hello to your poor old mother, 'cause you nev—"

Blanche sighed. Miz Cora's you-never-call-your-poor-old-mama riff was usually the finale of her talkathon. In a few minutes, Blanche would be able to get a word in.

"... sorry when I'm dead and gone." Miz Cora took a deep breath. Blanche spoke up:

"Well, I'm sorry to disappoint you, Mama, but I just called to see how you gettin along. You all right?"

The shocked silence that followed her words made Blanche grin, but Miz Cora was not about to be outdone.

"You just seen me t'other day, Blanche," she said. "You sure *you* all right? How's my grandbabies? You tell 'em to call their poor old granny. I still don't think it's right, you way down here and them children up there, in two different places where they aint got no family to look out for 'em, working for . . ."

When her mother finally released her, Blanche sat staring into space for a bit, amazed, as always, by her mother's ability to work her nerves, press her guilt button, and release a flood of affection in her all at the same time. She made herself a cup of recovery tea: fresh sliced ginger steeped in simmering water with a lemon slice and a lot of honey added to the cup.

15

One Out of the Can
and One on It

There was a moment's lull in the kitchen activity while the canapés and finger sandwiches were being served. Blanche washed her hands, untied her apron, and followed the sound of music through the house to a room that opened onto a patio overlooking a terraced lawn. The French doors were wide open, allowing people to flow in and out. The small combo, complete with a white Bobby Short imitator, was doing snappy versions of show tunes and what whitefolks called standards. "Strange Fruit" was a standard to her, but she doubted this lot would agree. She watched people dancing on the terrace, more than half of them moving as though they were working to hold an apple between their knees. There were three black couples on the dance floor trying hard to disprove the myth that all black people can dance.

Blanche recognized one of the dancing black men as a member of what she called the Andy Young Fools Club: civil-rights and other leaders and celebrities she read about who were foolish enough to go on those fact-finding trips for outfits like Nike and Kathy Whatshername. They always came back grinning about how happy those Asian workers were, and how much they loved being underpaid. Did those so-called fact-finders really believe that what they saw in those factories was what went on when they weren't around? Everybody cleans house when company's coming. Anybody who didn't know that didn't know a fact from a fart. The one she was looking at now was a Fayetteville boy who used to play football for the Panthers. Now he was spokesman for a chicken-processing company that ran plants where workers had been maimed for years. This good brother's job was to explain to the public that he'd talked to the workers and they were healthy, happy, and singing doo-dah all the day long. Just the kind of black man that would be invited in to celebrate the bicentennial of the ripoff of the land by slavers.

As she turned to go back to the kitchen, Blanche felt a flash of pain in the corner of her left eye, as though someone had shot off a flashbulb. Before her head was fully turned, she knew: David Palmer was standing with Seth and Jason Morris to the left of the French doors. She bit her lip and forced her eyes to stay open, ignoring her urge to run. Miz Minnie said it was her time to step up for herself, and Ardell said she had to get over it. No better time to start. Blanche took a deep breath, and looked him over.

Jason Morris had his arm around Palmer's shoulder as they talked for each other's ears only, their blond heads together—Palmer's bone-straight, and Jason's a curly cloud that made him look like Cupid.

David Palmer had been a young man when he'd raped her—not a boy, but young. She raised her hand and touched the place where he'd pressed the knife, just to the left side of her jugular vein. He'd nicked her while he'd thrashed through his ejaculation, his face twisted, acid sweat dropping from his forehead to her face. She pulled her mind back from what he'd done to her and looked at the man he'd become. She couldn't tell from here, but probably some of his blond hair had gone gray. It had receded from his face, which looked almost ball-round, with jowls he hadn't had back then. He had a slight, slack pouch and rounded his shoulders to hide it, like a young girl with too much bust. He didn't appear as wide as she remembered him from when he was filling her entire vision, back when he'd been in control of her life. In her mind she replayed the message he'd left on her answering machine. *No, you shit, I aint leaving,* she thought. *Not till I'm done with you, anyway.*

Palmer waved at someone Blanche couldn't see and was suddenly gone from view. Tension leeched from her body with such force she had to steady herself. She stepped into the hall and leaned against the wall, panting as though she'd just been running for her life. Great Ancestors, mothers of mothers, I thank you for your strength, she whispered. For, though she'd been rocked by the sight of David Palmer, she had not buckled. She had not run.

She stepped back into the terraced room and watched Seth Morris at the bar. He ordered a drink from Zeke without looking at him. Zeke made a Bloody Mary and handed it to Seth, who took it without a word of thanks or even an acknowledging nod. Blanche's eyes lit up. Maybe she couldn't yet get her revenge on Palmer right now, but this was the perfect time to give Seth that little surprise she and Clarice had talked about. Blanche hurried to the kitchen. Clarice was loading glasses into the dishwasher.

"Your boy's here and drinking Bloody Marys." They grinned in unison. Clarice got her handbag and took out the small plastic bag Blanche had told her to prepare and keep at the ready. There were about three tablespoons of grainy brown powder in it.

"I took ten of Mr. Henry's laxative pills and crushed 'em real fine." Clarice put the granules in a small glass pitcher. Blanche instructed her in the right proportions of vodka, tomato juice, lemon juice, Worcestershire, and pepper sauce for the Bloody Mary.

Twenty minutes later, Blanche poured the drink into a glass and carried it on a tray to the front of the house. She searched the crowd for Seth. The three of them—Palmer, Seth, and Jason—were back together again, like three magnets pulled toward each other. Palmer said something that made Jason laugh. Seth stood nearby looking like the third wheel on a date. He was holding a nearly empty glass.

Blanche beckoned one of the waitresses to her and exchanged the tray of champagne the girl was offering guests for the smaller tray with the Bloody Mary on it. She pointed Seth out to the young woman and directed her to collect his nearly empty glass and give him, and only him, the fresh drink. Blanche watched: without a break in his conversation or a glance at the person serving him, Seth set his old drink on the tray and lifted the new one, accustomed to having somebody anticipate his every need. Before the night was over, he was going to need somebody to anticipate his need for a couple extra rolls of toilet paper and a soothing salve for his very sore behind.

16

Visiting, Searching, and Dreaming

First thing in the morning, Blanche got busy on the vegetable bouquets—carrot tulips, radish roses, cauliflower and broccoli florets, and cherry tomatoes. The vegetables would be stuck on bamboo skewers slipped inside of green-onion stalks. She'd put half a cabbage in the bottom of each of the wicker baskets and arrange the skewered vegetables in them like flowers in a bouquet. The vegetable baskets would sit next to trays of dip at the affair that night. Ardell was picking her up in about an hour, time enough to make a dent in the vegetables. She hummed to herself while she worked and thought about how different catering was from what she usually did. She thought about her kids, too, where they were and what they were up to; she also wondered if she'd hear from Thelvin today. She dropped the last radish into the pan of ice water with the others and reached for the phone on the third ring.

"I'm sorry, Miz Blanche. I couldn't find a thing in David Palmer's accounts that's worth mentioning. Regular deposits to his checking account. His paycheck, maybe? Checks written to cash or on his debit card—maybe a thousand dollars every couple weeks. I guess he pays his other bills with a credit card. Regular deposits to a money market account and that's about it."

Blanche's mouth flooded with the sour taste of disappointment. "You couldn't have overlooked anything? He couldn't have some other kind of . . ."

"I'll check a little further, just in case, but I don't . . ."

"Thanks, honey," Blanche said, eager to hang on to one last bit of hope.

Ardell gave her a quick, sharp look when she picked Blanche up an hour later. She watched while Blanche double-checked to make sure her front door was locked and slipped a small piece of paper between the jamb and the door so she'd know if anyone had opened it while she was out.

"I'm glad to see you being careful," Ardell said. "You feeling okay?"

"I'd be fine if I wasn't being threatened and life was fair."

"You didn't get another phone call, did you?"

"Not the kind you mean. At least not yet. But that don't mean my other call was good news." Blanche told her what Mary had to say.

"Well, who knows? Mary might still turn up some dirt on that sucker that you can use against him."

Ardell turned off the highway onto a rutted one-lane road with trees lining it like watchers at a parade. Blanche tried to slow her racing mind. There was nothing she could do about Palmer at the moment. She looked out at the blue and gold summer day, felt the warmth of the sun on the back of her neck and her shoulders, then closed her eyes. A couple months ago, she'd found a book on Buddhism on the bus in Boston. She began reading it right away, sure that the book had somehow been left for her to find. Though she didn't understand a lot of it yet, she did understand about trying to live in the right now. Her way of practicing this was not as the Buddhist book said, by sitting and listening to yourself breathe, but by closing her eyes and simply listening to the sounds around her. She closed her eyes now. When she opened them, as usual, she was amazed by how absolutely perfect everything was when you didn't try to put labels and reasons on things. It gave her a kind of floaty feeling that always made her smile. In the moment, she understood and agreed with the idea that every moment, in and of itself, is perfect. She laid her head back against the seat and let herself become a part of the passing world until they pulled into Mr. Broadnax's yard.

Mr. Broadnax was sitting on his front porch, which was a weathered version of Mr. Broadnax himself: tall, lean, and watchful. He sat in a straight-backed armless wooden chair with his right leg crossed over his left, arms lying loosely across his raised leg. A hand-rolled cigarette dangled from his right hand. His spine went straight up from the seat of the chair, never touching the back of it. Mr. Broadnax the sphinx, Blanche thought. The only movement came from the smoke curling up from his cigarette in a slow spiral. Little round, dark sunglasses covered his eyes. His ever-present bow tie was dead-center. There wasn't a wrinkle in his short-sleeved white shirt, and the creases in his shiny black trousers were sharp as good cheddar.

"Hey, now, Mr. B.," Ardell called before she was fully out of the car.

Mr. Broadnax took a slow drag from his cigarette and released the smoke as though he hated to let it go. "Afternoon, afternoon." His voice was a whispery rasp.

Had he always sounded like Miles Davis? Cigarettes, probably.

"This my friend, Blanche. You remember her?"

Mr. Broadnax looked over the top of his dark glasses. "She a Farleigh girl?"

"Yes, sir. She Miz Cora White's daughter."

Blanche made herself relax and not jump down Ardell's and Mr. Broadnax's throats for talking about her as though she were a block of wood.

Mr. Broadnax turned toward Blanche. "Cora White's daughter, eh?" He took another drag on his cigarette and let the smoke leak slowly from his nostrils. "Now, aint that something?"

Blanche waited for him to tell them what was so special about her being Miz Cora's daughter, but Mr. Broadnax was once again silent and still.

Ardell cleared her throat. "Well, now, Mr. Broadnax, about them ducks."

"Inside," he said, but didn't move.

"Humm. Well, I'll just go on in and get them?"

Mr. Broadnax nodded.

Blanche turned to follow Ardell. The scent of the house—tobacco, hickory smoke, and something else familiar and slightly sweet—came to the door to meet them.

"How is that Cora?" Mr. Broadnax asked.

Blanche was stopped by that nose-twitching feeling that meant there was something interesting going on here even if she didn't yet know what it was.

"Mama's doing just fine." She stepped back outside. "Takes pretty good care of herself. Stays busy. Gets around."

Ardell gave them a curious look as she carried the first load of ducks out to the big cooler in the back of the van.

Mr. Broadnax made a noise that could have been a chuckle or a cough. Ash fell from his cigarette, just missing the cuff of his black trousers. A bit of white sock showed above his shiny black pointy-toed shoe.

"Cora always did know how to look out for herself."

A sharpness in Mr. Broadnax's tone gave Blanche the impression that, to his mind, being able to take care of herself was not one of Mama's better points.

"Woman who can't take care of herself is a woman looking to be treated like a child," Blanche told him.

Mr. Broadnax looked at her over the top of his dark granny glasses. His eyes were bloodshot. "There's the kind of taking care of yourself that's about keeping yourself together, and there's the kind that's about keeping other people away from yourself. It aint so smart to get them confused."

Blanche felt herself blushing as though Mr. Broadnax were talking about her, not Mama.

Ardell came out of the house with the last three ducks, each in a plastic bag. "I left your envelope on the table, Mr. Broadnax. I'll stop by in a day or so and bring you the ribs I'm gonna need for that job next Saturday."

Mr. Broadnax nodded.

"I'll tell Mama you asked about her," Blanche said.

Mr. Broadnax chuckle-coughed again and took another puff on his cigarette.

"Y'all take care, now," Ardell told him and gave Blanche a let's-get-going look. "What was that all about?" she asked when they were in the van.

"Beats me." Blanche told Ardell what Mr. Broadnax had to say. "You know I'm gonna ask Mama about it, for all the good it'll probably do."

Blanche, Ardell, and Clarice spent the next two hours wrapping prosciutto around spears of gingered pear. While they worked, Blanche told them about her meeting with Daisy.

"Sounds like she got a crush on that boy," Clarice said. "Mr. Henry say he nice enough, that Bobby."

"You really think he's got a alibi?" Ardell handed Blanche another tray of pear spears. Blanche arranged the finished ones on glass trays.

"Mr. Henry say he do, so I believe him," Clarice chimed in before Blanche could answer.

"Humm, well, time will tell, I guess, but I seriously doubt . . ."

The phone rang. Ardell wiped her hands and went to answer it.

Clarice turned to Blanche and spoke in a low voice. "I bet when she was a chile she was the one who tole the little kids there aint no Santa Claus." Blanche hooted at the memory of Ardell doing just that.

Blanche began pumping herself up as soon as she left Ardell's for home: Everything will be fine at the Miz Alice, she told herself. Palmer hasn't broken in. It was just a call to scare me off, and I aint going to let him stop me. To prove it, she was going to make some more calls about him.

Before she opened her front door, she checked for the paper between the jamb and the door. It was still there. She walked around the Miz Alice to make sure all the windows were still intact, then unlocked the door, went inside, and went right to the phone.

She hoped that already knowing the folks she had to call might make them more willing to talk to her. She'd gone to grade school with Miz Letitia's daughter, Marylyn, whose clothes—made by Miz Letitia—all the girls had coveted. Not only did they want Marylyn's outfits, they wanted their mothers to look like Miz Letitia: tall, thin, with beautiful red-brown skin, and always elegantly dressed.

"Hey, Miz Letitia, I don't know if you remember me, I'm Blanche White, I went to school with . . ."

"'Course I remember you. Cora's girl. How are you, chile?" Blanche brought Miz Letitia pretty much up-to-date with her life and asked about Marylyn.

"Big as a house, and no more taste in clothes than a jackrabbit," Miz Letitia sadly reported.

"Miz Letitia, the reason I'm calling is about the Palmer family," Blanche began after they'd talked about Blanche's mother's health, Miz Letitia's failing eyesight, and her ailing husband's bad back. "I was wondering if I could come over and . . ." Blanche could almost hear the woman squirming by the time she'd explained what she wanted.

"Well, chile, you know you always welcome in my house, but I don't want to get involved in no whitefolks' business. I keep my ears closed when I'm in those places," she said, as if Blanche didn't know that all the service people who kept their ears closed had long since been out of a job.

"I understand, Miz Letitia," she said. And she did: only the rich were in a position to eat without working. Hadn't she done the same thing when she chose not to report David Palmer for raping her?

She hoped for better luck with Mr. Jim, gardener to the Palmer clan. When Blanche was growing up, he and his wife and two sons lived a couple of doors away. He was a little man with long arms and a flattish head that made him look apelike—something he'd learned to use to his advantage at the poker table. As a child, Blanche had developed a kindness toward him because people teased him about his looks the same way they teased her for being true black.

"I works too hard to be listenin to what them peoples is up to. Anyways, I aint hearin all that good these days," Mr. Jim said, although he didn't seem to have any problem hearing Blanche. She tried to reach the Palmers' mailman, Roger Grainfield, but his wife said he was away at his uncle's funeral.

Okay, okay, she told herself, you knew it wasn't going to be easy. Would she have had a better chance of getting information from Miz Letitia and Mr. Jim if she'd been willing to tell them what Palmer had done to her? Maybe. Maybe outrage left over from times past, when the rape of a black woman by a white man was as common as a rainy day and just as accepted, would have loosened their tongues. Maybe not. Maybe the reality of a black community still too weak to protect its own would have kept them mute. Suddenly the feeling that she was wasting her time was stronger than hope. She lay down on her bed and pulled a thin blanket over her head, even though it was quite warm outside.

The party they were working that night was being held after the Bicentennial Awards Banquet, at the home-that-could-pass-for-a-hotel of the county's only state judge. Everyone who ever wanted to be anyone in that part of North Carolina was going to be there, including David Palmer. Blanche knew she'd have to make herself ready to see him again, but at least this time she'd put his presence to use.

Before the guests began to arrive, Blanche had a talk with Raheem and Rasheed, who were hired to park the cars. They were short, cute, plump brothers whose color and long necks reminded her of goose-necked squash. Ardell had told her both young men also did caddying and worked on cars at a dealership out on the highway. Blanche figured that gave them a fair acquaintance with the local men of means. She'd waved a ten-dollar bill under each of their noses and told them that later she was going to want to check out cars belonging to some local people.

Earlier, she'd told Ardell what she planned to do. "Probably won't find anything, but I feel like I gotta look everywhere I can."

Ardell hadn't looked happy. "Be careful, Blanche. Anybody catch you, Carolina Catering could . . ."

"I will," Blanche had interrupted, annoyed at feeling momentarily in competition with the catering business for Ardell's support.

When the party geared up, Blanche went out front to see if there were any chauffeur-driven cars. She found three balding black men ranging in color from nearly white to chocolate-brown to Blanche's own eggplant blackness. They greeted her invitation to a snack with grins and thanks. Blanche ushered them to a small table in the kitchen, out of the way of the catering staff and already loaded with enough food to keep them chomping for a day. She turned the TV on to a baseball game as extra incentive to sit and stay, then slipped back out front.

Rasheed and Raheem walked down the drive with her, telling her which car belonged to whom. David Palmer's big gray BMW was parked at the bottom of the drive in a row with cars belonging to Seth and Jason Morris. Archibald's car was nearby, as was the Mayor's brother's car and that of the host's sister. Blanche decided to check out a few of the cars, so the boys wouldn't know she was interested only in Palmer's, but she just had to check Palmer's car first. She took her rubber gloves from her apron pocket.

"I'm not going to take anything. I just want a look-see," she told the boys.

She made them stand near the front of the car, facing the house, so they couldn't see what she was doing, blocked her from being seen, and could warn her if someone was coming. She opened the front passenger door of Palmer's car.

"You looking for something special, Miz Blanche?" one of the boys asked over his shoulder.

"Not exactly. I'm just doing a little research."

"What kind of research?" he wanted to know.

"Sort of secret research. The kind I can't talk about, honey."

She felt but didn't care about his disappointment—as long as he stopped with the questions.

Palmer's car was neither spotless nor particularly dirty. It smelled of cigars. There were tapes in the compartment between the seats—some country, some white blues. She put her head out of the door and took a deep breath. Her skin recoiled from the car seat, from the knowledge that he had touched the very spot where she sat. She gritted her teeth and went on. There was change mixed with paper clips in the depression between the seats. The pocket in the door on the driver's side held a map and a roll of Life Savers. There was also a white handkerchief with a few dark-brown stains on an inside fold. She unlocked the glove compartment with the key in the ignition: a sleek black electric razor, breath mints, a clean handkerchief, a leather-bound notebook with attached pencil, but no notes, car booklets—nothing. Blanche pushed her disappointment away. It had been a long shot, after all. She closed and locked the glove compartment and moved on, keeping up her pretense of larger interests.

Archibald's Lexus was next. She felt a flash of the excitement she always got when searching her employers' things. She rifled through his Vivaldi and Chopin tapes. Like Palmer's, Archibald's glove compartment was also locked. She took the key dangling from the ignition and unlocked it. There was a Bible and a gun inside. Blanche didn't know which was the bigger surprise, but didn't touch either one. She looked down at Archibald's four keys on their plain silver ring. One was the ignition key, two others likely fit real locks, and the fourth was more of a key-looking ornament: a snake with most of its body extended and the tail loosely curled, giving it the shape of an old-fashioned door key. It held her eye for a moment before she put the keys back and moved on to the other cars.

Seth and Jason Morris's Mercedes were exactly the same, including their dark-blue color, which made her wonder which brother was the copycat. She voted for cheap-feel-copping Seth. She snatched Seth's keys out of the ignition. He had a snake ornament like Archibald's attached to his key chain. Jason had one, too. She turned it over with her finger. It had the markings of a snake with a wide black eye; a six-digit number was stamped onto the coiled portion of its body. She walked to the Mayor's brother's car. He had a snake ornament as well. She looked in the car parked behind him. There was a snake ornament on that key chain, too, although the host's sister didn't have one. Blanche went back to Palmer's car and checked his key ring again. Definitely no snake key. She didn't know what it meant, but she had that nose-twitching feeling for the second time that day.

She thanked the boys again and returned to the kitchen. The three chauffeurs were leaning back in their chairs, eyes glued to the game, stomachs seeming to bulge just an inch or two more than before she'd fed them. She waved to them and headed toward the front of the house.

The buzz of people talking mingled with music. She looked in the various rooms: the library full of men with cigars talking like they knew something; the billiard room, where mostly younger men and a few women were laughing and flirting across a pool table. There were dancers off the dining room, and Carolina Catering's excellent buffet in what was probably the breakfast room. Laughter erupted on the terrace outside the library.

The three inseparables were standing together near the bar. Had she ever seen Palmer, Jason, and Seth Morris at one of these things when they weren't together? Tonight they were joined by Nancy, Jason's wife, and a thin, long-faced, very pregnant woman who stood close enough to Seth for Blanche to believe she was his wife. Blanche watched herself watching Palmer. Did this mean she was getting stronger? She thought of all the black women who'd stood as she was standing, looking at their rapist, the raper of their daughters, black women who'd had to smile, to continue to serve in order to eat and feed their children. She wondered what David Palmer would do if she walked across the room and told him not to leave any more threatening messages on her machine. Act like he hadn't heard her, probably. So what? She took a step toward him, then another, before she was stopped by the reality of what getting in his face here might mean to Carolina Catering. While she watched, Jason said something to Nancy and waited for her to respond. Instead, Nancy turned her back on him and began talking to Seth's wife, who was holding her large belly as though she thought somebody might steal it. Fury flashed across Jason's face. Palmer put his hand on Jason's arm and began talking. This was the second time Blanche had seen Nancy Morris, who'd been so meek and mild with her, treat her apparently polite and decent husband like he wasn't any of that. Nancy and Seth's wife wandered away. Palmer's eyes never strayed from Jason. Blanche went back to the kitchen.

• • •

She was as tired as a sharecropper at sundown when she got home. The blinking light on her answering machine made her stomach clench in anticipation of what new threat might be waiting for her. She fixed herself a drink before she pushed the playback button.

First message: "Yo, Moms, whatsup?" Malik wanted to know. Damn! She'd been so freaked out by the threat that had followed Malik's message on the answering machine on Tuesday that she'd forgotten he was calling today. There was no more to his message, so she figured he was all right. There was no way she could call him, other than through the camp office, which he'd told her to do only in the most serious emergency, so she'd just have to wait until he called again.

Second message: "Big, fine, beautiful woman, where are you when I need to talk to you? I miss you, Blanche. Really miss you. Being with you makes me feel on top of the world. Thinking about you even makes these crazy whitefolks I work around less of a pain in the butt. Can't wait to see you," Thelvin told her, complete with train-station noise in the background.

Pleasure in his message, and in the fact that there was no threatening message following it, made her laugh aloud. How many men his age could just pick up the phone and say how they felt—and into a machine, no less? How many men of any age?

"Hey, Thelvin," she told his machine. "I'm real sorry I missed your call, but I plan to listen to your message over and over again. See you soon." She started to add an "I hope" to that but changed her mind. Overeager was for beavers. She took a long soak in the tub and cleared her mind of everything but the sound of her own breathing and the stillness of the evening outside.

Sleep came easily, along with a dream of keys that sang and messages on her answering machine that couldn't be heard in the usual way. She had to lay hands on the machine and feel the messages—not only the words but what the caller was thinking, feeling. When she woke, she remembered only one of the callers: Thelvin. She couldn't remember what his message said, but it felt like a combination of good sex and good food. She was ready for all of that.

Smoke, Flowers, and Backup

Blanche called Archibald first thing in the morning. His secretary said he was in a meeting. Blanche hardly had time to be disappointed and hang up the phone before someone tapped at her door.

"Hey, Miz Blanche, I was on my way to work, so I thought I'd drop by instead of calling you," Mary from the bank told her.

Blanche offered her some breakfast, but Mary said she didn't have much time.

"I just wanted to tell you that David Palmer's been writing checks to a flower shop. A lot of them. Every week, it looks like."

Blanche stood up a bit taller; the day seemed to brighten. "Flowers? From where?"

"Buckley Flowers, downtown."

Blanche saw it in her mind: silk birds-of-paradise on a pedestal in the window, green awning. "Thanks, Mary. You're a true sister."

"I'm just glad I could help. A man like that . . . Well, I hope you can do something."

"What church you belong to, Mary?" Blanche remembered Mary's mentioning church when they first spoke.

"Shiloh Baptist. Why?"

"Just curious," Blanche said. She thanked Mary again and gave her a big hug before she left.

As soon as Mary was gone, Blanche took out five of Archibald's twenties and reached for her notepad. "This donation is made in the name of Mary Lee in thanks for her kindness." She didn't sign it. She just wanted to show her appreciation for Mary's taking a risk to help her. She folded the note and tucked the twenties inside. She'd pick up some envelopes and mail the note when she got downtown, which was where she was headed. The flower thing wasn't much, but it made Blanche dance across the room. It was something, which was one hundred times better than nothing.

Downtown was still sleepy when she got there: shops were just beginning their morning opening routines: pavements being swept, awnings lowered, and doors unlocked. Blanche sat on a bench beneath a tree across the street from Buckley Flowers. The CLOSED sign was still in the window. A bouquet of silk flowers stood on the pedestal in the window. She could just make out the long glass-fronted flower case inside.

A stringy, olive-skinned white woman wearing a brown linen dress and beige pumps and carrying a matching bag came down the street. She stopped in front of the flower shop, fumbled in her purse for a set of keys, opened the front door, and flipped the sign in the plate-glass window to OPEN. The shoe store next door was also open now, but the tea room on the other side was still closed.

A short, fiftyish brown-skinned woman came out of the flower shop. Blanche sat up a little straighter. She figured the woman must have gone in by the back door. She wore a yellow smock over a print dress and carried a broom. Blanche looked closely at her face but found nothing familiar about her. Blanche watched her sweep the pavement with care, then rose to leave. She'd seen who was working there, which was all she'd come for. She'd stop by Miz Minnie's again on the way home.

"Flower shop, flower shop . . . Now, let me think." Miz Minnie tilted her head back and aimed her rheumy eyes at the ceiling, as though her list of acquaintances were written up there. The longer she was silent, the harder she rocked her chair. Finally, she sighed and slowed her rocking before she came to a full stop, like a pilot bringing in a plane.

She turned to Blanche. "Chile, I didn't even know a colored person was working in that there flower shop. Never thought I'd live to see the day in this town when a black woman would be waiting on customers in a downtown Farleigh flower shop." Miz Minnie sounded as though she were announcing the death of a loved one. Blanche realized that, in a way, she was. The changes in Farleigh were all over the place, more housing developments going up, more shops downtown, more cars, even a new motel out on the highway. But she hadn't realized until now how much that change had affected black Farleigh: there were blacks in and around this town whose people, jobs, children, and problems Miz Minnie didn't know. The two women sat observing a moment of silence for a way of life that was now deceased.

Blanche went home and called Ardell.

"Oh yeah, Aurelia. She moved here from Greenville. Went to school for flower-arranging or some such thing that don't sound like much of a living. Something happened in Greenville. Something about a married man, I think. Anyway, I remember hearing she got herself a job in the flower shop. 'Course, she just the type a Negro they would hire. She's one of the reasons I don't use them for flower arrangements. She act like every dime and flower is hers."

Blanche remembered Aurelia sweeping the pavement in front of the flower shop. Some things might have changed, but lots of things hadn't—at least not much.

"Thanks, Ardell. I'm gonna run by Mama's. I'll be back in about an hour."

First Blanche made some tea and thought about how to approach flower-shop Aurelia. Given what Ardell had said, it'd be a waste of time either trying to appeal to Aurelia as she'd done to Mary or offering her money. She finished her tea and left the house.

She tapped on her mother's screen door. "Mama? It's me. You home?" No answer. Blanche walked through the house. It smelled of lemon-scented furniture polish and bacon. She looked out the back screen door into the small yard lined with petunias. Her mother was hanging a tea towel on the clothesline. Her almost all-white hair glistened like snow in sunlight. She leaned over to pick up the clothespin bag. Then, one hand on her back, the other on her thigh, she slowly straightened up. Very slowly. Blanche's heart did a double beat. "Sweet Ancestors," she whispered, then stopped, unsure what to say to appeal for her mother's continued life without sounding selfish or asking the impossible. She stepped back, and her mother opened the screen door.

"Well, now." Miz Cora gave Blanche a rare smile. "It sure is a pretty day, aint it?"

For that reason, Ancestors, Blanche thought. Just so she can keep seeing beautiful days. "Sure is, Mama, it sure is."

Miz Cora went to the sink and washed and dried her hands. She looked at Blanche over her shoulder. "You want somethin to eat? I got some fresh biscuits and some of that slab bacon you like siting right there on the stove, and I just opened a new jar of apple jam this morning."

"Sure sounds good, but maybe I oughta move them boxes first." Blanche went upstairs to the small back bedroom that had once contained her life. Flashes of her child- and girlhood raced across her mind at the sight of that old dresser with her initials carved in the back, the wrought-iron bedstead that had always cooled her wrists on the hottest of nights. Her cane-bottomed rocker, picked up as a throwaway in front of some better-off person's house. None of the memories made her wish to be back then. She hadn't much liked being a child; she'd never enjoyed being under anyone's control. She opened the three boxes she'd left with her mother when she'd moved to Boston. There was nothing in them of value to anyone but her: a very dog-eared copy of Langston Hughes' poetry—the book that made her realize there were people like her to be read about; a flower press she'd made at church camp; her old skates. All things that she could easily live without now but that had helped save her life when she was a girl looking for a place to hide inside herself from the taunts about her blackness and from her mother's constant reminders to stay out of trees and fights. Now she carried the boxes downstairs and stored them on the little closed-in back porch so they'd be out of Sauda's way. Before she left her old room, Blanche couldn't help noticing the new blue-and-green floral curtains her mother had made for Sauda's arrival. Her own summer quilt, left to her by her grandmother, was folded at the foot of the bed. She'd only left it behind when she moved because Mama liked having it in the house. She blinked back tears as she was suddenly bushwhacked by her childhood belief that there was always someone her mother preferred over her.

When she was a child, it had nearly broken her heart to realize her sister, Rosalie, was their mother's favorite. But Blanche had loved Rosalie so much, Mama's bias had almost made sense. She also didn't mind when her mother preferred Taifa and Malik. There was a way in which she put them before Mama. But she'd expected that, after Rosalie died of cancer, she and her mother would find a way to move closer to each other. It hadn't happened. Now here was Mama making new curtains, putting out *her* quilt, and moving *her* things out to make room for a never-before-seen cousin. It stung Blanche like a wasp. She wiped at her eyes and chided herself for being foolish. Wasn't it time for her to be getting over all this hurt-child stuff? How would her life be different if her mother loved her just the way she wanted her to? Would it make her a better person? Would she be happier? More fulfilled? As if it mattered. Mama was Mama. No amount of tears, talking, or wishing was going to change her. Take it or leave it, she told herself. Take it or leave it. But she still snatched up her quilt and stuffed it into one of the boxes. Mama had other blankets Sauda could use.

Blanche washed her hands in the tiny bathroom before she went back to the kitchen. Miz Cora had put a bowl of her biscuits, along with the slab bacon, butter, and jam, on the kitchen table.

Blanche put the kettle on. "I saw Mr. Broadnax." She got the cups, sugar, milk, and teabags.

"Humph!" Miz Cora put a teabag in her cup.

"He asked about you." Blanche dabbed a large spoonful of jam on a biscuit half, topped it with a thick piece of bacon, and covered that with the other biscuit half.

"What he askin 'bout me for?"

"He said you always did know how to take care of yourself." Blanche took a bite from her biscuit.

Miz Cora rose from her chair so unexpectedly she startled Blanche.

"Royal Broadnax aint no judge of what I could or couldn't take care of."

"Royal? Is that his first name? No wonder he . . ."

"Why you talking to him about me in the first place? What else he say?"

Blanche thoroughly chewed her food, trying to think how to answer in a way that would lead to information from this woman who would talk you into deafness about almost anything but herself. Blanche had spent a considerable portion of her life trying to get her mother to talk about her own life and about Blanche's father. "He was a good father and now he's gone. Aint nothin else to say," was her mother's usual response to Blanche's questions about her father. "It weren't nothing special," or "I was young and foolish, but I had more sense than you, girl," were her mother's standard answers when Blanche asked about Miz Cora's youth. For a while, Blanche had given up on trying to get her mother to talk. She'd figured her father had walked off and left his wife and his children, too. So none of them owed him a thought, and her mother was entitled to keep her life as secret as she wanted to. Age had changed that: the older Blanche got, the more she believed it wasn't just her mother's and father's lives that were being kept from her, but part of her own. People who had or raised children didn't have sole rights to their own life story. Once you had a child, you became community property. Family property.

"Mr. Broadnax sounded like he knew you real well." Blanche eyed her mother, who'd sat back down at the table.

"Did he?" Miz Cora didn't look at Blanche.

"Was y'all friends or something?"

"You sure got a heap of questions today. Best eat that biscuit." Miz Cora poured the tea.

Blanche stared at her mother, refusing, with her silence, to accept what she'd been told. Her mother sighed.

"He was kind of like a friend of the family. Him and your daddy was . . . They ran around together some."

"A friend of the family?"

"He was kind to me when I needed a kindness. That's all I meant."

"What kind of kindness?"

"Lent me some money, if you got to know."

"For what?"

"Blanche! You aint even ast me how I'm feelin. My pressure was up when I went to the clinic yesterday."

Yeah, right. Blanche had heard this story before—whenever her mother wanted, or, like now, didn't want something, she'd break out the pressure story. "Did he give you a prescription?" Blanche took another bite of her biscuit.

Miz Cora gave her daughter an evil look. "He said I don't need to be gettin all upset, havin people bring up things I don't want to talk about without even askin me how I feel, when I'm . . ."

Blanche raised her palms in surrender. "Okay, Mama. I got to go anyway." She finished off her biscuit and put her dishes in the sink, then walked around the table and kissed her still-seated mother on the top of her head. "So long, Mama."

"Humph! Now you gon leave. I aint even had a chance to ask after my grandbabies!"

Blanche was out the door. Why should she be more willing to give out information than Mama was? The door was almost closed behind her when she turned around and went back in the house.

"Forgot something," she said.

"Humph! Never did have no memory! When you was ten years old you . . ."

Blanche retrieved her grandmother's quilt from the box and put it back on Sauda's bed. This was between her and Mama. Nobody else. Blanche's legs felt wobbly by the time she finally left, as though she'd actually been on a roller-coaster instead of just whipped around by Miz Cora.

There was a message from Melva on her machine that erased all thoughts of her mother and her Caribbean cousin:

"I was right about your boy," Melva's message said. "You up for potluck at my place? Junior and the kids are going to a game. Come on over about seven. Bring whatever you want. Okay? We can't do it no sooner, 'cause Patsy got to go over to Durham and can't get here no earlier. I'm on First Street, ten twenty-five."

Blanche remembered how Melva had looked both when Blanche told her about the snooping job and while Blanche was messing with Luella's mind. It was a close-attention, seriously interested kind of look that Blanche now recognized as the mark of someone who shared her own healthy interest in other people's business. Sure, Melva had liked the idea of getting a hit of cash for bringing Patsy and Blanche together, but Blanche knew Melva: she'd have done the same out of sheer curiosity.

On the way to Melva's, Blanche couldn't help fantasizing about what Patsy might have to say. She knew she was toying with disappointment. It wasn't likely Patsy had heard of another rape, or had seen Palmer beating up his future mother-in-law, or shooting up in the guest bathroom. If he was that out there with his stuff, she'd have heard about it by now. But if hope were hamburgers, she'd be stuffed.

Walking into Melva's house was like stepping into a ripe peach. The

sofa, the chairs, the lamps and shades, the walls, and the drapes that covered the entire front wall—even though there was only one small window
in it—were a peachy beige, as was the rug. The coffee and end tables were
rosy blond. Blanche found herself tiptoeing by the plastic-encased sofa
and chairs and realized how much the place reminded her of a funeral
parlor. She followed Melva back to the bright kitchen with its peach walls
and sparkling white café curtains and woodwork. Blanche set her bowl
of Vanessa's International Negro Spaghetti—the recipe of an old girlfriend—next to the fried chicken wings and the salad of lettuce, tomato,
and hard-boiled egg Melva had prepared. When Patsy arrived, she added
a large jug of red wine and two big bags of potato chips.

Blanche hadn't seen Patsy for years. She looked much the same, except
that she was ten pounds heavier and had given up the Jheri Curl she'd had
when last they'd met for hard-pressed hair done up in shiny loops that
looked like they'd give you a paper cut. Blanche knew it wasn't good to
rush a person with a story to tell, so she didn't object when, after the howyou-beens and a bite to eat, the first talk was about Maybelle Jenkins's
murderer.

"I'm surprised they even arrested that white boy." Patsy blinked at
them. "They been trying to find a likely nigger to blame it on since it happened."

Melva took another wing from the platter and a couple spoonfuls of
spaghetti and salad. "Yeah, but at least times is changed some. When we
was coming up, they just picked up somebody black and beat him into saying he did it."

"Yeah, well, this mess aint over yet," Patsy said from behind a cloud of
blue cigarette smoke that she at least had the decency to try to blow away
from the table.

Even though she'd told herself not to hurry Patsy, Blanche sighed loud
enough to make it clear that this was not the conversation she came to
hear. Melva gave her a quick look, then poured them all a jot more wine.

"So tell Blanche what you told me about that Palmer," Melva said to
Patsy.

Patsy put out her cigarette and sipped some wine. "Well, like Melva
told you, I useta work for them Gregorys, back before Miss Elizabeth
moved to gay Paree. She was engaged to that Palmer you askin about."

"Why'd they break up?"

Patsy swirled the wine in her glass. "Well, the official reason was that they was incompatic, you know, they was just too different." She sipped more wine. "But there was more to it than that, I think." Patsy reared back in her chair and picked something from between her side teeth with her little finger. "What I mean is, Miss Too-Cute-to-Be-True Elizabeth was what you might call highly sexed. The girl acted like she *discovered* the nasty. But I heard her say sex with David Palmer wasn't all that. She said . . . Wait a minute, it'll come to me." Patsy put on an I'm-thinking look and drank some more wine. Blanche clenched her fists in her lap to keep from trying to shake the words out of Patsy.

"Oh yeah, I got it! She said he was a emotional retard and needed some lessons in foreplay. More like taking a nap than having sex. Them's her exact words. Or almost."

"When was this?"

Patsy thought for a minute. "Let me see, now. I stopped working for them about three years ago . . . two and a half, and Elizabeth had been gone from home—oh, let me see—it's been about six or seven years now, I guess. Lord! Where does the time go?"

Blanche was about to ask Patsy how come she remembered so well after so long, but Patsy wasn't finished:

"I always remember what Elizabeth said when I see him, 'cause it sure aint the vibe I get from him. The Palmer place aint far from where I'm working now. He be driving by. Sometimes jogging when I'm walking the dogs. He don't ever look at me, but I don't take my eyes off him."

"Why?"

Patsy shrugged. "'Cause he the kind of man you got to watch, else who knows what'll happen? I useta see him when he come to see Elizabeth," Patsy said. "From jump street I thought there was something, I don't know, creepy about that man. I just don't trust him. Something about him made me always want to be with somebody when he was around. I don't know why, just something about him." Patsy stopped to light another cigarette. "And since he had that breakdown, I don't know. He looks weird to me."

Blanche was so moved to finally hear some other woman say something she recognized about Palmer that she had to stop and think about what to ask Patsy next.

"Breakdown? That don't sound like a rich-Southern-white-boy kind of a thing. What was that about?"

"About him losin it! She said David Palmer's stuff got so raggedy his daddy had to slap the poop outa him at some party. Then his daddy put him in the mental hospital. Yeah, girl. They had to hog-tie that boy and drag his sorry ass off. I heard Elizabeth talkin about it. Right after that, Elizabeth left and aint come back since either."

"Damn! Run the girl clean out the country!" Melva said, and slapped palms with Patsy and burst out laughing.

Blanche was too stunned by what Patsy had just told her to laugh. She was sure that those three events—the rape, the breakdown, and the breakup—had all happened around the same time. In Palmer's mind they were probably related. To her mind, it wasn't the because that mattered. She had no way of knowing whether Palmer had raped her before or after he was jilted by Elizabeth Gregory and she didn't care. She didn't know whether he'd broken down before or after he'd raped her and she didn't need to know. No breakdown or breakup was reason to rape her. There could be no reason for raping her. None. All that mattered to her was the act. Knowing how he might have justified it to himself only made her hate his weak, sneaky ass even more.

Patsy stood and stretched. "Oh! Miss Elizabeth say she think David Palmer's daddy wanted his son to marry her as much as David Palmer did hisself. I gotta pee," she announced.

Blanche looked up at Patsy with serious thankfulness in her eyes—not for having shown her Palmer's twisted path to raping her, but for letting Blanche know there were at least two other women in the world who understood that there was something basically wrong with David Palmer.

Blanche turned to Melva. "You did good, honey." She handed her two twenties. When Patsy came back from the bathroom, Blanche told her, "I appreciate this, Patsy, I really do. Here's a little something for your trouble." She was about to give Patsy Archibald's twenties, then remembered their true purpose.

"Did Elizabeth ever say anything about his sisters?"

"Lord! Did she ever! She couldn't stand either one of them cows. Said the oldest one, the one that moved to Florida, would do anything for money. But Elizabeth Gregory and her friends talked about the younger one like a dog."

"What they got against her?"

"She a dufus! She do everything they do. One of them change her hair color, Karen Palmer changes hern. Same with clothes. She try to find out what her friends is wearing so she can get something as near to it as possible, if not the same damn dress! Now, is that pitiful, or what?"

Blanche and Melva shook their heads in wonder over a woman with money enough to develop her own style and too lame to do it.

Patsy leaned forward over the table. "Oh, you aint heard the best part yet. They call her Tester Cunt!"

"What!?" Blanche and Melva shouted in unison.

"Oh yeah, some of them so-called high-tones got mouths like cesspools."

"But what the hell is a Tester Cunt?" Blanche asked.

Patsy lit another cigarette. "I didn't get it either, at first. It's, you know, like they have at the perfume counter in the BonBon. The bottle that's open so you can try the perfume or hand lotion. That's what that Palmer girl does, tries on all her friends' men! But she engaged now, I hear. Some fool with no brains and too much money, they say."

Blanche handed Patsy the twenties.

Patsy quickly counted the money, then grinned. "Girl! I wish I'da known you was gonna be askin, I'da taken me some notes!" Patsy high-fived Melva, and all three women laughed.

Melva picked up the jug. "Y'all want another taste?"

Blanche and Patsy held out their glasses.

"Y'all remember the time we went down Greensboro to that New Year's Eve party?" She looked from Patsy to Blanche.

"You mean the one where that woman poured a pitcher of ice water over her man's head to cool him off from dancing with you?" Blanche asked her.

Melva nodded. "Yeah, and y'all went off with that crazy Ardell and left me with that . . ."

"No such a lie!" Patsy shrieked. "You wanted to stay with that wild boy—what was his name, Blanche?"

"Richard? Or Richie? Something like that. Melva, you was so hot for that boy we could hear you sizzle, girl!"

"Oooh! Y'all oughta be 'shamed of yourselves, lyin on me like that! Ask Ardell. She'll tell you! He was the one after me. I swear! All I did was . . ."

And they were off on a trail of memories of the days when they were faster than they were wise.

18

Balance, Lunch Hours,
and Canapés

Six-thirty the next morning, Blanche put that old goose/gander saying into practice and called Archibald, who acknowledged her early-morning call was payback for his.

"I saw this snake thingy on a man's key chain the other day. You know what I'm talking about?" Blanche asked after they'd said their good mornings and had shown a passing interest in each other's health and welfare. "It looks like a half-coiled-up snake. It's got a number on it."

"Does this have something to do with, er, uh . . ."

"I don't know yet," she told him.

"It's the membership key to SOF. Not a real key, more symbolic of . . ."

"S-O-Who?"

"The Sons of Farleigh. A men's club."

"A club for men like you? Rich men?"

"Well, yes, if you want to put it that way."

Blanche rolled her eyes at the ring of self-congratulation in Archibald's voice, like heavy coins clinking together.

"Who in town don't belong?"

"No women, of course, but I can't think of any man in my social circle who isn't a member."

"Thanks, Archibald. I'll be in touch. Oh, one more question. What happens if you lose your key?"

"You're given another, with a new number, and your old number is struck from the log."

Blanche had no idea why she was so interested in Palmer's missing key, but, having dreamed about keys the night before, she couldn't help feeling she was on to something. She saluted her Ancestors, exercised, ate, and dressed before she called Miz Minnie and invited herself over. "I'll bring you some apple tarts," Blanche said. She didn't mention they were left over from a catering job.

"Club been there, oh, maybe seven, eight or so years now," Miz Minnie told Blanche. "I hear it started as a way for the decent rich white mens to show they was different from they Klan-joining brothers—although none of them seem to want to do right by us, no matter which club they in." Miz Minnie shot a streak of tobacco juice into the label-less can beside her chair. She wiped her lips with the back of her hand, then went on talking: "Leroy Sacks been workin there must be since the thing started," she added when Blanche told her what she was after. "I believe his oldest boy's workin there, too. He about your age."

"Bunnie Sacks, who lived over by the high school?" Blanche saw a lanky, honey-beige boy with bedroom eyes and perfect lips. Bunnie had been more interested in studying than in going to dances and parties, which had made him all the more fascinating to the girls in their class, including Blanche. She wondered if he remembered her.

It was still early when Blanche got to Ardell's to do her share of today's prep work for the cocktail party they were working that evening. She needed to get her work out of the way: she had other plans for the bulk of the day. She'd already made fifty each of miniature ham and cheese puff-pastry tarts for tonight. They were in the freezer and would only need glazing before being popped in the oven. Now she prepared a huge pot of her mini ground-turkey-and-chicken meatballs simmered in a hot garlic-and-soy sauce—a spicier version of one she'd found in an old Julia Child cookbook many years ago.

"Humm. Sounds like the old mistress thing," Ardell said when Blanche told her about Mary's visit and the flowers Palmer was sending.

"Don't it, now? 'Course, he could have a real sick friend or a lonely maiden aunt he cheers up with weekly flowers," Blanche said, "but I doubt it."

"What you gonna do?"

"Find out why a single man like him is backstreeting at all. These old families is as used to men screwing around out of their class as they are to having money, so I don't think that's it. I aint seen him with a woman at the bicentennial things either. Makes me think he's banging somebody's wife."

"Humm, if she is somebody's wife, I sure would like to hear what kinda story she tells her husband about where all them flowers come from."

"I'll be glad if I can just find out who she is."

As soon as she was done, Blanche grabbed her bag. She stopped on her way out the door to call Bunnie Sacks. His line was busy.

"Good hunting!" Ardell called after her.

Blanche knew she should try to curb her hopes. This flower thing could lead her to another woman who may have seen some of the Palmer Blanche knew, instead of the Mr. Likable people kept talking about. But if that woman was Palmer's lover . . . Just find out what you can find out, she told herself, then figure out what to do with it.

She hurried downtown and once again settled herself on the bench across from Buckley Flowers, with a newspaper and her thermos of tea to keep her company. She opened the paper, then ignored it in favor of the tea. Three people went in and out of the shop while she watched: a young white woman, an elderly white man, and a younger black man. The woman came out folding a piece of paper she put in her purse. The elderly white man came out with a bunch of flowers wrapped in blue-and-white striped paper tied with a red ribbon. The black man came out with a bucket and squeegee and began washing the front window. Yes, indeed, some things hadn't changed a bit.

At eleven-thirty, Aurelia stepped out of the flower shop. She came back promptly at quarter past twelve carrying a grocery bag. The brunette white woman who'd opened the shop yesterday left at twelve-forty-five. She didn't get back until two-thirty. Blanche thought she saw a bit of a sway in the woman's walk. She had a feeling that if she got close enough to

Flower Shop Lady she'd pick up a whiff of one of the milder-smelling liquors—gin or vodka—favored by a number of genteel lady drinkers she'd worked for in the past. In one case, it had taken her two days to realize the constant glass of what her employer said was ice water was that and more. Blanche put the lid on her thermos and folded the newspaper. She'd seen what she'd come to see; now she had to get ready for work.

Although she didn't have a minute to spare, she was happy to hear the phone ringing when she walked into the Miz Alice.

"Hey, Malik, how's it goin?"

Malik showed no surprise that she knew it was him before he spoke.

"Hey, Moms. I'm cool. What's up with you?"

"Everything is everything. How's camp going? How was Outward Bound?" She settled back in her chair, her mind cleared of everything but learning as much as she could about what was going on with Malik and concern for his well-being—except for the part of her mind that was always surprised by her ability to let Malik and Taifa take up the center of her life even though she didn't ever give them all of herself and didn't think she should.

"Man, Outward Bound was da bomb diggity. I mean it, Moms! We had to climb up the side of this cliff. One guy almost fell."

"But you were fine." She spoke with confidence even as a picture of him hanging by one ankle over a height so high there was no bottom to be seen zipped through her mind.

"Yeah, I did all right. And guys really had each other's backs, you know? So if you messed up or something . . . It was cool, Moms."

"Make any new friends?" Blanche tensed once the question was out. She waited for Malik to get on her about always trying to get him to make friends outside of the neighborhood, but he fooled her.

"Maybe," he said. "A guy named Ray. He's from Cambridge."

"It's nice he's so close."

"Yeah, we been talking about maybe doing handball this winter if . . . But I'm not the only one making friends, or so I hear. I tried to call you, but you were out."

Blanche hesitated, trying to get a hold on all that was being said and not said. "Ardell's been keeping me hopping," she said finally, deciding to take the neutral road and see what happened. "She's got a lot of catering business because of the town's bicentennial."

"Unh-unh. I got a letter from Ifa. She told me you were seeing some guy." Malik sounded half tempted to make a joke of it and half tempted to accuse her of something.

"His name is Thelvin Lewis. He's a conductor for Amtrak."

"A train conductor? Cool." He hesitated for a few moments. "So—what's up with you two? I mean, Taifa said . . ."

Blanche cut him off before he could tell her what Taifa had to say on the subject of Thelvin. It would only irritate her, and, anyway, this was Malik's time. "There really aint nothing much to tell, Malik. We went out a couple times. We're just having fun."

"You're not thinking about . . . I mean, Taifa said it sounded like you and him were getting real tight. I mean, like . . ."

"If I decide to elope with him, I'll give y'all at least a week's notice. I promise. But I don't see it happening anytime soon. Okay?"

"Okay, Moms, I get it," Malik told her.

Blanche changed the subject to how she liked living in the Miz Alice. "When I was a kid, I used to pretend I lived all alone in this little house. It's as much fun as I thought it'd be. I'm just not getting to spend much time in it," she told him before she explained that she needed to get ready for work.

She had to hurry through her shower. She knew that once she got to the job she was going to be run off her feet serving cocktails and canapés to forty people. It was just her and Clarice working the floor tonight.

On the job, Blanche circulated, smiled, offered her tray of goodies, re-filled the tray, and started all over again. About halfway through the party she took a moment to look the crowd over—pretty much the same bunch she'd been seeing at most of the bicentennial events. There was the beyond-middle-aged woman who always wore pink; the young couples working so hard to seem gay and carefree while their eyes brimmed with boredom; the women alone who fiddled with their little clutch bags as though they were prayer beads, and looked so grateful when someone approached them; the folks who seemed always to be in a spot where fresh drinks were being offered and whose complexions grew rosier, hand gestures larger, and laughter merrier as the evening went on. Over there, by the window, was the snorer. He and his wife separated at the door, she to mingle, he to find a quiet corner with a chair where he slipped off to sleep until his wife roused him to go home. The dancing show-offs were there, too, looking dejected that there was no musical center stage for them to occupy. In her mind, Blanche redressed them all in polyester; she moved the party to the Holiday Inn and appreciated how little difference money made to who people really are at heart. The rich could afford better psychiatrists, but they were still as crazy, as low on self-esteem, as bored, sleepy, and lonely as everyone else.

The job had gone well, but by the time she got home, the whole evening was a blur of heavy trays, spilled wine, the hostess and her husband arguing in hissy whispers in the pantry, and a guest too drunk to leave the bathroom. Blanche fell into bed without brushing her teeth and found nothing but sleep, deep and comforting as the womb. She woke full of a plan for how to approach Aurelia and find out where Palmer's flowers were being sent.

19

The Mistress of Disguise, Part One

Blanche pulled out the housecleaning uniform she'd brought along: old and gray with frump written all over it. She put on the black, lace-up oxfords she usually wore only when it rained, mashed a straw hat over her cornrows, and grabbed her handbag. It was just one-ten when she opened the door to the flower shop.

Inside, it was cool and smelled of fresh green and that nose-tingling essence of flowers that was more peppery than sweet.

"Afternoon, miss." She gave Aurelia a shy smile.

Aurelia looked at her as though she thought Blanche might have wandered into the wrong place. "May I help you?" Her voice was as cool as the shop, and Blanche was prepared to bet her tone was a cheap imitation of that of the woman Aurelia worked for.

"Yes, ma'am." Blanche lowered her eyes in seeming deference. Whatever works, she told herself.

"Well, my missus told me to pick up the cleaning, ya see."

"Yes?"

"Well, the young mister, he was there at the time, ya see, and he heard her say it and . . ."

"Does this story eventually have something to do with flowers?"

Blanche could see the pleasure in Aurelia's eyes at having made this snappy remark.

"Yes, ma'am. I'm sorry, ma'am." Blanche began wringing her hands. "Like I was sayin, ma'am, the young mister, he give me this note and ast me to stop in here on my way to pick up the cleaning and put in this order for these here flowers, ya see."

"Yes, all right." Aurelia held out her hand. "Let me see the note."

"Well, you see, that's just the problem, ma'am." Blanche opened her handbag and rooted around in it. "I done took everything outa this here pocketbook of mines and I can't find that note nowheres." She gave Aurelia a pitiful look. "He don't like it when ya mess up," she mumbled. "The young mister, I mean." Blanche could feel disdain oozing out of Aurelia like fat from bacon.

"Well, if you don't have the note, there's nothing I can do."

"Well, now, ma'am, ya see, this aint the first time. I mean, he done it before, ya see. Couple times. Give me a note to bring y'all 'bout them flowers he all the time sends."

A pitchfork-shaped frown marked Aurelia's forehead.

"That nice white lady with the long brown hair was here last time. She say, 'Oh yes, the usual. He send them every week, same address, same flowers,' she say, and didn't even take the note, just looked it up someplace or somethin, I guess, or . . . Well, maybe I just oughta talk to her. She here?"

"What's your employer's name?" Aurelia pulled a large ledger out from under the counter.

"Why, Palmer, ma'am. It was the young mister, Mr. David, who gave me the note and tolc me . . ."

"Yes, all right." Aurelia turned pages sharply. "All right. David Palmer. Yes, I have it right here."

Blanche moved as close to the counter as she could get and coughed as hard as she could, holding her chest and doubling over. Aurelia moved back and looked at Blanche as though her first name was Typhoid. Blanche panted for a few seconds while she worked not to laugh. Then:

"Ma'am, I wonder if I could trouble you for a drop of water?" She began coughing again.

Aurelia turned and stepped behind a screen to her left. Blanche spun the ledger around and looked quickly down a column of names until she found Palmer's. She heard a faucet running. In the Deliver To column was written "14 Decatur Street, Durham." There was no name. The water stopped running. Blanche flipped the ledger back to its original position. Aurelia returned with a small paper cup half full of tepid water.

"Lordy, ma'am," Blanche said when she'd finished her water. "I done troubled y'all for nothin. The young mister done sent me in here without a penny to pay y'all with and Lord knows I can't spare a dime."

Aurelia gave her a puzzled and suspicious look. Blanche thanked her and hurried out of the shop. She made sure not to break out in a grin until she was out of sight of the shop. She could hardly wait to tell Ardell about her little scene with Aurelia and the way she'd used Aurelia's uppityness to work her ass. Silly cow. Aurelia was black enough and old enough to know better than to judge people by how they dressed and talked. Anybody that stupid deserved to be played. Shoulda figured out a way to get myself a flower or two, she thought, giggling to herself.

Saturday afternoon, Blanche borrowed Ardell's car and drove to Durham. Decatur Street turned out to be a small, working-class-looking street not too far from Duke University. Most of the mid-sized houses on one side had two or more mailboxes, which made her think this might be a student area. The other side of the street had fewer houses. A weeded lot took up the corner space. Next to it was number 14: a small brick two-story house mostly hidden by trees and shrubs. It felt like nobody was home. The street was deserted except for a few cars at the curb. She was tempted to knock on the door of the little house, but what if someone answered? She turned the corner and continued down a similar street, still thinking how to approach number 14. She was going to have to come back.

She took the car back to Ardell's and headed for her mother's: Cousin Sauda had arrived from Angelica yesterday.

Blanche didn't know what she'd expected her cousin to look like, but Sauda Leon was quite a surprise. Although her long flat nose and large shapely lips came straight from Africa, her skin was the color of rich cream, her hair red-gold and just slightly wavy instead of kinky. Mama looked dazzled, as though she'd been out in the sun too long. Blanche doubted if there would ever be a time in America when color went unnoticed.

"I'm pleased to meet you, Cousin Blanche," Sauda said with a lilt in her voice that reminded Blanche of steel-drum bands in the park on Harlem summer nights.

"Auntie Cora says you might be able to help me get some work. I got a scholarship, but I need money for . . ."

Blanche looked at her mother.

"With the catering, I was thinkin," Miz Cora had the nerve to say.

"It's Ardell's business, Mama, I can't just . . ."

"Already talked to her." Miz Cora looked as satisfied as a dog with two bones. "She say maybe y'all could use somebody to help out."

Was Ardell out of her mind!? This girl might not know a cutting board from a washboard! Blanche jumped up from her chair. Or, more likely, Ardell didn't have the guts to say no to Mama and had left it up to her to do it. "Well, I just dropped by for a hot minute, to meet Sauda and say welcome. I got a lot to do this afternoon, but I'll stop by tonight, or maybe tomorrow, and we can talk about it." While she was speaking, Blanche was also inching toward the front door. Now she opened it.

"Wait a minute, Blanche! We can settle this right now! Ardell said you . . ."

"Sorry, Mama, I gotta run." Blanche snapped the door closed behind her and hurried down the street, feeling beat on by family and friend alike.

20

Thelvin, Thelvin, Thelvin

This was the first time Blanche could remember a man inviting her to his place for Sunday brunch prepared by his own hands. She stopped at the Quick Mart and picked up the Sunday *Durham Herald Sun*. She looked at the skimpy array of regional papers in the store and longed for the *Village Voice* or even the *New York Times*. It was funny about the New York things she still missed after having been gone from the city all these years: the speed of underground travel that Boston's subway system just didn't seem to match; the sound of three or more languages being spoken in her multicolored neighborhood; black people dressed in ways that were neither American nor European; the particularly oily, sweet, foody smell of busier parts of Harlem.

Thelvin opened the door before she rang his bell. He'd wanted to drive over and pick her up, but she'd borrowed Ardell's car for the short ride to Durham. The big old house where Thelvin lived had a feeling of protection about it, as though anyone welcomed inside would be well taken care of. It had likely once been a single dwelling but was now a duplex. Thelvin was waiting in the doorway, a big fluffy white cat lolling in his arms.

"Hey, beautiful woman." Thelvin leaned over and kissed Blanche's cheek.

"Miss Ann," he said, nodding toward the cat.

Blanche chuckled at that old nickname for a white woman. The cat jumped from Thelvin's arms and strutted away, her bushy tail held high.

"Who takes care of her when you're out of town?"

"Oh, Miss Ann's got the run of the place. She thinks the couple upstairs belong to her as much as I do. A real lady of the plantation." He took Blanche's hand and led her through the house to the kitchen.

Thelvin had the whole first floor, which was filled with dappled light shining through the trees outside his windows. Red and orange throw rugs and pale-yellow walls brightened the place. The living-room sofa was the long, plump kind that whispered, "Fall on me." Blanche gave it a regretful look as she passed by, only to notice a chair big enough even for someone her size to curl up in; a pile of cushions on a window seat that looked like a nap; a rocker with a plump hassock in front of it. The whole place was an invitation to relax, settle in. Everything in it seemed to want to be touched, caressed, leaned on. Another gold star in Thelvin's crown.

Miss Ann reappeared in the kitchen. She sniffed around Blanche's ankles, looked up at her with a haughty squint, then shifted her gaze to something only she could see, just to the right of Blanche's shoulder.

Thelvin leaned down and gave Blanche a real kiss. "She likes you, too."

"How can you tell?" She put the newspaper on the table.

"She didn't nip you on the ankle."

"She bites?!"

Thelvin nodded. "Only people she don't like. She just ignores the ones she does, the way she's doing us right now." Thelvin ran his hand down Blanche's back. "Of course, how any living creature could ignore you . . ." He lowered his head to hers again. Blanche was jolted as much by her own eagerness as she was by the feel of his lips—soft, yet determined to hold her, draw her even closer to him. And closeness was what she craved: arms around her to dispel the chill of so much time spent thinking about David Palmer, to soothe the achy place where loneliness sometimes lurked. She stood up and leaned into him. He tightened his arms around her.

Later, Blanche wondered how they'd made it to the bedroom with their bodies glued together.

With his hands, his tongue, his penis, and his talk, Thelvin flowed in and over Blanche while she breathed him in, sucked and licked, kissed and touched him everywhere she could reach, savoring all his textures and tastes. When he pulled her on top of him, she matched her rocking hips to his until they moved together as though they had always been doing this. Without a word, she opened up to him in ways that pushed her deeper into and out of herself until she was as naked and wide open as a cloudless, star-filled night. And she could tell from the pleasure and surprise spilling from Thelvin's eyes, from the way he touched her face, and said her name, as though it were the source of all goodness just discovered, that he, too, was feeling the delicious shock of a closeness that was more than expected. Blanche's pleasure was so intense, the longing it answered so strong, she couldn't resist the urge to lean down and bite his shoulder. His soft moan of minor pain and major pleasure came just as she did—the first time. Five orgasms later, she lay beside him, damp and limp and slightly light-headed, her crotch still throbbing. She admired their complementary blacknesses—her skin full of shades of plum and deep blues, his red-tinged and rosy. Thelvin rolled onto his side toward her. He leaned his elbow on the bed and propped his head up on his hand. His face was relaxed, but his eyes were questioning.

"No regrets?"

Blanche laid her hand on his thigh. "It was wonderful. I mean it."

Thelvin grinned. "For me, too. But that's not enough."

"What else?" She held her breath, uncertain whether she really wanted to know.

"No regrets," he said.

"Oh." Blanche looked away, then made to rise. Thelvin stretched his arm across her waist and stopped her. His smile was mischievous. "You're a runner."

Blanche relaxed against the pillow, relieved by the change of subject. "I used to be. I loved it when I was a kid. I still remember running just to be running."

Thelvin rocked her gently. "I don't mean when you were a kid, Blanche. I don't mean that kind of running."

"Oh." As hard as she tried not to, Blanche felt herself stiffen beneath Thelvin's arm. She couldn't help remembering what Ardell had said about her being unwilling to let anyone get close to her. She consciously relaxed, took a deep breath, and made herself stay right where she was—and not just her body, but her mind and feelings, too.

"Maybe sometimes," she said, "but I'm more concerned with running toward you a little too fast than I am about running away from you, Thelvin." Goose bumps rose on her arms in the aftershock of her frankness.

The look on Thelvin's face was her reward for honesty. He laughed a soft, deep chuckle.

"You think that's funny?"

"I think that's wonderful." He leaned over and kissed her lightly on the lips. "I think it's wonderful that you let yourself move a little faster than usual and that I had something to do with that. I was about to bust, girl! I'm too old for that soapy-palm-in-the-shower routine." Thelvin lay back and stretched.

Blanche wondered how many other women and, for all she knew, men were currently satisfying him. Of course, they'd just used condoms, but if he'd spent the last ten years screwing drugged-out, needle-using prostitutes with the letters HIV tattooed on their thighs, or was infected himself, it would have been nice if she'd asked an hour or two ago. She still needed to know. She gave him a sober look. "Wanting to wait a little longer before we got this far wasn't just about finding out if we really liked each other," she said. "I mean, I want to get to know you better, but it's not just about getting to know you."

"You mean it aint just my personality that you're curious about?"

"Well," Blanche said, "it's like they say, even nice people get AIDS."

"No joke." Thelvin pulled himself up. Leaning against the carved wooden headboard and looking off into space, he began to speak in a barely audible voice, as though he were really mumbling to himself: "I didn't have sex or even see a movie with another woman for four years after my wife died. We were high-school sweethearts, see? She was big, like you. A whole handful of woman. Big-hearted, too. We got married right out of school and stayed that way. She was . . ." Something sad happened to Thelvin's voice. "I thought I loved her when she was alive, but when she died . . . it was like everything in the world turned gray. The kids kept me going, kept me busy."

Thelvin stopped speaking and closed his eyes. He heaved a sigh that seemed as heavy as the bed they lay on, then continued.

"One day I woke up and Ruth's name wasn't the first word that popped into my mind. After that, I felt too guilty to think about another woman. Not only had Ruth died, I was forgetting her, which meant she was really and truly gone. So I decided to do everything I could to keep her memory alive. I set a place for her at the table on holidays, on all of our birthdays, and on our anniversary. I talked to her about the boys and how to raise them right. I put pictures of her everywhere, even in the bathroom and the cellar!" Thelvin moved his hands as though trying to grasp something Blanche couldn't see. "But she kept slipping away, slipping away. First her eyes, then her voice, then the way she laughed." Thelvin shook his head. "When the boys grew up and went off to school, every last bit of Ruth that was left walked out on me." Blanche could see the years of misery still alive in his eyes. He turned his head away and laughed. "So I joined the church." He laughed again. "Lord, Lord, Lord. One of the biggest singles clubs in the world! Half the women in that church were on the make for a permanent mate. And the men! Dudes who couldn't get a date with a donkey showed up at church knowing sisters were looking for men. I aint just talking kids and young people. I mean people our age!"

Blanche had a flash fantasy of a passel of pastel-clad colored ladies of various ages and sizes in their feathered and frilled Sunday-service hats, chasing Thelvin up the front steps of the church.

"Anyway, I went out with a couple righteous, pious sisters." He shrugged. "It just didn't work. It was like I was trying to punish myself by only seeing women I wasn't all that attracted to, who I knew I couldn't love and didn't even want to screw." He slid back down into the bed beside her. "There's been a couple women since. I been real careful with the condoms, but nobody special. Until now."

Blanche reached over and took his hand, acutely aware of Thelvin's deep and probably everlasting ache for his dead wife. She also had a wondrous respect for his willingness to show his feelings and was relieved that, according to what he'd said, Thelvin hadn't been living the life of a sex dog. She wondered if his having lost someone he loved dearly had anything to do with his pushing her to say she would see him into the future.

Thelvin hunched her with his elbow. "Now you. You know how fickle you gap-tooth girls are supposed to be."

Blanche told him about the men she'd gone out with in Boston over the last three years. "They were nice enough, but if they weren't looking for a doormat in a woman's body, they wanted a mama or a cook."

While she was talking, Blanche realized that, despite Thelvin's openness with her, she didn't want to talk to him about Leo. She didn't mind Thelvin's knowing about her and Leo—she'd only had sex with him once, a couple years ago, since he'd been married; she was a grown woman and it was her body. But something felt wrong about telling Leo's business to Thelvin. "Only one other lover in all that time, and then only once," she said.

"Didn't you leave somebody out?"

She didn't pretend she didn't know who he meant. Some part of her was glad Thelvin hadn't spoken Leo's name.

"No. Leo was the last one I mentioned." She shrugged. "It was always an off-and-on thing."

Blanche could feel Thelvin tensing up. "Yeah, but since high school?!"

"Well, for most of that time it was off. I was living in Harlem and Leo was down here. I'd see him when I came to visit Mama, and once in a while he . . . You met his wife."

"So?"

Blanche stretched. "I'd be embarrassed to be going with a man married to that limp sister! Make me look bad!"

Thelvin chuckled and rolled toward her. He put his arm around her waist. "Man's a fool, no doubt about that." He snuggled closer.

"I haven't had much of a love life these last few years."

"How could that be, a good-looking woman like you? I know it wasn't about not having no takers."

"Well, you're a man. You know who's out here for a woman my age. Brothers think they can run any old kinda game and I'll be so grateful they noticed me, my legs'll spring right open."

"Yeah, there's some dogs out here, all right. But a big, fine woman like you, baby . . ."

Blanche leaned over and kissed him. Men were so cute. If they wanted you they figured everybody else had to want you, too. After all, wasn't each and every he the center of the universe? She pressed her belly against him. "You hear that noise? It aint a thunderstorm coming. It's my stomach. I need some of the other kind of nourishment."

"Coming right up." Thelvin bounded out of bed.

• • •

Thelvin tried to persuade her to spend the night, but Blanche explained that an overnight needed to be a planned thing, so she could bring her necessities and be comfortable. He had finally given up trying to get her to change her mind at just the moment she could feel her left nerve beginning to twitch.

She'd expected to see Ardell when she took the car back, but Ardell wasn't home. Blanche slipped the car keys through her mail slot. Once she was home, she immediately wished she'd stayed with Thelvin. Her desire to be back in his bed doubled when the phone rang. This was not a good time for her to be quizzed, but because she knew who it was, she didn't even think about not answering it. That probably wouldn't happen for another ten years after Taifa was grown and gone from home.

"Hey, Taifa, how you doin?"

"Great, Moms."

"How's the job going?"

"Actually, it's getting boring! I never thought I'd get the hang of it, but now that I've got a routine, I can do the job in my sleep. And I'm sure glad I don't have to do it, you know, for a living, like a career."

"But you're still having fun?"

"Most definitely having a blast! There's a couple of girls here who . . ."

Blanche half listened, although a bit of her was closely attentive to anything that smacked of fast cars, late-night parties, and college boys.

". . . and her dad took us to dinner at this really nice restaurant."

"Well, I'm glad you're having a good time."

"Thanks, Mama Blanche." Taifa was quiet for a few moments, then: "What about you? Still going on dates?"

"You and Malik been talking about me, I hear."

"Well, yeah, I mean, well, are you?"

"Am I what? Still seeing Thelvin?"

"Thelvin. Yeah."

"I am, as a matter of fact. I really like him." Yes, she really did like him. The thought made her smile.

"What do you like about him?"

A flutter in Blanche's crotch reminded her of one thing she liked about him, but it wasn't the only reason, or the most important. "He's a gentle, affectionate person. I think he's probably a real good person," she added, feeling lucky to be able to say it. She admitted to herself that Thelvin was the kind of sweet, romantic man it would be easy to love, but didn't say it. Blanche didn't think that was what Taifa wanted to hear.

"Has Aunt Ardell met him yet? I mean . . ."

Blanche laughed. "Girl, get a grip! I promise not to get too serious about Thelvin until you meet him. Okay?"

"Well, I'm not trying to . . . I, we just don't want you to get hurt or anything."

Anything like laid. "Well, I appreciate that, honey, but there's nothing to worry about. I promise." At least not yet, she added to herself.

"Okay, well, have a good time, but remember your promise."

"My promise?"

"You know, what you just said about not getting serious until we meet him."

Blanche shook her head at someone young enough to think such things could be controlled.

"Okay, sweetie, okay."

Poor Taifa—like most people her age, she wanted both her independence and her mommy, and she wanted her mommy on the job twenty-four/seven. Blanche took a long hot shower and went to bed to dream of trying to dance with Thelvin while Taifa kept tapping her on the shoulder to cut in.

"You don't even need to tell me what happened, and I wish to hell you'd stop grinning like that!" Ardell said when she opened her back door to Blanche on Monday.

Blanche took a chair at the kitchen table. Ardell poured her a cup of tea and pushed the milk and sugar toward her. "Now." Ardell slipped into the chair across from Blanche. "Tell me everything." She put a teaspoon of sugar in her own cup.

"Everything?"

"Don't get cute, Blanche. You know what I mean." Ardell paused. "It was good, hunh?"

"'Good' is not the word, girl! The man's got magic fingers, a tongue that knows its way around a woman's parts, and a penis that keeps perfect time to my tune!" Blanche laid her arm across the table, palm up.

Ardell slid her own palm across Blanche's in that amen way. "You look like you been on a month's vacation, skin all glowing and shit."

"Yeah, but I still wish I'd had the willpower to wait a little while longer before dropping my drawers."

"Girl! You know damn well you didn't have no drawers on! But it was a bit early," Ardell added when they stopped laughing.

Blanche rolled her eyes. "I tried to hold out, but . . ."

"Yeah, I know how that is."

Both women were lost in reverie for a minute. Blanche was about to signify about her sexual encounter with Thelvin being proof she wasn't afraid to let a man get close to her, as Ardell had claimed, but Clarice showed up, and they got down to the business of baking five hundred individual pastry shells.

By the time they were done, Blanche didn't even want to hear the words "pastry" or "oven." She was practically out of her shoes before she was in the Miz Alice. She plopped down on the sofa. Fatigue throbbed through her body. She laid her head back and quickly relaxed into sleep.

Her eyes were wide open almost before the broken glass hit the floor. The thing that came hurtling through the window rolled across the room and stopped inches from her feet. Something hard and tight squeezed her chest and made her gasp. She wanted to kick the round, paper-and-string-wrapped thing on the floor away from her, but she could neither feel nor move her limbs. She took a deep breath and let the air out slowly, took another breath, then rolled off the sofa and stooped low so that she couldn't be seen from the windows. She made her way across the room in a crouch, reached up and turned off the lights. She slid to the floor, what little strength she'd had flowing from her body like sweat. "Don't panic, don't panic, don't panic!" she told herself again.

Despite the darkness, the baseball-sized bundle on the floor glowed as if spotlighted. Shoulda expected something like this, she told herself. She wrapped her arms around her body and held on tight. Didn't I know there'd be more than just that one phone call? she asked herself, as though she should have been, could have been prepared for this. She leaned her head back against the wall, waiting for her heart to slow, for her mind to clear and focus.

When her heart was no longer trying to escape from her chest, she rose and closed the curtains. She lifted the side of the curtain at the front window. Cracks radiated from the hole in the glass. A faint breeze blew through it. She gulped air like a person fresh from near drowing. The street was empty and quiet, except for the night creatures that were supposed to be outside her door. She would put bars on the window tomorrow. She would . . . She turned on the light and stared at the bundle on her floor. She walked slowly toward it, braced herself, picked it up. Heavy. A rock, of course. She got a knife and cut the string. The paper was yellow and lined. The bottom edge was torn and crooked. The letters were printed. Big fat red capital letters:

I'LL HURT YOU IF I HAVE TO.

Blanche fought hard not to drag her suitcase out from under the bed and start packing. She knew that he could hurt her, had hurt her, could put his hands on her again. The rock and the note slid to the floor. Her stomach roiled. She flew to the bathroom and vomited up all that she'd eaten since lunch, then rose on wobbly legs to wash her face and hands. Turning her face from the things on her floor, she went directly to her Ancestor altar and lit candles and a stick of incense with fingers cold as snow.

"You see it," she told her Ancestors. "I don't have to tell y'all about rocks through the window at night. You know, you know. So please give me . . ." In her mind she once again heard glass breaking, the thud that could have been a beer bottle filled with gasoline, and a flaming rag landing at her feet instead of a rock. She'd been about to ask her Ancestors for the strength and courage to get through this battle with Palmer. But she realized she didn't want to have the grit to go on; she didn't want to have to go on at all. She wanted to believe this rock and note were meant for someone else in some other house. She wanted to believe the rock was thrown by a girlfriend of Thelvin's trying to run the competition out of town. She wanted to believe that Palmer had nothing to do with this note and if she couldn't convince herself of that, she at least wanted the sense to stop, to quit mucking around in Palmer's business while she was ahead. While she was still alive. But she moaned at the realization that she couldn't stop. It was too late. If she had not seen Palmer, if Archibald hadn't given her the idea of pawing through Palmer's life, if she'd acted like she knew he was dangerous when Palmer warned her off with that phone message—any one of those things might have stopped her. But now . . . He wouldn't be threatening her if there weren't something he wanted to stay hidden, something he was afraid she would find out or had already found out. Why else try to scare her off? What was it? What was it? She turned and looked at the note lying on the floor. Rotten fucker!

She picked up the rock, opened the front door and looked around: no one in sight. She spit on the rock and threw it as hard as she could. She closed and locked the door, then found a small plastic bag, stuffed the note in it, sealed the bag, and put it in the freezer of her small refrigerator, believing the cold would contain its evil. She peed in the scrub bucket, added five times as much water and some Jean Naté—ready to try any- and everything. She wiped the window and door frames with the mixture, then mopped the floors, hoping this provided the protection Madam Rosa had told her it would.

She emptied and washed the bucket, rag, and mop and hung her rubber gloves on the shower rod. She looked at the phone, longing to talk to Ardell, to not be alone, to have had someone there with her when the rock came through her window so she wouldn't even have to describe it. Of course, she didn't have to describe it, did she?

She wanted to tell Ardell about the note and the rock, and maybe Archibald, too. But what would they do? Ardell would go off! She'd do everything she could to stop Blanche from nosing around about Palmer. She didn't know how Archibald would react. She realized she'd have to tell him everything—about the rape and how she was using his money. Forget that.

She put the kettle on for tea and downed two shots of gin while she waited for the water to boil. He hasn't changed a thing, not a thing, she told herself. It wasn't true, of course. Everything, from the way she left her house, to the way she crossed the street, to the way she breathed, had changed.

Mistress of Disguise,
Part Two

Blanche was at the hardware store when it opened in the morning. She bought a canister of pepper spray, a pane of glass for her broken window, and, spending more than she could afford, a set of inside shutters for three windows and a piece of plywood to be held in place by a couple of bricks for the small bathroom window. Though she was sweaty and hungry by the time she was done, her spirits were lifted by her efforts to protect herself, and she was ready to get back into Palmer's business by the time she left for Ardell's.

Ardell was hunched over a small calculator when Blanche arrived to borrow her car.

"Don't stop," Blanche told her.

"Humm." Ardell punched in some more numbers. "You okay?" she asked without looking up.

"Had a restless night," Blanche told her.

Ardell shook her head and went on working. Blanche was relieved not to have Ardell's full attention. The more time she could put between the

rock through her window and having a sit-down with Ardell the better—
unless she wanted Ardell to see through her like cellophane.

"I'll only be a couple hours." Blanche took Ardell's car keys from the
hook in the kitchen and kissed her on top of her head. She strapped
Ardell's aluminum ladder to the car roof and took off for Durham.

Blanche parked in front of the cottage to which David Palmer sent
weekly flowers. The place still had that nobody-home feeling. She
climbed out of the car and pulled the seat of her coveralls away from her
sweaty back. The coveralls belonged to Mr. Billy, who worked at the gas
station; Blanche had paid Mr. Billy's wife ten dollars for their use.

She cranked an old-fashioned doorbell and heard its grating ring from
inside, but no one came to the door. She rang again, waited, then went to
a front window and looked inside: sofa and chair covered in a blowsy rose
print, a multicolored braided rug, a potbellied lamp on a flimsy-looking
end table in a small room painted white with dark woodwork. Blanche
spun around.

The woman approaching her was tall, with a beaky face and watery eyes
behind pink-framed glasses. Shoulder-length dark-blond-and-gray hair
swung around her face in a way that said, "Wash me!"

"Kin I hep yew."

"Mornin, ma'am. I'm lookin for the owner. Said he gonna meet me
here. I got two other jobs."

"Jobs?"

"Yeah, windows. I do windows."

"I aint never seed no woman window-washer before." She looked
Blanche up and down.

Blanche put her hand on her hip. "Neither did I, before I needed me a
second job." She looked back at the house. "I guess I can start on the outside. Maybe he'll show up by then." She walked around the woman toward
the back of the place.

"Water spigot around here?" There were two windows in the back.
Blanche went to the curb and pulled the ladder from the top of the car. Go
on, girl! she told herself as she easily carried the ladder to the back of the
house. She returned to the car and got her bucket, squeegee, cloth, and
cleaner, then put some water in the bucket. By the time she was ready to
climb up the ladder, the neighbor had grown bored and left. Blanche
stepped up onto the second rung of the ladder and tried to open the clos-

est rear window. It didn't budge. She dragged the ladder to the other rear window and tried it. Stuck. But it lifted a bit. She hammered the wooden frame and loosened it enough to push the window up. First, a quick look around the corner of the house to check on the neighbor across the street, then she put on her rubber gloves and climbed in the window.

The old-fashioned kitchen, with its skirted sink and 1950s stove, looked as though it wasn't used for much. There were no dirty dishes, or even glasses, in the sink. She opened the fridge: two bottles of Moët & Chandon White Star Champagne, a jar of black olives, some Brie, and a dried-up chunk of pâté. There was a box of water crackers in a kitchen cabinet with four water glasses and two champagne flutes.

The only other downstairs room was the living room she'd seen from the front window. She went up the enclosed stairs. They opened into a bedroom that was clearly the center of activity. The brass bed was queen-sized, high, and covered with a paisley velvet duvet in red, purple, and green. The sheets were red satin. Purple and green pillows of various sizes and shapes were bunched at the head of the bed. A white porcelain vase of yellow roses, their dead heads hanging like rejected lovers, stood in the middle of the dresser. A full-length mirror in a chrome frame was angled to reflect the bed.

Blanche stood at the foot of the bed and slowed her breathing, relaxing into herself so that she could feel the room around her. She took a deep breath: dust and a light perfume that could come from soap. No people smell. No smell of skin on skin, fluids. She looked around her. The room told her nothing. Whatever went on here, the house didn't think it was any of her business. It was wrong. She was going to find its secrets, with or without the house's help.

She opened the bureau drawers. All but one were empty. It was full of expensive-looking underwear of the see-through and crotchless variety in black, red, peach, and midnight blue. She held up a red thong and wondered how she'd look in one of those. Why should the skinny girls have all the fun? There was a sheer black negligee and matching mules in the closet, along with a man's black-and-white-striped silk robe and black leather backless slippers.

A mini stereo system and a smallish TV/VCR sat atop a large table at the foot of the bed, between the two front windows. In the small bathroom beyond the bedroom, Egyptian-cotton towels were stacked like banked clouds on an open bamboo étagère. A wicker basket overflowed: bars of fancy soap, a back brush, and loofahs. There were bottles of expensive-looking bath oil, bubble bath, and flavored massage oils—cherry, peach, raspberry. Thelvin would taste good in peach. The floor was covered in overlapping small sisal rugs. The shower stall was mirrored. A razor, some shaving lotion, toothpaste, and two toothbrushes in a small glass sat on the ledge of the sink. There was an old razor blade in the wastebasket. Blanche went back to the bedroom and opened the drawer in the night table: an emery board, six condoms in foil packets, and a slightly curved rectangular gold-colored bar that looked like a piece of some sort of jewelry, maybe a large brooch. She picked it up. It was painted to look like metal, but something like black plastic showed through a scratch at one end. The back of the bar had what looked like clear glue stuck to it. The front side was covered with a row of gold-painted rosebuds. Cheap, she thought.

A door slammed nearby.

Blanche looked out the front window. The blonde woman across the street had just closed her door behind her. She was carrying a tray and heading in Blanche's direction. Blanche slipped the rose-covered bar in her pocket, closed the night-table drawer, and ran down the stairs. She hoisted herself up on the sink—truly grateful for all those push-ups she'd been doing lately—slid out the window, and made it to the side of the house just as the woman reached the front of it.

"I thought you might like a glass of fresh lemonade." The woman held out the tray with its two tall green glasses.

Damn! Of all the times for Southern hospitality to kick in! "Why, thank you." Blanche was panting a bit. "That's mighty nice of you." She took off her gloves and picked up the lemonade. The woman raised her own glass to her lips, all the while watching Blanche, obviously waiting for Blanche to taste hers.

"This is really delicious!" Blanche said. And it was. "Something unusual in here, aint it?"

The woman beamed. "My own special ingredient. Just a drop or two of grenadine."

Blanche nodded her approval. The woman sat on the front step of the cottage.

"Don't see nobody over here much," the woman said. "I see lights some nights. And the car once in a while."

"That so?"

"You can get to the back through the alley. They mostly use that. That's why I don't see them much."

How much is much? Blanche wondered. "They got kids?" she asked.

"Oh no, no. They're not regular . . ." The woman's eyes glittered. "It's a love nest," she whispered loud enough to be heard across the street.

Blanche mustered her considerable acting ability. "A what?!" She made sure to widen her eyes and leave her mouth slightly ajar. No sense doing a half-assed job.

"Well, I aint positive. I mean, I never seen them doing nothing or . . . But they aint a regular couple. They aint here every day, for one thing."

"Well, maybe they travel for work."

"That's another thing—I never see them around the times people usually come from work and go to work. It's always off hours when they're here."

"They spend the night, though."

"Not so's you'd notice."

"Sounds like you're right about *the love nest*." Blanche mimicked the woman and whispered her last three words.

"Well, live and let live," the woman said.

Blanche was surprised. She'd thought the woman wanted both to talk about her neighbors and to judge them.

"I only spoke to him on the phone," Blanche said. "I always wonder what a person looks like when I don't get to meet them face to face. Know what I mean?"

The woman shrugged. "They aint neighborly, that's for sure."

"They been here long?"

"About a year now, I reckon. Place used to belong to old man Johnson. He died not too long 'fore these folks came. Most of the old families around here is dead or moved out. His kids all moved away. I don't know if they sold this place or they're just renting it. I didn't realize anybody was over here, but I kept seeing this big gray car. I waved to him once, but . . ."

"Is he . . . ?"

The woman was as puzzled as Blanche expected her to be.

"Good looking?" Blanche said. "The man? I thought he might be, 'cause he sounds like . . ."

"Oh yes, very handsome, very nice-looking. Of course, he wears a hat or a cap so I couldn't see . . . Blonde, though, I did see that. She's very petite, from what I could see of her. Very refined, both of them."

Blanche drank the rest of her lemonade. "That sure hit the spot. I thank you kindly." She handed the woman the glass and stood up. "Well, I'm 'bout done here. I aint doin no more till I get paid!" She stood up. "I'm just gonna git my things."

Much to her disappointment, the woman just sat there, sipping away. Blanche had hoped to get back into the house. Maybe there was something else besides this thing in her pocket, something that would move her closer to knowing who Palmer was shacking up with and why he didn't seem to want it known, since nobody she'd talked to had mentioned this setup or even a current relationship with a woman. She hesitated, hoping the woman would leave. She didn't.

Blanche went around to the back of the bungalow, closed the window she'd left open—careful not to slam it—and carried the ladder out to the car. The woman smiled up at her from the stoop. Blanche gathered her bucket, mop, and squeegee and took them to the car.

"Well, thanks again for the lemonade," she said.

"Why, you're more than welcome," the woman said, but still didn't stand.

Blanche suddenly understood. She wants to take a look around, too, she thought, and gave up.

"All right, now, y'all take care."

The woman waved. Blanche jumped in the car and drove off. When she stopped at the light on Main Street, she slipped the metal bar from her pocket. She didn't know what it was, but she knew it had belonged to a woman, and, according to that underwear in the bureau drawer in the cottage, she wasn't Palmer's sick and aging aunt. Blanche gunned the engine when the light changed.

A Ride and a Release

Ardell was opening mail when Blanche arrived to return the car.

"Look! I found it in Palmer's place in Durham." Blanche held out the rose-covered piece from the cottage.

Ardell laid down the letter she was holding and took the gold-colored bar from Blanche. She turned it over a couple of times. "Humm. About as much help as a bucket with a hole in it." She handed the bar back to Blanche. It suddenly looked dull and even cheaper, and was now littered with lint from Blanche's pocket.

"Well, at least I know something I didn't know before."

Ardell picked up another envelope and slit it open with a table knife. "And just what might that be?"

Blanche told her about the underwear she'd found in the bungalow bureau drawer. "So I know for sure he's shacking with somebody over in Durham. He coulda been using the place for a poker stop or something."

"Humm. With that piece of information and a ham sandwich, you got lunch." Ardell frowned at the letter she took from its envelope.

It was all Blanche could do not to tell Ardell that maybe this was the thing Palmer wanted to hide enough to throw a rock through her window.

"But I aint through yet," she said. "There's something out there on that pig, and I'm gonna find it. Palmer is in for one big surprise."

"And so is that damned florist over in Raleigh." Ardell sat down at the kitchen table and waved the bill at Blanche. "Look what he's charging me for the arrangements for tonight! I know he's cheating me. I got a good mind to call around some places and check his prices." Ardell threw the invoice down, picked up a pencil, and put big question marks beside certain numbers on the sheet of paper. Blanche patted Ardell's shoulder and kissed the top of her head. "I'll see you later," she said, and headed for home.

She felt a bit better as she walked. For a few minutes, Ardell's lack of enthusiasm for the broken piece from the cottage had made Blanche wonder if she'd wasted her time searching the place. But Ardell was too distracted by business to understand how important the piece and the sexy underwear could be. Ardell also didn't know just how badly Palmer was trying to scare her off. No, there was no reason to be down. She'd even gotten a little bit of a description of Palmer's lover. I'm on it! she declared to the street, which remained silent except for the chitter of birds and the gentle hiss of a light breeze. So much quiet in a poor working people's neighborhood in the middle of a weekday was a good sign. It meant people had paid work. But after last night, she'd just as soon all her neighbors were outside to bear witness. She checked to make sure the small piece of paper she'd stuck between the jamb and the door was still in place and all the windows were fine.

She went inside and called Bunnie, her old high-school mate who Miz Minnie said worked at the Sons of Farleigh Club. The man who answered the phone said Bunnie was out of town for a week. She left her name and number, then debated taking a cup of tea out on the stoop and enjoying the day, but convinced herself she should wash out some underwear first. She was filling a small plastic washbasin at the sink when a kind of pulse beat at the base of her brain: someone she cared about was coming or about to call. Half a bit later she knew it was Leo tapping on her front door. A part of her—the part that liked to keep things neat and avoid pain and foolishness—urgently whispered to her not to answer, but she was already turning the doorknob.

"Hey, Blanche. I was . . . I was in the neighborhood, so I thought . . . How you doin?"

Blanche held the door open and stepped back. Leo took a giant step inside.

The Miz Alice wasn't large enough for the flock of memories that marched in on Leo's heels, so Blanche suggested they take a ride out into the country. It didn't help: Leo's car was even smaller. Blanche found herself breathing in the remembered smell of that night thirty years ago when they'd skinny-dipped in Mudflat Pond, then lay on a blanket in a field of new grass, the moon turning them both to black silver. Now, sitting beside Leo as he drove along the back road toward Hokeysville, both of them in their fifties, her lips still remembered the velvety softness of their first kiss, when she was twelve and he thirteen. She heard the murmur of years of their talk about everything from what life was really about to why plaid skirts made her legs look funny. Blanche rolled down the window as far as it would go and fanned herself with her hand. Leo didn't glance at her, but she could still feel him examining her as though he could see her through his skin. Blanche looked straight ahead; all she saw was a blur of green with a ribbon of black slicing it in two.

She turned to look at him. "Damn you and your needy-assed self!" she shouted so loudly Leo jumped in his seat. He gave her a quick puzzled look, his bottom lip caught between his teeth.

"If you hadn't up and married Luella, we . . ."

Leo reached over and grasped her hand. "I know," he said. "I know it every minute of every day."

Blanche felt her heart melting like so much chocolate left out in the sun. She snatched her hand away and faced forward. "I never would have done that to you, Leo. I . . ."

Leo laughed with no mirth. "No, you wouldn't have gotten married on me, Blanche, but you wouldn't marry *me* either."

"I didn't need to marry you, Leo!"

"That's just what I'm talking about! Even if I wasn't with Luella, you . . ."

"Leo, why you got to be with me in a married way? I just don't understand it. You act like being married is more important than what goes on between two people."

Leo slowed the car and glanced at her. "You talk like you don't believe in marriage, but you act like mine is holy or something. My being married aint got nothing to do with you and me. We could still . . ."

"Maybe we could, if you'd been married when I met you, but not now. Leo, me and you . . . Well, let's just say I know you, Leo, and I know you don't no more love that weak, silly, mousy-voiced woman than a chicken wears shoes. And it deeply hurt my feelings that you would pass up what we had for . . ."

Leo pulled the car over and parked on the side of the road. He turned in his seat and looked at her. "We aint getting no younger, Blanche. I aint like you. I don't want to be a old man on my own."

Blanche's mouth fell open. She'd thought Luella had just caught Leo at a weak moment and roped him into marriage, but it was worse than that. "Is that what this is all about? You trying to make sure you got somebody to push your wheelchair?" She couldn't help laughing, even though she could see that Leo was not amused. "I'm sorry, Leo, but you're old enough to know there aint no guarantees, no matter how many insurance policies you think you got. Luella could land in the nursing home before you, or die and leave you to do the best you can. Too bad you didn't think to ask me if I was interested in the job, no wedding ring attached."

Blanche turned her head away and wondered if Leo knew that there was more distance between them right now than there'd been when she was in Boston and he was down here: he didn't trust her to hang in with him if the hard times hit without the government and some preacher amening the deal. She'd thought Leo knew she had his back down the line, as she'd assumed he had hers—before he married Luella. How could he not know that what they'd had was so strong she'd have no choice but to be by his side if he needed her? She couldn't understand how she had known these things and he had not. Yes, she'd refused to marry him; yes, she had made sure he knew that she was and always intended to be her own woman. But she had also given him all that she knew of herself that was givable. How could she have known him and cared for him since she was a girl and never really understood how much of a blind fool he was? She'd long been aware of the difference between the man in her head and the one in her bed, but she'd thought her relationship with Leo too deep for her to have mistaken him for some make-believe lover. Maybe I'm wrong, she thought, maybe there really is no other kind.

She told Leo she had to get home. As he turned the car around, it occurred to her that all of this might have turned out differently if she'd said everything she'd felt straight out. And why hadn't she? Leo was afraid of growing old alone. Was she afraid of growing old *with* someone? She laid her head back and closed her eyes, fully aware that it was not too late. But what would happen if she spoke now? Would Leo leave Luella for her? Did she want him to? Did she want him? Or did she just want him to want her? Or to pull her back from the scary, soul-naked place she was headed with Thelvin? Leo was safer. At least she knew him—or so she'd thought until today. They were both silent for the rest of the trip back to town.

"Blanche, look," Leo said as they neared her house. "I know you're down on me right now. I know, far's you're concerned, it's all over between us. But it aint like that. It aint that easy and you know it." He put his hand on her knee. The flash that always passed between them leapt through her body.

"We two peas, Blanche. Whether you like it or not. That aint changed since we was kids. Luella don't change it. Your new friend Thorston don't change it neither."

Blanched opened her mouth to tell him he was wrong, then stopped. There was no sense trying to convince Leo that he'd been replaced by Thelvin. Leo wouldn't believe it. Did she?

"Thelvin."

"What?" Leo looked confused.

"Thelvin. His name's Thelvin."

Leo slowed to a stop in front of the Miz Alice. Blanche immediately opened the car door.

"You giving me a headache, Leo. I got to go." She slammed the door behind her.

While Leo was driving away, Blanche made sure she had her pepper spray in her pocket, then left the house. She looked around for zooming cars and unaccounted-for strangers before setting out to walk at a fast, arm-swinging clip. She needed to move around, to air herself out. These days her life seemed to bounce back and forth among men—Leo, Thelvin, David Palmer, Mumsfield, Archibald, even Bobby Larsen—like she was the ball in a game of Ping-Pong. She deliberately turned her attention to the trees, shrubs, and grass around her, taking in the different shades of green from just beyond yellow to nearly black. It only half worked. Neither Thelvin nor Leo would go away, and the shadow of David Palmer floated between her and the sun. She went home, checked to make sure the slip of paper was in place, and washed and changed for work.

She was looking forward to the distraction of the dinner for twelve they were serving that night—a nonbicentennial event for some couple having their third anniversary. Blanche wondered if Palmer would be there and visualized an "accident" in which boiling-hot soup was spilled in his lap.

"Mr. Henry say it was just like Bobby Larsen tole 'em," Clarice began as soon as she stepped into the kitchen where they were working that evening.

"Girl, what are you talking about?" Ardell asked.

"That Bobby Larsen. He out."

Blanche came to attention. "You mean they let him go?"

Clarice looked from Blanche to Ardell. "Is you two been hittin the bottle? That's what I said, aint it? He out 'cause that rich fella from New York City say him and Bobby was huntin over by Milford when Maybelle was killed, just like Bobby say. Mr. Henry say Sheriff don't know what to do now. He say they aint got no more suspect. Some of 'em thinkin the perp'trator done got clean away. That's what Mr. Henry say."

"Perp'trator"! It was bad enough for the cops and military to use cover-up names like "perpetrator" for killer and "collateral damage" for the bombing of innocent people. It was too much to hear that mess from Clarice, who couldn't even pronounce the word.

"You mean the murderer, don't you?"

Clarice put her hand on her hip and sighed with impatience. "That's what I said."

Blanche had to hold her breath to keep from arguing with Clarice. She didn't know if she was just getting cranky and ill-tempered as she got older and more menopausal, or whether the way people used words without thinking what they meant was getting worse.

Blanche pictured Daisy dancing with delight at Bobby's release.

"What about that, Ardell?" Clarice said. "You the one say he didn't have no alibi."

"Okay, I was wrong. Now, let's get this . . ."

Blanche remembered what else Daisy had told her and interrupted Ardell.

"According to Daisy, Bobby's got something on the man who really did it," she said.

"Mr. Henry didn't mention nothin 'bout that," Clarice said.

"All right, y'all," Ardell said. "We got work to do."

Blanche had time to wonder who it was that Bobby had the goods on before she turned her mind to food.

Dessert was being served when Blanche stepped out the back door to catch a bit of the evening's breeze. She strolled idly around the side of the house, admiring the way the blossoms in the flower beds glowed in the evening light as though lit from inside. She was turning back to the kitchen when she heard voices. A man and a woman? She couldn't be sure. She stepped into the deeper shadow of the house and stood still, trying to figure out where the voices were coming from.

And there they were, at the other end of the garden, walking in her direction. Shit! She didn't feel up to having to be pleasant to guests. Blanche stepped back even farther and felt her shoes sink into the soft dirt of a flower bed. The couple turned and headed toward the other side of the house, then stopped, turned toward each other, and began talking. The woman folded her arms across her chest. The man put his hands on the woman's shoulders; then, even though she didn't resist, he yanked her toward him with force. The strength of his kiss pressed her head back. He let her go so abruptly the woman swayed for half a second. He said something to her, then turned sharply away. The woman reached out a hand as if to stop him but he continued toward the house. Blanche watched him leave and so did the woman. As he came into the glow from a window, Blanche recognized Seth Morris. I shoulda known! she thought. Bugging some other female, poor woman. Was she all right? Blanche turned toward her. The woman was still standing where Seth had left her. She turned her head in Blanche's direction as though feeling herself watched. Blanche squinted her eyes. Mindless of the flowers beneath her feet, she stepped closer to the woman. Well, I'll be! Blanche's lips spread into a grin. She stepped boldly out onto the path, now wanting to be seen even more badly than she'd wanted to stay hidden just a few moments ago. Her step was springy with delight at the shock slowly registering on the woman's face as Blanche walked toward her.

"Why, Karen, honey, I thought that was you." She put her hand on her hip. "Tell me, does Mumsfield know you're out here exchanging bodily fluids with Seth Morris?"

Karen opened and closed and opened her mouth before she turned and stumbled hurriedly toward the house.

"Have a good night, now, Karen," Blanche called after her. "And give

Mumsfield my best." She laughed her way back to the kitchen. It seemed Archibald was pretty good at smelling a rat after all.

Blanche figured Karen must have left the party before they'd finished breaking down to be already sitting in her car outside Blanche's door when she got home that night. Blanche saw her but didn't speak. She put the key in the lock and had just opened the door when Karen spoke.

"Please. Please, just let me talk to you." She got out of her car and joined Blanche on the stoop.

Blanche was definitely interested in what Karen had to say, but she didn't intend to make it easy for her. All of Karen's mousy softness was gone, her lipstick had worn off, and she looked at Blanche with eyes that were far from girlish. The first of those tiny little lines, like hairline cracks, that some older white women develop around their mouths were just beginning to show. She looked well used.

Blanche opened the door wide enough for Karen to come in, then changed her mind. She could feel the Miz Alice shiver at the idea of letting Karen's vibe loose inside.

"We can talk out here," she said, and closed the door.

Karen turned to face her. Blanche crossed her arms and waited.

"Do you want me to beg? Do you want money?" Karen opened her purse and took out a checkbook. "How much will it take?"

Blanche still didn't speak.

Karen's shoulders slumped. "You probably think I'm some kind of slut, or just after Mumsfield's money. But it's not like that. I swear."

"Oh? Was that mouth-to-mouth resuscitation you were doing on Seth Morris?" Blanche remembered the train station where she'd first seen Seth deep-kissing a woman. She pointed at Karen. "It was you with Seth at the train station!"

Karen didn't deny it. "Marrying Mumsfield means everything to me. Everything. I broke it off with Seth. I told him so. Tonight, when you saw us. I'll make Mumsfield a good wife, a . . . respectable wife. I'll . . . I do care for him. I do. Seth was just . . ." Karen lowered her head and rubbed her forehead.

"What do you want?" Blanche asked her.

Karen's head snapped up. "Just . . . please, don't tell Mumsfield. I'll push back the wedding, if you like. Give you time to see that I . . . I'll . . ."

Blanche put her hands on her hips. "If you aint after his money, what is it?"

Karen stared at her for a few moments. Blanche could feel her trying to decide what to say, what bit of mealy-mouthing would get her over.

"You don't know what it's like living in my father's house," she hissed in a low, frantic voice. "He . . . I just want my own home, to be my own . . ."

Blanche had expected something more in the line of wheedling and whining but didn't show her surprise. "You could get your own place instead of . . ."

Karen's laugh was both wild and harsh. "My father doesn't believe in that kind of independence. As he says, 'We're a family. We live together. Anyone who doesn't live here is not a member of this family. Anyone who is not a part of this family will not inherit,'" Karen said in a deep voice, mimicking her father. "He's everywhere!" She looked over her shoulder as if she expected to see him at the end of Blanche's street, then turned back to Blanche with the faintest shimmer of tears reddening the rims of her eyes. "When we were kids, Daddy . . ."

Blanche both wanted Karen to say what it was her father had done and didn't want to know. She folded her arms tightly across her chest, warding off the distress swirling around Karen like a dust devil. "There aint no law against you getting a job and taking care of yourself."

Karen looked at Blanche as though she'd never seen her before, then lowered her head. When she raised it, her tears were gone and defeat was written like fresh wrinkles on her face. "I should have known when I first met you, the way you behaved. . . . I tried everything I could think of to get rid of you, but you . . ."

Blanche took a step closer to Karen. "Everything you could think of? What do you mean? What did you try?"

For a bit of a second, Karen's eyes shifted to Blanche's front window, then quickly away. Blanche heard glass breaking, saw a paper-wrapped rock sailing into her life like fear made solid.

"It was you! You!" she pointed her finger at Karen. "You're the one who . . ."

Karen held her hands out in front of her. "I . . . Please, I just wanted you to go away before you . . ."

"You hired somebody to threaten me on the phone and throw a rock through my window! Or were you at least woman enough to do it yourself?"

Karen blushed so violently, Blanche knew the answers to her own questions. "Your boyfriend, that asshole Seth! You got your boyfriend to do your dirty work for you! Why? What did I do to you? Did your brother . . ."

"My brother? He's got nothing to do with this. If he knew about me and Seth he'd . . . Mumsfield told me you were going to be asking questions about me. He thought it was a fine idea, a way to mollify that damned Archibald!"

Blanche felt like she was trying to hold a fistful of water. Karen, not David. Karen. She worked to get her mind around this idea.

"Being scared I'd find something on you sure as hell didn't stop you from showing your racist ass when you thought you were safe!" Blanche put as much belligerence as she could get into her voice. She thought of the sleepless, fear-filled nights she'd spent because of this woman, the nightmares she'd suffered when she could sleep, the shutters on her windows and the lead pipe by her bed. This bitch! "I ought to slap the shit out of you!"

Karen scurried from the stoop to the walkway, as if she thought Blanche couldn't reach her there, but then she turned back toward Blanche.

"I could say I'm sorry for all the things I said to you at lunch, but you wouldn't believe me. No matter what you think of me, I beg you, please, think about Mumsfield. For all his money, he hasn't had much happiness, you know. For all his money, I'm the only woman he's ever been with. Did you know that? He's lonely. Did you know that? You think he'll be happier knowing about . . . about something that I swear is in the past? Do you think he'll be happier without me?"

"You mean would he rather be lied to, cheated on, and probably robbed by you and your half-assed boyfriend? If you two are low enough to throw rocks in my window, what're you planning to do to Mumsfield when he gets in your way?"

Karen shook her head. "No. I'd never let . . . I'd never . . ." She sighed and shook her head again. "Whatever you decide to do, there'll be no more . . . I know I can't make you leave. I won't try anymore. I promise you that." Karen climbed back in her car and drove away.

Blanche was almost dizzy from the mix of feelings roiling around inside of her: fury with Karen for scaring her and for having the nerve to come here and try to cop a plea; relief that she didn't have to watch her back anymore; and disappointment that it was Karen and not her brother who'd been threatening her. She looked at the phone. She'd call Mumsfield right now if it weren't so late. She used her anger to fight her disappointment. She knew it was weird to be sorry that somebody wasn't after you, even while you were glad about it, but she couldn't help it. Knowing that Palmer was desperate enough to threaten her to keep her out of his business was part of what had given her the energy to stay after him. Now . . . She shook her head, but it didn't clear. Well, no matter how confusing her feelings might be, she knew one thing: she sure as hell wasn't looking forward to bursting Mumsfield's bubble.

Connecting the Dots

Blanche tried her best to call Mumsfield the next morning, but she couldn't make herself do it. Let him enjoy another day of pleasure in Karen and his upcoming marriage. Once Mumsfield—and Archibald, because she had to call him, too—knew about Seth and Karen, Mumsfield would likely end up with his money but not his happiness. Archibald would see to that. She wondered which one Mumsfield would choose. Even if Karen could convince Mumsfield that her thing with Seth was over and the attempts to scare Blanche were due to fits of hot monkey love, Blanche was sure Archibald wouldn't be impressed. Could he force Mumsfield not to marry Karen? Poor Mumsfield. She really had to call and tell him about Karen and Seth, she just needed to decide the best way to do it.

The next couple of days passed so quickly they ran together in Blanche's mind like melting scoops of ice cream. She worked, she talked to Ardell, she sent cards to Malik and Taifa, she called her mother, and she missed Thelvin. She'd taken to carrying around the broken piece of that something she'd found in Palmer's bungalow as a way of reminding herself that he had secrets; maybe one she could use, although she hadn't made a bit of progress toward getting any more information. She also hadn't called Mumsfield or Archibald about Karen, and she had a heavy feeling in her stomach that she associated with things going wrong. Some out-of-doors was always a cure for the glums. She left the Miz Alice for downtown to buy some insoles for her favorite work shoes. She'd nearly passed the cleaners on Main Street when something made her turn her head and look inside.

"Daisy!" The sight of the rosy-faced blonde fired Blanche's curiosity. Bobby had been out of jail a couple of days, and there hadn't been a word about new evidence in the case or someone else being under suspicion or arrested. Blanche opened the door to the cleaners and stepped inside.

Daisy came to stand across the counter from Blanche. "Why, Miz Blanche! It sure is nice to see you!"

Blanche went on alert. Was there something not quite sincere in Daisy's greeting?

"Hey, Daisy, how you doin, honey?"

"I'm just fine, Miz Blanche."

"I know you got to work," Blanche said, "so I won't keep you. But I was just wondering about what you told me. Remember? About Bobby having proof that somebody else was with Maybelle when she died."

Daisy's face went white. "Shhh!" She looked around as though the place were full of ears. "I told you. I aint supposed to talk about that!"

"I know, I know." Blanche lowered her voice even more and talked faster as she went on, as if she could outrace the look of rising panic on Daisy's face. "But you already told me he found something, so there's no harm in telling . . ."

Daisy was shaking her head from side to side so fast her hair flew around her head like a propeller.

A short, elderly white woman, like a bleached raisin, came in. "Hello, Daisy. How are you today?"

"Why . . . why, just fine, Mrs. Carson. How're you?"

"Just fine, thank you, Daisy, just fine." She handed Daisy a receipt and gave Blanche a brief nod, which Blanche didn't return. Blanche was aware of the woman's assumption that she would be waited on immediately, regardless of Blanche's being there first. Blanche wasn't surprised; old habits were hard to break, even in the New South. If she'd been a real customer, she'd have given the woman some practice in changing her ways, but as things stood, she didn't even waste the time to roll her eyes at the woman. Daisy turned to the metal rack behind her and found a woman's suit, pink, plaid, and ugly.

"Y'all come back, heah?" Daisy called out in the soppy drawl that went with that phrase like ham with biscuits.

"So, Daisy . . ." Blanche began as soon as the door was closed.

"Why you asking me about all this, Miz Blanche?" Despite the air conditioning, tiny beads of sweat pocked Daisy's upper lip.

Blanche fingered the piece in her pocket. She'd been so intent on what she wanted to know, she'd forgotten Daisy was likely to have questions of her own. She absentmindedly took the piece out of her pocket and fiddled with it. "I was just curious, is all," she said, but Daisy wasn't listening.

Daisy was staring down at Blanche's hands on the counter as though they'd suddenly turned to gold.

"Where'd . . . How . . ."

"What?" Blanche held the piece out to Daisy. "This?"

Daisy reached out and gently ran her index finger across the gilt rosebuds, then drew her hand back as though the roses had heated up beneath her finger.

"We both had one," she said. "See?" She turned her head to the side.

Blanche looked at the gold-toned rosebud-covered barrette in Daisy's hair, then down at the piece in her hand. Something lurched in her belly, like somebody knocking on her insides. She caught her breath.

"You mean you and Maybelle," she said without a question in her voice or mind.

Daisy nodded. Blanche shut her eyes for a moment, dizzied by the realization of what this piece of junk she was holding could mean. If this belonged to Maybelle . . . Blanche suddenly saw not Maybelle or Palmer but Palmer's key ring, and heard Daisy once again telling her that Bobby had found something with Maybelle's body. Blanche's knees went weak. She clutched the counter in front of her. Did Daisy know about Maybelle and David Palmer?

"I had mine first," Daisy said as though this were something to be proud of. "Maybelle said she liked it. I tried to give her mine, but she was kinda funny about used things. She always wanted new. So I bought her one." Daisy touched the broken barrette again. "Where'd you git this, Miz Blanche?" Daisy looked as though she wasn't sure she really wanted to know—or perhaps that was really suspicion in her voice. "I ast her where hers was when she stopped wearing it. She told me it broke. Said it was cheap."

"Tell me what Bobby found and I'll tell you where I found it." Blanche held up the barrette piece.

Daisy shook her head. "I cain't! I cain't!" The more upset she became, the more North Carolina laced Daisy's accent.

Blanche tapped on the counter with the piece of barrette. "Look, Daisy, I'm on Bobby's side. On your side. I want them to catch the person who killed Maybelle. I want it all to be over so you and Bobby can help each other get through your grief and . . . I maybe even know what Bobby found, so . . ."

"Well, if you already know, there aint no need of me . . ."

Blanche had no intention of leaving that place until Daisy had confirmed what she thought she already knew. But how to get Daisy to talk?

Blanche thought of the gimmick she and her childhood friends had used when they wanted to tell something that they'd sworn not to tell.

"I know you want to keep your promise to Bobby," she told Daisy, "so you don't have to *tell* me. All you got to do is turn your head away from me if I guess right. Okay?" Daisy didn't look like it was really okay, but she didn't say anything.

"All right," Blanche said. "Is it something you wear?"

Maybelle blinked straight at Blanche.

"Okay," Blanche went on. "Is it something you eat?" She thought a couple of dumb questions might relax Daisy a little.

Daisy shook her head.

"Is it something you can fly?"

Daisy looked puzzled.

"All right, is it something off a key chain?"

Daisy turned her head away from Blanche and toward the door at the same time the door opened. A tall, blond, muscular man with ears like sheets of crumpled pink paper came into the cleaners, some white shirts thrown over his arm. He aimed his eyes at Daisy, then at Blanche, although Blanche doubted he saw either one of them.

"Medium starch throughout, heavy on the collars and cuffs. I need them tomorrow." He pushed the shirts across the counter at Daisy as though she were the opening of a washing machine.

Daisy glanced at Blanche, who nodded her head. Yankee, Blanche thought, and was pretty sure Daisy was thinking something similar.

Daisy took her time inspecting the man's shirts for stains and writing up his receipt. Every once in a while she shot Blanche a worried look that finally made Blanche realize that what she'd taken as Daisy's slowing down to put Mr. No-Manners Yankee in his place was really Daisy playing for time.

When the customer left, Blanche leaned over the counter and gave Daisy a hard look. "Did you turn your head because of *him*"—she jerked her head in the direction of the departed customer—"or because what Bobby found was from a key chain, like I said?"

Daisy looked as confused as if Blanche had suddenly begun speaking Dinka or Ibo. "Maybe I should just ask Bobby what he found, tell him you . . ."

Daisy shook her head again. "No, ma'am. No, you can't do that!"

"Then tell me right now, Daisy, or . . ."

"I already did what you tole me about turning my head! Why you . . ."

Blanche slumped against the counter, weakened by the meaning of Daisy's action and words, closed her eyes, and thanked her Ancestors. It might be a coincidence that Palmer's girlfriend had a barrette like Daisy's, although she couldn't see any of the women in his circle wearing one like it. It also might be a coincidence that something was missing from Palmer's key ring and Bobby had found something from someone's key ring when he found Maybelle's body. But both things together were a bit more than coincidence. Was this why Maybelle's death had moved her so, because somehow she'd sensed that they'd had the same attacker? She remembered how the woman across the street from the cottage in Durham had described Palmer's girlfriend and pictured small, blonde, dainty-looking Maybelle climbing out of Palmer's big gray car. Blanche gagged at the thought of him deciding which of his victims to kill and which to rape.

"You okay, Miz Blanche? Miz Blanche?"

Blanche heard her but couldn't pull herself away from her own thoughts long enough to answer. She shivered at the knowledge of what Palmer was capable of, what he might have done to her in addition to raping her. Blanche wanted to rush right home and light candles all over her Ancestors' altar in gratitude for this gift of information, as terrible as it was. First, she expected Daisy to ask her to keep their bargain and tell where she'd found the piece of Maybelle's barrette, but Daisy had other things on her mind:

"Miz Blanche, you gotta promise me you won't go near Bobby. If he finds out I told you anything, he . . ." The girl's eyes widened even more.

"He don't have to find out. But when is he planning to tell somebody about this? I know he don't trust the Sheriff, but he's got to tell somebody."

Daisy didn't answer.

Blanche thought about what the papers and radio had said about Maybelle's family. The phrase "poor white trash" hadn't been used, but it had been hinted. Bobby was likely from the same kind of people: folks who followed their own ways and didn't look to the law for justice any more than she did.

"Bobby aint thinking about doing nothing dumb, is he? Like trying to get revenge himself?"

Daisy tightened her mouth and lowered her eyes. Blanche leaned a little closer.

"Honey, you better tell Bobby to stay away from that man unless he wants to end up like Maybelle. David Palmer's already killed once. He . . ."

Daisy's eyes widened.

"Everything all right out there, Daisy?" a man called from the back.

Daisy jumped and spun around. "Yes, sir. Just fine. I'm just straightening up a bit." She turned back to Blanche and waved frantically for her to leave.

Blanche leaned over the counter and whispered: "Tell Bobby if he don't talk soon I'm gonna tell the Sheriff!" A threat only someone who didn't know Blanche would believe.

Blanche could have tap-danced home if her happiness weren't related to Maybelle's death. She chanted a string of thank-yous to her Ancestors. To think she could have left the piece of barrette behind thinking it was just junk, never knowing that it was exactly what she'd been looking for. Her smile faded. She'd thought that being a rapist made Palmer likely to have other sins he'd want to hide, she hadn't thought murder would be one of them—maybe because he'd had a chance to kill her and hadn't. Poor Maybelle.

Blanche was so full of images of Palmer's face when he was finally caught that she was startled by the three little girls, once again lined up on the top step of her stoop, as solemn-faced as undertakers. The biggest and, Blanche assumed, oldest girl sat in the middle. They were wearing another set of cotton dresses with the amateur look of homemade.

"Hey, y'all, nice to see you again. What's up?"

The biggest girl reached for her sisters' hands and made to rise. Blanche held out her arms to stop them. "Hey, now, don't run off. I was just thinking about going indoors and finding them cookies."

"Cookieth?!" the smallest one said.

"Lucinda!" the biggest one hissed. "You know better!"

"But she didn't ask me for a cookie," Blanche said, guessing they had parental instructions not to ask people for things. "She just said the word 'cookies.' Aint that right, Lucinda?"

The child moved her head up and down with feeling and smiled wide enough for Blanche to see she'd lost her two front teeth.

A loud crash caused them all to turn their heads toward the house where the girls lived.

"Bitch! I'll break your fuckin . . ." Another loud crash. Blanche looked back at the girls. The oldest now had an arm around each of her sisters. They sat pressed tightly together, their heads bowed as though they'd done something they were ashamed of.

"I got some milk to go with them cookies," Blanche said on impulse. "Why don't y'all come on in and have some?" She felt uncomfortable inviting children whose parents she didn't know into her house. If they were in her care, they'd be in big trouble for going in a stranger's house. But Farleigh, for all its growth, was still a small town. Things not allowed in the city were commonplace here. And which would their mother want right now? For them to sit here and listen to her getting beat up or for them to be inside, safe and out of earshot? Blanche remembered the way the girls' mother had responded—or, rather, not responded—when Blanche had waved to her. I could get in trouble for this, she thought. Another crash and a loud wail from their house made up her mind. "Come on, I need me a cookie right now." She opened the door and herded the girls inside.

They stood around Blanche's table as still and quiet as 3:00 A.M. in the cemetery. Their thin arms rigid at their sides, they seemed hardly to breathe, although Blanche could smell confusion and fear like waves of sourness pouring from their bodies. Tears crowded into her eyes. She turned away. What had these children seen and heard? What was being done to them? She blinked back her tears while she got out some of the Hasting twins' shortbread cookies, milk, and lemonade. "My name's Blanche." She brought plates and glasses to the table.

"I'm Doretha," the one who hadn't spoken said, then pointed at the tallest girl. "This is Murlee, and that's Lucinda."

"I'm four yearth old," Lucinda volunteered.

Blanche set cookies and drinks in the middle of the table. "Would you girls like milk or lemonade?"

"We'll all have milk," Doretha told her. "It's better for us." Her voice and look dared her sisters to disagree.

"It goes better with cookies, too," Murlee added.

"I want milk *and* lemonade," Lucinda said. Both of her sisters gave her a shut-up look.

Blanche poured three glasses of milk, a glass of lemonade for herself, and a small one for Lucinda. She set a plate and paper towels, quickly folded into hats, in front of each girl. They giggled their delight with the napkins in little-girl gasps, then watched her, waiting.

"Help yourselves to the cookies, please." She nudged the cookies closer to them. From the looks of surprise on their faces, Blanche figured helping yourself to the cookies was not a regular event in their lives. Their thank-yous were breathy and real.

They didn't so much attack their cookies and milk as concentrate on them. Every bite and sip was taken with full attention and care. No crumbs were allowed to escape. They wiped their mouths gently, as though unwilling to bruise the paper towel.

Doretha finally looked up from a cookie long enough to gaze around the room. "We like your house," she said as though they'd all conferred.

"It'th pretty," little Lucinda said. Murlee nodded her head and finished her milk.

Blanche didn't ask if she'd like more, she just refilled Murlee's glass, which got her another look of surprise. Blanche was starting to get pissed off at the thought of girls too poor to expect a second glass of milk. Or *was* it poverty? Blanche used the pretext of getting a glass of water to check as much of their bodies as she could see for bruises.

"We have to go now," Murlee announced so suddenly Blanche wondered if they'd caught her examining them.

"If y'all don't help me eat these cookies, they're going to go to waste. You help yourselves, and I'll go tell your mama where you are."

"It's all right now," Doretha said. The other two nodded in agreement.

"Well, at least have a couple cookies to go."

The girls looked up at Blanche, then at each other, and finally at the plate of cookies.

"Okay," Murlee said for all of them as she reached for another cookie.

"I'll walk you home." Blanche opened the door for them, each with a cookie in each hand. She wasn't about to let them walk in on their parents fighting.

"No!" Murlee and Doretha said in unison.

"It really is all right now. Really," Doretha said.

"Daddy went off in the car," Lucinda added.

Blanche remembered hearing a car go roaring down the street a bit ago.

"And Mama"— Murlee looked to her sisters for the end of the sentence but got no help— "doesn't like us to bring home company," she said.

Blanche wanted to grab the child and hug her to safety. Instead, she stood on the stoop watching the girls walk across the street. She still felt she should introduce herself to their mother, but didn't want to disrespect the girls' wishes. They likely knew more about how to handle this situation than she did, poor things. Their mother stepped out onto the porch; she raised her hand to the left side of her face as the children grew close to her. Trying to hide a bruise or a cut that couldn't be hidden for long? Blanche remembered reading that most women were liable to get hit by a man at least once in life. But wasn't once enough? The girls ran to their mother, their faces turned up to her like pansies to the sun. As she talked, Murlee gestured over her shoulder toward Blanche, then turned and waved to her. Their mother raised her hand and nodded in a way that

Blanche decided meant thanks. Blanche waved back and was relieved to go in the house and shut the door behind her.

When Ardell arrived, Blanche was still so upset about the girls, she hardly gave Ardell a chance to get in the door before she started talking about them.

"These three little girls from across the street come to visit today. Well, not exactly come to visit." She told Ardell about the girls and what was going on in their house. "I feel real bad for them. They must be scared half to death."

Ardell set the two shopping bags she was carrying on the table. "Their mom's scared, too," she said, turning toward Blanche.

"Yeah," Blanche agreed. "But she can do something about it."

"Like wait until he's asleep, bash him with a iron skillet, then run like hell, like you told me after the first time Harvey slapped me?"

Blanche sighed. They'd been over this too many times before. As usual, Ardell was just making excuses for women who stayed with men who beat them as regularly as the clock struck five. Over the years, Blanche had heard women give every reason from "I know I can change him" to "I worked too hard to get this house to leave and let him have everything," with a whole lot of "But I love him"s in the middle. None of it made any sense to her. She joined Ardell at the table and began unpacking the bags full of raisins, sweet red and green peppers, and chickpeas for the cold couscous salad Blanche was to make for tomorrow.

Ardell fiddled with the stem of her spectacles. "You still think all a person has to do is walk out. That aint how it works. You oughta know. You didn't press charges against Palmer!"

"If Palmer had been raping me three times a week, do you think I'd have hung around and waited for him?!"

"Oh, I get it! It's okay to let somebody rape you *once* and get away with it."

"I didn't let Palmer get away with raping me! What was I supposed to do? You think the cops would really have cared? You think I ever woulda got another job around here if I turned him in? What the hell did you expect me to do?"

"Well, did you ever think that maybe that woman across the street don't have no more choice than you had?"

"She could up and leave! If Palmer had turned his back on me for one second . . ."

"She's got three kids!"

"That's all the more reason to get the hell out of there!"

The two old friends stared at each other, neither willing to back down. Blanche could feel misery rising around her calves like flood water. It had been so long since she and Ardell had had a real fight, Blanche had forgotten how it made her feel: like she was trying to rip off her right arm and beat herself over the head with it.

"I gotta go pick up some tablecloths," Ardell mumbled. "I'll talk to you later."

"Hey." Blanche held out her hand, but Ardell was gone. Blanche went to the sink and washed the peppers. Shit! She didn't need this! She grabbed her sharpest knife and began whacking the peppers in half as though they were the cause of her fight with Ardell. She hadn't even had a chance to tell Ardell about Maybelle's barrette.

She turned from the peppers to the phone before it finished its first ring, glad for the caller and the distraction.

"Malik. How you doin, honey?"

"I'm okay, Moms. You should see me. I'm really bulkin up!"

"Don't come home no hulk, now! How's camp goin?" She felt a slight change in the vibe coming through the phone, and it focused all of her attention on him.

"Moms," he said, in a pay-attention voice. "These little guys. I don't know, it's weird. The ones I'm in charge of, they follow me around and act like . . . I mean, most of them are almost my age, but they treat me like I'm a . . ."

Like I'm a man, Blanche completed his unfinished sentence in her mind. Was she ready for this? Did it matter? "Well, that's why you got picked for the counseling job, honey. I told you, you're a good leader."

"Yeah, but these guys come to me with their problems. I mean real problems. Like this kid who wets the bed, and the one who cries all the time and says his parents dumped him here 'cuz they don't want him around. Another boy didn't change his underwear for a week, and I had to talk to him and . . ."

Blanche was aware of a kind of heaviness in Malik's voice, as though he was feeling the weight of his coming adulthood. Manhood. She didn't know how to help him with that particular part of his growing up, but a good person was a good person. She was certainly up for helping him with that.

"It's a lot of responsibility, Malik. But I know you can handle it. And you're smart enough to ask for help when you need it. Those kids are lucky to have you, and I bet they know it."

"Man! What I wouldn't do for a piece of your baked chicken and a biscuit and some garlic mashed potatoes and broccoli with . . ."

Blanche knew there were mothers who'd be thinking about how to send this boy a care package full of his favorite foods about now. She felt fortunate not to be one of them. "Soon's you come home we'll have an all favorites dinner," she said.

They talked a minute or two more about the food and the state of Malik's socks and underwear. When she hung up, Blanche felt cushioned from the sharp edges of her fight with Ardell. Malik was a child who made parenting worth the effort. She didn't know where he was going, but she knew he'd get there.

She washed and seeded the peppers and began slicing and chopping them, giving herself over to what she was doing until she, the knife, and the peppers performed a perfect dance whose tempo was set by the movements of her hands and arms. She rested in the comfort of her momentarily quiet mind until the phone rang again.

Blanche gasped as she realized who it was. She excused herself to the knife and the peppers and answered the phone.

"Woman, you are harder to reach than perfection," Thelvin told her.

"Hey, Thelvin, how you doing?" Blanche was a tad flustered. She'd known it was Thelvin on the phone before she answered. There was no denying what that meant. "I got your message," she said.

"And I got yours, but I'm tired of messages and thinking about you. And I needed a break from those crazy Amtrak white boys. So I switched schedules with a brother who owed me a favor. I'm back in town for a couple days. What say I pick you up in an hour or so."

"Sounds interesting, Thelvin, but not tonight, thanks." Despite the distance Malik's call had put between Blanche and her fight with Ardell, Blanche was feeling a bit too needy to play fast and loose with Thelvin. She also didn't like his thinking that, just because he'd decided to change his schedule, she'd be waiting for him. He should have called her first.

Thelvin was silent for so long Blanche asked if he was still on the line. "Sorry. Just disappointed, I guess."

He sounded like it, too. She could change her mind. But every one of her slave ancestors set up a howl at the very idea of letting somebody else decide who she should see and when. It was more important for Thelvin to understand this about her than it was to play out some romance thing where he had to see her when he decided he had to see her.

"What about tomorrow?" he asked. "You still too busy to see me?"

"I didn't say I was busy. I just said not tonight."

"So you're not busy. You just don't want to see me, is that it?"

"Hey—where you going with this, Thelvin? You aint trying to say the only reason I can have for not seeing you is being busy? What about being tired? Or having a headache? Or just wanting to stay home by myself? You got to understand, I like you a lot, but I can't be on call. I . . ."

"Leo got anything to do with this?" he asked as if she hadn't even spoken.

"You're way out of line, Thelvin, way out. This aint about Leo, it's about who I am."

"You didn't answer my question."

"I'm hanging up now," she told him. "You give me a call when you aint got me confused with a piece of property you own somewhere."

She didn't wait to see if he was going to call back, just slammed out her front door, needing either to walk or to scream. Damned stupid-assed male! Who the hell did he think he was? Just because she liked him, just because he'd screwed her until she'd run out of orgasms, didn't give him the right to think she was going to leap every time he said *Up!* If she saw him every time he wanted, he'd probably take that to mean he could tell her what to do with the time she didn't spend with him. Men!

She walked the perimeter of Farleigh's black community—over to First Avenue, around the corner to Cornwell, and along Green Street. She was calmer now and willing to admit, at least to herself, that part of her irritation with Thelvin was due to her having known he was on the phone before she answered it. This only happened when she cared about people. Was she ready for him to be this important to her? She stepped up her pace as if affection could be outraced. Tiredness overtook her on the way down the hill on Mulberry Street behind Shiloh Baptist Church. She reduced her speed, hardly glancing at the pickup truck turning slowly onto

Mulberry from First Street. She was thinking about how Shiloh Baptist Church, like so much of the town, seemed smaller to her now than when she used to get in trouble for playing in the ditch that . . . The truck sped up. People drove like they didn't have as much sense as a warthog! Good thing she was on the opposite side of the road. There were no sidewalks here, but she was well out of its way.

Except that the truck was veering in her direction, heading right for her.

Blanche ran toward the remembered ditch that had separated the church's property from the street and hoped it was still there.

A car horn blared.

Sweet Ancestors! She didn't see the ditch. The truck was so close she was sure she could feel the heat from its headlights. There! There! She threw herself into the narrow weed-filled furrow just as the truck rolled over it. She lay sideways, looking up at the wheel of the truck, not five inches from her head. Was it stuck? Would the driver come at her on foot? She choked on fumes as the truck's engine revved, the truck reversed. Should she get up? The blaring car horn made it harder to think. She was wedged in too tightly to reach her pepper spray. She braced herself.

"Stop! Stop," a man shouted.

Blanche heard the truck moving but it didn't come toward her. She lay there panting.

"You cracker bastard!" A car door slammed, footsteps came running toward her. Thelvin was standing over her with a baseball bat in his right hand. He threw it aside and dropped to his knees. "Are you all right, Blanche? Oh Christ, are you . . ."

She managed a nod to let him know she was better than she'd expected to be. He helped her out of the ditch that was both more shallow and narrower than she remembered.

"I saw him heading for you, that son of a bitch. He coulda killed you! Fucking racist dog! They beat a young black kid half to death last year!" Thelvin's voice sounded stuck in his throat. He hugged and stroked her, rocking her gently. Blanche laid her head on his shoulder. Thelvin held her while she cried from the pain in her side; over almost being run down; and for joy at the sight of Thelvin. She cried so hard she nearly drowned the question of what he was doing there.

Thelvin was still ranting about the racists in and around Farleigh as he helped her into the house. While he rattled on, he helped her undress, filled the tub with perfect-temperature bathwater, helped her ease into the tub, brought her a drink, and sat with her while she soaked away most of the soreness, although she was left with a large, tender bruise on her right thigh.

"Blanche, you got to be more careful. You can't be roaming around alone at night! Farleigh's changed," Thelvin said, helping her out of the tub. "More people, more crime. And these racists! We gon have to do something about them. I swear they must be breeding like minks, so many of 'em popping up around here. A brother I know in Rocky Mount told me . . ."

Blanche looked down at the top of Thelvin's head while he patted her legs dry and continued to talk. I gotta tell him, she thought. It felt like bad luck to let him think she'd been attacked for racial reasons when she knew otherwise. But before she did anything else, she wanted to talk to Mumsfield and Archibald.

When Thelvin had settled her in bed, Blanche asked for the phone and her handbag. Thelvin gave her a quizzical look but handed them to her without comment. She found Mumsfield's number and called him. No one answered. She tried again.

"What's going on, Blanche?"

She looked up at him and saw worry written on his face plain as a strawberry birthmark.

Blanche put the phone down. "I know who did it."

"Did . . . You mean who tried to run you down?" Thelvin moved closer to the bed. "Who? Tell me."

"It's . . ." She motioned for him to sit on the bed beside her. "I've been doing a favor, well, some work, really, for somebody who . . ."

"Why the hell you talking about work? You said you knew who'd tried to run you down. I want to know . . ."

"I'm trying to tell you, Thelvin!" Slowly, she explained to him what she'd been doing for Archibald, and her last conversation with Karen Palmer, but didn't mention David Palmer.

By the time she'd finished, Thelvin had jumped up from the side of the bed to pace the room. "A threatening phone call and a rock through . . . You should have told me, Blanche! I could have . . . That no-good bitch! I don't believe in striking women, but if I could get my hands on her I might change my mind."

"Not to worry," Blanche told him. "I intend to take care of that myself."

Thelvin stopped and stared at her. "You got more parts than a airplane! Why the hell didn't you tell me . . . And why're you even fooling around with some white man who . . ."

Blanche told him about her relationship with Mumsfield and his family. "And I'm getting paid, too."

Thelvin squinted at her in a way she didn't like. His lips curled into something that was definitely not a smile. "Damn! You a regular *Murder, She Wrote*! I'm scared of you!"

Blanche cringed. She hated that scared-of-you talk from men. She knew "I-don't-think-I-can-control-you" when she heard it, no matter what words were used.

Still no answer at Mumsfield's number, so she called Archibald. She'd wanted to tell Mumsfield first, but it was more important for her to get hold of somebody with enough clout to stifle that girl right now.

"Forgive me for not calling you," Archibald said when she announced herself. "I had every intention of letting you know as soon as I heard, but . . ."

"Excuse me, Archibald. I don't know what you're talking about. I called because you got to do something about that Karen Palmer. She . . ."

"You mean Karen Palmer Carter don't you? Or if you prefer, Mrs. Mumsfield Carter III."

"What? What? When?"

"What's going on?" Thelvin whispered. Blanche motioned him to be quiet.

". . . telegram, of all things, from Mumsfield. Yesterday. He said they'd decided not to wait. They're honeymooning in Hawaii. They may go on to Tahiti. Mumsfield always wanted to travel. What was it that you wanted me to do something about?"

Blanche felt bad for Mumsfield. She hoped his marriage worked out, but he wasn't her major concern. If Karen married Mumsfield yesterday, she had no reason to try to have Blanche run down tonight. She'd already gotten what she wanted. But if not Karen, who? It could be David Palmer, but Blanche didn't think so—or maybe she only thought that because he hadn't been responsible for the phone and rock threats. But if not him . . .

"It's . . . it can wait till the morning. I'll call you." She hung up.

She looked up at Thelvin, who was fidgeting by the bed, watching her closely.

"Looks like you may be right." She told him about Mumsfield and Karen eloping. "Maybe it was just your everyday American-as-apple-pie racist nut who tried to run me down."

"Thank God!" Thelvin sank back down on the bed. "I mean, at least it wasn't somebody out for you personally, somebody likely to keep trying till they get it right. Those crazy crackers attack whichever black person they happen to see. That's why you can't be strolling around after dark like . . ."

Blanche nodded and half listened and thought of telling Thelvin about David Palmer. She didn't know what Thelvin would do with that information, but, judging from the you-need-to-stay-in-after-dark-and-let-me-protect-you bullshit he was giving her right now, she was pretty sure she wouldn't like it.

Do Friendless Orphans
Have More Fun?

Blanche was tempted to pretend to herself that she'd simply let Thelvin spend the night as opposed to having wanted him to spend the night. But she was never good at self-lies.

She was relieved that she hadn't had to tell him that being nearly run over did not put her in the mood for sex. It wasn't until morning that she'd felt his hardening penis knocking against her thigh. They made slow, gentle love without getting up to brush their teeth first. Afterwards, they lay with their hands and legs touching. Blanche listened to the early-morning quiet laced with birdsong and enjoyed the relaxation and sense of well-being that multiple orgasms produce. She lay that way for as long as her mind allowed, then turned on her side to face Thelvin.

"I'm sure glad you were over here last night, but why were you?"

Thelvin shifted his eyes toward her but didn't move his head. She fought the urge to play with the scant and graying hair on his chest.

"I was heading here."

Blanche sat up. "Why? I'd already told you I didn't want to go out."

Thelvin looked away. "I know. But I thought if . . ."

"If I saw you I'd fall down drooling?" Blanche reminded herself the man had probably saved her life last night, but it was too late to keep her voice free of irritation.

Thelvin just looked at her in the way she'd seen other men do—as though they could stare her into either agreeing with them or forgetting what she was pissed off about. Blanche got out of bed, put on her robe, and went to the bathroom. She was a bit sore, but better than last night.

Thelvin was sitting on the side of the bed when she came out. "Now you're mad." He sounded as though she couldn't possibly have any reason for being so.

"You want to use the bathroom before we have us a little talk?" she asked him.

Wariness squinted Thelvin's eyes. Once in the bathroom, he took the time to have a shower. Blanche concentrated on doing her exercises to keep from getting even more angry. She began talking the moment he opened the bathroom door.

"Thelvin, when I say I don't want to see you, I also don't want you to show up at my house to try to change my mind. No means no. You got a problem with that?"

"Don't be mad, baby." He tried to put his arms around her waist. Blanche held him away.

"I'm not a baby or a sex nut, so a laying on of hands aint going to help the situation. I need for you to take this seriously. You have to understand that . . ." Something that looked to her like guilt flickered across Thelvin's face, and Blanche lost her thought to another, more upsetting one. She jabbed her finger at him: "You were coming over last night to see if Leo was here, weren't you?"

Thelvin shifted his eyes away from her. "What makes you think that?"

"Just tell me, Thelvin."

Silence.

"Thelvin!"

"I just wanted to know if you two were still . . . I thought maybe you didn't want to tell me, so . . ."

The air in the room changed. All the little wisps of leftover lust dissolved. The last tendrils of the tenderness and peace of afterglow dribbled out the window.

"Sit down, Thelvin. Let me tell you about Irma, a woman I worked for when I lived in Harlem." She sat on the bed next to him. "Irma was about my age, but had a different life. College, Peace Corps. She was a schoolteacher when I worked for her. She could only afford me once a month or so and needed me every day. She was married to a city bus driver, a widower with six small children. They'd been married about a year when I started cleaning for her. To make a long story short, it turns out that bus driver was a suspicious man. He listened in on her phone calls, followed her, checked up to make sure she was going where she said she was going. The last time I worked for her, she told me he'd took to coming to her class, just sitting in the back of the room watching her. Next thing I heard about her was some man on the radio talking about how her husband had blown her brains out."

Thelvin looked as though she'd slapped him. "I know you aint thinking I'd do no crazy shit like that!?"

"Irma's husband didn't start out by shooting her. He started out being jealous, not trusting her, checking up on her. Then he lost it."

"Yeah, Blanche, but I would never . . ."

"I know most jealous people don't go crazy and kill somebody. That aint what I'm saying. But how's a person supposed to know which kind of jealous person they're dealing with? I mean, being suspicious of somebody all the time is still . . ."

"Well, maybe he thought he had a reason, maybe she really was cheating on him, maybe . . ."

Blanche stood up and glared down on him. "No matter what she was doing, he didn't have a right to treat her like she was a old shirt he could rip up to keep somebody else from wearing it!"

"No, Blanche, no. I'm not saying he was right. I'm just saying . . ." Thelvin frowned at her. "I useta go with a woman who was always on me about how I didn't care what she did. Now I'm being accused of . . ." He shook his head again.

"We aint all the same, Thelvin. Although I doubt there's many women out here who want somebody checking up on them like they're a child or a . . . and, anyway, it don't matter what some other woman wants. I aint speaking for women, I'm talking about Blanche. My body and my time is my business. *My* business, not yours or anybody else's. I got a right to do what I want with any willing adult I like, anywhere and anytime I feel like it."

"Blanche, don't talk like a . . . I know you aint that kinda woman."

"That's where you're wrong, Thelvin. That's exactly the kind of woman I am! And if you . . ."

Thelvin held up his hands. "Wait a minute. If I hadn't come by last night when that truck was trying to run you down . . ."

Blanche walked across the room and looked out the window without seeing a thing before turning back to Thelvin. "I'm not saying I aint grateful for everything you did last night. But I'm prepared to take my chances in the world without being protected. And you were wrong to come over to spy on me, or whatever you was planning to do!"

Thelvin looked at Blanche in a way that made her mouth go dry. "I don't know, Blanche. Maybe I aint . . . I know you aint weak. I know you don't want nobody trying to run your life. I respect that. I like that about you. But what about needing somebody sometime? Aint that important, too? I mean, if you can't lean on me a little when somebody's trying to kill you, then when?"

They stared at each other, trying to maintain stoniness without cracking at the prospect of ending what they'd only just begun.

"I gotta go," Thelvin said when Blanche didn't answer him. He slammed the door as he left.

It wasn't stubbornness or anger that had kept Blanche silent. So much had gone through her mind she couldn't sort out what to say. Thelvin's questions had nothing to do with her demand that he not check up on her. His questioning her might just have been his way of changing the subject. But what he'd asked had plenty to do with who she was and where they were headed. Maybe she was wrong. Maybe, despite her belief that she'd quarantined Palmer and what he'd done to her in such a way as to keep his poison from seeping into her relationships with men, there'd been some leakage. More suspicion. And caution. But that was okay. Probably normal, and hadn't stopped her from seeing him, or other men before him. What concerned her was the recognition that if she'd never been raped Thelvin would still have had cause to ask those same questions. She flipped through the mental album of her relationship with Leo over the years, and with other men she'd known, and saw herself guarding her borders even when she wasn't under attack. My own little third-world country, she thought. She knew she wasn't alone in keeping a sharp lookout where men were concerned. She didn't know a woman with sense who wasn't riding shotgun on her own feelings, on guard against men who borrowed money and disappeared, who claimed to be madly in love with her while a woman across town was carrying his baby, who were looking for a mama, a tit, a free ride. It was a lot for one man to overcome, and a lot for a woman bent on not being anybody's fool to overlook. But had this carefulness become something harder, sharper, and so second-nature to her that Ardell was right—she was afraid of letting a man get close to her? She thought back to her car ride with Leo and remembered asking herself if she was afraid to grow old with someone just as Leo was afraid of growing old alone. She hadn't given herself an answer. She still didn't have one.

More than anything, she wished she could call Ardell, talk all of this mess out with her, but she and Ardell hadn't talked since their argument. Blanche hadn't even had a chance to tell her about David Palmer and Maybelle Jenkins. Blanche picked up the phone and put it down again. She wanted their next contact to be face to face—when Ardell came to pick up the couscous salad.

What could be worse than being on the outs with her best friend and, yes, damnit, her man? That final admission sent her scurrying for Archibald's phone number. Anything to distract her from where these thoughts might lead.

When she got him, she told him about Karen and Seth, the leave-town phone message, and the rock through her window.

"Good God! You should have told me immediately! This is an outrage, a . . ."

First Thelvin, now Archibald. Blanche knew Archibald was just showing his concern, but she vowed to throw up on the shoes of the next man who told her she should have reported the threats to him. "Calm down, Archibald. At least she wasn't responsible for last night." She told him about the truck.

"Blanche! Really! I . . ."

"Wait, Archibald. Just listen. I thought Karen was behind the truck that tried to hit me, but since she'd already got Mumsfield . . ."

"Yes, I see what you mean. However, the other threats are serious enough in themselves to . . . And she still might have wanted you dead to make sure you didn't tell Mumsfield. The fact that they're married doesn't . . ."

"Look, Archibald, none of this is going to make Mumsfield give her up, I'd bet on that," Blanche told him. "And it's just her word against mine."

"Yes, you're probably right. But surely . . . Was there anything else?"

"Nothing as serious as this." She justified not telling Archibald about David and Maybelle on the basis that it had nothing to do with Karen, although she doubted Archibald would agree. Anyway, Archibald and everyone else would know all about it as soon as Bobby spoke out.

"Tell me what else you found," Archibald said.

"Well, she's got a reputation for sleeping with her girlfriends' men." She didn't tell him what Karen's friends called her, because she didn't want to have to explain what it meant. "Seems she's hardly ever had a man who wasn't going with one of her girlfriends. They make jokes about it." Blanche took a couple sips of water.

"Regular little round-heels!"

Blanche couldn't remember the last time she'd heard that old easy-lay term. "She's got some kind of copycat thing, I guess."

"Pitiful but not certifiable, unfortunately," Archibald said.

"And I know from having had the pleasure of her company at lunch that she don't think much of black folks, although that probably makes her average around here, and most black folks probably feel the same about her. I sure do." Blanche waited for Archibald's chuckle to subside before she went on. "Karen's so-called friends are probably happy she finally got a man of her own, although they say Mumsfield's a fool with no brains and too much money. Some of the younger menfolk in your circle talk about her as very used goods."

"It's not too late to get her to sign an agreement, armed with this information. I thank you, Blanche. I may not have been able to stop the marriage, but all is not lost. I'm indebted to you."

"No need to be. I'll send you a bill later this week." She'd considered charging him less since she'd used his money to dig up dirt on David Palmer, but, after having to deal with Karen, Blanche decided she deserved combat pay.

"Fine, fine. Send it to my home." He gave her his address.

Blanche hung up the phone. "Well, that's that." She felt as though she'd finally dropped a heavy bag she'd been toting for weeks. It was all over—not just the Karen/Mumsfield business but, more important, the David Palmer piece. Bobby was soon to turn Palmer into dead meat—or at least arrested meat. She was looking forward to the day when Palmer's name was plastered all over the newspapers. But what was taking Bobby so long? Cold feet? Or had Palmer convinced him to keep his mouth shut?

"We gonna fight today?" Ardell asked when she walked in an hour later. She fiddled with the stem of her spectacles, the way she did when she was nervous.

Blanche held out a hand to her friend. "Maybe not today, but soon enough."

Ardell took Blanche's hand. "Yeah, 'cause we both got too much mouth," Ardell said.

Blanche nodded. "We worse than family."

"And just as good," Ardell said.

Blanche got up to give her a hug.

"Why you moving so stiff?"

Blanche told her about the rock through her window, and finally the close call with the truck.

"Damn, Blanche! How could you not tell me, how could you look me in the face knowing your life was in . . . I thought you got the shutters because of the phone call when all the time you . . ."

"I didn't really think my life was in danger, not until the truck; then . . ."

"I don't care! You should have told me about the rock when it happened. I'm your best friend! You can't keep stuff from me like that!"

"You're right, Ardell, you're right." Blanche knew that she'd feel exactly the same if their positions were reversed, but she wasn't a total fool and wanted Ardell to acknowledge that. "If I'd really thought I was in danger, I'd have told you about it right away."

"Thought! You didn't think, that's the problem. You just shut me out without—"

"No! I didn't want you to worry, Ardell. Okay? It was that simple. I know how you are, you'd want to—"

"Bullshit! This isn't the first time, Blanche! You remember when you thought you had a lump in your breast, the time you—"

"I'm not a child, Ardell. I don't have to report every—"

"You're getting as closemouthed as your mother!"

Her mother! Blanche was dumbstruck. She'd thought Ardell was going too far with her, holding out complaints. But if she was comparing Blanche with Miz Cora, and finding them near twins, this was serious, at least to Ardell.

"I apologize, Ardell." Even though she wasn't sure Ardell was being totally fair, she recognized Ardell's need for their friendship to be all that it had always been. It was a need Blanche shared.

Ardell shook her head in a way that seemed to dispel some of the tension between them. "Sometimes you act like you aint got as much sense as a . . . Where's Karen Palmer now?"

"Hawaii, Archibald said."

"I hope a big wave washes her ass to West Hell!" She sighed and looked at Blanche. "Well, aint nothing I can do about her, no sense going on about it now, but I swear, Blanche, if you ever . . . if anything had happened to you . . ."

"I won't hold out on you again," Blanche told her. "I promise."

Ardell didn't look like she necessarily believed her.

Blanche was eager to get on to her other news. "I got something else to tell you, Ardell. Daisy says that piece of thing I found in Palmer's place in Durham is from a barrette she bought for Maybelle Jenkins!"

"Humm. How does she know it's the same barrette?"

"Well, she doesn't *know* know, but she's sure. And you saw the thing. It aint likely it belonged to somebody in Palmer's social set, is it?"

"So you think Maybelle's the woman Palmer was buying flowers for and . . ."

"Sure looks like it. Woman across the street from the place even described Maybelle, only I didn't make the connection at the time. But that aint all! Daisy says Bobby's got proof that somebody else was with Maybelle the night she died, and guess what that proof is?"

Ardell looked blank.

"Daisy said it was something from a key chain!"

Ardell still looked blank.

Blanche realized she hadn't told Ardell about David Palmer's missing Sons of Farleigh key.

"And you just now telling me about this, too?" Ardell looked disgusted. And hurt. "What else you hiding from me, Blanche? How long's this been going on? I thought we . . ."

"I'm sorry, Ardell, but there was so much happening with the catering business, and I wasn't really sure the key thing was important, even though I had a feeling . . ."

"But how do you know that's what Bobby found?"

"Well, what else could it be? I mean, Bobby finds something from a key chain when he finds Maybelle's body, and the man Maybelle's screwing around with is missing something from his key chain. What else can it be? There aint that much coincidence in the world!"

"Oh yes there is!" Ardell said. "But if you're right about what Bobby's got, you're home free! All you got to do is wait and watch Palmer go down, the no-good bastard! The whole damned family sucks!"

"Yeah. I'm just sorry somebody had to die for David Palmer to get his."

"Humm, well, I'm just glad *you* didn't get hurt." Ardell gave Blanche a look full of the affection that went with that gratitude. "You were real lucky, Thelvin showing up like that, I mean."

The muscles in Blanche's shoulders tightened. "Yeah, lucky. But, like everything else, it's got its down side."

"So you weren't expecting him," Ardell said, as if she'd guessed as much.

"I'd already told him I didn't want to see him. He admitted he was coming over because he thought Leo might be here."

"Uh-oh. I know that stressed you out!"

"I told him about Irma."

"Humm, did he get it?"

"Time will tell, but I aint putting no money on it."

"Humm, well, you wouldn't, would you?"

"What's that supposed to mean?"

"I talked to my cousin Nadine," Ardell said instead of answering Blanche's question directly. "She lives over Durham and is in everybody's business."

"And?"

"I asked her did she know Thelvin."

Blanche leaned forward. "What'd she say?"

"Humm, well, she knows a woman, I think Sheila's her name. Anyway, this woman went out with Thelvin for a while. It didn't last long."

"What happened?"

"He didn't want to get married, for one thing, and she didn't like his work schedule either."

Blanche waited for her to go on.

"Well, she did say his jealousy thing seriously got on her nerves. Nothing violent," Ardell hurriedly added. "But a whole lot of questions and checking up on—kinda stuff that makes you think he thinks you're some kinda slut or liar, is what she said."

"See? See? That's just what I'm talking about! Maybe it's time for me to back off."

"Humm, yeah, but Nadine also said Sheila wishes she had him back. She's still talking about all the flowers he sent her and the dinners and dancing and whatnot. Don't find a lot of men his age up for that kinda thing."

"Oh, you his mouthpiece now?"

"You know better. I just don't want you to make your move too soon, know what I mean?"

"Yeah, but I don't want to hold on to him just because somebody else thinks he's a prize!"

Ardell pushed up her spectacles, leaned in close, and gave Blanche's eyes a thorough search. "Something else happened. What?"

"He asked me if leaning on . . ." Blanche hesitated. Just talking about it made her want to squirm. "He wanted to know if needing somebody aint as important as being independent," she said all in a rush, as though the words might burn her tongue.

"Damn! He's serious, Blanche. Black man singing 'Lean on Me' is sho nuff . . ."

"Unless he's a joker just waiting for me to have a lean so he can jump out the way and let me land on my ass!" There was a rawness in her own words and voice that startled Blanche.

"Maybe," Ardell said. "But there's only one way to find out."

Blanche turned away from Ardell's steady gaze. "I don't know, Ardell, I don't know." But she did know that, despite his jealousy and his asking questions that made her want to run, she liked him, really liked him.

Ardell was gone when Blanche became aware that her mother was at the door.

"Come on in, Mama," Blanche called before her mother could knock or open the door.

"I wish you wouldn't do that, Blanche. Knowing people are coming before they get here is the work of the devil and not the Lord."

"It aint really work at all, Mama. It just happens. You know that."

Miz Cora rolled her eyes and sucked her teeth with a loud "Tsk."

Blanche was sure her mother was sorry for the day Blanche had heard her admitting that Blanche had inherited the ability to sense the nearness of loved ones from Miz Cora herself. It was one piece of their shared history that was out of Miz Cora's control.

"You lookin kinda peaked. You gittin enough sleep? You aint comin down with nothin, is you?"

Damn! The woman didn't miss a thing. Never had. She might not know exactly what was up, but she always knew when something was going on. "No, Mama. I'm fine. I fell last night, is all. Got a couple bruises." Blanche held her breath and hoped her mother wouldn't ask for details that would force Blanche to be creative in avoiding telling either the truth or a lie.

Miz Cora shook her head and began removing covered dishes from her bag. "You always was clumsy as a newborn calf. Never understood it. Don't take after me! Why, when I was a girl, I was just as sure-footed as a mountain goat; why, I remember one time . . ."

"How's Sauda doing, Mama?" Blanche had already heard the story so many times she could lip-sync it.

"She's fine. Settlin right in. Good company, too, but eats like a sick bird. That's how come I got all these here leftovers. I know you aint eatin right, and I don't want this food to go to waste. I brought you some potato salad, some of my meatloaf, and these here greens cooked with smoked turkey, just like you like 'em."

Blanche was pleased and surprised that her mother had taken her advice about not using fatty pork in her greens.

"I been cooking greens like this ever since Doc Pinkney told me I needed to watch my diet if I wanted to keep my pressure from going up. I cut out some salt, too, even though I aint worried about no high blood pressure. I'm too old to be lettin things get on my nerves till I break out in a sweat. Even when I find out my own chile is runnin around this here town gittin in some rich white man's business like she forgot who she is and what world she live in, I don't allow myself to git all upset. No, I don't. I git down on my knees and ask the Lord, who is known for protectin fools and sinners, to take my child under his wing and keep her from doin somethin that will get her hurt, thrown in jail, or make me any more worried than I already am, and her a grown woman who shouldn't be causin her poor old mother so much grief!" Miz Cora pried off another lid.

Blanche had wanted to set her mother straight on a couple of points, but as Miz Cora continued to talk, Blanche was more mesmerized by her mother's ability to talk nonstop than she was interested in interrupting. Please, please, sweet Ancestors, let this moment stay in my mind when Taifa or Malik gives me the blues. Let me turn into a floor lamp before I drive them screaming out of the house to block out my voice. She took a deep breath.

"Somebody's paying me," she told her mother. She knew her mother would be impressed, or at least surprised, whether she admitted it or not.

"What!?"

"That's right, Mama. Somebody's paying me!" Blanche said again, even though David wasn't the Palmer she'd been paid to check on and her stint snooping on Karen was officially over.

"Payin you!? Payin you!? There's a fool out there payin you to sneak around askin people questions like you own a sheriff's uniform? Well, whoever it is needs somebody to look after his money, and you"—she pointed a bony finger at Blanche—"need somebody to look after your life!" Miz Cora looked at Blanche as though she thought her daughter had finally lost the last of her mother wit.

Blanche pulled herself up to her full seated height. "I got somebody to manage my life, Mama. Me! It is *my* life, remember?"

Blanche could tell from Miz Cora's expression that she was as surprised by Blanche's tone as Blanche was herself. There was no anger in Blanche's voice, none of the whininess that crept in when she felt reduced to little-girlhood by her mother. Instead there was certainty, and just a hint of "I'm sick of this shit," in her tone. Miz Cora was looking at Blanche as though it had been a long time since she'd seen her.

"Well," her mother said in a way that was as much a sigh as a word, "you is a grown woman. You *s'posed* to know what you doing. I hope you do, 'cause I sure don't, and I . . ."

"Thank you, Mama, for your good wishes. Now, how about some of them greens?" Blanche gave herself a mental pat on the back.

Miz Cora looked like she had more to say, but she just pursed her lips and turned to the cabinet. She opened doors until she found the plates, took one down from the shelf, and dished out some greens. She put a slice of meatloaf and two spoonfuls of potato salad on the plate as well. "Need to keep up your strength," she said. "All that snoopin around you got to do." She handed the plate to Blanche.

Blanche laughed. "Mama, you a mess!" She took the plate from her mother. It was possible to get a foothold in an argument with her mother, as she'd done a moment ago, but there was only room for one of them to have the upper hand, and Mama had that solidly covered. Still, Blanche was pleased with how their conversation had gone—something almost as rare as free money.

"How's my grandbabies?" Miz Cora put the kettle on and found the tin of teabags.

"They're all right." Blanche told her mother some of what she'd heard from the children—one topic of conversation that kept her mother all ears and no mouth. Talk of children moved Blanche's mind in another direction.

"There's some kids who live across the street," Blanche began. "Three little girls, just as cute and bright as they can be." Blanche went on to tell her mother the story of the two visits from the girls and what was going on in their house. "I don't understand a woman like that, let her girls see some man using her to polish the floors." She looked at her mother. Miz Cora was standing at the sink, her back to Blanche.

"Ardell gave me all kinds of grief for not going over there and trying to help that woman," Blanche said. "I told her I thought it was the kids who needed help." Her words sounded cold and mean dropped in the room just drylongso. "I mean, I know she's the one who's getting beat up, but the kids don't have nobody on their side if both their parents are . . ." She wasn't sure if her words sounded lame because they were or because of the loudness of her mother's silence, a silence Blanche couldn't read.

"After all," Blanche said, "she's a grown woman. All she's got to do is leave!"

Miz Cora drew herself up well beyond her normal height and turned to face Blanche. "You don't know nothin 'bout it! Not a blessed thing!" Each word was as sharp as a well-honed blade. Blanche was all attention.

"You aint never even lived with no man! You don't know how . . . and you aint had no kids either! Not your *own* kids. You don't know what . . ."

Blanche opened her mouth to protest.

"No!" Miz Cora shouted before Blanche could speak. "I know you love them two you raisin, but you didn't birth 'em. You didn't have 'em with some man who turned on you like . . ." Tears shimmered in Miz Cora's eyes but seemed unwilling to fall.

"Mama?" Blanche rose and went to stand in front of her mother. "Mama?" Blanche put her hands on her mother's shoulders. Miz Cora's body jerked. She made a sound, more like a strangled scream than a sob, as those reluctant tears finally tumbled down her face. Blanche put her arms around her mother and held her close while Miz Cora sobbed in a way Blanche had not seen since Rosalie, Blanche's sister, had died.

"I never wanted you to know," Miz Cora said when her tears subsided. "But when you started talkin all stupid 'bout that poor woman across the street . . ." Miz Cora wiped her eyes and nose. "You were too young to re-member him much. He never struck me in front of you. Especially you. He loved you both, but you were his favorite. So I . . ."

Pain pricked Blanche's entire body, as though all of her circulation had been cut off. Her mother's words ricocheted around her brain, bouncing off Blanche's attempts to make them mean something other than what her mother was saying. Her mother. Her father.

"Did Rosalie know?"

Miz Cora took another tissue from the box on the bureau.

"Did Rosalie know?"

"I wasn't going to tell you," Miz Cora said again. "He loved y'all like you was made of gold, especially you. You look so much like him you coulda spit you outa his mouth."

Blanche recalled pictures of her father and wondered why she'd never noticed their likeness. Too busy wanting to find Mama in me, she thought.

"He said he loved me, too," her mother went on, "but when he was mad about somethin on the job, or foolin around with that alcohol, he acted like I was the most hateful, ugly black thing in the world. Just like he said I was. That's what he always called me when he was mad. A ugly black thing."

Something in the way Miz Cora said "thing" nearly stopped Blanche's heart.

"Oh, Mama! I'm so sorry. So, so sorry."

Miz Cora sat down while Blanche made her a cup of tea. "Is he still living" she asked.

"Nah. I heard he died a year or two before Rosalie. Up in Cleveland. Heart attack."

Blanche poured tea for both of them. She added extra sugar to their cups, as though they were shock victims in need of a boost. They drank in silence. Blanche had plenty she wanted to ask, but her mother looked worn out from what had already been said. "You all right, Mama?"

Miz Cora sighed and nodded. "Got myself all worked up. Wears a body out."

Blanche reached across the table and patted her mother's hand. "I know it was hard for you, Mama, I . . ."

Miz Cora pulled her hand away and rose. Her eyes reminded Blanche of locked gates, as though Miz Cora had barricaded herself inside and wanted no visitors. "I got to be goin."

Blanche nodded. Of course. Mama was still the same person. Before the night was over, she'd probably be kicking herself for having talked at all. Blanche offered to walk her home, or call Ardell and get her a ride, but her mother insisted on leaving the same way she came. Blanche watched her walk away, her head high, her back as straight as a plumb line.

"Thanks for telling me, Mama!" It didn't make her happy to know her father was a wife-beater, but there was no part of her own history she didn't want to know.

If Miz Cora heard Blanche, she didn't act like it.

When she shut the front door, all that Blanche had been feeling and had held back from her mother was waiting for her. She closed her eyes and laid her head against the door. Her chest was so tight she could hardly breathe. All her adult life she had been asking and searching for a glimpse of the person who was Cora, not Mama. Today, she'd gotten her wish. She now had a picture of Miz Cora the woman, a picture that sent Blanche rushing across the room to fling herself on the bed. She pulled the pillow over her head, but it didn't stop her from seeing her mother being slapped and called a *thing* in her own house by a man who claimed to love her. Here was independent, take-no-prisoners, stronger-than-truth Mama wailing and cowering in a corner of her own kitchen.

She added her mother to the circle of bruised women that included

Blanche herself, her neighbor across the street, poor dead Maybelle, Daisy, even Ardell, back in the days. She wondered if there were women in the world who hadn't been slapped, or probed, or punched, or shouted out or down, or at least scared for half a second when some man—on purpose or by accident—let her see, in the way he stood over her, or punched his fist into his open palm, or inflated his chest and moved a step closer, just how their argument or difference of opinion could easily be solved and who would win and how.

Blanche threw the pillow across the room so hard the case made a popping sound when it hit the wall. She jumped up to pace the floor as if her feet were trying to keep time with her flying thoughts. What was she going to do with this knowledge, and what was it going to do with her? Was it possible both to want to know and not to want to know something at the same time? She wanted to scream, to, yes, scream at Mama, until she . . . what? Was no longer a woman who stayed with a man who beat her? No longer a woman who married such a man? No longer a woman who had caused Blanche to lose her father? Unfair, unfair. She knew that, but what if Mama had left after the first time he'd hit her? What if, after that first time, Daddy had decided to change his ways to keep his family? But he could have decided that at any time. Just like he decided to beat the woman he claimed to love. Mama didn't create him.

Her father! It explained so much, like why Mama never wanted to talk about him. And dead now. The last of Blanche's barely acknowledged hope of someday knowing him sifted from her heart like ashes blown from a hearth, leaving a fine dusting of grief behind. He was still her father. And I look like him. What did Mama think when she looked out at me, her child, and saw the man who'd scared and beaten her? Did Mama worry that, looking so much like him, I'd be like him? Grow up pulling the wings off butterflies and bullying little kids? Is that why Mama was always on me about getting in fights and being a tomboy, about being too rough and mannish for my own good?

But why hadn't Mama ever told them? No, not them, her. Blanche was positive her sister, Rosalie, had known. Rosalie and Mama had been closer than flesh and bone. And Rosalie never told me, either. She felt a twinge of that old left-out feeling she'd had as a child when she'd come upon Mama and Rosalie huddled together, their heads almost touching, as they worked over a piece of sewing or put together a pie. The shape of their heads and their smiles were so much alike that Rosalie seemed to be a miniature of their mother. Blanche suddenly remembered playing a game with Rosalie in which they made a tent with the blankets on their bed and sang songs inside it, their voices bouncing off the blankets and doubling in strength. Was that to keep out the sound of blows, of her mother begging for mercy? And had Rosalie gathered her up and taken her outside to wait out their father's storms the way the older girls across the street now did for *their* younger sister?

"Oh, Mama!" she shouted. "Damn both of y'all!"

25

Reporting and Bonding

Blanche went out on her stoop the next morning to wait for Ardell to pick her up. She looked down the street toward the house where Doretha, Murlee, and Lucinda lived. All was quiet, no one in sight. Their father's car was parked out front, though, so who knew how long this sense of peace would last. Were the girls huddled together inside, holding their breaths, tiptoeing around the house to avoid waking the monster? Blanche was both sorry and glad to be getting off the street for the rest of the day. She'd have liked to stay around to offer cookies and shelter to the girls if something jumped off over there. At the same time, she was relieved to leave. She felt the girls drawing her into a place she didn't want to go and, as an outsider, didn't belong. The pull was only made stronger by knowing what her father had done to her mother when she was a child. She began telling Ardell about him the minute she was in the car.

"Oh, sugar, I'm so sorry." Ardell reached over and patted Blanche's hand. "I always thought one day you might go looking for your daddy. Now to find out he . . . Poor Miz Cora. Who'd have thought she . . ."

"Yeah. That's just the problem I been having. It's like she's a different person from . . ."

"Well, sure," Ardell interrupted. "You still thinking about your *mother*. It was Cora White got beat up by her man—and would have whether she was your mother or not."

Leave it to Ardell. Of course. Wasn't that what she'd been thinking when Mama told her? "You're absolutely right! All these years I been wondering who Cora really is, what I was looking for was a woman who is as big, bad, and strong as my mama. There aint no such woman."

"That's right," Ardell said. "Nobody's as big and bad as your mama. Miz Cora's just a woman like any other—making mistakes, being scared, moving on anyway. Just like the rest of us."

Blanche made a mental note to call her mother later. Just to check.

Clarice was waiting outside Ardell's house when Blanche and Ardell drove up. The three of them were going to prep for a cocktail party—making finger food, slicing cheese, and so forth. Now Clarice was shifting from left foot to right and wearing a look that changed her usually pleasant face to something painful to see.

"You better get that door open before Clarice pees all over your pavement," Blanche told Ardell.

Once Clarice had emptied her bladder, she was full of talk, and had already started before she was fully in earshot: ". . . dead, Mr. Henry say." Ardell and Blanche were washing their hands at the kitchen sink as Clarice continued talking. ". . . and him not a week out of jail!"

Blanche spun around, spraying soapsuds across Ardell's spotless floor. "Dead?! Bobby Larsen? When? How?"

"Mr. Henry say last night. Car accident. Truck, really. Old piece of pickup truck come apart right under him, Mr. Henry say. Out there on Sumter Road, where that nasty curve is."

"Whole lotta people had accidents out there on that road," Ardell said. "Five or six of 'em been killed. They need to really do something about it."

"They keep sayin they going to, but . . ." Clarice shrugged.

Blanche dried her hands and went to the phone. She asked Information for the number of the cleaners where Daisy worked, then called the number and asked for Daisy.

"She's not working today," a man told her in a voice edged with irritation.

"Well, my missus said I should talk directly to her, 'cause she was real helpful," Blanche told him.

"She's supposed to be sick," the man said, his voice switching from irritated to disbelieving.

"Well, my missus don't want me to talk to nobody else, she say. . . ."

"Hold on a second." The man left the phone, then returned and gave Blanche Daisy's number.

Blanche thanked him and called Daisy. "May I speak with Daisy, please?"

"This is Daisy," she said in a voice flat as a cast-iron skillet.

"Hey, Daisy, it's Blanche White. I heard about Bobby. I just wanted to tell you how sorry I am. I know you was real fond of him."

Daisy burst into muffled sobs, as though she was trying to keep her voice down even if she couldn't stop crying.

"Ah, honey, I'm real sorry." Blanche hadn't realized that Daisy's crush on Bobby was so serious. "I know you must feel . . ."

"Don't nobody know, not even my papa. Only me, only me," Daisy said between sobs.

Blanch hesitated. Her call had been made out of concern not for Daisy but for the information Bobby had had that she hoped would nail Palmer. Just because there was no more Bobby didn't mean there was no evidence, and Daisy was her only road to it. But she was reluctant to tread on the girl's grief.

"Look, when you coming back to work? I'll come by and see you. Or maybe we could meet at that place where we had a Coke?"

"I'll be in tomorrow," Daisy said in a whisper. "I'll meet you at twelve. I gotta hang up. . . . Comin, Pa," Blanche heard Daisy call out before the line went dead.

"What's that all about?" Ardell wanted to know. Clarice seconded the question with her eyes.

"I told y'all about Daisy." Blanche repeated what she'd already told them.

Ardell looked as though she might have another question, but Clarice spoke instead.

"Oh yeah," Clarice said. "Daisy the one got a crush on that Bobby. Mr. Henry say . . ."

Ardell didn't let her finish. "Girl! If I had a nickel for every time you said 'Mr. Henry,' I could retire to a life of luxury. What's the matter? You think you gonna forget the man's name?"

Clarice looked puzzled for a few seconds, then: "No, I aint scared I'll forgit it. I just like to say it." Clarice's smile was sweet and secretive.

"And what makes him worth all that?" Ardell asked.

Clarice didn't hesitate for a second. "My feet git real tired from standin mosta the time. Mr. Henry, he rub 'em every night 'fore we go to bed. With sweet oil." Clarice lowered her eyes and giggled. "Mr. Henry say I'm pretty. I know it aint true," she added as though wanting to say it before Ardell could. "But that don't matter, do it?" She looked from Ardell to Blanche. Neither of her listeners disagreed. Blanche noticed the comfortable, sure way Clarice took up her space.

Clarice turned toward the sink, then looked over her shoulder at Ardell and Blanche. "Don't never have to ask Mr. Henry to put the toilet seat down neither." She turned on the tap and washed her hands.

"Humm. You right," Ardell told her. "Man deserves to be called Mr. Henry. I'm gonna call him Mr. Henry myself!"

"I aint tryin to say he perfect, but . . ." Clarice hesitated as though she couldn't think how to say what she wanted. Finally, she shrugged. "He try to be good," she said as though that said everything, and turned back to the sink.

Blanche looked at Ardell, sure that they were both thinking about their last Thelvin conversation.

"Excuse me."

Blanche went back to the phone. She cleared her throat when Thelvin's machine came on, then said: "It's me, Blanche. I don't know the answers to your questions yet, but I'm thinking about them. What are you thinking about?"

Blanche decided to stop by her mother's instead of calling. Sauda answered the door and gave her a guilty look.

"You aint come about the job have you, Cousin?"

Damn! She'd completely forgotten to talk to Ardell about a job for Sauda. 'Cause I didn't want to deal with it, she chided herself.

"I'm sorry," Sauda said. "I should have let you know I got a placement at the school. In the library"—a word she made sound like "lie-Brie."

Blanche relaxed. "I'm glad. 'Cause I forgot to deal with it," she said, being careful to tell the truth. She couldn't afford cheap power trips, they always somehow brought her down before long.

"Your mama gone out," Sauda told her.

"Well, I guess I'll get on home, then. You take care, Sauda, and tell Mama I stopped by." Blanche turned to leave.

"You want a cool drink? I mean, I got no business asking you, it's your mama's house, and I . . ." Sauda looked away from Blanche. "I don't know nobody here, you see. Except you and Auntie Cora, and . . ."

She's lonely, too, Blanche thought. Just like Mama. Both of them here together.

"I could use a glass of water, if you don't mind." She turned and headed into the house.

"So they got other black students over there at the art school?"

"One or two." Sauda shot Blanche a look. "Stuck-up type. Speak to me once, long enough to find out I aint Michael Manley's niece and that's the end."

"I'd have thought they'd take you up. Being foreign and everything."

"Some of the whites do. Want to talk to me about reggae. I don't know a ting 'bout reggae, and that a fact. They think *I'm* stuck up."

"You getting it from both ends, girl. That's too bad."

Sauda shrugged. "I didn't think was gonna be no bed a roses. I used to sell my small pieces on the beach, wood carvings, small stone pieces, things like that, you know. I met lots of Americans. Blind as bats, most of them. Only looking at the world for how it is for them, not for other people, but . . ." Sauda shook off whatever she was going to say, and went another way. "Auntie Cora say you and Miss Ardell been friends from girls."

"Yeah, honey. We got history, me and Ardell."

"I got me a friend like that. She live in London. Trying to make it as a singer."

In the silence that followed, Blanche felt the tug on the cord that connected her to Ardell and what that connection had meant in their lives. She realized that she and Ardell hadn't spent any real fun time together since she'd been back in Farleigh. They'd been in each other's company a lot, but mostly on gigs or getting ready for gigs, where their attention was taken up with work. She decided to make a date with Ardell just to hang out.

"Ardell's got a cousin about your age, I think. I'll ask her to give you a call, show you around."

Sauda looked as though Blanche had just saved her life. "I appreciate that, Cousin."

Blanche rose to leave.

"Wait. I got a bit a something for you. It's not much, but . . ."

Sauda went upstairs and came down again. She handed Blanche something small wrapped in wrinkled tissue paper. Blanche unwrapped a dark-gray marble oval the size of a large chicken egg. But it wasn't smooth. A woman's face, heavy-featured and haughty, was carved on all sides of it in such a way that as you turned it the expression changed from haughty, to laughing, to tears and a frown. Blanche turned it over and over in her hands, wowed by both its beauty and its cleverness.

"Girl, you got something goin on here!" She gave Sauda a hug along with her thanks.

Blanche was dressing for work when Thelvin called. She took a deep, shuddery breath before she picked up the phone.

"I miss you, Blanche. I can't stand being on the outs with you," Thelvin told her before she could speak.

"Me, too," she said, aware that she was grinning fit to split her face. "I can't talk long, I gotta go to work."

"Me either. I just come in. I been out my sister's place, helping my brother-in-law put down a floor. I figured since you and me wasn't together I might as well . . . I got to go back out there, so . . ."

"What about tomorrow?" Blanche asked him. She felt shaky the minute the words were out of her mouth. She wanted to see him, but it was like a sore tooth: it didn't hurt as long as she didn't touch it. Although they still had plenty to work out, she wanted a rest from it for a minute. A little space where everything was all right. "I know!" she said. "It's time for you to meet Ardell."

26

Meeting of the Blanche
Fan Club

As the afternoon moved toward evening, Blanche became more and more tickled by her own nervousness. Anybody'd think Ardell was Mama. No. If it were Mama, she wouldn't care so much; Ardell's opinion of Thelvin was second only to Blanche's own. Don't expect her to trust him, she warned herself. You know how Ardell is. But, though Ardell wasn't exactly a cheerleader for maleness, she liked sharp people, quick people, and Thelvin was all that. And gentle, too. Blanche laid down the spatula, mindless of the smear of cream-cheese frosting it made on the table, caught up in remembering his delicate touch as he held her on the dance floor, the way his eyes seemed to light up when he saw her, as though he was both surprised and happy to be with her.

The carrot cake was ready and so was she when Thelvin came to pick her up. The three of them were going to watch *Eve's Bayou* at Ardell's house. Blanche was bringing dessert.

Ardell opened the door before they were parked. "Hey, y'all." She took the cake from Thelvin and carried it to the kitchen.

"Ardell," Blanche said when she returned, "this is Thelvin. Thelvin, this is my best friend, Ardell."

Ardell put out her hand and Thelvin shook it, but neither of them smiled. Blanche imagined she heard a sound—metal grating on metal like a fast-braking train. Oh shit! She looked from one to the other and could almost see both their backs go up. This was not love at first sight.

"I got the movie," Ardell said before Blanche could get a line on what was going on. "Sit down, sit down. Y'all want something to drink?"

They were quiet during the movie except for a chuckle, a grunt or shrug, a nod of approval. They took an intermission about halfway through so that everyone could go to the bathroom and get fresh drinks. No one had anything to say beyond "More ice?" and "Thank you," as if they'd silently agreed to keep their minds on the movie. Yet, beneath the quiet calm, Blanche could still hear that grating sound, as though Ardell and Thelvin were rubbing each other the wrong way just by being in the same room. She looked from one to the other and hoped she was imagining things.

When the movie ended, Thelvin and Ardell both stood and stretched as though it were part of watching the video. Blanche went off to the kitchen to cut the cake.

"So—what'd you think?" she asked when they all had cake in front of them and the coffee was almost done.

"I think it was . . ." Ardell and Thelvin said in unison.

"Ladies first," Thelvin said.

Blanche cringed. Ardell gave her a smirky smile.

"It was the best black movie I've seen," Ardell said.

Blanche didn't think it was better than *Daughters of the Dust*, but she didn't say so.

Thelvin stared at Ardell as though she'd just announced she was a serial killer. "How can it be the best black movie you ever seen when the major black man in it is a womanizing . . ."

Ardell shrugged. "It's life. That's what . . ."

"I know you aint goin to say that's what all black men is like?" Thelvin asked. "Just because some men run around on their wives and girlfriends don't mean . . ."

"A helluva lot of them *is* cheaters, it seems to me," Ardell snapped. "All you have to do is look at . . ."

"That still aint *all* black men," Thelvin told her. "Anyway, if we doin all that cheatin, who're we doin it with? Some black women aint no better than . . ."

Each time they spoke, Ardell and Thelvin seemed to puff up a little higher and stiffer, like competing bowls of egg whites being whipped to peaks.

Oh shit! Whose idea was this, anyway? "Hey, you two! You aint the only ones saw the movie. I thought it was real good. And it wasn't really about his running around so much as . . . Well, he was a good doctor and tried to be a good father and loved his wife in his way, but couldn't keep his . . . It shows how all people got a weakness." Blanche knew she sounded like Miz Movie Critic, but she couldn't stop for fear the two of them would start nipping at each other again. "You know, kinda like a beautiful bronze statue but when you turn it around it's got a scratch on it. It's like . . ."

Thelvin and Ardell stared at her as though she were drooling.

"His womanizing was just one kinda scratch, sorta." She looked from one to the other.

"Beautiful bronze statue? You talkin about the movie or the man?" Thelvin asked.

Ardell looked amused. "The blacker the berry, the sweeter the juice. Didn't you see how they darkened Samuel Jackson up for the part? Blanche likes her juice on the supersweet side. Don't you, Blanche?"

Blanche glared at Ardell.

Thelvin frowned.

"What I liked about the movie," Blanche went on as though the movie was all they were talking about, "was that they seemed like *real* black people. Most of the time when you see what's supposed to be black middle-class people in the movies, they're just white people with deep tans. All well-off black people aint like that. In this movie, folks acted like black people, believed like black people. They were as much black as they was well-off."

"Yeah, and they didn't go for the totally happy ending," Ardell said. "I like the way it ended, with both daughters knowing they did things they wished they hadn't."

"What you got against happy endings?" Thelvin wanted to know.

"Not a thing." Ardell turned so that she was looking right at him.

"Long's it's real and not some Hollywood-type phony happiness that looks good on the outside and is full of shit on the inside."

Blanche choked on her coffee. Damn! What did Ardell think she was doing?

"Oh, I thought maybe you didn't like to see other people happy because you're afraid it might rub off on you." Thelvin rose, stacked and carried his plate and cup to the sink.

Blanche turned her head to look at him so quickly her neck hurt.

"What the hell does that mean?" Ardell asked.

Thelvin crossed his arms. "Well, you know, Ardell, some people seem to like . . ."

Blanche stood up and stared at him, her hands on her hips.

"Sorry, Ardell. I didn't mean anything by it," Thelvin said to Ardell, then turned to Blanche. "Blanche, what say we make tracks? I got a early morning."

"You go ahead," Blanche told him. "When Ardell takes a break from her unhappiness, she can give me a ride."

For half a second Thelvin's face squinched together like he had a quick-passing pain. "Look, I'm sorry. I apologize. To both of you." His eyes pleaded with Blanche to come with him as surely as if they spoke.

Ardell was studying the kitchen table as though the answers to all life's questions were written there. Blanche looked from Ardell to Thelvin.

"Both of y'all just as simple as you can be. You know that? Act like two little kids fighting like . . ."

"Sorry, Blanche," Ardell said, squeezing Blanche's arm.

"Me, too," Thelvin said. "Just tired and a little evil, I guess."

"Sure, both of us," Ardell added. Blanche appreciated it, but she didn't believe it. She'd been concerned that Ardell wouldn't like Thelvin and, as it turned out, for good reason. It hadn't occurred to her that the feeling would be mutual. After all, who could not like Ardell?

Blanche was quiet on the way home. Thelvin seemed to be holding his breath. When they reached her house, he switched off the engine and turned toward her. She already had the car door open.

"Don't get out," she told him.

"Blanche, please, I'm real sorry. I don't know what got into me."

"I do," Blanche said, one foot reaching for the ground. "It don't take much to see that, for whatever reason, you just didn't like her."

Thelvin gave her a sour look. "She didn't give me much reason to, did she?"

Blanche had to admit that Ardell hadn't exactly been the gracious hostess. "But it was more than that," she said.

"It wasn't about you, if that's what you're thinking," Thelvin said. "I'm not jealous of . . ."

Blanche thought of the feeling she'd gotten when Thelvin and Ardell first met. "No. I don't think you're jealous of her exactly, but . . ."

Thelvin interrupted her. "Maybe next time me and Ardell'll both act like . . . I don't know what got into me, Blanche. There's just something about her. I promise it won't happen again."

Blanche took his hand, pulled him toward her, and kissed him.

Thelvin grinned. "What was that for?"

"For owning your shit and being just who you are."

They both got out of the car. He walked with her toward her stoop.

"I'll be gone all week," he said. "So . . ."

"Well, I'll be here when you get back," she said, and watched disappointment pull down the corners of Thelvin's mouth. She might have changed her mind and invited him in, but it felt too much like choosing sides.

She waved to him as he drove away.

As she took off her shoes, she wondered how long it was going to take Ardell to call her, so she was ready when the phone rang.

"*I'm* hard on a man, *I* want him to be Mr. Perfect!" she told Ardell. "You really showed out, girl. I know Thelvin was out of line, but you . . ."

"Okay, okay. I'm sorry. He's probably a nice person. I don't know what it was, but the minute I met him . . ."

Blanche once again remembered that flash of friction she'd sensed when Thelvin and Ardell first shook hands.

"I don't know, but something about him just got my back up."

Their mutual dislike was so balanced they talked about each other in the same way. But there might be something more to Ardell's dislike of Thelvin.

"Maybe because there's not enough wrong with him. Maybe that's what bothers both of us," Ardell added.

Blanche gasped. "You sounded just like me when you were talking to him, like you were just waiting for him to step wrong and prove you right!" The realization both startled and depressed her.

They were silent for a few moments before Ardell spoke.

"Damn! You think we're that . . . that . . . ?!" Ardell couldn't seem to find the right word.

Blanche didn't help her. "I'm gonna leave you to think about that one, honey. I'm going to bed."

A Pressed Flower

Daisy looked squashed when Blanche saw her the next day, as though some large weight had descended from the sky and leveled her. Her face looked spongy, her eyes red-rimmed and bloodshot. She scattered crystals across the table as she tried to put sugar in her tea. "I couldn't tell anybody," she said. "He was Maybelle's boyfriend and she was my best friend. I woulda died before I let on that . . ."

Poor Daisy. Any chance she'd thought she had of winning her heart-throb had, according to Clarice and the morning radio newscast, ended with a steep embankment, a hairpin curve, and a snoutful of liquor.

Blanche resisted the urge to lean across the table and take Daisy's hand. Enough eyes were already on the two of them having tea together across the color line. Blanche also didn't want to give Daisy so much comfort she no longer needed to talk out her pain and do something about it.

"I don't mean to be disrespectful," Blanche said, "but it seems a double shame that Bobby should die now that Maybelle's gone and you and him might have . . ."

Daisy leaned forward and looked intently at Blanche from watery blue eyes. "Don't say that, don't say it, Miz Blanche, it's an evil, evil thought!"

One you been thinking a lot, Blanche added to herself. "Exactly what happened? I mean, if you're up to talking about it."

Pain overcame propriety, and Daisy grabbed Blanche's hand. "It happened out on Sumter Road. Bobby was drinking!!" Daisy released Blanche's hand. She took a soggy tissue from her pocket and blew her nose in it. Blanche quickly moved her own hands to her lap and sat back in her seat.

"I bet Bobby's been driving around that curve on Sumter Road, drunk or sober, all his life. Maybe this one last time he had some help."

"What you mean, Miz Blanche?"

"Daisy, honey, don't you get it? Bobby was going to hurt Maybelle's killer, either by going to the Sheriff or trying to do something else to him for killing Maybelle. Now, all of a sudden, Bobby's dead."

"That curve's real nasty, Miz Blanche, and Bobby always did drive like a hellion, and . . ."

"I don't know much about trucks and cars," Blanche told her, "but anyone who reads the papers or watches TV knows you can do things to a truck that can cause accidents and that it aint always easy to tell when that happens." She went quiet, letting what she'd said sit with Daisy for a moment or two.

"It aint fair!" Daisy groaned. "Bobby shouldn't be dead because of *her.*"

Daisy made "her" sound more like an enemy than a friend. She gave Blanche a look full of so many emotions that Blanche couldn't read them—except that they included something other than love and mourning for Maybelle.

Blanche flung a little kerosene on the fire. "The news reports all said Maybelle was real sweet." She said it like she believed it.

A wash of crimson rose up Daisy's face and neck like an Easter egg dipped in red food-coloring. Beads of sweat peppered her forehead. "Well, Maybelle wasn't exactly what everybody thought she was, you know." Daisy spoke in a loud whisper. "I knew her better than anybody. Better than Bobby. She told me everything. And I mean *everything!*" Daisy's eyes were slitted; her mouth was set in a firm line.

Blanche fanned the spreading flames again: "Well, I'm sure Bobby knew her better than you, honey. After all, he was her man."

Daisy shook her head almost wildly from side to side. "No! No, he didn't! Bobby was too sweet for his own good. He didn't even know she was messing around on him until . . . She told me all about it, though, all about the rich man who . . ." Daisy clamped her mouth shut as though it were set on a timer that had just gone off. She closed her eyes.

Blanche felt a change in the air, something not yet well enough formed to be fully felt. She looked more deeply at Daisy, searching for something in the girl's face, replaying Daisy's words. There was nothing there—except the feeling that Daisy was probably the one who'd told Bobby that Maybelle was cheating on him.

Daisy opened her eyes. "I just got to put all this behind me. Forget all about it, all about it." She gave Blanche a watery smile.

Blanche slapped the table lightly with her open hand. "Forget about it! Forget that some rotten dog killed the man you loved?" Blanche took a deep breath. She knew from the startled way Daisy was looking at her that she needed to take some of the heat out of her voice. She sat back a little.

"Listen, Daisy, honey, don't you want this man punished for what he did?"

"Yes, ma'am, but there aint nothing I . . ."

"Just because David Palmer killed Maybelle and Bobby don't mean he's got whatever Bobby found."

Daisy blinked rapidly, an uncertain look on her face, when Blanche mentioned Palmer's name.

Blanche went on. "Maybe Palmer thought he didn't need it as long as Bobby wasn't around to use it against him." She watched Daisy's face closely—willing her to pay attention, to agree. "It might still be in Bobby's things." Daisy was paying attention but beginning to frown. Blanche hurried on: "Maybe you could get a look at Bobby's things. See if . . . Or maybe you could tell the Sheriff what Bobby . . ."

Daisy looked stricken. "Miz Blanche, I don't want to get in no trouble with rich folks in this town. You know how they is, all sticking together. I could lose my job if . . . They need my paycheck at home. I can't take no chance on . . ." Daisy held her hands out to Blanche in a pleading way. They were shaking.

"All right, Daisy, all right. You don't have to make up your mind right now."

Blanche knew she'd lost her when she'd mentioned the Sheriff. But it was too important for Blanche just to give up.

"At least think about it, Daisy. You don't want Palmer to get away with killing Bobby, do you?"

Daisy shifted her eyes around the room as if the walls knew what she should say. Blanche admitted to herself that Daisy wasn't about to go rummaging through dead Bobby's things. Even if she did, what good was the key without Bobby to say where and when he'd found it? But she wasn't finished yet. She'd found the barrette, noticed Palmer's missing Sons of Farleigh key, and tied him to Maybelle. There might be something else out there that would confirm the connection between Palmer and the dead girl.

28

A Fond Goodbye and a New View

There was a message from Taifa when Blanche came home from doing a little grocery shopping—not a call-me message, but a don't-worry-I'm-okay kind of message. It reminded Blanche that, even though Taifa might be changing in ways Blanche didn't necessarily like, the girl continued to be more sensitive to Blanche's feelings than Blanche often gave her credit for. The phone rang while she was rewinding the tape.

"Hello, Blanche, this is Mumsfield. How are you, Blanche?"

"Hey, Mumsfield. This is a surprise. I'm okay, all things considered. How about you?"

"I am well, Blanche. I am calling from Hawaii. From my honeymoon."

"Yes, Archibald told me." She couldn't bring herself to congratulate him on his marriage to Karen.

"Karen told me the bad things she did to you, Blanche."

"Did she, Mumsfield?" Blanche wondered exactly what and how much Karen had told him.

"I am very sorry Karen did those things, Blanche. Karen is very sorry also."

"Um-hum." Blanche kicked off her shoes and sat down by the phone. "Did Archibald call you?"

"Yes, Blanche."

"Did he tell you to call me, Mumsfield?"

"Yes, Blanche. He said you had important things to tell me."

She'd charge Archibald extra for making her the bad-news messenger. "Um-hum. And when did Karen tell you about what she did to me, Mumsfield, honey?"

"Last night, Blanche."

After a night of screwing your brains out, I'm sure, she thought. "Does Karen know you're calling me, Mumsfield?"

"No, Blanche."

"Did she tell you why she did those things to me?"

"I understand, Blanche. Karen was afraid you would not like her, that you would make me not like her."

"Is that what she told you?"

"She said she did some things that she did not want you to find out about."

"But you told her that I was asking around, didn't you, Mumsfield?"

He was silent a moment. "Yes, Blanche, I did."

Blanche didn't say anything. If he didn't understand that he had set Karen in motion against her, Blanche wasn't going to explain it.

"Blanche, have you found out very bad things about Karen? Did you, Blanche? Did you learn very bad things about Karen?"

Blanche grimaced and shook her head. The word "very" told her how much Mumsfield really wanted to know, but she wasn't about to cover for Karen Palmer.

"Well, you weren't her first and only lover, but you knew that, didn't you?"

"Yes, Blanche."

"She was seeing somebody else while you were engaged. Did she tell you that?"

"Yes, Blanche. Karen explained. She told me it is over now, Blanche."

There was no sense asking him if he believed Karen. That was obvious. "Well, I didn't hear anything worse about her than what you know now, Mumsfield. What else did Archibald tell you?"

"He said I did the wrong thing to marry Karen without a pre . . . He said Karen . . . he said Karen maybe married me for my . . . for not good reasons. What do you think, Blanche?"

"I don't know, Mumsfield. She wasn't poor before. Maybe she does just want her own household, her own husband. Maybe . . ."

"Archibald is making an agreement. He will take care of everything. Then I won't have to worry about . . ."

And if she doesn't sign, Blanche thought, Archibald will somehow manage to unhook her from Mumsfield. Blanche was sure of that.

Mumsfield was silent for a few moments, in which Blanche fought the urge to hang up. What the hell was she doing sitting here trying to explain why his racist-bitch wife might not want to steal his money? There was no way Blanche could move Mumsfield from the someone-I-know-and-like to the friend category. Karen made that impossible. How could he ever be her friend and not understand this very basic part of who she was? Would he have a friend who chose to marry someone who hated people with Down's syndrome? But, of course, whitefolks in this country are trained to believe they can have it both ways, like stealing the Indian's land while claiming to admire the Noble Savage.

"Listen, Mumsfield, honey, I'm kinda in the middle of something right now, so . . ."

"All right, Blanche. I understand, Blanche. Remember, you promised to have dinner with me. Just the two of us."

"Sure, honey, we'll make a date soon's things slow down with the catering business." She wondered if Mumsfield realized she was lying. She supposed she could tell him the truth, but there were limits on how much energy she could put into race relations without getting stressed.

"Goodbye, Blanche. Don't forget me," he said, as if answering her question.

"Goodbye, Mumsfield, honey. You take care of yourself, now."

She felt drained and sweaty when she got off the phone. Sad, too. She really liked Mumsfield.

Ardell, she thought. Every time the subject of friendship had come up lately, it had called some part of her relationship with Ardell to mind. Now she remembered she'd never made that hangout date with Ardell. She dialed Ardell's number.

"Hey. Let's go over to Chapel Hill to the movies. We aint done that since Hector was a pup."

"You kidding? Girl, I got so much work to do I can't see straight! Invoices to send out, bills to pay, working on a new brochure, and these bicentennial people want to see a piece of paper for every time we folded a napkin. I don't know what I'm . . ."

Blanche could hear the tightness in Ardell's voice. No wonder they weren't having any fun together. Ardell was nose-deep in the business. And I aint even thought about the paper end of things, she scolded herself. Acting like I'm working for some stranger instead of thinking about being a partner in the business with my best friend. "I'll tell you what," she said. "I'll come over and help you for a couple hours, then we can go somewhere."

"Deal!"

Ardell's kitchen table looked like a portable office on which Ardell had marked off a spot for Blanche, complete with the bicentennial contract; menus from events; receipts for ingredients, flowers, linens, and so forth; and the bicentennial report forms. Blanche found that she enjoyed filling in all the little details about money spent and materials used that the contract with the Bicentennial Commission demanded. Around noon, she and Ardell took a back-and-lunch break.

Blanche made chicken sandwiches while Ardell squeezed lemons for lemonade. Feels good to be here, Blanche thought. She arranged their meal on the small table in front of the sofa, then watched Ardell fiddling with the radio. She loved this woman. Couldn't imagine life without her. They were not so much alike as they were complementary parts. She thought of the many years and ways in which they'd shored each other up when the shifting slipperiness of their lives threatened to sweep their feet out from under them. Now they settled down on the couch, just like old times. We've taught each other a lot, she was thinking when the local newscaster began a story about a fire out on Rochester Road. Blanche only half listened to what sounded more like a put-down of the folks who'd been burned out than a straight news report.

"Neighbors stated that the family is in a long-standing feud with another branch of the same family in the Dolly Point area. Members of the Dolly Point Larsen clan have been implicated in arsons in the past. The Sheriff is investigating. Mrs. Delvinia Larsen, the matriarch of the burnt-out Larsen clan, says the Sheriff is wasting his time." The voice of an elderly woman, cracked but clear, came next: "That there fire started in my great-grandson Bobby's bed in the lean-to. It's a sign. A message from my Bobby from beyond the grave, tellin these menfolk to mend their sinful ways." The newscaster ended with a smile in his voice: "And that's the news."

The weatherman was well into guessing tomorrow's temperature and pollen level before Blanche was struck by the lightning of what she'd just heard.

"That was Bobby's house!"

"Bobby who? Oh, you mean the dead alibi boy? What'd they say?"

Blanche repeated what she'd heard, half irritated that Ardell hadn't been listening even though she herself had missed the first part of the story.

"Damn! Can you believe it? First Bobby and now this!"

"Yeah, he's even worse than I expected him to be."

"You think Palmer burned that house down?"

Blanche nodded. "And it looks like I was right about him not getting the key before he killed Bobby. Now he's made sure nobody else will find it either."

"Humm. I guess, if you go so far as killing somebody, burning out their family aint a problem. What you gonna do now, Blanche?"

Blanche sighed. "I don't know. If I had any sense, I'd just forget about it." She stared out the window and tried to remember life before she'd seen Palmer at that dance. She turned to her friend. "You were right, Ardell. I should have done something about him right away. At least I could have marched around in front of his house with a sign saying, This man raped me. Even if nothing happened to him because of it, I'd at least have called him the rapist he is. He'd have been talked about for a little bit, whether people believed me or not. Maybe Maybelle would have heard about him and picked another sugar daddy. Maybe he'd have left town and never met her."

"Humm. And maybe the sun will turn into a bullet-sized pellet and shoot him in the butt! Girl, you got better sense than to do that couldawoulda what-if shit. Anyway, you had a living to make, as much as I wanted you to nail that sucker. And . . ."

"And what?"

"Well, you didn't really want nobody to know about it, did you? And we both know why, don't we?"

Blanche almost thanked the phone for distracting Ardell from her questions, although Blanche couldn't avoid the answers. She didn't want to see that look of pity on people's faces, or hear that tone in their voices—equal parts relief that what had happened to her had not happened to them, and curiosity about just how it had happened and how awful it had been. She and Ardell both knew she couldn't handle that.

". . . and how many guests do you anticipate?" Ardell grabbed a notepad and pencil from the table and turned her back to Blanche.

By the time she got off the phone, Ardell had promised to get together with whoever she was talking to about a catering job.

"I'm sorry, Blanche. But this sounds real promising. A bridge club. They have their meeting catered every month. Their regular caterer died. It's just the kind of steady gig I need, and just the kind of women who'll recommend me to their friends." She offered to drop Blanche off at home on the way to her meeting, but, as usual, Blanche wanted to walk.

"We'll do something together real soon, I promise," Ardell said before she drove off.

Blanche hung somewhere between depression and rage that the key was gone. She'd already given up on Daisy's looking through Bobby's things for the key. What could she have done with it anyway? The burning of Bobby's house didn't really change anything. It was all still on her to tie Palmer to Maybelle's murder. When she got home, the red eye of her answering machine winked at her from the shadows of the living room:

"Blanche White! It's Bunnie. I could hardly believe my ears when I heard you and your wild self was back in town. It's almost two now, and I got to get a haircut, but if you got a hot minute, come on by Miz Mackey's around four this afternoon. If that aint good, call me back and we'll work something else out. Can't wait to see you, girl." At least he remembered her. She wondered if women still panted after him the way they did in high school. She hoped Palmer spent enough time in the bar at the Sons of Farleigh Club where Bunnie worked so Bunnie would have something useful to tell her.

There was no legal public bar in Farleigh where black people congregated, only Miz Mackey's blind pig, or speakeasy, as they say up North: a basement "paneled" in gray plywood and carpeted in unnatural green indoor/outdoor carpeting. The jukebox against the wall was an old domed yellow-and-gold one with plastic bubbles cascading up and down its insides. It was a weekday, so the place was far from full. Two men sat at the small bar, one at each end, one reading the newspaper, the other drumming his fingers on his thigh like he was thinking at a fast rate. There was no one at any of the square metal tables.

"How you doin, Miz Mackey?" they both called out to the wrinkled and rouged woman behind the bar. Miz Mackey didn't take her eyes off her story on the little TV in front of her, but raised her hand in greeting. She managed to fix their drinks, take their money, and give them change and thanks without ever looking away from the TV screen.

Blanche watched Bunnie's pert behind as he preceded her to a table. He was just as cute as he'd been in high school. They sat at the table farthest from Miz Mackey's TV.

"Girl, it sure is good to see you, although why you come back to this one-horse town I'm sure I don't know." Bunnie took a long drag from his cigarette and sipped his Jack Daniel's with water, no ice. His big, soft brown eyes were even longer-lashed than she'd remembered.

"It aint that bad, Bunnie. You still here."

"Yeah, well, it aint nothing to be proud of. I'd leave if I wasn't such a lazy, triflin heifer."

"Heifer?!" Blanche laughed. "So that's why nobody could snag you in high school!"

Bunnie winked at her. "At least none of the girls. But I sure had the hots for Melva's brother!"

Blanche could feel surprise reordering her face. She raised her glass in salute.

They caught up on what Blanche had been doing all these years, on Bunnie's life, the death of his mother, and his sister's sudden decision to move to Atlanta last year and leave her kids with Bunnie. Then Bunnie said: "Your message sounded like you had something particular you wanted to talk to me about."

"I wanted to ask you about somebody who belongs to that club where you work. David Palmer."

Bunnie nodded. "What you want to know?"

"Oh, I don't know, exactly."

"Well, why you want to know?"

"Because he raped me." Blanche gave Bunnie a startled look, shocked at her own words, yet feeling suddenly like she wanted to laugh. She hadn't ever been able to say those words out loud without feeling exposed and somehow wrong. Now they only felt like the truth. She didn't know why this should happen with Bunnie. Was she taking advantage? Assuming it was safe to confide in him because he was gay? Or maybe she'd told him the truth because Ardell had been right when she'd said Blanche hadn't wanted anyone to know about her having been raped. But it wasn't true anymore. What she hadn't understood until now was that saying what had happened to her out loud changed her rape—changed it from being her secret problem to being the crime against her that it really was. She had not raped herself. She felt as though she'd just loosened a brassiere so tight it had restricted her breathing.

Bunnie reached out and took her hand. "That no-good . . . You should have him arrested! Even though the law don't give a shit about people like us, especially when we go up against people like him."

"It didn't just happen. It was a while ago, but . . ."

He squeezed her hand. "I should have sent his drunken ass out to play in traffic last time I saw him, instead of getting him a ride home," Bunnie said.

"When was that?"

"Oh, I don't know, couple weeks ago. No. I remember. It was the night that white girl got murdered. Mabel, or something like that? I remember reading a couple days later about her being killed. I don't know why, but sometimes when I see stuff like that, I think about what I was doing when the murder happened. I figured out that when that girl was being killed, I'd probably just served pigboy Palmer his ninety-ninth drink. Yeah, girl, he was wild that night! Crying and shit, mumbling to himself. His buddy dropped Palmer off early and he stayed till closing—almost got in a fight with somebody's guest from out of town. I finally got the night manager to drag his behind on outa there."

Blanche could hear herself panting.

"What's wrong, Blanche?!" Bunnie looked as alarmed as he sounded. "You look . . . You okay?"

Blanche nodded her head, not trusting herself to speak. She took a couple of deep breaths and let them slowly out of her mouth, then gulped a mouthful of her drink. Later, she didn't remember much of what they'd talked about. Her mind was totally caught up in the meaning of Palmer's being at the Sons of Farleigh Club while Maybelle was being killed. She just hoped Ardell was home by now.

"Life!" she said, laughing without a drop of humor, after she'd told Ardell what Bunnie had said. "I shoulda known in the beginning that it was too easy. It was like I was being led to his hanging. I was so sure, so sure! I thought maybe it was the Ancestors making it all work out for me. Now Bunnie tells me Palmer was at the Sons of Farleigh Club while Maybelle was being killed. Even if he'd left the club in time to kill her, he'd likely been too drunk to do it. Damn! I had it all worked out: Palmer's flowers, the place in Durham, Maybelle's barrette, the missing Sons of Farleigh key, and the fire at Bobby's place."

Ardell handed her a glass of fresh lemonade. "Humm. You got proof of something, but maybe you aint got the right person."

"What do you mean?"

"Well, for example, what about Jason Morris? Didn't Bunnie say Palmer was dropped off by a friend? Was it Jason?"

"So what if it was?"

"Well, maybe Palmer and Jason are the kind of friends who'd kill for each other. Maybe Jason left Palmer at the club so Palmer would have an alibi since Maybelle was Palmer's girlfriend, then went off and killed her."

"But Bunnie said the friendship was mostly on Palmer's side, so why would Jason kill Maybelle for him?"

Ardell shrugged. "Humm, well, Bunnie don't know everything."

Blanche didn't think much of Ardell's idea but she didn't have one of her own, so why not check it out? She got Bunnie on the phone.

"Bunnie, you said Palmer's buddy dropped him off at the club the night Maybelle died. Did you mean Jason Morris?"

"Yeah, that's who it was. He only stayed a minute but he was supposed to come back. When I tried to get Palmer out of the club, he said Jason had his car and was supposed to pick him up, but he never did."

"Why didn't Jason have his own car?"

"Who knows? Maybe it was in the shop. But now that I think about it, I seen Palmer give his car keys to Jason more than once. Couple times a week, sometimes. Funny thing is, they didn't always come together, so Jason's car was probably sitting right outside."

"What's with Jason? You know anything about him?"

"Nothing much. He used to be a true dog. I think his family may be on his case about that because I don't hear him talking so much about how many women he's tricked into screwing him the way he used to. Which reminds me, one night, oh, back I don't know how long now, I heard Palmer make a toast to Jason. Some long, drunken bullshit about Jason being a real romantic and willing to do whatever was necessary to keep the woman he loved, or something like that. Palmer acts like he thinks Jason's piss is holy water."

"Thanks, Bunnie. You been a great help." Blanche hung up the phone and stared at Ardell while she tried to process this new information.

Ardell could be right. Jason might be involved somehow. But just because Palmer had been at the club the night Maybelle died didn't mean he wasn't responsible for her death. He could have hired somebody else. That could be why he was so upset at the club that night: because he knew his girlfriend was being killed while he was getting sloshed. Maybe Jason had been out delivering the payoff money because Palmer couldn't face it. Why had he killed Maybelle in the first place? Was she asking for money, or threatening to tell his wife and family? Maybe she just got on his nerves. Or maybe I'm just feeding myself a bunch of junk 'cause I don't want to give up on getting Palmer, she told herself.

She tried to remember every time she'd seen Jason Morris, going back to the first time, when Jason had gone all over furious about what Seth was trying to pull on Clarice. Or at least he'd seemed to. Was that all an act? But who was it for? His wife? Was it all an act to keep Clarice or the catering company from making a fuss? She tried to dredge up a separate memory for each of the other times she'd seen him, but her collective picture was of him laughing, and talking with his brother, Seth, and David Palmer. She was going to have to do a little check-around on Jason.

"I got a feeling you're right and these bad boys is in the mess together," Blanche said when Ardell came back from the bathroom. She told Ardell about her call to Bunnie.

"Well, be careful, Blanche. You already know what Palmer's like."

"Don't worry. I'm taking it all serious." And she was—she'd become

more than careful while crossing streets; she made sure the little piece of
paper she'd stuck between her front door and the door jamb was still in
place before she went inside and her length of steel pipe was always at
hand.

She didn't have a lick of trouble finding out what she wanted to know
about Jason Morris once Ardell told her who to talk to.

"Oh, he's a devil, all right," Katie Crumbley told her. Katie had worked
for the Morrises every summer while she was going to high school. This
was her last summer. She was off to Spelman in the fall.

"Both his daddy and his wife were deep in his stuff about his chasing
women. He says, 'I promise,' but nobody in their right mind believes that
boy when it comes to women. You talk about addicted! Miz Blanche, he
got sex on the brain. I learned early not to be alone with either him or that
brother of his, Seth."

Blanche thought about Jason's kindness to Clarice. "I thought he was
decent."

"Oh, he is, when his wife or his daddy's around. His daddy threatened
to cut Jason out of his will if he don't straighten up, and his wife is talking
about walking out and taking all her money with her."

Pieces of an idea began to come together in Blanche's mind.

"When you go back to work," she told Katie, "I want you to do me a favor, if you can. I'll make it worth your while." Blanche didn't feel bad asking, since Katie Crumbley was leaving her job anyway. "Just a little story I
want Jason Morris to overhear." Blanche told her what to say and punctuated her instructions with three twenties. She told Katie that she needed
to say her lines by noon the next day. Blanche knew it was tricky, but Katie
was game. And she didn't have any other ideas for the moment. She pictured the alarm in Jason's eyes when he heard Katie gossiping about the
Sheriff's having found evidence related to Maybelle's death in a bungalow
in Farleigh—something that probably came off the killer's key chain. She
hoped the mention of the key chain would generate a few drops of sweat.

29

Up Close and Universal

By the time she talked to Thelvin again, Blanche was missing him so
badly he could have told her any old kind of bull hockey. But instead of
trying to oil his way back into her good graces:

"Look, Blanche," he said on the phone, "I know I'm skating on thin ice
with you. I know I made a lotta wrong moves. But don't you see? I like
you, woman! I want to be with you, and it makes me act stupid! It's been a
long time since I've felt this way about anybody, and I guess I just forgot
how . . . how *delicate* this kinda stuff is."

Who could resist?

"You haven't had any more near misses or threats, have you? I know
you don't want to hear it, but I still think you need to . . ."

Blanche cut him off with an invitation to come over.

She'd made them a dinner based on recipes she'd found in a cookbook
called *Intercourses: the Aphrodisiac Cookbook.* She couldn't afford the book,
so she'd jotted down some recipes in the store. Of course, she'd changed
some of the ingredients, like substituting catfish for red snapper—she
wanted sexy, but she needed colored, too. They'd just finished the baked
oysters, grilled catfish with avocado sauce, rosemary-cheese grits casse-

role, and mixed green salad. Neither one of them was quite ready for the strawberry shortcake.

They plopped down on the sofa and sighed in unison.

"You can burn, woman. I never even knew grits could taste like that!" Thelvin took her hand, kissed it, then held it on the sofa between them.

"Just one of the many, many things I do well," Blanche teased. "But what about you? I watched you do that conductor thing, Thelvin. You got it down to a bust-out."

Thelvin grinned his pleasure, but his smile didn't last. "My uncle was a redcap in Baltimore in the old days. He useta tell me stories about how they got treated by some of the white people who rode the trains. But he didn't tell me how bad it was on the inside."

"Why, do you think?"

Thelvin shrugged. "I don't know. Too proud, maybe. It was one thing being mistreated by riders, but the people who were supposed to be your brother workers . . ."

"How long you been working for the railroad?"

"Thirty-one years. I was fresh back from the merchant marine when I got hired on. Long time. Long, long time. Too long."

"Would you quit, if you could?"

"In a heartbeat."

"Oh yeah! I remember hearing about some black folks suing Amtrak over discrimination stuff. Problem is, it's everywhere."

"That's why I gave up thinking about quitting," Thelvin said. "On my run, I talk to men who work construction, work for hotels and in shoe stores, work for big corporations. They all going through some brand of the same hell I'm catching. It aint like somebody's in your face calling you a nigger, or putting KKK pamphlets in your locker, although that happens, too, believe me. It's the other shit. Like I always got to follow the rules like God hisself gave 'em to me, and if you step wrong, then . . . All the union wants is your dues to use to make sure the leadership stays white. Look how long a lotta the unions kept us out."

"Sounds to me like business as usual in the good old U.S. of A."

He rubbed his hands across his face as if to wipe away his worry. "The funny thing is, it's your own hope that trips you up. I worked with white men before. I knew how bad some of them act. But every job, every trip, you start out hoping this'll be better than the last. That there won't be nobody in this bunch of people who's bound and determined to make you feel like shit or like you want to rip their fucking . . . and then the race crap starts and you feel bad, when you should have known all along that . . ."

Blanche could feel Thelvin's weariness, stretched nerves, and disappointment like a vibration in the room. Did white people have any idea how much energy and hope and downright stubbornness it took to live and work and try to find some fun in a place where you were always the first to be suspected, regardless of the crime? She thought of the two little boys who'd been arrested for rape in Chicago a few years ago, even though doctors said they were too young to produce the sperm found in the dead girl. Would that have happened if they'd been two little blue-eyed blond white boys? Would any cop anywhere in America have been half as eager to arrest Palmer if she'd reported him as the Farleigh Sheriff had been to find a black man responsible for Maybelle's death?

"I wish every white person, just once, could spend a day being followed around a store by Security like they got 'thief' printed on their foreheads. I wonder how they'd deal with not getting a job or an apartment because they got white skin."

"That's why they so scared of us. They know how they act aint right. They're scared one of these days we're gonna give 'em what they know they deserve." His voice was full of the smoldering coals that glowed in most black people's voices when they got on to this particular subject.

Blanche and Thelvin were both silent for a few minutes, but Blanche's mind rang with remembered slights and taunts, and echoes of that awful, heartbreaking instant of fear that was a part of every trip into the white world—a fear of being refused or given poor service because she was black, stopped by a cop because she was black. And it wasn't simply her fear: it was so much a part of what it meant to be black in America it mostly no longer showed itself as fear—it showed up as stress, high blood pressure, asthma, tuberculosis, heart disease, and cancer. It's like our bodies have been taught to discriminate against us, Blanche thought.

"It's good you can talk about it." She figured some woman in his life was responsible for that. Most men she'd met didn't come to talking about their feelings through heart-to-hearts with the boys.

"It's good to have somebody to talk to about it. Since Ruthie died . . ." Thelvin squeezed her hand. "I don't know, seems like a lotta women want you to play the strong black prince no matter how you're being . . . no matter how scary shit gets out there."

Blanche nodded. Of course, like most man/woman stuff, it wasn't all one-sided. Who was the famous black woman who, when somebody asked her why she only married and dated white men, said she couldn't handle black men's pain? The sister got a lot of back talk from black folks about that, but Blanche respected her for being honest enough to save herself and some black man a lot of grief.

She moved closer and put her arms around Thelvin, who melted into her as though he needed to be relieved of his own weight for a while. She wondered how much his jealousy had to do with all of this. A person had to feel powerful someplace, even the wrong place. Maybe being a black man—the most hated human being in the country—and mostly working jobs where somebody else had all the say had something to do with wanting exclusive ownership of a woman's life. Of course, absolutely none of that made it healthy or all right. She didn't know if jealousy was a thing that could be cured, but she certainly hoped so. Or maybe it wasn't as big a problem as she thought. She did know there was nowhere for her and Thelvin to go if he couldn't get beyond it. He was at least worth a couple more conversations on the subject. She opened her mouth to speak but changed her mind. Let him rest with the fact that he could talk to her, trust her to understand and be on his side. She let her mind float free and gave herself over to giving and receiving the healing comfort that holding provides.

Action

Blanche decided to make her calls early in the morning, before either man was likely to have left his house. As the Palmers' number rang, it occurred to her that she didn't have a plan for what to do if Palmer himself answered. She needn't have been concerned. She could tell from the tone that it was help and not family she was talking to.

"Morning, ma'am. I'm calling for Mr. Jason Morris?" She made sure to make the statement sound like a question, since she was supposed to be of the class that didn't have any answers. "He say y'all should remind Mr. David to meet Mr. Jason at one o'clock at the big bench at the Japanese Teahouse in Eno Park?" She remembered the Teahouse from the picnic they'd catered there. It was secluded without being too far away to make shouting for help a total waste of time.

"Yes, ma'am, I'll tell him. One o'clock. Eno Park Japanese Teahouse."

"Y'all take care, now," Blanche called out before she hung up. Then she called Jason Morris's house and left the same message for him from David Palmer.

She now had three and a half hours to get ready. She remembered the tape recorder she'd used in Boston to help find out who'd killed Ray-Ray.

How much would a tape recorder cost that could do what she needed? She counted her money. Forty-five dollars and sixty cents she couldn't really spare, plus twenty dollars of Archibald's money. Wondering if Ardell had a good one, she punched in her phone number.

"What?! You're gonna do what?! Are you out of your mind?" Ardell screeched. "Even if I had a tape recorder, I wouldn't lend it to you. If those boys catch you, they'll chew you up and . . ." Ardell stopped shrieking like somebody had just snatched her handbag and spoke more slowly, in a calmer, softer tone, as though she were trying to talk Blanche down off a tenth-story window ledge. "Blanche, think about this. If one of those two really did kill Maybelle and Bobby, what do you think they'll do to you if they catch you eavesdropping on their conversation? That's if they even show up. And who's gonna believe anything you say you heard if the two of them say different? That aint changed, you know."

"I don't intend for them to catch me, and I don't expect nobody to take my word for anything. That's why I want a tape recorder, the kind that starts right up as soon as somebody starts talking. I guess I'm going to have to buy one. I hope they don't cost too much. I'll put it someplace near that bench that goes around that tree in the middle, remember? It's the biggest bench there and the only place it makes sense for them to meet. I'm gonna try to find a place to hide inside, but if I can't, I'll just leave the tape recorder and get it when they're gone."

"You're taking a terrible chance, Blanche."

"I don't think so. But I need a ride to the mall to buy a tape recorder. How about it?"

"You need more than a ride! You need to be put in a straitjacket for being so damned . . ."

"Didn't you tell me I needed to do something about David Palmer?" Blanche reminded her.

"Yeah. But I was thinking something more like, well, I don't know what I was thinking, but I know it wasn't this!"

"It's the best I can do, Ardell. I can't sneak up on him and hit him in the head with a baseball bat, 'cause I aint prepared to do no time for him. Even if I wanted to, I can't afford to pay nobody to mess him up for me, and, like I said, the dead don't suffer. So this is all I can see to do. It don't show him up to be the raping bastard he is, but it could give me enough information to cause him harm. Even if he never knows I had anything to do with it, I'll be satisfied."

"All right, Blanche. All right. But I'm going with you. I'll pick you up in half an hour."

"Thanks, Ardell. I'll be ready." Blanche decided to wait until after the mall to tell Ardell that this was a one-woman job. If there was any danger, no sense both of them being in it.

Ardell gave Blanche the $4.68 she needed to make the price of the recorder and to buy a tape and batteries. Ardell also gave her a paycheck from the catering company, although payday was still days away. Blanche stopped in the hardware store and bought a length of clothesline.

They went straight from the mall to the Teahouse for a practice run. As Blanche had hoped, there were only a few people around and no one in the Teahouse. They scoped out the wooden bench that surrounded the gnarled ficus in its huge terra-cotta pot in the center of the Teahouse. They dithered back and forth, trying to decide if the tree pot was the best place for the recorder, and then decided to put it under the bench. They approached the bench from different directions, and Blanche even stooped in front of it as if to tie a shoelace, to make sure the recorder couldn't be seen. They went behind the shoji screen in the corner and piled the clay pots and trowels back and angled the screen so that, when Blanche stood behind it and peeped from the side, her face was so deep in shadows she couldn't easily be seen from the area around the ficus, although she could see that area clearly. When they were satisfied their plan would work, Blanche tied the clothesline she'd bought at the mall across the doorway of the Teahouse.

"To make people think they're not supposed to go inside," she explained. Ardell dropped Blanche off at home and promised to pick her up at twelve-thirty sharp.

Blanche was too hyped to do much more than pace the floor. She read the tape-recorder manual as she walked, trying out various buttons and recording a snatch of her own voice to make sure she knew how to operate it. By twelve o'clock she was so wound up she was sure she could electrocute someone with a touch. Things could go wrong, like Palmer or Jason saying something that made them realize neither one of them had set up the meeting. But there was no backing out now.

"Aint no sense getting a bad case of the nerves now," Ardell said as she drove them toward Eno Park. "We got plenty of time to get the tape set up and get situated."

"Not we, Ardell. Me. It's easier for one person to hide than two. Anyway, if they do something to me, won't nobody know where to look for me if you get caught, too."

"Blanche, I aint about to let you go in there by yourself!"

Blanche was pleased that Ardell had thought about her before the business, but that didn't stop Blanche from using Carolina Catering to twist Ardell's arm: "You aint thinking smart, Ardell. What about the business? If they catch us, it would be *real* bad for business."

Ardell eased the car into a parking space in the free lot attached to the park. "It don't feel right letting you do this by yourself."

Blanche looked at her watch, fifteen minutes till one, then gently tapped the back of Ardell's hand. "I'll be fine. You can wait right here. If I aint back by two, come looking for me. Okay?"

"No, it aint okay, but you aint giving me no choice."

"Wish me luck!" Blanche jumped out of the car and headed for the Teahouse. She put the tape recorder in its hiding place. She had just decided to relieve Ardell's mind by leaving the tape recorder unattended and coming back for it but there was Jason Morris heading toward the Teahouse. She barely made it behind the paper screen in the corner.

Jason paced around the Teahouse, a pale beast sniffing the air, trying to gauge the level of danger. He circled the bench, looking intently at everything he passed. He lit a cigarette and seemed to relax some, but he didn't sit. When he saw Palmer heading toward him, Jason pulled his shoulders back and sucked in his gut like a model about to hit the runway, but he didn't move from where he stood. He waited for Palmer to come to him.

"You heard about the Sheriff?" Jason skipped the Southern-gentleman niceties that would normally have eased them into conversation, which proved to Blanche that he was seriously concerned about what the Sheriff might have in his possession.

"Heard what?"

Jason told Palmer about the Sheriff's having found something belonging to Maybelle in the bungalow over in Durham and also having something that might be from the killer's key ring—Katie Crumbley had earned her money.

Jason spoke with much more ease than he'd shown earlier. "It's only a rumor. I heard it from one of the maids."

"Maybe. But those downstairs darkies always seem to know . . ."

"No need to panic, Davey boy," Jason said as though David was pissing in his pants.

"Oh, pardon me, Jason, I guess I'm just not used to being an accessory to two murders."

Blanche clamped her hand over her mouth to help stifle her desire to whoop with delight. She congratulated herself on thinking of the tape recorder.

Jason's only response was to drag on his cigarette.

"Tell me what happened, Jason. Was she going to leave you? Did she want money? Threaten to tell your old man if you didn't pay up? She wasn't pregnant, or the newspapers would have said."

"I told you, Davey, I didn't kill her. She was just a piece of poor white tail. There was no . . ."

Palmer turned his back. "When that boy Bobby was arrested, I thought maybe, just maybe, I was wrong about you. Now he's dead, too." Palmer turned back to face his friend. "I wish to God I'd never told you he'd come to see me!"

"That's bullshit, old buddy. You expected me to do something. You wanted me to. It was your SOF key he said he had, not mine. I was protecting you!"

"He wouldn't have had it if you hadn't given it to Maybelle. Why the hell couldn't you have rented a car instead of . . ."

"I didn't give it to her, dear boy, I swear. Maybe she took it off the ring while I was in the shower, or . . . She loved trinkets, that girl."

Blanche wanted to scream at the way Jason talked about Maybelle, as though she'd been a favorite puppy run over by a car.

Palmer shook his head and ran his hands through his hair. "All for a piece of ass! Two people dead, the Sheriff . . . Christ! I actually believed you loved her, that you couldn't live without . . ."

Jason laughed and put his hand on Palmer's shoulder. "You know, you've been sappy ever since your little episode. That broken-hearted romantic role you're determined to play has gotten a bit stale. So some woman jilted you ninety-nine years ago, so what? She was just another cunt, just like all those ball-breaking . . ."

Palmer shrugged off Jason's hand. "Fuck you, Jason. I wash my hands of you and all this . . ."

Jason took a drag from his cigarette and let the smoke out through his nose. "Well, you can't exactly do that, can you, dear boy? I mean, the flowers, the cottage, the presents, all in your name. On my behalf, but . . ."

Palmer took a step back. He looked like he'd been sucker-punched, which made Blanche grin.

"I can't believe I'm hearing . . . After all I've done, all . . . I can't believe you'd be so . . ."

"Come on, Davey, you know what kind of position I'm in with my old man! You can handle this. It'll all blow over if you just don't panic and . . ."

"You'd leave me holding the bag for all of it, when you're the one who . . ."

Jason spoke in a softer, more soothing tone. "Davey, Davey, don't worry so much. It's just backstairs talk. If there's really a problem, you can talk to the Sheriff. I'm sure he . . ."

"*I* can talk to him? Shouldn't that be *we*, Jason?"

"Well, dear boy, why would I talk to him?"

"Seth always said you've never cared about anyone but yourself. I thought it was just a jealous-brother thing, or maybe liquor talking. I told him you and I have been friends since . . . that we've always stuck together and you'd never do anything to . . ."

"All right, Davey, all right. You've made your point."

But Palmer hadn't, not yet: "But, you know, I got to thinking about what old Seth had to say. After all, he *is* your brother, your blood. He's lived with you all his life. So, just in case old Seth knew what he was talking about . . ." Palmer pulled a small piece of paper from the outside breast pocket of his blue blazer. He unfolded it and held it out to Jason. "This is a copy of a card you wrote and signed and had me stick on a bouquet for your ladylove."

Jason snatched the paper, read it, and turned the color of good curry powder.

"'Sweet Maybelle, can't wait to light your fire. Love Jason' doesn't sound like she's *my* mistress, now does it? But no need to panic, Jason, my boy," Palmer said, mimicking Jason's words and tone.

"And just in case you're thinking of getting me drunk and running me off the road the way you did Bobby, or throwing me down a ravine like

Maybelle"—Palmer nodded at the paper in Jason's hand—"that's my insurance policy. Anything happens to me, the original will be sent to the Attorney General and . . . Even if he lacks interest, I'm sure the copies that'll be sent to your wife and your father will cause at least a minor stir in your domestic and financial life. So you better just hope the Sheriff hasn't got anything that belongs to me, and you'd better fix it if he does."

The two men stared at each other as though each believed some way around their stalemate must be written in the other man's eyes.

Jason spoke first: "I'm sure there's a dollar amount that would make all things possible in the Sheriff's Office."

"That's not my problem, Jason, old buddy. I'm not interested in the details."

Blanche noticed the way Palmer had taken on Jason's buddy-boy way of talking as though it belonged to whoever had the upper hand in the conversation.

Jason dropped his cigarette and stepped on it. "I'll talk to Harold in the morning. As my granddaddy always said, 'The function of a good lawyer is to help you break the law as legally as poss . . .' "

By the time Jason looked up, Palmer had already turned and stalked away.

"Don't take it like that, Davey boy!" Jason called out in a slightly surprised and bewildered tone.

Blanche waited a minute or two after Jason left before she came out from behind the screen and dived for the tape recorder. She was breathing as though she'd just run there from across town. Her hands shook so badly she could hardly rewind the tape. She wondered if that reporter who'd exposed Mumsfield's family for her some years back was still around. She knew she should get back to the car, but she sank down on the bench and rewound the tape, unwilling to wait another moment to once again hear David Palmer admit to knowing his friend was a killer and not doing a damned thing about it.

All she heard was static. She wound the tape ahead a bit—more static. She wound it until she'd counted to ten, then to thirty. More static. Tears stung her eyes like sweat. She blinked them away, frantically pushing buttons, winding, rewinding, forwarding, hoping the damned thing would speak. She looked over her shoulder when she felt Ardell nearby.

"I saw them leaving. What happened?" Ardell asked in a loud whisper.

Blanche slumped over the tape and moaned as though disappointment had punched her in the gut.

Ardell grabbed Blanche's shoulders. "Ohmigod! What did they do to you? I knew I should have come with you!" Ardell was all over Blanche, looking for bruises and blood.

Blanche held up the tape machine. "It aint me, it's this goddamn piece of shit! It didn't work!" She raised her arm to throw the tape player. Ardell snatched it out of her hand. "Let me try." She repeated all the button-pushing and listening Blanche had already tried, then gave up and sank to the bench beside Blanche. She put her arm around her friend's shoulders. "Ah, Blanche, I'm so sorry."

Blanche nodded, and laid her head on Ardell's shoulder. She was too disgusted to cry.

"So what're you gonna do now?"

Blanche sat up. "Nothing, I guess. Nothing *to* do."

"Well, you could . . ." Ardell thought for a while, then gave up. She patted Blanche's shoulder. "Well, you tried."

Blanche just wished that were enough.

Disappointment and Understanding

For the next four days, Blanche walked around with a bitter taste in her mouth that couldn't be killed by saltwater rinses, mouthwash, toothpaste, or the freshening effect of a crisp apple. She knew the cause, of course: Palmer and Jason had said enough for her to know that Palmer hadn't murdered Maybelle or Bobby, even though she wished he had. Still, accessory to murder was trouble enough. Or it would have been, if the tape had worked. Now she had nothing. Nothing. In two days, the bicentennial celebration would be over. Ardell had been asked to cater a small goodbye party for Jason and his wife, who were off to the Greek islands to rest up from the ordeal of having had to attend so many galas. And murders. Ardell had turned down the job.

Two days ago, Blanche had seen David Palmer and Jason Morris at a cocktail party she'd worked. At earlier events, the pair had seemed to move toward each other from different parts of the room as naturally as petals closing on the same flower. That evening, they'd avoided each other. Blanche had noticed Nancy Morris looking from her husband to David Palmer and back again, as though trying to figure out what was up with them. Blanche had fought hard to keep from telling her. She'd thought back to the other times she'd seen Nancy with Jason and guessed that Nancy had seemed so distant and cold toward Jason because she wasn't one of those wives who were the last to know. If Nancy had only been watching her husband, she might not have been suspicious. Jason had lost a friend, but, to judge from the way he'd laughed and flirted, he clearly wasn't letting one monkey in any way interfere with his show. Palmer, on the other hand, really looked as if he'd lost his best friend. Blanche hoped he was truly suffering.

She was still in bed on the morning the man on her radio announced that David Palmer was dead. For a few moments, she seemed to be floating, weightless with joy above her bed. I will never have to see him again, she thought. She rolled out of the bed and walked around the Miz Alice while the newscaster went on about the numbers of people who'd died and been injured over the years in taking that particular curve. He was followed by a little speech from the management of the radio station demanding that the highway department do something about the killer curve on Sumter Road. "Never, ever again!" Blanche roared, throwing her arms toward the ceiling and twirling around. Everywhere she looked—the bureau, the bed, the sink—everything seemed brighter, sharper, as though her eyesight were improved by the knowledge that she'd never be forced to look at David Palmer again.

The phone rang.

"I just heard," Blanche told Ardell. "It's over." She was surprised by the tears that followed those words.

"Yes, Lord! Sometimes bad things do happen to bad people. It's enough to make a . . . You want me to come over? I've got to run to the . . ."

"No, no. I'm okay. It's just . . . I feel like I just escaped from somewhere. And scared."

"Scared of what?"

"I don't know, like I . . ."

"You didn't want him dead, remember? It's like a gift. It didn't have nothing to do with you."

Blanche looked over at her Ancestor altar.

"Like you said, Blanche, it's over. He is out of your life, big-time. I gotta hurry. I'll call you later. Celebrate, girl!"

Blanche hung up the phone and thought back to how she'd cringed in the Miz Alice the first night she'd seen David Palmer, how afraid she'd been of every sound and movement. She felt the last of that fear dissolve. Whoever was at the door or out there waiting for her in some alley, it was not him. It would never be David Palmer again.

She thought about sitting outside the flower shop, calling Mary at the bank, bugging Miz Minnie for names of people around Palmer, setting up that piece-of-junk tape recorder, all her sad little efforts to find a way to rid herself of the last slick of scum that Palmer had left under her skin. "And all I had to do was wait for today," she said aloud.

She didn't know what to make of Palmer's having died in the very place Bobby had been killed. It was too much coincidence, too much balance—except real balance would have put Jason Morris in the car with Palmer. What had happened? Had Jason decided to get rid of his ex-friend despite Palmer's warning about the letter Palmer had left with his lawyer? But for all she knew, Jason and Nancy had already left for Greece. Suicide? She liked the idea of Palmer's putting himself out of his own misery, but why would he? Truly he'd lost his best friend and was a party to murder, but being a rapist hadn't made him drive his car off a bluff, and he hadn't sounded like suicide was where he was headed when she'd heard him talking to Jason at the Teahouse. Maybe it really was an accident. However it had happened, he was gone. Dead gone.

She stretched and grinned at the same time, so caught up in her thoughts the knock on the door made her jump.

Damn! Mama was the last person she wanted to see right now, but if she didn't answer the door, Mama would know she was inside just as surely as Blanche knew that it was her mother knocking.

"I guess you heard," Miz Cora said instead of "Hello" or "How are you?"

Blanche just stared at her. Miz Cora stepped by her into the house. She set her small plastic shopping bag on the table, took a pint of gin, a lemon, and a liter of tonic water from the bag, and held up the gin. "This still your drink, aint it?" Without waiting for Blanche to answer, she went right to the sink and washed and dried the lemon. "You know I aint much

of a drinkin woman, but seemed to me we ought to drink a toast to celebrate that man's passin."

"Mama, what . . . ?"

"Oh, that's right," Miz Cora said, "I aint s'posed to know what he done
to you, is I? It's all right for other people to know, but I . . ."

Blanche was too stunned to do more than lean against the table with
her mouth hanging open.

"Why you lookin like your behind's draggin the ground 'stead of dancin
in the street? That's what I'd be doin if I didn't have this here arthyritis.
Person don't often git to see they dream come true. I wished that man
dead and now he is. Thank you, Jesus, even though I know it aint a Christian thing, wishin people dead."

This wasn't the first time Blanche had seen her mother step out from
behind what she said she believed, to do or say what she thought was right.
Miz Cora stopped slicing the lemon, laid the knife down, and looked at
Blanche.

"Why you aint tole me what that nasty dog did to you, baby? Hurt me
to my heart when Miz Minnie . . . I feel bad gittin on you 'bout checkin
round about him, now I know what he done to you." She poured gin and
tonic in both glasses, topped each of them with an ice cube and a slice of
lemon, and handed a glass to Blanche.

"To dreams that come true," she said. The clink of glass on glass was
like a period at the end of a long, sad sentence.

Blanche eased into a chair. "Did my daddy ever . . ."

Miz Cora shook her head and sat down at the table. "Naw. He kept his
pants up when he mistreated me."

"How'd y'all break up?"

Her mother looked a little surprised by the direct question, but from
the way she leaned back and crossed her arms, Blanche knew that for once
she was going to get a real answer.

"Don't know why it is that a person can put up with a thing year in and
year out and then one day . . . one day you just know you got to do somethin or . . . It was usually the drink with him, but not always. That last
time, I knew he was comin home drunk. One of the neighbors told me
they saw him staggerin toward home. I hurried up and took you and Rosalie over to Mae's. You remember her? She was a good friend to me even
though she was cousin to your daddy, God rest her sweet soul." Miz Cora

sighed and then went on. "When I got back home he was waitin for me. Puke on his shirt and meanness twistin him into somebody I didn't want to know. He was hardly in the door before he grabbed me by my hair and knocked my head against the wall 'cause dinner wasn't on the table. I knew where he kept his bottle, and I fetched it for him, poured him a big glass, and then another, until he could hardly make his way to bed. When he finally passed out, I gathered up our clothes and left." She stopped talking for a bit, then: "He didn't even come looking for us for three days. Too drunk."

"That's what Mr. Broadnax gave you money for?"

Miz Cora nodded. "That's right. He helped me out till I got on my feet. We stayed with Mae for a week or so. You probably don't remember that. Then I rented Royal's—Mr. Broadnax's—mama's house. She'd died a year before, and the place was empty. He fixed it up and . . ." Miz Cora stared into her glass.

"It didn't start out with your daddy just hittin me. He was real sweet in the beginning. For a long time. Long time. Before and after you was born. Then he brought us over here when he got work at the sawmill. All my people, my friends, was over Fayetteville way. I didn't have nobody I could depend on but him. I was never quick to make friends, you know. But things was pretty all right, until he started havin trouble on the job. Bossman talked bad to people, made fun of 'em. Then your daddy start talkin bad to me, callin me stupid and lazy. He started drinkin more, too. Pushin me around, laughin at my country ways, as he called 'em. Then, one day, he just hauled off and . . ."

Miz Cora looked at Blanche. "Why'd I let him do that to me. Why? If I'da stood up for myself the first time, maybe . . ."

"But you didn't have nobody to . . ."

"I had my girls, my children to look out for. I shoulda bopped him with a frying pan the first time he . . ."

And why hadn't she? Blanche wondered. What had made this woman whose temper could reburn Atlanta let a man mistreat her? "You were young, Mama," she said, trying to find an answer to her own question.

"Naw. That weren't the reason." Miz Cora took another sip of her drink, then leaned across the table toward Blanche. "There I was, s'posed to be some kinda upstandin, decent woman with a mind of my own, raisin two girls, dressin every day in my nurse's-aide uniform and goin to the hospital tryin to help people. Then I goes home with my knees tremblin and my heart jumpin for fear that man was gon wipe the floor with me, and maybe even in front of my girls next time. But I didn't want to be run outa my own house! Have to let on I couldn't handle my own . . . I was 'shamed. So 'shamed I couldn't a raised my head if the Lord called me by name."

Blanche went to her mother, leaned down and put her arms around her. "But you left him, Mama."

"Yeah, but I waited too long. Just like you tryin to do somethin 'bout that dog that hurt you after all this time. Both of us waited too long."

Yes, Blanche thought, and for the same reason: the shame of the wounded. What was it that the rapists, batterers, and torturers did to make women they hurt feel ashamed of what was done to them, to suspect, at least for a moment, that they deserved to be raped, maimed, and bruised?

"It's all right, now, Mama. We both got free. Both of us."

Miz Cora stood up and patted Blanche's shoulder. "Thank the Lord, chile. Thank the Lord." She swayed a bit when she moved away from Blanche. She put her glass in the sink and picked up her handbag.

Blanche threw on a skirt and sweater and walked her mother home.

On the way back to the Miz Alice, Blanche thought about all her mother had said and how she'd always wished something would bring her and Mama together. The thought made her laugh with bitterness. She would rather she and Mama never spoke again than that either of them should have suffered in the way they had, no matter how much closer it might bring them. Both of them assaulted, disrespected. Both of them keeping quiet as though it was their fault. But at least they'd healed enough to say their hurt out loud.

Daisy, Daisy, Tell Me
Your Answer True

Blanche pulled the sheet over her head. She didn't particularly want to get out of bed. She needed time to rest up, to let her life settle down a bit. But there was still Daisy. Blanche made herself get out of bed, exercise, eat, and go downtown.

"Miz Blanche!" Daisy grinned to see Blanche waiting outside the cleaners when she got off.

"Hey, Daisy, how you been?"

"You just caught me," Daisy said. "This here's my last day at the cleaners."

Blanche fell in beside Daisy. "You got a new job?"

"You might say that." Daisy turned to look at Blanche. "I just want to git away from all the . . . you know, all that's happened. To Bobby and Maybelle and . . . and all. So I'm going to the army." She gave Blanche a snappy salute but her eyes remained sad. "Me and Maybelle useta talk about joining up before her and Bobby, and then . . ."

Blanche hesitated. What difference would it really make to Daisy that Jason Morris and not David Palmer had killed Bobby? This whole business was running Daisy out of town. Leave the girl alone, Blanche told herself. By the time the Attorney General got Palmer's note, if it really existed, Daisy would be living another life. And as far as she knew, Palmer's message to the Attorney General didn't say anything about how Bobby had died. From what was being said on the radio and in the papers, Bobby's crash and David Palmer's were just two more in a long string of accidents on a curve in the road that had already killed a number of other people. Nobody was likely to be charged with deaths that happened there. Better warning signs, guardrails, and even a straightening of the road were being talked about. So it was probably all over. A let-sleeping-dogs-lie kind of situation as far as Daisy was concerned, Blanche thought. But she couldn't stop herself from asking: "You heard about David Palmer?"

Daisy blinked and nodded.

"He didn't do it," Blanche said as if she hadn't been in on her own thinking. "He wasn't the man Maybelle was seeing. He didn't kill her. Or Bobby. Although he did know about . . ."

Daisy buckled like a piece of bent cardboard.

"Daisy, what's wrong?" Blanche took her arm until she was steady.

Daisy clutched her chest and stared at Blanche. "Oh my god! Oh sweet Jesus!" She hid her face in her hands.

"Daisy, what is it?" Blanche pulled on Daisy's arms, trying to uncover her face.

Daisy lowered her hands and stared at Blanche. "It's like Maybelle put a curse on us. First Bobby and now me."

"What are you talking about?"

Blanche looked around. There was a bench half a block down; she took Daisy's arm and pulled her along toward it.

Daisy's eyes were wide and blurry with tears. "It was a accident, Miz Blanche, I swear! It was a accident! Bobby just pushed her. He didn't even slap her or . . . He didn't mean to really hurt her, but she fell and hit her head. And she . . . died." She sank onto the bench.

"Wait a minute, wait a minute." Blanche was suddenly short of breath. Her bowels grumbled. "You trying to tell me that Bobby . . . ? But what about his alibi?"

"We didn't know what to . . . Bobby put Maybelle in the car and I drove her to where they found her. I carried . . . I rolled her body down the . . .

so nobody would know she'd been up there in the woods where Bobby and that man was hunting, so . . ." Daisy was sobbing now.

Blanche remembered the feeling she'd gotten from Daisy last time they'd talked about Maybelle. There'd been something stiff and strange in Daisy's attitude that Blanche hadn't been able to identify. It made sense now. She felt weak and dizzy. "But how did Maybelle get . . . ?"

"Bobby said he had to talk to Maybelle. He asked me to bring her up to Briarmount to meet him that night. This New York yankee was payin Bobby to take him huntin, so Bobby didn't want to leave him up there where they was campin 'cause he hadn't been paid yet. But Bobby knew that city man'd be tuckered out early, so he told me to bring Maybelle to . . . He wanted to talk to her about . . ."

"About running around on him," Blanche said.

Daisy nodded.

"What did you mean about Maybelle putting a curse on you?"

"Oh, Miz Blanche, I feel so awful. . . . I . . ."

"Daisy! Tell me what the hell you're talking about!" Blanche shouted. Two people across the street stopped and stared for half a second before going on.

"All right, Daisy," Blanche said in a quieter voice. "Just take a couple of deep breaths. Now tell me."

"I told Bobby what you said, and I told them others, too."

"What do you mean, what I said? What did you tell Bobby? Them who?" Blanche could feel the last of her patience drying up and blowing away like dust. "What did you tell Bobby, exactly?"

"I told Bobby what you said!" Daisy hissed. Her face was flushed. Her eyes were angry, and something else Blanche didn't understand. "About that David Palmer bein the man Maybelle was runnin around with."

Blanche looked at her with surprise. "But, Daisy, you're the one who said . . ."

Daisy shook her head vehemently. "No, no, Miz Blanche, *you* said. Maybelle told me she had a boyfriend with plenty money, but she wouldn't tell me who."

Blanche's head was beginning to throb. "But, Daisy, don't you remember? You told me Bobby found Palmer's Sons of Farleigh key and that Bobby . . ."

Daisy shook her head again. "No! *You* said."

Blanche tried to dredge up all the times she'd talked with Daisy. Had she been so intent on nailing Palmer, so intent on finding some part of his life that matched what he'd done to her instead of the good-guy crap she'd been hearing about him, that she'd heard more in Daisy's words than had actually been said? All the time that she'd thought Daisy was giving her information, was it really the other way round? She couldn't make herself remember. She did remember what Palmer had said at the Teahouse, about Bobby's coming to see him and saying he had something of Palmer's.

"But Maybelle *did* have the key!"

Daisy frowned at her.

"The key from Palmer's key chain," Blanche said.

Daisy shrugged. "Bobby didn't know nothin 'bout no key." Her face got even redder. "He didn't find nothin! I was just saying that 'cause I was tired of Bobby being bad-mouthed. He didn't know nothin until I tole him what you tole me."

"So you told Bobby that Palmer was Maybelle's other man and that Palmer was missing something from his key chain." Rocks had settled in Blanche's stomach by the time she finished speaking.

Daisy bowed her head. "I begged Bobby not to go near that Palmer, but Bobby wouldn't listen. He said the least Palmer could do was pay for taking Maybelle away from him. So Bobby went to see him, and . . ."

Blanche heard Jason Morris telling Palmer that he'd taken care of Bobby.

Daisy was still talking. ". . . then Bobby was dead, and I was so mad and so hurt, I didn't know what to do. When you told me how Bobby's accident wasn't no accident at all, well, all I could think about was that dog Palmer walkin around free, actin like he was somebody when he . . . So I tole Maybelle's daddy and her brothers and Bobby's brothers and uncles about Maybelle and Palmer and the key Bobby was supposed to have."

"But you didn't tell them that Bobby pushed Maybelle, and that you moved her body, did you?" Blanche didn't know why she asked, since she already knew the answer.

Daisy looked up and down the street as though searching for a place to hide. "I didn't tell 'em about what happened to Maybelle. Or about Bobby tryin to get money from . . ."

"So you told Bobby's and Maybelle's people that Bobby found Palmer's key when he found Maybelle's body."

Daisy nodded.

Blanche waited for her mind to stop spinning. "Well, that doesn't mean the families . . . You don't think . . . Maybe it was just a . . ." There was no way of really knowing. Maybe Bobby's and Maybelle's families had gotten revenge. Maybe Palmer had really had a car accident before the families had time to do anything to him.

"Oh, Daisy, I'm so sorry. I was so sure Palmer was the one who killed Maybelle and Bobby that I . . ."

"It don't matter how sorry you are! I still got the wrong man killed." Daisy's voice was thick with tears.

Blanche had no intention of telling her that Bobby would likely still be alive if he hadn't tried to get money out of Palmer. She'd already made enough grief for poor Daisy. "You don't know that for sure, Daisy. Palmer could have just had an accident."

Daisy wiped her eyes with the backs of her hands. "Like Bobby," she said.

Blanche couldn't look at her. If she was going to tell Daisy who had really killed Bobby, this was the time. But she couldn't do it. What good would it do Daisy to know? She couldn't go back to Bobby's people and tell them she'd made a mistake about Palmer and she now knew who'd really killed Bobby. She couldn't go to the Sheriff, because then she would have to tell the truth about Maybelle. So why tell her? Why should both of them carry it around? "Right," Blanche said. "Like Bobby."

The two women stared at each other. Blanche could see misery circling around Daisy like buzzards around roadkill.

"Oh, Miz Blanche, I feel so bad about telling Bobby about that Palmer."

"I know you feel bad, Daisy, honey, and I feel bad for getting you involved in all this. But I want you to remember, Bobby didn't have to push Maybelle. Bobby didn't have to try to get money out of David Palmer just because you told him Palmer killed Maybelle. We all played a part in this mess, but we aint all equally responsible. You understand?"

Daisy looked uncertain, but she'd stopped crying. "I guess."

Blanche rose from the bench; Daisy followed her.

"Well, goodbye, Miz Bl—"

"Daisy, I gotta ask you something else. Somebody in a truck tried to run me down. Do you know . . ."

Daisy hid her face again, sighed, then looked at Blanche. "I wasn't really tryin to hurt you, Miz Blanche, I just wanted to scare you off. You was talkin about goin to the Sheriff and tellin him Bobby had something when he didn't. I was hopin you'd think that Palmer knew you . . . I thought . . . I was just tryin to make everything work out for Bobby and me. I'm real sorry." She put out her hand for Blanche to shake, then changed her mind and hugged Blanche instead.

"Look out for yourself, Daisy."

Daisy stepped back. "I'll try, Miz Blanche, I will." She turned and walked quickly down the street, her pink floral dress waving like a flag around her substantial thighs.

Blanche watched Daisy until she turned the corner, then sank down on the bench again. She thought about what Miz Cora had said about David Palmer's death and the pleasure Blanche should and, to some degree, did take in it. But at the very, very center of herself she knew that she'd rather Palmer were still alive. She didn't want him alive so that his life could go merrily along, or even so that she'd have another chance to try to bring him down. She wanted him alive so that she wouldn't have to carry the weight of knowing she was partly responsible for his death, no matter how light the load.

No More

Blanche lived so deeply within herself for the next few days that she felt as though a Plexiglas wall stood between her and everyone else. She sleepwalked through her work. When she wasn't working she was either sleeping—much more than usual—or doing what she could only call sitting with herself: in a chair by the window or on the stoop, letting herself be, unattached from everything that had happened. Thoughts of Palmer and Bobby and Daisy and Jason attempted to take center stage in her mind; she didn't let them hold her attention but, rather, pass through her mind like balloons sailing slowly across a meadow and then up and up until they disappeared.

She'd had a long talk with Ardell about how she was feeling, but it hadn't changed anything. She was still locked in some outer room of herself, waiting for the time when it would be okay for her to take up her life again. Before this could happen, she knew that she needed something she couldn't name but would know when it came to her.

There'd been no story in the newspaper or on the radio about Jason's involvement with Maybelle or about the Palmer note. But Clarice brought the scuttlebutt to their last bicentennial catering job:

"Yeah, chile. Mr. Henry say Attorney General over there in Durham got a letter from the dead man saying his best friend was messin round with Maybelle Jenkins. Well, they looked into it and seem like the dead man was messin with her hisself. Mr. Henry say Sheriff figure to let sleepin dogs be."

Blanche nearly dropped a plate when Clarice used the same phrase Blanche had used in thinking about telling Daisy the truth about Bobby's death. Blanche didn't have room for any more disappointment, so the news from Clarice hadn't rocked her. Her attempt to hurt David Palmer was truly over. Summer was passing on. She decided that tomorrow she would clean the entire Miz Alice and give both of them a fresh start. Thelvin was gone for another couple of days; she needed to do something with all of her unused sexual energy.

Mid-afternoon the next day, she stepped out onto her front stoop to give the floors inside time to dry. Gwennie, her neighbor, and another woman were standing down the street. They were facing the girls' house, talking and shaking their heads. Blanche sat down on the stoop.

"Bitch! I'll make you wish you was dead!" a man's voice boomed from the house across the street. Blanche could feel that house's distress like a hot wind on her face.

She looked up and down the street, hoping the girls were outside and safe, but they were nowhere around. Something crashed against a wall in their house, and a woman shrieked like a kicked dog.

Blanche hurried back inside and slammed the door. She leaned against it as though this could block out sound, then covered her ears and moved to the corner of the room farthest from the door.

"Why don't you run, you stupid cow?" she thought, as though she had direct access to the woman's inner ear. She lowered her hands and stood up straight, shocked by the stupidity of her own question. How could she not have seen that this woman was under the knife, just as she'd been, just as Ardell and Mama had tried to explain to her? They were all the same, those raping, kicking, punching, killing motherfuckers. This was what they wanted: a woman cringing in a corner, a woman begging, begging him to be careful with that knife, that gun, that rope around her neck, that threat to destroy her face, hurt her kids, or whatever else the rotten shit

used to scare her out of herself, to keep her from running. Sweet Ancestors! Even in death, how she hated that man. She pushed herself away
from the wall.

She looked wildly around, finally flinging open the kitchen cabinet. She
grabbed a large pot and searched the drawer for a wooden spoon, rushed
out of the house and across the street, and stopped directly in front of the
little girls' porch. Big things, like chairs, were being thrown around inside,
punctuated by slaps and groans. Blanche raised her pot and banged its
bottom with the spoon as hard as she could, over and over and over.

With each bang, Blanche felt something loosening inside—like she'd
felt when she'd told Bunnie she'd been raped—something opening up and
letting her breathe more deeply, be more present than she'd felt in a while.
Her questions about whether Palmer would have raped her if she hadn't
been taking a forbidden bath on the job, if she'd remembered to lock the
bathroom door, if she had tried to fight despite his knife—all her secret
worry that it was these mistakes, her mistakes, that had caused her rape—
were revealed to her as utter and total bullshit. If she'd been strutting
down the street buck-naked, he didn't have a right to touch her. No. If
that woman across the street told her husband he was the worst fuck in
history and gave him dog food for dinner, he didn't have a right to hit her.
No. Just because women were blamed for everything but good luck didn't
give nobody a right to do them wrong. And it didn't mean they were supposed to take it when they were done wrong. All this woman-hurting shit
had to stop.

"Stop!" she shouted for herself as she banged her pot. "Stop!" she
shouted for Mama. "Stop!" she shouted for poor, lovesick Daisy. "Stop!"
she shouted for dead Maybelle.

Maybe the only way to end this mess was for every woman to stand up
for every other woman, even if she couldn't stand up for herself.

"Stopstopstopstopstop!" she shouted as she banged on her pot.

A short, wiry, red-brown man rushed out of the house and glared at her.
His fingers formed and unformed fists; sweat marked the armpits of his
shirt.

"Bitch! Is you crazy?!"

Blanche kept banging and shouting.

"Get the fuck away from here before I . . ."

"Kiss my big black ass!" she screamed at him, ready to run if she had to—after she gave him a shot of the pepper spray in her pocket—but he didn't move toward her.

"Shame on you! Shame on you! Shame on you!" Gwennie and the other woman across the street began shouting, clapping their hands in time.

The man stood on the porch breathing hard as the women from across the street came to stand beside Blanche. She watched his eyes shifting from woman to woman.

"All you bitches is crazy!" he screamed and brushed past them. He jumped into his car and sped off down the street as though he expected as well as deserved to be chased.

Blanche was glad Gwennie said she'd go inside and check on the girls and their mother. Blanche didn't want to see. One more bit of rage would surely burn her alive. But she did go home and call information. She wrote down the name and the number of the new women's shelter, then slipped the piece of paper with the number on it under the woman's screen door.

Later that evening, Blanche once again went out and sat on her stoop. There was no one else around, and everything was quiet, not a lingering vibe from that afternoon. Even the house across the street felt less miserable. Blanche watched the night chase the day away and wondered what would come next for her, in a year or so, when the kids were gone.

She liked catering work, but she didn't think Ardell really needed a partner. Anyway, after all that had happened since she'd been back, she didn't know if she could stand living in Farleigh again. Maybe the town was once again giving her a "Get out!" message, as it had when she rushed away from here for Boston. She just didn't know. She also wasn't sure Carolina Catering could support them both without the bicentennial business. She didn't want to have to do day work to support herself as a caterer. And there were the kids' school needs to consider. Even with scholarships, loans, and jobs to go along with her education insurance policy, they still might need her help. Ardell had started catering lunches for business meetings, but how much could you make on sandwiches? And if business *was* strong enough to support them both, Blanche didn't know if she was ready to give up city life—or to work with Ardell. She didn't doubt they still loved each other, but she wasn't sure it was a love that could take daily in-person contact around a business that Ardell expected to change her whole life. Only one thing was sure: once the kids were in college, she'd be out of that racist Boston in a heartbeat. But then what? The idea of trying to establish herself in New York again made Boston look good. The problem was that she had no idea what would be better. The question of Thelvin hung in the back of her mind, but she didn't feel she had to answer it now. One thing about a railroad man, he could get to her pretty much wherever she was—if she wanted him to.

A car not their father's drew up in front of the house where Doretha, Lucinda, and Murlee lived. A woman and a man got out and went inside. A few minutes later, the girls and their mother came out of the house. The mother had a suitcase, each of the girls a big green plastic bag. The man was carrying a box. The woman opened the trunk for the box and bags, then got behind the wheel. The three girls piled into the back seat with their mother. As the car passed Blanche's house, the three of them waved and Lucinda called out the window:

"Bye, Mith Blanche. Thankth for the cookieth!"

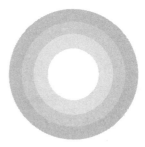

Blanche's Gig from Hell
Dessert Sauce

4 egg yolks
1/4 cup sugar
7/8 cup muscat or any other sweet dessert wine
1 cup heavy cream, whipped
2 tablespoons lemon juice

Whisk the eggs and sugar in a metal bowl until pale yellow. Add the wine and continue whisking until frothy. Place the bowl over a pot of simmering water, being careful not to let the water touch the bottom of the bowl, and whisk until the sauce thickens slightly. Continue simmering and whisking until the sauce reaches 165 degrees on a candy thermometer. Cool immediately by putting the bowl in a second bowl of at least the same size half filled with ice. Whisk occasionally until cool. Just before serving, fold in the whipped cream and lemon juice.